T0283402

ALL THE WAY GONE

Also by Joanna Schaffhausen

Dead and Gone

Long Gone

Gone for Good

Last Seen Alive

Every Waking Hour

All the Best Lies

No Mercy

The Vanishing Season

ALL THE WAY GONE

A Detective Annalisa Vega Novel

JOANNA SCHAFFHAUSEN

MINOTAUR BOOKS
NEW YORK

First published in the United States by Minotaur Books, an imprint of St. Martin's Publishing Group

ALL THE WAY GONE. Copyright © 2024 by Joanna Schaffhausen. All rights reserved. Printed in the United States of America. For information, address St. Martin's Publishing Group, 120 Broadway, New York, NY 10271.

www.minotaurbooks.com

Designed by Gabriel Guma

The Library of Congress Cataloging-in-Publication Data is available upon request.

ISBN 978-1-250-90414-0 (hardcover)
ISBN 978-1-250-90415-7 (ebook)

Our books may be purchased in bulk for promotional, educational, or business use. Please contact your local bookseller or the Macmillan Corporate and Premium Sales Department at 1-800-221-7945, extension 5442, or by email at MacmillanSpecialMarkets@macmillan.com.

First Edition: 2024

1 3 5 7 9 10 8 6 4 2

For Professor Joseph DeBold, whose biopsych class
changed the trajectory of my career

ALL THE WAY GONE

ONE

··········

THE DAY THE GIRL FELL FROM THE SKY STARTED LIKE ANY OTHER FOR RUTH GOLD BERNSTEIN BECAUSE SHE PREFERRED IT THAT WAY. She ate the same breakfast Sunday through Friday, which consisted of a soft-boiled egg, a slice of wheat toast, and half of a navel orange. She and Marty used to split a grapefruit and the *Chicago Tribune,* but he'd had the temerity to develop pancreatic cancer and die on her three years earlier. Ruth blamed the bacon. She was an observant Jew and never touched the stuff. Marty had been less observant, although he'd often joked, "I'm observant. I observe bacon tastes damn good and I plan to eat as much of it as possible." In the weeks after his death, Ruth had carefully wrapped up Marty's half of the grapefruit to save it for the next day, right up until her daughter, Meredith, informed her that grapefruit didn't mix with Ruth's medications and forced her to switch to the orange—a small resentment Ruth choked down every morning with her toast and black coffee.

Meredith lived in California now, with her husband and Ruth's two grandsons. She wouldn't know if Ruth sneaked the occasional grapefruit, but Ruth gave her word she'd stick to oranges and Ruth's word was gold like her name. After breakfast, she washed and dressed and opened the sliding balcony door to tend to her plants. In late April it was finally warm enough to move them back out into the fresh air. Weather permitting, Ruth took her afternoon tea on the expansive balcony, watching the comings and goings of the courtyard below, and she swore she could see the plants unfurl their tender green leaves toward the sun, exhaling at the arrival of spring.

She felt a touch upon her leg and looked down to see her white Persian cat, Duchess, meowing and sliding her ample furry body along Ruth's charcoal-gray trousers. Duchess had been a surprise present from Marty the year before he died. They had never owned a pet before; it didn't seem fair given the amount of traveling they did. Ruth didn't like surprises, but surprisingly, she did like the cat. She admired the grace and fastidiousness of the animal, the way Duchess perched in a regal pose upon the cushion of the armchair, her front paws crossed and her fluffy tail licked into submission alongside her. Ruth had to admit, especially on cold nights, it was nice to have another beating heart in bed with her. Like the plants, Duchess welcomed the change of seasons because it meant that Ruth left the slider open to the balcony and she could watch the birds flit around from their vantage point, fourteen stories up.

Of course, Duchess had seen the girl, Victoria. *Call me Vicki,* she'd said to Ruth the day she'd moved into the apartment next door two years ago. Ruth could not understand why someone given the name of queens would instead choose to go by the moniker of a shopgirl, but she kept this opinion to herself. Vicki liked to lie out on her balcony, engaging in loud, chatty phone conversations about the various men in her life, all of whom were riffraff from what Ruth could make out. The girl was friendly enough, though, and helpful. Once, Duchess had seized on the open front door and zoomed out to have an adventure in the hallways. Before Ruth could stop her, the cat had climbed into an elevator and ridden it to Lord knows where. Vicki had helped Ruth track down Duchess by the pool area. *Aren't you the most gorgeous kitty,* Vicki had cooed, which meant she had impeccable taste in felines even if this discernment wasn't evident in her sartorial choices. Indeed, the girl had been wearing what looked like fuzzy hot-pink house slippers at the time. Ruth thought perhaps she'd been in such a hurry to help she'd run out of the apartment not yet dressed. But no. She'd seen the girl wearing the horrid slippers out on the street. Upon a closer look, Ruth noticed they said UGG on the sides and she thought that extremely fitting.

Still, she liked Vicki in a vague sort of way and she wished the girl could find a mate worthy of her. Sometimes Ruth would glimpse one of the no-good men slinking out of Vicki's apartment before noon, unshaven and carrying his shoes. Ruth would fix him with her most icy stare so he'd know quite well what she thought of that behavior. But they need not have bothered to sneak, Ruth knew. The girl was never awake in the early morning, certainly not before ten, which is what made her fall that day all the more mysterious.

Ruth took her walk as usual when the grandfather clock struck 8 a.m. She had a set one-and-a-half-mile route around the Gold Coast that she did in rain or shine precisely at the same time every day. The rest of the world did not adhere to her constancy. She had different companions in the elevator every day. This particular morning, it was that handsome doctor from across the courtyard. Dr. Canning. He'd received big press last year when he'd separated twin girls born in Thailand who were conjoined at the head. The manager of the property had cut the article out of the newspaper and pinned it on the community notices board by the mailroom, but of course, Ruth had already seen it in the metro section.

"Mrs. Bernstein," he said, smiling down at her with his even white teeth. "You're looking well turned out this morning, as always."

She couldn't really say the same. He wore jeans and sneakers and what was that frightful thing called again . . . oh, yes. A hoodie. She overlooked his wardrobe because no doubt he was on the way to the hospital to save someone's life and that took precedence over one's clothing, even in Ruth's estimation. "Do you know the name of every single person in this building, Dr. Canning?" she asked as the elevator glided to a stop.

"No, just the cute ones," he replied with a wink.

"Oh, get on with you," she said, waving him off with both hands, but her face warmed at his words. She'd never turned a lot of male heads—Marty's was the only one who mattered—and now at age eighty-four she was almost invisible.

Dr. Canning went to the garage entrance while Ruth walked to the front door. Damon Young, the doorman, hurried to open it for her, favoring her with one of his trademark wide smiles. "Morning, Mrs. Bernstein."

"Good morning, Damon. How did your forensic psychology paper turn out?"

"Got me an A," he said with pride.

"Of course you did." Damon was taking night classes to earn a degree in criminal justice. He would be graduating soon and leaving them, which was the way of things. More change. If you lived as long as Ruth had, change became inevitable, but that didn't mean she had to like it.

"And how are things with your new lady friend? When am I going to meet her?"

Damon chuckled. "Aw, Mrs. B, you wouldn't approve."

Ruth peered up at him with a serious gaze. "You're a young man, and it's fine to have fun while you're young. But be careful with your heart—it's the only one you'll ever have."

"You're telling me. It's a war zone out there. Not everyone gets lucky like you and Mr. B."

Damon had not known Marty. What he knew of their relationship came only from Ruth's tales. "You'll know," she told Damon. "When it's the right girl, you'll know."

She left Damon and took her usual route over to Michigan Ave by the old water works, from there walking north toward the Hancock Center. Only it wasn't the Hancock Center anymore, she had read in the papers. It was nameless now, just a number like any other building on the block. She remembered it being built in the 1960s, how excited Marty was to see it climbing to its towering one hundred stories. Ruth had never much cared for the skyscraper in its heyday. It was black and looming and the shape reminded her of that movie villain, Darth Vader. When she'd told Marty this, he'd laughed and hummed the theme music at her. Now when she saw the hulking, brutish structure it made her smile and remember his voice. Maybe she even pitied the poor anonymous building a little. The second-tallest building at the time, now it was only the fifth-tallest in Chicago. *If you survive long enough,* she thought, *time will tell you—you're not so special after all.*

She took Oak Street toward home. The city had hung out cheery baskets of spring flowers on every light post and the riotous colors lifted Ruth's mood. She was humming to herself and mentally preparing for her next task—catching up on her electronic correspondence—when she approached her luxury apartment building from the rear. The back entrance had no doorman, which meant Ruth had to carry her key card to get in through the gate to the courtyard, but she felt the extra bit of nonsense was worth it for the view. The large stone fountain in the middle was not yet operational for the season but was nonetheless intriguing to behold, with its three life-sized buffalo heads and the manicured bits of greenery around it. She made eye contact with one, was contemplating its laconic gaze, when a single terrified scream jerked her attention upward.

Ruth raised her eyes just in time to see the girl fall through the air and hit the pavement with a horrible noise that echoed off the marble façade of the U-shaped building. She froze in the moment because it felt impossible. Surely that had not just happened. It could not be. Ruth quivered, her bones shaking, and she thought she might fall to the earth herself. "Help," she wheezed, tottering in the direction of the lobby. "Somebody help her." She stumbled on the path and dragged herself into the building. She made it to Damon before collapsing in his arms. "Vicki," she managed to say. "She—fell."

Thus began a seemingly endless parade of fire trucks, ambulances, and police cars, a small army of men and women who arrived after the battle had already been lost. Ruth knew the instant she'd heard the awful thud that there would be no saving that girl. Still, she had to relive the death over and over as she recounted what she'd seen to a dozen different people in uniform. They asked her the same repeated questions, only some of which Ruth could answer. How had Vicki seemed lately? Was she depressed? She couldn't say. She thought she had heard her weeping on the phone to someone last month, but Ruth had chalked it up to boyfriend trouble. Had Ruth heard anyone else in the apartment with Vicki that morning? No, but that wasn't unusual. Vicki's overnight guests often rose when she did, at midday.

Someone brought Ruth a paper cup of tea that went cold in her hands. Eventually a nice young man who introduced himself as Detective Carelli took the tea from her and disposed of it. "I'm very sorry for what you've been through today," he said as he took a seat next to her on the bench in the lobby. Ruth shuddered. They had carted out Vicki in a bag not a half hour earlier.

"I'll be fine. I just can't figure out what happened to that poor girl." The idea that Vicki might have leaped to her death when she seemed so outwardly happy was almost too much to bear. Maybe Ruth should have paid more attention. Been more neighborly.

"We think it was an accident," Detective Carelli said as he consulted his notebook. "Ms. Albright was apparently alone in the apartment, hanging wind chimes on her balcony when she slipped."

"An accident," Ruth whispered. "How terrible."

Detective Carelli accompanied her back to her apartment. He offered to call someone for her but Ruth waved him off. What could Meredith do from California at this point? No. Ruth would make a pot of Earl Grey tea and put on some soothing music—no, maybe something raucous, like Saint-Saëns, loud enough to drown out the echo in her head of that poor girl hitting the ground. Ruth had scarcely removed her jacket when she felt an odd stillness in her home, a total silence she hadn't felt since Marty died. "Duchess?" she ventured, beginning to explore the six rooms in search of her companion. "Duchess kitty, where are you?"

She looked everywhere, including the balcony, but Duchess was nowhere to be found. A great sob rose up out of Ruth, then a keening she'd been holding back all day. Vicki had helped her find Duchess the last time. Who would help her now? She was so overwhelmed with grief and worry she forgot the one bit of memory that had been niggling at her since her conversation with Detective Carelli. It had been silent in the courtyard before Vicki fell. Ruth had not heard any wind chimes.

TWO

············

THE GOLD PLATE WAS SO NEW AND SHINY THAT ANNALISA COULD SEE HERSELF REFLECTED IN IT. She noticed her crinkled, worried gaze and rearranged her features into a smile before she turned around, drill still in hand, to face Nick and his teenage daughter, Cassidy. "Ta-da," she said, gesturing like Vanna White to the nameplate she had affixed to the wall next to her office door. "What do you think?"

"Vista Investigations," Nick read off, his brow slightly wrinkled. Cassidy had the same wrinkle. In fact, they even stood alike, their arms folded, fingers landing in identical fashion at the elbow, shoulders at the same slope. When Cassidy had appeared in front of Nick last fall saying she was his daughter from a long-ago affair, Annalisa had counseled him to get a DNA test to be sure. Nick had so far resisted and Annalisa had to admit it was pointless anyhow. They were plainly related. "Why not Vega Investigations?" Nick asked as he nodded at the name. "It's a one-woman show here."

"The *A* and the *V* are for me," Annalisa replied. "The *S* and the *T* are for Sam Tran." Her last case at the Chicago PD had been Sam Tran's death and now she'd taken over his PI business. "The *I* is for what we have in common . . . investigation. Add it up and you get Vista."

Nick smiled and moved to put an arm around her. "Proud of you," he said, giving her a squeeze. Annalisa looked down at his hand and saw the wedding band she'd slipped on his finger just two months ago. *There are no second acts*, F. Scott Fitzgerald once wrote, and Annalisa hoped like hell he was wrong. She'd quit her job as a police detective to hang out her own shingle and remarried the ex-husband who'd run around on her like an alley cat during their first union. Annalisa had placed a lot of faith in sequels.

"Yeah, congratulations," said Cassidy with a burst of enthusiasm and perhaps a touch of awkwardness. The teenager was a product of one of Nick's earlier affairs, unknown to him for years, and now they were all trying to figure out a new family configuration. Their interactions so far were polite and careful. "I think it's super cool you're going to be a PI," Cassidy told her. "All my friends agree."

"Wait a sec. Are you saying a PI is cooler than a cop?" Nick pretended to be offended, and Cassidy immediately looked contrite.

"No, I meant—"

"Relax, kid, he's just yanking your chain," Annalisa told her and Cassidy relaxed.

"Oh, in that case . . . yes. Way cooler. Annalisa's done the cop thing already and now she's going out on her own to take on cases the police won't. That's badass."

"I agree," Nick said, eyeing the gold sign.

"Let's not get carried away," Annalisa said as she went back inside the small waiting room and then into the larger office. "I don't even have any cases yet." The lack of income made her nervous. Nick had moved in and they were trying to sell her condo, but the market had cooled and there were no bites yet. Nick told her not to worry, that he could float them both for a while, but Annalisa had always made her own way and did not want that to change now.

"Still, we should celebrate," Nick said. "Take-out Thai and cheap wine?"

"That's what we usually have on Friday nights," Annalisa replied as she shifted through the paperwork that had somehow amassed on her desk.

"We'll put the wine in real glasses this time," Nick replied.

"Okay, it's a date." Annalisa eyed Cassidy. "Not like a romantic date," she clarified. "You're welcome to join . . ."

"Oh, no no. I have to be getting back to my mom's anyway." Nick's phone rang and he excused himself to take it. Cassidy watched him go. "I think your date may be canceled," she said to Annalisa. "That sounds like work."

Annalisa knew the drill. "You're a quick learner."

"I never realized that people got killed every single day." Cassidy walked to the window and looked out at the street. "You only think about it when it happens to someone you know."

Annalisa opened her mouth to reply but no words emerged. Cassidy's mother was dying of ALS; no one was sure how many days she had left. Nick poked his head back in before Annalisa could formulate a response. "I've got to go. Shooting in West Garfield Park, and the guy they caught is one I'm looking for. Order the Thai anyway and I'll be home as soon as I can."

It was no fun drinking alone. "I will."

He pointed at Cassidy. "You need a lift?"

"No, I'm good. I'll hang here with Annalisa for a bit and then take the bus."

Annalisa raised her eyebrows as Nick disappeared. She and Cassidy hadn't really spent any time alone together, and she figured the kid liked it that way. "I'm not going to be doing anything very interesting," she cautioned the girl. "I've got to do some paperwork and establish a filing system."

"I can help you," Cassidy answered brightly. "Actually, I was thinking I could help you on a regular basis."

"What?"

"Nick said you were hoping to hire a part-time assistant."

"He told you that?" Annalisa froze in her paper shuffling. Nick had been nagging her to spend some one-on-one time with the girl. Was this Nick's idea?

"If it's just filing and phone stuff, I can do that no problem."

"But don't you have . . . school?" Cassidy was a junior in high school, only sixteen.

Cassidy moved around the desk to face Annalisa, resting her hands with their chipped polish and bitten nails on the edge as she pled her case. "Yeah, but I'm done by two-thirty, and there's nights and weekends and stuff."

Eating off that nail polish isn't healthy, Annalisa thought. *My mother would have had a fit if I pulled that.* Immediately as she thought of her own ma, Annalisa remembered why Cassidy's mother wasn't able to battle something as minor as her daughter's nails. This kid shouldn't be shuffling paper around right now; she should be with her mother. "But your mom must need you . . ." she said aloud and Cassidy's expression turned stricken.

"Mom is fine," Cassidy said, her chin lifting. "I mean she's stable. She has aides to help her. She—she wants me to get a job. She says it will look good on my college applications."

Annalisa bit her lip and tried to think of another excuse. Before she could come up with one, her gaze fell on a stamped envelope peeking out from under her new file folders. She cursed and grabbed it. "I can't talk about this right now. I have to get this in the mail today." It was her insurance paperwork and she couldn't operate as PI without it.

"I can do it," Cassidy said eagerly. "The post office is on my way home."

"Oh, that's okay." Annalisa didn't want to encourage Cassidy's assistant idea; she wasn't looking for her own personal Veronica Mars. She reached for her jacket, intending to shepherd the girl outside the office, when a woman appeared in the doorway. Somehow, she had entered without making a sound, and she looked out of place amid the mess. Her pink headscarf, tailored beige overcoat, and large sunglasses suggested a Hollywood starlet who didn't want to be recognized, but this was Chicago, not Los Angeles. Still, there was a diffidence about her, a vulnerability that triggered Annalisa's protective instincts.

"Can I help you?" Annalisa asked.

"I hope so." The woman's mouth, set in a tense smile, gave an odd twitch. "I apologize for barging in like this without an appointment, but my situation is fairly urgent. The door was open so I just came in . . ." The tote bag hanging from her shoulder rose and fell with her helpless shrug. "You are a private investigator, yes?"

Annalisa glanced around at the chaos in the office, which included a filing cabinet without drawers assembled, the empty bookshelf, the papers on her desk, and the two paint swatches on the wall where she was trying to decide between olive green and desert sand for the new color. She had passed the licensing exam with no issues but had yet to receive the actual license in the mail. Technically she wasn't yet open for business, and she still had that insurance check that had to be posted by five. "I have to run a time-sensitive errand at the moment," she said to the woman. "But if you'd like to leave your name and number, I could get back to you after the weekend . . ."

"I need help now," the woman insisted, clutching her bag. "Please. Next week will be too late."

"I can run the errand." Cassidy seized the opportunity. "It can be my first official task as your assistant."

Annalisa hesitated. The woman checked her delicate gold watch. Whatever this woman's problems were, money wasn't one of them. She would be a paying client. "Unofficial," Annalisa said as she grudgingly handed Cassidy the envelope. "We'll discuss more later."

"I won't let you down." Cassidy gathered her things in a whirl and left Annalisa alone with her mysterious visitor. The woman had yet to remove her dark glasses.

"Okay," Annalisa said, taking a breath. "How can I help you?"

"First you have to promise me one thing." The woman reached for her sunglasses and Annalisa half expected to see a black eye underneath. But no. The woman's bright blue eyes were intense but unharmed. "Whatever happens, whatever you find out . . . you can never let him know I was here."

THREE

....

I ASSURE YOU I KEEP ALL MY INVESTIGATIONS CONFIDENTIAL." Annalisa still assumed she was dealing with a battered spouse. The woman wore a wedding ring.

"All?" The woman sat across the desk from Annalisa and arched an eyebrow at her as she gestured at the paint swatches on the wall. Her lips twitched again but this time it felt like teasing.

Annalisa ducked her head with an answering smile. "Well, yes, that's how I mean to do it going forward. You caught me on opening day, Ms. . . ." She still didn't know the woman's name.

"Doctor," the woman supplied. "Dr. Mara Delaney. But please call me Mara."

"Great. I'm Annalisa Vega."

"I know. I saw the news stories about you a couple of years ago . . . when you caught the Lovelorn Killer? That's why I'm here."

Annalisa's shoulders tensed and she forced herself to sound pleasant. "I see. And why is that exactly?"

"You've met one," Mara replied flatly. "You've met one and you know it. I feel like that gives you a better starting place than most other people."

"I'm sorry?"

The woman took out a hard-backed book and slid it across the desk to Annalisa. The glossy cover read *The Good Sociopath* in bold letters above a shadowed male figure rendered somewhere between a photo and an illustration. The lighting effect made his dark eyes stand out but the second *o* in *Sociopath* was colored yellow like a halo behind the man's head. Annalisa set the book back down.

"If you read the news stories, then you know the Lovelorn Killer had nothing good about him," she said coolly.

"No, of course not. But he was unusual."

Annalisa chuffed. "I should say so." The man had murdered ten people.

"I mean he was unusual among sociopaths. Most aren't homicidal or even especially violent. In fact, they may be helpful to us in some capacity."

"Good sociopaths," Annalisa said with skepticism as she picked up the book again. This time she registered the author's name: M. J. Delaney. "This is your book?"

Mara answered with a wry smile. "Yes, technically. I conceived the concept, carried out the research, and wrote the text. But he's the reason the book exists." She pointed at the male figure on the cover. "Craig Canning. Maybe you've heard of him. He's a local neurosurgeon and the soon-to-be poster child for desirable sociopathy."

Annalisa suppressed a shiver as she imagined the shadowy figure on the cover wielding a scalpel. "A surgeon? I'm not sure I'd want a sociopath operating on me."

"You might be surprised. It takes a certain kind of nerve to cut into another human being—to crack open their skull and muck around in the blood and brain matter." This time, Annalisa did squirm, and Mara pointed a finger at her. "Aha, see? You can't even stomach imagining it, let alone going through with the act. But what if you had a brain bleed or a tumor that had to be removed? You'd be desperate for someone with a scalpel and the wherewithal to use it."

"Enter Dr. Canning." Annalisa fingered the edge of the book. In her experience, sociopaths were violent predators to be eliminated at all costs.

"Him and others. Sociopathy rates are higher among surgeons and other types of doctors." She held Annalisa's gaze. "They're higher among police officers as well—around double the numbers you see in the general population, which is around one to four percent."

"I'm sorry . . . you're saying one out of every twenty-five people is a sociopath?"

Mara smiled again and nudged the book closer to Annalisa. "Intrigued yet?" When Annalisa didn't answer, Mara sighed and leaned back in her seat. "Yes, that's the starting point for my argument. If sociopathy weren't somehow beneficial to society, why would it persist at such high levels? It turns out, once you start looking at some of the core traits in another light, you can understand why we might want them around. Think about a funeral director, for another example. To do his job well, he has to perform empathy for his clients—the deceased's loved ones—but he cannot go to pieces every time a new family walks through the door. If he's breaking down crying with them, if he cannot bring himself to embalm the body, then he's useless to the family. They need him to retain a certain emotional distance."

"So funeral directors are all sociopaths too?"

"Of course not. It's possible for an empathic person to develop a hardened shell, to compartmentalize enough to carry out an otherwise difficult job. But my point is that sociopaths naturally fit these roles. They thrive in them. Craig Canning has saved hundreds of lives." She hesitated a beat. "He just doesn't care that he's saved them. Not really. He's in it for the skill and the challenge. He enjoys beating death at its own game, if you will. He views every patient saved as a kind of trophy, which is abnormal thinking, I grant you, but the end result is a win for the patient too."

"This is fascinating, really," Annalisa said as she pushed the book back toward its owner. "But I don't know what it has to do with me."

Mara glanced over her shoulder like she was afraid she'd been followed. Her voice dropped to a stage whisper. "My publisher is a university press. They've bet big on this book—on me and Craig—and they have sunk more money than usual into the print run. Needless to say, my grant money is tied up in this too. If the book sinks, my career is shattered. So I need to be absolutely sure."

"Sure of what?"

Mara waited another moment before taking a newspaper clipping from her bag. "This young woman, Victoria Albright, fell to her death the other day from the balcony of her penthouse apartment."

Annalisa didn't need to read the newspaper article. Nick had mentioned the case at the Parkview apartment complex. "And?"

"Craig Canning lives in the same building. I need to be sure he had nothing to do with Miss Albright's death."

"What makes you think he was involved?" As she recalled, Nick had ruled the whole awful incident an accident.

"I don't think it. At least, I don't want to think it. Craig Canning has no record, no history of violence. I wouldn't have centered the book around him if he did. He's well-liked in his field, and most people who know him refuse to believe he could ever be a sociopath. He's charming and delightful most of the time."

"What makes you sure he is one?"

"I've run both brain imaging studies and psychological tests on him. It's as close to certainty as one can get about these things."

"But you're less sure he's good, is that it?" Annalisa asked as she looked at the book cover again.

"We're slated to appear on *Good Morning America* next month for the book's launch. *The New York Times* is sending a reporter." She sounded pressured. "There are going to be a whole lot of people out there trying to prove me wrong, looking for any kind of dirt they can dig up on Craig. I need him squeaky clean."

"But this woman's death . . . it was ruled an accident. Do you have any reason to believe otherwise?"

"Nothing concrete," Mara admitted. "But the newspaper report says she was hanging wind chimes when she fell."

"So?"

"So wind chimes are Craig's go-to move when he's trying to bed a woman, and he tries to score with all of them. He even tried it with me and he knows quite well I'm married. He has a charming story about how the wind chimes remind him of his grandmother's farm back in Iowa. He says she hung a set she made herself, and he used to play in the yard with the baby goats and listen to the chimes blow in the breeze. He'll tell you that the tinkling sound makes him feel like her spirit is watching over him."

"Sounds sweet," Annalisa agreed.

"It's bunk," Mara said flatly. "His grandmother worked at Marshall Field's. But he'll make you believe the story when he's telling it."

"So you think because Victoria Albright had wind chimes, she must have been involved with Craig Canning? And that he pushed her over the edge of that balcony? Why?"

"I told you—I don't want to believe it. I am hoping you find out that the two of them never even rode in the same elevator together. But whatever you do, you can't let him know it's me who hired you. You can't let anyone know. If it got out that I had doubts about my star subject . . ."

"But you do have doubts," Annalisa pointed out. "Doesn't that negate the whole premise right there?"

"No. I could very well be wrong. I probably am. Besides, it's a proven fact that Craig saves lives. He—he's ultimately a force for good no matter what his motives."

Annalisa fingered the edge of the newspaper article. Victoria Albright's smiling face peered out at her, a candid photo taken at some recent society benefit. "What do you think would happen?" she asked. "What would Craig Canning do if he found out you were investigating him?"

She gave a brittle laugh. "Sociopaths hate to lose. Craig's hospital already didn't want him doing this project, but he overruled them. It caters to his narcissism. He's expecting a big bestseller and some bad-boy notoriety. If the project goes south, it will be my career but Craig's ego will take a hit. A hit that he can't, and won't, withstand."

"What does that mean?"

"If he suffers, then I do too." Her gaze flickered over Annalisa. "Me and anyone else he blames for the downfall of his big coming-out party."

"Me?" Annalisa asked, sitting up straighter. A prickle broke out across her neck. She had barely survived her last encounter with a sociopath.

"You understand then why I came to you," Mara said with a grim nod. "You know the risks. You'll be prepared."

Annalisa turned the book back around so she could study the dark, enigmatic eyes of Craig Canning. He didn't look dangerous, but then again, they never did. Mara Delaney was right that Annalisa wouldn't be fooled this time. "Okay," she said with a long exhale. "I'll take the case."

FOUR

··········

Annalisa picked up a brochure from the marble counter as she loitered in the lobby of the Parkview apartment building. *Timeless beauty with the luxuries of modern living,* read the cover. The glossy photos showed residents enjoying a crystal-blue pool, sitting in a landscaped garden, and admiring the skyline view from an expansive balcony. "Thinking about moving in?" asked the uniformed doorman in a friendly tone. "We've got a penthouse apartment opening up."

"Uh, maybe," Annalisa hedged. She and Nick were in search of a new place, but they could never afford to live here. Technically, Victoria Albright had lived and died in the same Chicago that Annalisa was raised in, but the ritzy Gold Coast bore little resemblance to the boxy, low-lying brick houses found in Norwood Park. The city's priciest neighborhood had started out as undesirable swampland until tycoon Potter Palmer set his sights on it in the 1870s. He built himself a forty-two-room mansion, as big as a city block, which had then attracted his wealthy buddies to the region and sent real estate soaring. Now the place was a mix of sleek high-rise condos, row houses, and historic buildings with fancy façades that had been converted to luxury apartments years ago. If you still pined for an old-timey mansion, you could get one if you had a spare five million dollars lying around, which Annalisa assuredly did not. She put the brochure back down. "I'm not sure how safe it is here," she confided to the doorman, whose name tag read DAMON. "Didn't some girl die here just the other day?"

He made a sympathetic noise. "Yeah, Vicki Albright. But it was a freak accident, nothing against the building."

"But I read she fell from her balcony," Annalisa said, going wide-eyed at him. "That suggests there's an issue with the building codes—or at least the railing."

"Nah," he replied. "Building's fine. Vicki wasn't always the most careful girl around, you know?"

"What do you mean?"

He looked like he considered saying more but then shook his head. "I just wouldn't worry about the apartment being unsafe, that's all."

Annalisa gave him points for refusing to gossip. She tried another tack. "Well, if I were interested . . . do you know who might be selling?"

"Not sure. She had a brother, but he lives out in L.A. and I'm pretty sure he likes it that way. Doubt he'd want to move here away from all the sunshine and movie stars."

"Movie stars!" Annalisa leaned over the counter and tried to act impressed. "Does he really get to hang out with them?"

"Sure does. He showed me a pic of him and that chick who just won the Oscar—like, from the after-party? He got to hold the statue and everything."

Annalisa did not get to reply further because Nick walked in the front doors holding a folder in one hand and a hot dog in the other. "Really?" she asked him as she gestured at their tasteful surroundings. "You brought a street dog in here?"

"You said to meet you here for lunch. I assumed that meant I had to bring my own."

"Hey, you're that cop," Damon said, pointing at Nick. "We met the other day when Vicki . . ." He trailed off and then looked at Annalisa with suspicion. "Does that mean you're a cop too?"

"Nope," Annalisa said, feeling freer at the word. "I'm just his wife. Thanks for all the information on the building. We're just going to look around a bit if that's okay."

"Fine by me," Damon replied, although he seemed faintly puzzled.

In the elevator, Annalisa snatched the folder from Nick's hands as he finished off the last of his hot dog. She paged through the witness statements from the morning of Vicki Albright's accident and winced as she got to the photos. Vicki had landed face down on the stone pavers near the fountain in the courtyard. "Zimmer would kill me if she knew I was showing you this stuff," Nick said, referring to her old boss.

"She'd hate it more if you missed a murder."

"That's the only reason I'm here. Hey, check it out." He touched a handmade flyer tacked to the elevator wall. *Lost cat*, it said. *Reward for safe return*. "How much do you think the reward is in a place like this? Like, a week's salary for you or me? Two?"

Annalisa glanced at the photo of the white cat with the blue eyes. "You're a detective," she told him. "Find the cat and you'll have your answer."

The elevator gave a soft ding as they reached the fourteenth floor. "It's number 148," Nick said as he fished the keys from his pocket.

"Wait a sec." Annalisa stopped him before he pushed open the door. She pulled out two sets of latex gloves from her jacket pocket and handed one pair to Nick. He stared at them as she put on her gloves. "We don't want to disturb the scene," she said. "In case forensics needs to take a look."

"They took a look. They found nothing. The same nothing we're about to find." He made a show of putting on the gloves and then entered the apartment. The scent of stale, slightly perfumed air hit Annalisa in the face. It only took a few days with no circulation for a space to feel alien and stifled, and Vicki had been dead for nearly a week. Annalisa stalked the perimeter of the huge apartment to get a feel for the layout. Burnished hardwood floors, cobalt paint on the walls with a white coffered ceiling. The place had to be three thousand square feet at least, and Annalisa counted three spa-like bathrooms. She repressed an eerie feeling at imagining Vicki at the vanity getting ready for her day. No matter how many times she had visited a deceased person's home, Annalisa never got used to being a voyeur, an unwelcome guest. Vicki would have stocked the bar, picked out the oversized white sofa, hung the giant painting of Audrey Hepburn on the wall, never imagining these would be the artifacts left at the scene of her death.

"The front door was locked from the inside?" she asked Nick as she drifted to the kitchen.

"Correct."

The kitchen was magazine-cover beautiful, with no dirty dishes to be seen. It had modern walnut-colored cabinets with brass pulls and a large quartz island. The huge fridge was dressed to match the cabinets. Annalisa opened it and found a bunch of expensive cheese, half-eaten, prewashed salad wilting in the bag, various types of alcohol, and three single-sized bottles of fancy pomegranate seltzer water. The freezer held stacks of Lean Cuisine entrées and Annalisa smiled a little as she saw them. Maybe she and Vicki had something in common after all.

"Who gets this place?" Annalisa asked as she moved to the living room. It featured wide glass doors that led to the huge balcony, which was presumably the point of Vicki's demise.

"Not sure. Maybe her brother, Gavin. He's out in California."

Annalisa turned to look at him. "You spoke to him?"

"He took the news hard. Started sobbing on the phone."

"Hmm. Still, if this is a murder, he'd have to be a suspect. The money's all his now."

"That's a big if," Nick replied. "And like I said, he's in California. He hasn't seen her since Christmas and I got the feeling that was how she liked it."

"Hmm," Annalisa said again. She consulted the photos in the folder and went out to the balcony. Nick followed. "Nice view," she remarked as she looked out at the blooming trees in Washington Square Park.

"I guess that depends on which way you're looking," Nick said, peering over the edge to the courtyard below. Annalisa looked too. Management had cleaned up any trace of Vicki's fall. The garden was pristine.

"So," she said to him, "walk me through it."

He narrowed his eyes at her. "This is supposed to be your show, not mine."

"You say it was an accident. Tell me how it went down."

He gave a heavy sigh. "She'd dragged one of the chairs over to this corner," he said, pulling out a metal chair from the set Vicki had on the balcony. "You can see the hook on the ceiling here where she was hanging the wind chimes."

Annalisa squinted where he'd indicated and saw a cheap-looking temporary white hook stuck to the bottom of the cement overhang. She pulled out the photo to compare and noted Nick had the wrong chair. The one in the photo was missing one of its tiny iron feet. "Use this one," she told him, dragging over the correct chair.

He rolled his eyes and went on with his demonstration. "Okay, so Vicki Albright put the chair here and climbed up with her wind chimes. Only she lost her footing . . ." The chair wobbled as he stood on it.

"Careful," Annalisa cried.

He steadied himself. "As you can see, the railing is down past my knees, well below my center of gravity. If I stumbled in the wrong direction, I'd go right over the edge."

Annalisa saw a bar set on wheels sitting in the corner. "Was she drinking?"

"No alcohol or other drugs in her system," Nick said as he climbed back down.

Annalisa's cell phone buzzed in her pocket and she drew it out to find a text from Cassidy. It included a selfie of Cassidy dropping the envelope in the mailbox outside the post office with a grin and a thumbs-up sign. *Dropped off ytday*, she wrote. *All set. I need 2 talk 2 u abt new case.*

Annalisa shook her head but had to smile at Cassidy's persistence. The kid had verve. Nick saw the photo and frowned. "Is that Cassidy?"

"Yeah, she ran an errand for me yesterday and now she thinks we're in business together."

"Ha," Nick replied, but then he narrowed his eyes. "You're not, though. Right?"

"Not what?"

"I mean, you're not going to make a habit of using her for your errands and stuff. She's a kid."

Annalisa halted her poking around to stare at him. "She's your kid. You're the one who said I should get to know her better."

"Yeah, I meant like take her out for coffee or a manicure or something."

"Since when have I ever gotten a manicure?"

"Just . . . leave Cassidy out of your work, okay? She doesn't need to see that kind of stuff." He nodded at the file folder she held in her hand. "Especially not with everything going on with her mom."

"Hey, she's the one badgering me for a job, not the other way around."

Nick frowned. "I'll talk to her." He took a deep breath and spread his arms. "Well, have you seen enough? I told you that everything here points to an accident. It all adds up."

Annalisa wrinkled her nose at her surroundings. "Except for the wind chimes."

"What are you talking about?"

"Look around. Vicki Albright's got high-end, modern taste. The teak chaise loungers, the wrought-iron table and chair set. Why is she hang-ing some kitschy wind chimes out here? It destroys the vibe."

"I'm sorry," Nick said cupping one hand behind his ear. "Are you arguing my conclusions based on *vibes*?"

"You have to admit wind chimes don't fit the aesthetic." Even if Vicki had wanted some tinkling accompaniment on her balcony, An-nalisa felt sure she wouldn't have picked the version found at the scene. The file folder held two photos of the garish decoration, each depicting the face of a stained-glass jungle cat—a leopard, maybe—with crystals and chimes hanging down. One photo showed them in disarray on the ground, as Nick had described, and the other showed them laid out flat on a counter with an evidence tag. "There's a crystal missing," Annalisa observed.

"Yeah?" He came to look over her shoulder.

"This one. See?" A teardrop-shaped crystal was missing from the end of one of the strings. She started searching the ground for it, drop-ping down on her hands and knees to examine under the chaises. "I don't see it anywhere," she reported after a thorough exploration.

Nick gestured over the railing. "Maybe it fell down over the edge with her."

"Maybe," Annalisa said, unconvinced. "I still say she didn't buy those wind chimes herself. Too tacky."

"But she hung them up," Nick argued. "She must have liked them well enough."

"I'm going to check the bedrooms." She walked through all of them, pausing here and there to take photos with her phone. She discovered Vicki had converted the smallest bedroom into a giant closet, com-plete with a rose-gold sofa, a three-way mirror, and a ring light to help capture it all. Annalisa pulled out the closest gown, a shimmery black number with a killer slit up the side.

Nick let out a low whistle as he joined her in the room. "I guess the rich have to spend their money on something, huh?" he asked as he contemplated her floor-to-ceiling rack of shoes.

"Did you see the engraved thank-you notes tacked up in the office? American Cancer Society, Protect the Great Lakes, Oxfam, and a bunch of others. Vicki must have given a bunch to charity, which no doubt meant she had a lot of chichi parties to attend." Annalisa had taken her own pictures of all the notes and photos to look through them later. So far, she saw no trace of Craig Canning. There was no evidence that the neurosurgeon and the socialite even knew each other.

Nick took out his phone to check the time. "I've got to get back. You need a lift?"

"No, I want to look around outside. Maybe talk to a few of the residents." Like Craig Canning, if she could catch him. "I'll let you know if that missing crystal turns up."

"Yeah," Nick said with an odd tone.

She tilted her head at him. "What?"

He took a breath. "Look, I don't want to piss all over your first case or anything, but it's bunk. This doctor guy, Canning? He didn't do anything to Vicki Albright. The witness says Vicki fell at 8:52 on the dot. Canning was in surgery across town at 9:15 that morning. He couldn't have done it."

"How did you know that? About his alibi, I mean."

Nick shrugged. "When you told me you were looking at him for Vicki's death, I called the hospital to check his whereabouts. No big deal."

"It's a huge deal. I never asked you to contact the hospital or look into Canning's alibi. Who did you talk to? Did you mention my name? This investigation is supposed to be confidential."

"You're the one who looped me in, remember? Excuse me for trying to help."

"Mara Delaney was very clear that Craig Canning cannot find out he's being investigated for this. I can't believe you butted in—this isn't your case."

"Actually, it is. And it's closed." He grabbed for the folder but she held it back. He dropped his hands and his expression turned apologetic. "At least you can tell your client that her 'good psychopath'—whatever that is—didn't do it."

"Yeah, thanks." Annalisa glanced at the folder. "You might want to do a little more investigating, though. One of your suspects is lying to you."

He drew back in surprise. "What suspect? Who?"

"Vicki's brother, Gavin? You said he told you he hadn't seen her since Christmas. But the doorman downstairs said Gavin showed him a picture taken at the most recent Oscars party, which would have been only about four weeks ago." She smiled and patted his middle with the folder. "Thanks again for the tour, Detective."

FIVE

....

ANNALISA SCOURED THE GROUNDS BELOW VICKI ALBRIGHT'S BALCONY, BUT SHE DID NOT FIND THE MISSING CRYSTAL FROM THE WIND CHIMES. The landscapers could have picked it up while tending to the gardens, she supposed. Or perhaps a crow spotted it glinting on the sidewalk and made off with it. Eventually she told herself she had stalled enough and it was time to make direct contact with her target, Dr. Craig Canning. Mara Delaney had told her he drove a black Jaguar and even helpfully provided the plate number. Annalisa found the car parked in his slot in the underground garage, which suggested he would be home. His apartment was directly across from Vicki's on the other side of the courtyard, although he was two floors down. Annalisa paused outside his door to consider her approach. Mara had said Dr. Canning liked his women and pursued pretty much every one in his path. Armed with this knowledge, Annalisa slipped off her wedding ring. The more distracted he was, the better.

She knocked and waited. No reply. She put her ear to the door and heard muffled noises on the other side, like music or the television was playing. She knocked again. This time, the door opened to reveal a barefoot, bare-chested man wearing doctor's scrubs for pants. He was toweling off his wet hair and paused when he saw her standing there. "Well, hello," he said with a slow smile. "I hope you haven't been waiting out here too long. You caught me in the shower."

"Not long, no."

"Good, good." He looked at her with a half smile, like he was waiting for her to say something. She made him wait. "Did we have an appointment?" he asked, still friendly. "Because Damon usually buzzes me when guests arrive."

"No, I've just been going door-to-door talking to people in the building."

"Huh." He leaned on the open door and looked her over appraisingly. "You don't look like a salesgirl."

"I'm not. Your powers of deduction are strong." Annalisa gave what she hoped was a dazzling smile. "I'm an insurance investigator. We're handling the incident with Victoria Albright."

"Ohhh," he said frowning. "Awful thing. Just the worst."

"Do you mind if I ask you a few questions?"

"You're welcome to come in, but I'm afraid I won't be of much help to you." He started walking into the apartment, leaving the door open for her to follow. "I wasn't here when it happened," he called over his shoulder, his voice echoing off all the hard surfaces. "I was at work."

"Oh? What do you do for work?"

He didn't reply right away so she lingered in the living room, a mirror to Vicki Albright's with the same sliding doors leading out onto the balcony. She walked to the glass and looked out. He had a fake potted ficus tree, a single lounge chair, a big metal grill, and, waving gently in the breeze, some wind chimes. She took a quick picture with her phone and turned to study the rest of the room.

Craig Canning's walls were gray, with custom walnut bookshelves on either side of a massive television. He had an L-shaped black leather sectional and a coffee table that appeared to be made from a slice of a giant redwood tree. The coffee table had a few books stacked on it and she picked them up. The second one down was an advance copy of Mara Delaney's title, *The Good Sociopath*. She flipped it open and saw an inscription. *To the best bad boy I know—we did it. XO Mara.*

"I'm a neurosurgeon," he said, emerging as if from the ether. He had a sweatshirt on now.

She nearly fumbled the book since she hadn't heard him approach. "Oh, ha," she said as she set it back down. "I always wondered what brain docs say when the rest of us joke, 'It isn't brain surgery . . .'"

He grinned. "We say, 'It's not like talking to women.'"

She did laugh then. "Somehow I don't think you have trouble with that either."

"You just bring out my chatty side," he answered with a conspiratorial wink. He nodded at the coffee table. "I see you found my book."

"Oh, it was lying here so I took a quick peek. I hope you don't mind. Such an interesting topic . . . who would imagine a good sociopath?"

"You want a copy? I've got tons." He went and pulled one off the shelves. "It doesn't come out for another few weeks, but you can be one of the first readers."

"Wait," she said, pretending to be confused. "Are you M. J. Delaney then? This is your book?"

"M. J. is just the writer," he said as he handed her a copy. "I'm the star." He tapped the cover with his stylized image on it.

"Oh, wow. That's you?"

"Crazy, huh? I don't believe all that psychobabble stuff, but the press can't get enough of it, let me tell you. We've got the *Tribune*, *The New York Times*, the *L.A. Times* . . . even *People* magazine is doing a feature."

"On you? Because you're . . ." She hesitated on purpose and lowered her voice to a whisper. "A sociopath?"

He laughed as he sat on the sofa. "It's okay to say the word. Lord knows Dr. Delaney reminds me enough what I am."

"Okay, but you're not, uh, you're not going to cut off my head and stick it on your mantel, are you?" She gave a nervous laugh as she perched on the edge of the opposite couch. "Because my company knows I'm here doing interviews."

"No, no," he rushed to assure her. "I don't kill people. I save them."

She looked down at the book in her hand. "Ah. That's the good part?"

"Oh, honey," he said with a grin, "I'm more than good." He reached over and tapped her knee, an affectionate, flirty gesture that made her cheeks warm. "Now, what did you want to ask me about?"

She set the book aside. "Victoria Albright. Did you know her?"

"We may have said hello in the elevator once or twice. Seemed like a nice girl."

"When was the last time you saw her?"

"A couple of weeks ago, maybe. I'm not sure."

"And what time did you leave the apartment building on the day she fell?"

"I had surgery that morning so it must have been on the early side. Eight-fifteen? Eight-thirty?"

"And you didn't see Vicki at all that day?"

"Not a glimpse." He spread his hands. "Told you I wouldn't be any help to you. I didn't know the girl. Why are you investigating her death? She had an accident, is what I heard."

"She fell hanging wind chimes," Annalisa replied, watching him closely for a reaction. His dark brown eyes showed only sympathy. How was this possible? Mara had told her Craig Canning didn't feel normal human emotions.

"Tragic." He shook his head like he couldn't believe it. "And so young."

"You must lose patients sometimes," Annalisa ventured.

"Yes, but it's expected. Part of the job. You don't expect a young, healthy person to die climbing a chair and falling over a balcony."

Did the news stories say Vicki had been on a chair? She wasn't sure. "Did you know any of her friends? Someone else I might talk to?"

"I'm afraid not. Hey, I'm completely dehydrated. You want something to drink?" He stood up and she followed him to a blindingly white kitchen with lacquered cabinets. He opened the refrigerator for perusal, making sure she got an eyeful of his tight rear end.

"I've got to ask," she said. "Why does that author lady think you're a sociopath? I mean, you seem plenty nice to me."

He stood ramrod straight and turned to face her. "How did you know M. J. is a woman?"

"Uh . . ." Annalisa froze and cursed herself for the slipup. Mara had warned her she had to be careful. "The book," she said, thinking fast. "There's a bio of her on the back flap." Her heart hammered while he processed this and she hoped like hell it was true.

Craig's eyes crinkled as he smiled and he wagged a finger at her. "You are an astute investigator, Ms. Vega. I like that. To answer your question, Mara ran a psychological battery on me and put me through an MRI machine. According to her, I'm a textbook sociopath."

"Yes but . . ." She couldn't resist asking. "How does that make you feel?"

"Feel?" He looked at her curiously, as though he didn't understand the question.

"Being labeled like that," she clarified.

"It makes me feel sorry for Mara and all her little mind-doctor friends. Psychology shouldn't really be considered a science, you know. It's got more in common with astrology . . . or witchcraft." He paused to admire his own humor. "So she has this little theory about me. Good for her. It doesn't mean she's right."

"But what if she is?"

He considered, his eyes growing hooded. "If she is? Then maybe you're right to be worried, being here alone with me." He watched her face for a reaction and she couldn't hold back a startled blink at how quick the steely line of menace crept into his voice. Just as quick, it was gone. His face became open and friendly again. "No worries, though, because Mara is full of it. Let me get you that drink, shall I?"

He turned around to the fridge again and produced two bottles of seltzer. Annalisa recognized the obscure brand, Ora, and the flavor, pomegranate, as the same drink she'd seen in Vicki's apartment. "Pomegranate," she said as he held out one bottle to her. "How unusual."

"I'm addicted," he admitted. "Can't get enough of the stuff, and it's impossible to find. You have to special order it or go to this one bodega I frequent over by the hospital. They're the only place in the city that stocks it. Cheers," he offered, touching his bottle to hers.

Annalisa felt the cold travel from her hand to her stomach. She made herself smile at him. "Cheers."

SIX

....

ANNALISA'S LAST STOP AT THE COMPLEX WAS THE UNIT DIRECTLY ADJACENT TO Vicki Albright's, an opulent apartment owned by Ruth Bernstein, who happened to be the one to witness Vicki's fall. When Annalisa went to knock she found another flyer for the lost cat, Duchess, affixed to the door. She noticed Ruth's name as the contact and determined it must be her cat that had gone missing. The door flung open almost immediately after Annalisa's knock, revealing an impeccably dressed, impossibly tiny woman with cloud-white hair. "Yes?" she said eagerly. "Do you have news?"

"News?"

"Of Duchess," the woman replied, faltering at Annalisa's confusion. "My cat."

"No, I'm sorry. I haven't seen your cat. Has she been missing long?"

"Since that awful day, when Victoria fell."

"Victoria Albright," Annalisa said. "Yes. She's the reason I'm here. I'm investigating her death." She introduced herself and gave the same ruse she'd invented for Canning, that the insurance company had sent her.

"Insurance? Don't tell me her brute of a brother stands to collect." She scowled at her own words and waved one delicate hand. "Oh, listen to me and my terrible gossip. It's not my business what happens to that poor girl's money. Come in, won't you?"

Annalisa entered in, past a ticking grandfather clock and an antique coat stand displaying a man's wool coat and fedora hat. The placement of the living room was now familiar to her, with the glass sliders leading out to the balcony. Ruth Bernstein's apartment was furnished like Annalisa's own parents' might have been, if they were wealthy Gold Coasters: sturdy, classic furniture in a traditional L-shaped arrangement. Annalisa paused to admire a colorful Tiffany lamp. "Your home is beautiful," she said to Ruth.

The woman's answering smile didn't quite reach her eyes. "Thank you. It's too big for me now that Marty's gone, but I've lived here for fifty years and can't imagine being anywhere else. Can I offer you some tea? I've got a hot kettle in the kitchen."

Annalisa had already downed a bottle of pomegranate seltzer but she said yes anyway. The kitchen was open to the living room so Ruth called back to Annalisa as she assembled the tea. "I guess it makes sense that the insurance company would send their own investigator, given how shocking and unexpected Vicki's death was. I have pet insurance for Duchess, but a fat lot of good it does me now. There's no one to call, no one to investigate. Just . . . poof! She's gone."

"I'm sorry," Annalisa said with sympathy. "I know you must miss her."

"Someone must have taken her. That's all I can think. She got out into the hall and someone snatched her up. She's friendly and would go with anyone, especially if they offered her a treat. I swear I'll find who took her. I'll go door-to-door through this whole building if I have to—I'm going to find her."

"I hope you do."

Ruth gave a wry smile as she handed Annalisa a cup of tea. "I apologize for my rambling. I'm afraid Duchess is foremost on my mind these days. But you're here about Victoria. How can I help you?"

"I heard you witnessed the incident."

"The incident," Ruth repeated, her mouth tight. "Yes." They returned to the living room where Ruth set her tea on the end table and then carefully lowered herself into a Queen Anne chair. "I had just returned from my daily walk when it happened. I heard a horrible scream, and when I looked up, I saw Vicki tumbling from her balcony." She shuddered. "Poor child."

"Did you see anyone else?"

"On the balcony? No."

"Anyone else in the courtyard or otherwise nearby?"

"No, it's a quiet time of day. Usually it's just me and the birds outside. Duchess, she likes to watch them so sometimes I take leftover crumbs in a little baggie to drop for them in the courtyard. It keeps them flitting about."

"And you say this happened a little before nine a.m.?"

"Yes, must have," she agreed with a short nod. "I leave for my walk promptly at eight, when Ben says so."

"Ben?"

"The clock by the door? He was a wedding present from Marty's parents. He bongs out the hour, and when he bongs eight, I get my coat. By the time he's done his business, I'm out the door. It takes me fifty minutes to do my loop and I'd just finished up when . . . when Victoria fell."

If the timing was true, then Nick was right: Craig Canning couldn't have done it. He was in surgery by nine-fifteen and it was at least a twenty-minute drive to the hospital. "Could I take a look at Ben?" Annalisa asked, setting down her china cup. Maybe the clock had been wrong.

"Of course," Ruth replied, rising somewhat stiffly and escorting

Annalisa to the clock. Annalisa checked the time against her phone and found it was the same. "Ben still keeps perfect time," Ruth said with pride. "He only needs winding once per week."

"He's beautiful," Annalisa said, meaning it. "And you go for your walk every day at the same time?"

"Eight sharp, rain or shine. I used to go in the snow too but these days the icy sidewalks are too treacherous for me."

"And Vicki—Victoria Albright . . . did she like to go for walks?"

"No," Ruth said as they returned to the sitting room. "Not that I saw. She liked to entertain guests, sometimes overnight, and she went out a lot. She did love her balcony. She would lie out and talk on the phone at all hours. It was the kind with just earphones—only they're called something else now—anyway, it would look like she was talking to the air. Sometimes she would stand by the railing, gesturing as she talked, and I swear someone watching her from the other side would think she was doing a theater production."

"So you could hear her conversations."

"Some of them," Ruth demurred. "I tried not to listen."

"Oh, of course, but it must have been difficult not to hear. Your balconies are so close." Annalisa estimated the ends had only about four feet between them.

"She talked a lot," Ruth admitted. "That's why I was surprised when they told me she was hanging wind chimes. Who would want that racket while trying to hold a telephone conversation?"

"It does seem odd," Annalisa agreed. "So, that morning, when you left for your walk, did you see anyone in the hall?"

"No. As I said, the working folk tend to depart even earlier, so it's quiet around here by eight o'clock. I did run into Dr. Canning in the elevator."

"Craig Canning?"

Ruth gave her first real smile. "You know him? Such a handsome fellow. And brilliant too. I can't believe some woman hasn't snapped him up yet." Her gaze dropped to Annalisa's ring finger, which was still bare from where she'd removed her wedding band.

"Maybe Victoria Albright could have made a play for him," Annalisa suggested.

"Well, she certainly was holding plenty of auditions." Ruth pursed her lips. "But no, I don't think they would have made a match. Victoria was too flighty and dramatic for someone like Dr. Canning. She was sweet enough, and lovely to look at, but a man like that needs a woman of substance. Besides, after that incident with her brother last fall . . ." She broke off with an embarrassed grimace. "Oh, here I am going on again. You don't care about this stuff."

"No, really. Anything you can tell me about Victoria Albright is helpful. We're trying to, ah, assess her state of mind at the time of the accident."

Ruth's dark eyes grew wide, popping out from the rings of wrinkles. "You don't suspect she might have jumped?"

"We have to look at all possibilities."

"The only source of strife I'm aware of was her brother—Gavin is his name. He was visiting from California last fall and he got into an accident while driving Victoria's BMW. He was unharmed, but the car was totaled and the couple he hit sustained injuries. I gather the husband who was driving was relatively unharmed, but the wife had to have brain surgery."

"Brain surgery," Annalisa mused.

Ruth gave a knowing nod. "Dr. Canning was the surgeon. So you see, he would have known about the chaos going on in Victoria's life. That couple is suing for damages, and I expect they'll win. Gavin expected Victoria to pick up the charges and she wasn't having it."

"He doesn't have his own money?"

"Not enough of it, apparently," Ruth said with a dismissive sniff.

"But he's just lucky that Dr. Canning saved the woman's life. Otherwise, Gavin would be looking at murder charges. Now, I guess, he'll get Victoria's money after all."

Annalisa looked out at Ruth's balcony, which held an array of potted plants and a pair of comfortable lounge chairs. "Do you mind if I go out there to take a peek?" she asked.

"Go right ahead. I haven't been able to bring myself to go out since it happened."

Annalisa went out and felt an immediate breeze in her face. At fourteen stories up, the wind chimes would have gotten a continual workout. She noted that Ruth was correct at how close her balcony came to Vicki's next door. She wondered if maybe the cat, Duchess, had made the leap to the neighbor's place on the day Vicki fell. Of course, then someone should have found her there, unless she'd managed to escape during the parade of the forensic team going in and out. Annalisa went to the railing and slid her gaze across the units on the other side until she located Canning's apartment. With a start, she jumped backward. There he was on his balcony, watching her. When she looked again, he gave a little wave. Ruth came out onto the balcony, having put on a sweater. She joined Annalisa at the railing and followed her gaze to find Canning across the courtyard. "Oh, speak of the devil," Ruth said as she waved back. "There's Dr. Canning now. Isn't he just the nicest man?"

SEVEN

....

MARA DELANEY STOOD AT THE LECTERN, TWO HUNDRED PSYCHOLOGY STUDENTS SPREAD OUT AROUND THE AUDITORIUM IN FRONT OF HER. They were more upright than usual; the syllabus said they would be starting the unit on sociopathy, which was a class favorite. Normally it was her favorite topic too, but this unpleasant business with Craig Canning made her voice strident as she started the lecture. "What is conscience?" she asked them. "How do you know if you have one?"

A hand shot up in the front row. Brittney Geller. She always did the reading, always had the answers. Mara nodded at her. "Conscience is moral reasoning," Brittney said. "The little voice inside your head that tells you right from wrong."

Mara smiled. "It might surprise you that plenty of people—maybe as high as one in four—don't have any kind of inner monologue. No voice that narrates their behavior. Does that mean these people lack a conscience?"

Brittney looked perplexed that she hadn't given the correct response. *Gotcha,* Mara thought, scanning the darkened room for another hand.

Jason Fuentes didn't wait for her to call on him, just yelled out his reply. "It's when you do good things to help other people."

"Maybe," Mara countered. "But what if you help other people but you don't feel good about it?"

"What do you mean?" Brittney asked.

"I mean maybe you give money to the poor to lower your own taxes. Maybe you take care of your elderly neighbor hoping she'll remember you in her will. Or maybe you'd like to kill your spouse, but you know you'd go to jail for it so you don't do it. Are you still a good person?"

"Conscience is a deeply held set of moral principles," called a male voice from the shadows. Mara froze. She couldn't see his face, but she recognized him nonetheless. *Canning*. "Alongside the desire to act on those principles," he continued. "It requires empathy, self-knowledge, restraint, and reason. Absent any one of these and the individual in question will never develop what we consider a 'normal' conscience." He said this with assuredness, but also a hint of humor, and some of the students twisted in their seats to look at him.

"That—that's right," Mara said after a beat. "Conscience is a collection of traits, not an all-or-nothing status."

"But it is possible to have nothing," Canning called out. "A blank space where conscience would be. Isn't that so, Doctor?"

"A sociopath," Jason chimed in with enthusiasm. "Right?"

"Yes," Mara said, still looking in Canning's direction. Why was he here? He never visited her campus unless she'd specifically summoned him. "Estimates are that one to four percent of the population meets the criteria for sociopathy."

"That means in a room like this, we'd expect four to eight of them," Canning said, spreading his arms.

The students looked around at each other warily. They were all paying attention now. Mara normally liked to try to pick out the sociopaths in her class. Canning was wrong about the numbers; psychology pulled a lower percentage of sociopaths than other majors. They were, as a rule, incurious about what made other human beings tick. A sociopath assumed everyone was like them—calculating, empty inside—or else they were a patsy. But Mara did typically get one or two in her larger classes. They were the ones who didn't attend class and then showed up at her office angry about their poor grade. Some tried to charm her into changing it. *I totally love your class, but it's been a rough semester for me because my grandmother died . . . can we just round up the grade this one time?* Others tried threats. *My parents pay your salary. This C-minus is on you, not me. You didn't teach the material well enough. I'll be reporting you to the dean.*

"So what causes it?" Brittney wanted to know. "Are they, like, brain damaged? Genetically deficient?"

"Maybe they're superior," Canning said before Mara could answer.

"They certainly believe they are," she agreed. "As to why these individuals lack the normal traits that make up conscience, no one yet understands completely. Their brain scans show more impulsivity and a low response to fear. Why these changes happen is not clear. Growing up in a chaotic environment may contribute. But it is becoming clear that some people are just born that way."

"And you can't fix it?" Brittney wanted to know. "You can have a little baby sociopath and there's nothing you can do about it?"

Wait and buy my book, Mara thought with a flash of irritation. She caught a glimpse of Canning, his arms folded, looking smug at catching her off guard. She decided to give it right back to him. "Well, consider the case of Phineas Gage," she said to the class. "Gage was a well-liked and responsible man, a born leader. In 1848, he was foreman on a crew that used dynamite to clear boulders out of the path of the coming railroad tracks. It was a risky job. One day, there was a terrible accident and the tamping rod used to insert the dynamite into the rock blew back on Gage and went straight through his head.

Remarkably, Gage survived. He could walk and talk just as before, but something had changed in him. Where before, Gage had been an upstanding citizen with a steady job and many friends, he became foul-mouthed and lazy. He couldn't keep a job. His behavior was selfish and impulsive. He did not care about other people. It was like his conscience had been removed. Gage's injuries were about here"—she pointed to her forehead just above her nose—"suggesting that this part of the prefrontal cortex is necessary for the human expression of conscience. Furthermore, Gage never recovered. Once eliminated, conscience does not return."

"What happened to Gage?" Jason called out. "Did he start killing people or what?"

"Most sociopaths do not kill people," Mara said, feeling the weight of Canning's gaze on her. "As for Gage, he became a circus freak. A human curiosity and nothing more."

Her zinger landed. Canning rose and stalked out of the auditorium. He didn't like being compared to a degenerate circus act. *Good,* she thought, breathing easier again. *He's gone.* Sociopaths often refused to accept the truth about themselves. It was their one weakness. The same huge ego that made Canning a brilliant doctor made him blind to other people and their own motivations. Now she had to hope that her own ego hadn't botched everything, just when it had finally fallen into place.

···········

THE LATE AFTERNOON AIR HAD TURNED NIPPY, WIND ROARING OFF THE LAKE, AND MARA TIGHTENED THE BELT ON HER OVERCOAT AS SHE HURRIED TO HER OFFICE. Turning the corner, she found Craig Canning waiting for her. He leaned against the stone wall, vaping, and from this distance he could have been any other student. Mara squared her shoulders as she approached and he pushed off the wall with a grin when he saw her. "Classes done for the day?"

"Yes," she said, hoisting her bag higher on her shoulder. "Although I noticed you didn't stick around for the ending."

"You were getting kind of rough in there, doc." He took a puff. "Sociopaths are foul-mouthed, lazy, selfish. That doesn't sound like someone who has a book coming out next month about the societal benefits of lack of conscience. What happened to the good sociopaths?"

"Some are useful," she said brusquely, pushing past him to use her key card at the door. "Not all."

"Don't I feel special, then." He followed her into the building and down the hall to her office, where he lay his beautiful, lanky body across her worn-out brown leather sofa. Mara went behind her desk and powered up her computer. She had a dozen emails to answer before Paul arrived, and she did not want Craig to be here when he did.

"What are you doing here?" she asked him as he picked up a psychology journal and started paging through it. "You were done with school a dozen years ago."

"I thought I might take you to dinner."

She looked away from her computer screen. "What?"

"I have a medical society function tonight. I want you to be my date."

"I can't," she said, returning to her work.

"Sure you can." He sat up. "Won't it help the cause, if the pair of us are seen socializing together? People will believe you when you tell them I'm harmless fun."

"I have work to do."

"I am your work," he said, his tone flirtatious as he stood up and approached the desk. "I'm your biggest project. What could you possibly have to do that's more important than me?"

"I'm also married," she reminded him.

"Oh," he said, picking up the photo of her and Paul from the desk. "Right. I keep forgetting that detail. Maybe it's because you keep forgetting it too."

She grabbed the picture away. "Stop it. I told you, that was a mistake."

"I don't make mistakes."

She glanced at the clock on her wall. Paul was due in five minutes. "If you want this book to succeed, I have to maintain my professional objectivity. I'm the researcher, and you're my subject."

"Sure, okay. It's just . . . here I am offering to donate my body to science, and you're saying no." He leaned over the desk. Dammit, he still smelled good. "Don't you wonder," he murmured, "if one of those interviewers is going to think to ask how we met?"

For a second, her blood went cold. He couldn't be ruining things now, could he? "We met as part of the study," she said firmly, pushing her chair back.

"That's not how I remember it. I remember a helpless woman broken down by the side of the road, at two a.m. in a rainstorm. You were lucky my surgical schedule ran late that day. I was there to pick you up and . . . dry you off."

She narrowed her eyes at him. He was right, this was a vulnerability in her story. She laid out convincing evidence in her book that he was a sociopath, but no one had yet thought to ask her how she knew he was a sociopath in the first place. Why had she included him in the study? She had told Annalisa that Craig had given her wind chimes, like he did with all the women he pursued, but she hadn't been honest about the circumstances. "That was almost two years ago," she told him. "Ancient history. Why are you even bringing it up?"

"I told you." He picked a chocolate from the ceramic bowl on her desk, the one she kept for anxious students. He unwrapped it without asking and ate it. "I need a date."

"Try Tinder."

"Okay," he said agreeably, "but I don't think a Tinder date is going to give me half a million dollars."

Her jaw dropped. "And I am?"

He shrugged. "I have alerts set up for my name."

Of course he did.

"And this funny one arrived the other day—it says the book has a new deal? The international rights have sold at auction, and there's an audiobook deal now too. The news story said that author compensation would range more than seven figures."

Crap. She hadn't told him about any of this. "*Author* compensation," she said crisply. "I'm the author."

"But what would you have to write about, if not for me? Frankly, I'm hurt that you would use my story and then refuse to share in any of the profits." He gave her a thin smile and picked up her photo again, the one with Paul. "Unless maybe you were planning to use that cash to divorce this loser and run off with me. Then I could understand."

She heard footsteps in the hall and her heart went to her throat. But it wasn't Paul who came through the door. It was Miles Dupont, and his face was splotchy red over his sculpted beard. "They've pushed my book off the spring calendar," he bellowed at her. "I hope you're happy."

"Of course not. I'm sorry."

"They made the decision weeks ago, apparently, but did not bother to tell me. Your print run was doubled and that leaves no room at the presses for me. That's what they're saying." He paced near her sofa.

"Doubled the print run?" Craig said with a grin. "That's fantastic."

"Miles," Mara said, raising her voice over Craig's chortling. "I'm sorry about your book. But it wasn't personal, and it wasn't my decision."

"Yeah, Miles," Craig echoed with a waggle of his eyebrows. "Maybe your book was just boring." He chuckled at his own remark as Mara sent him a warning glare.

"Go ahead and laugh," Miles said acidly. "You'll burn with the rest of us when the planet goes up in flames. Climate science is a real, actual problem, the most important issue of our time—not some made-up fairy tale about nice psychos." Craig looked surprised at this remark, and Miles advanced on him. "That's right, I read the book, at least enough of it to know what you are."

"If that's true," Craig reasoned, "you might want to step back."

"I'm not afraid of you."

"Then you're dumber than you look."

"Gentlemen," Mara called loudly. "Zip 'em back up, please."

Paul walked into the room just in time to hear her say it. He blinked behind his glasses. "I'm sorry, did I have the wrong time?"

"No, honey, they were just leaving."

"He was leaving," Craig said, pointing at Miles. "Not me."

"This is breach of contract," Miles said, looking from Craig to Mara. "My book was supposed to come out in July and now it's not, thanks to you. Maybe fall, they said. The earth can always wait, right? It's been here 4.5 billion years—what's a few more months? Instead, let's spill a bunch more ink on sexy, rich bad boys and why they're *sooo* fascinating. Well, maybe you don't care about carbon dioxide levels or clean energy, but I bet you care about money. I'm going to find the nastiest legal team around and sue you all for damages."

"Not very eco-friendly," Craig said to Mara in a stage whisper. "Think of all the wasted paper."

"I'd tell you to go to hell," Miles said, flicking a disgusted glance at Craig. "But I think you'd enjoy it there."

He stalked off and Paul sneezed into his handkerchief. "My," he said as he wiped his nose. "He seems rather worked up."

"He'll cool off," Mara said. Miles had no other choice. He could try to sue the publisher, but she'd bet his case would not be successful. At the moment, she had bigger problems as Paul was eyeing Craig with curiosity.

"I'm Paul Delaney," he said, extending his hand.

"I know," Craig replied, and Mara held back a squeak. He wouldn't dare say anything.

"You do?" Paul asked, puzzled. "Have we met?"

"We work out of the same hospital," Craig explained. "And of course Mara's mentioned you. You're into feet, right?"

"Podiatry, yes." He turned watery eyes to Mara for more context. "I'm sorry, my allergies are terrible this time of year. I'm afraid the medication makes me a little fuzzy-headed."

"This is Craig Canning," Mara said, forcing a smile.

"Oh." Paul jerked upright and looked at Craig with fresh eyes. He knew about Mara's project and he didn't approve. *Even if it's true what he is,* Paul had said to her, *why do you need to advertise it? It's not good for the hospital. And what's bad for the hospital is bad for us, remember?*

She had accepted this little reminder about who paid the bills in their household. Her university teaching career paid an okay salary, but it was nothing compared to the quarter million Paul pulled down annually as an experienced podiatrist. The book was about to change that power imbalance, if only she could hold everything together. Craig had to show he was the real deal.

"Your wife has kindly agreed to accompany me to a boring dinner where we all get to hear about some new kidney drug," Craig said, smooth as ever, daring Mara to overrule him now.

Mara was stuck and she knew it. She looked at Paul with apology. "It's a last-minute thing," she said. "His date canceled."

"His date?" Paul repeated quizzically. "You're going as his date?"

"Purely business," Craig assured him. "Right, doc?"

Her answer was pure steel. "Right."

Paul sighed heavily and blew his nose again. "I guess I'll just order soup from the deli, then, and have an early evening. Hay fever is the worst."

"You should see a doctor," Craig deadpanned.

Paul actually chuckled. "Good one," he said with a wheeze. Craig's charm worked on everyone, it seemed.

"I'll drive home," Mara announced. To Craig, she said, "Meet you there?"

"I'll send a car," he told her.

When the Lincoln pulled up outside their town house, Mara was ready in her ankle-length black dress with the slit up the side. Paul had taken an allergy pill with his dinner and passed out in a recliner in front of the television. She would never admit it to Craig, but the evening ahead excited her more than staying home to grade papers while Paul snored away in his La-Z-Boy. She took her sparkly silver clutch and went to the car, where she was surprised to find Craig waiting for her in the back seat.

"You look ravishing," he said.

"Look but no touch," she reminded him. "This is business, remember?"

"If it's business, then we should definitely revisit the financial terms now that the book is taking off," he murmured as his hand came to rest on her knee. He squeezed lightly and Mara held her temper.

"You know," she said as the car pulled into traffic, "if you make trouble for me, that would harm the success of the book. It would potentially wreck the whole project." This was the way to deal with him, she knew: remind him of his self-interest.

"I realize that." He slid his hand up her thigh. "And it's the same for you, yes? You'd be risking everything if you made trouble for me."

Her abdomen tightened like a boa constrictor and she had to force her tone to remain light. "Why would I want to make trouble for you?"

He leaned in and nuzzled her cheek, his breath whispery across her skin as he replied. "Believe me, sweetheart, you don't."

EIGHT

···········

ANNALISA'S NEXT MOVE WAS TO CHECK THE OTHER END OF CRAIG CANNING'S ALIBI. Ruth had met him in the elevator a few minutes past eight the morning Vicki Albright fell to her death. She saw him heading to the parking garage and presumed he left for the hospital at that point. But did he? Annalisa had printed up a few fake business cards that read BETH THOMAS, ACE INSURANCE and she took them with her to the hospital where Craig Canning worked. She drove from his apartment building, the most direct route, and the trip clocked in at twenty-two minutes. He should have arrived at about eight-thirty the day that Vicki went over her balcony.

Annalisa found a young man working in the office near the entrance and exit to the hospital garage. Or at least he was supposed to be working. Instead he was deep into a paperback copy of *American Gods*. Annalisa introduced herself as Beth, gave him a card, and told him she was investigating a claim that Dr. Canning had made about vandalism to his car. The kid scrambled to sit upright. "Dr. Canning's car was damaged? He just got here."

"Not today. A week ago Tuesday. He's not actually sure where the damage took place, but the car is parked here frequently. I wondered if you might have security footage to see if the vehicle was damaged when it arrived or if it could have been dented on hospital property."

"Yeah, of course," he said, still sounding concerned. "He never said anything to me about someone wrecking his car."

"Dr. Canning prefers we take care of it," Annalisa replied pleasantly. "And who knows? Maybe the footage will reveal nothing and the damage occurred elsewhere."

"I'm sure. Has to be." He picked up his keyboard and opened what looked like a log of times and dates. "Okay, here you go . . . on the date you're talking about, Dr. Canning drove in at 9:02. He left at 7:33 p.m."

"Can we see him parking the car?" At his puzzled look, Annalisa explained, "I want to make sure Dr. Canning himself didn't damage the car while parking it."

"No way." The kid hit a few more keys. "Dr. Canning drives a Jag coupe that goes for more than a hundred Gs. If I had a ride like that, I'd put it to bed like a newborn baby. Okay, here you go. This is his reserved slot on the second floor."

Annalisa leaned down to watch the black Jaguar slide neatly into the spot and Craig Canning emerge from the driver's seat. He wore jeans, sneakers, and a blue sweater, and he seemed to be in a hurry. He started walking out of the frame before he triggered the locks on the car, causing its headlights to flash. Annalisa caught a flash of something else too. "Wait," she said. "Go back. Now stop."

The kid froze Dr. Canning crossing in back of the car on his way to the hospital. His right hand held the keys, but she saw an odd white patch there as well. "What's that?" she asked, pointing at it.

The kid squinted. "Looks like a bandage."

Annalisa stood up, her gaze still on the screen. "Yes," she mused. "It certainly does."

....

Back at her office, Annalisa tacked blown-up versions of her photos of Vicki Albright's place to the wall. She scrutinized each one, jotting down all the names she could find from the various pictures and notes Vicki had displayed in her apartment. She also had taken a photo of the wind chimes picture Nick had shown her from the case file. So far, she had not been able to identify the brand or where they might have been purchased.

She was standing in front of the photos when she heard young female voices out in the hall. A moment later, Cassidy burst through the door with another girl in tow. "Sorry I'm late," Cassidy said, a bit breathless. "I had to pick Naomi up from the train station. Naomi, this is Annalisa Vega."

The other girl, a thin teen with shoulder-length dark hair streaked blond around her face, gave an awkward wave. "Hi."

"Hi." Annalisa frowned. The assistant gig would never work if Cassidy thought the office was some kind of hangout pad for her friends. To Cassidy, she said, "I thought you wanted to work here."

"I do. I am," Cassidy replied brightly as she lowered her school backpack to the floor. "I told you I'd rounded up some business. Naomi wants to hire us."

Annalisa tamped down her annoyance and put aside her work on the Albright case. "You need a private investigator?" Annalisa regarded the second girl with intrigue. "You don't look old enough to have a cheating spouse."

"I'm eighteen," Naomi said. "If it matters."

"I don't know. Does it?"

"And I can pay." She looked worried after she said the words. "Assuming you're not too expensive."

"Let's talk daily rate later," Annalisa said dryly as she indicated the chairs for the girls to sit. "Tell me what the problem is."

"I need to find my mother." Naomi reached into her bag and pulled out a folder. "Her name is Elizabeth Johnston, and she left before I turned three. The last postcard she sent me was postmarked from Chicago."

Annalisa accepted the card. "This is dated two years ago."

"It's the most recent I have."

Annalisa checked the address on the postcard. "You live in Lafayette?"

"Yes, ma'am. My father teaches tenth-grade history."

"At your school?" Annalisa guessed, and Naomi made a face. "Tough gig," Annalisa concluded. "Does he know you're here, trying to find your mother?"

The two girls exchanged a look. "No," Naomi muttered at length. "He said . . . he said I shouldn't chase her. That I'd only get hurt. But I really need to find her."

"Why?"

Neither girl said anything. Naomi twisted her hands in her lap. When she didn't speak, Cassidy took a deep breath. "Maybe it would help if I told Annalisa how we met," she said to her friend. Annalisa had wondered about their connection. Lafayette, Indiana was more than three hours away by car. Naomi gave a tight shrug, which Cassidy took as permission to launch into the story. "Well," she said, "you remember a few years ago when everything shut down?"

"I vaguely recollect that, yes," Annalisa said, folding her arms across her chest.

"Everything went online—school, church, and therapy appointments. I'm in a group for kids with parents who are, uh, really sick. You know, like they probably won't get better?"

"I know the kind of group, yes." Dread blossomed inside Annalisa like a corpse flower. Maybe this other girl's father was dying, like Cassidy's mom, and they wanted Annalisa to track down her deadbeat mother. A woman who took off on her toddler was not likely to step up to the plate now.

"Anyway, my group met online back then and one day the hospital tech people screwed up. They put us in the same room as the kids who are sick themselves. Because of the mix-up, no moderator showed up, and most kids left. But a few of us stayed to chat, including me and Naomi. She had a poster of Frida Kahlo and so did I. We're both, like, obsessed with her." The two girls shared a smile. "After that, Ni and I chatted on our own. We text all the time, mostly about silly stuff, but it can help, you know, having someone who is used to talking about heavy medical stuff."

"I bet." Annalisa wasn't quite making the connection between this story and the girls' presence in her office.

"So when Ni said she had to find her mom to ask her for a kidney, I thought we could help her."

"Wait a sec . . . a kidney?"

Naomi looked like she wanted the floor to open up and swallow her. "I was born with a rare genetic mutation that slowly destroys my kidney function," she said, her voice barely above a whisper. "I was fine until about age five, but they've been getting worse over time, and last year, they pretty much gave out for good. Without dialysis, I'd be dead already. If I don't find a kidney donor soon, I might still be."

"I'm sorry," Annalisa said.

"I'm on the registry, but there's been no match," Naomi explained. "My dad got tested, but turns out, he has only one kidney himself. They think maybe it's related to the same weird gene thing I have. Anyway, he can't give me his or he'll die."

Annalisa was willing to bet the dad would be happy to turn over his kidney no matter what it meant for him. "You think your mom might be a match?"

"Ni's dad is Japanese and her mom is white," Cassidy said. "That makes it harder to find a match on the general registry. A relative is her best chance."

"I see."

"So will you take the case?" Naomi asked with anxious eyes. She pulled out an envelope that held a thick stack of cash. "I've saved all my birthday and Christmas money for three years. I don't know if it's enough, but I have a college savings account too . . ."

Annalisa already knew two things: one, Naomi's father had certainly tried to find her mother already, so either he'd failed or the woman had said no to being tested; two, if she declined to help Naomi, the girl would find someone else who would gladly take all her cash whether they could locate Elizabeth Johnston or not.

"I'll take the case," she said, and Cassidy's face broke into a wide smile.

"I told you. I told you she'd help."

Annalisa held up one finger. "I do have a condition."

"What is it?" Naomi asked, wary.

"I am going to need to talk to your father."

"No," Naomi blurted. "He—he won't agree. He hates her for running off on us, says no good can come from letting her back into our lives. I only got the postcard she sent for my birthday because I reached the mailbox before him. He doesn't even know I have it."

"Does she have other relatives . . . mother, siblings . . . someone who might know where she is staying?"

Naomi shook her head. "Her parents are dead. They died in an accident before I was born. No brothers or sisters."

"Then your father is our only link to her. He would know her old friends, maybe her Social Security number, past addresses—information that could tell us where she is now."

Naomi slumped in her seat. "He's afraid it will hurt me if she says no," she murmured. "But it's a no right now anyway since we can't even find her. If she turns me down, I'm no worse off. I'm still gonna die."

"You're not going to die," Cassidy said with such vehemence it took Annalisa aback. Cassidy grabbed her friend's hand. "You're not."

"I'll see how far I can get without talking to your dad," Annalisa said. "But if you really want to find her, we're probably going to have to loop him in at some point." Elizabeth Johnston was not an easy name to trace. Too common.

"Okay," Naomi said with a tight nod. "Whatever it takes to find her."

"We can get started right now," Cassidy said, jumping to her feet. "What should I do first?"

Annalisa wanted to run her initial database searches without Naomi looking on, so she told the girls to go across the street to get her coffee. "Get yourselves a snack too," she said, handing Cassidy a twenty. "Consider it a signing bonus."

While they were gone, Annalisa ran Elizabeth Johnston's name through her usual search sites and came back with more than fifty thousand hits. She was definitely going to need more information to start winnowing the field. When the girls returned with her coffee, Cassidy handed it to her along with a paper-wrapped cookie.

Naomi sipped her drink as she perused the photos on Annalisa's wall. "Why do you have a picture of Miles Dupont up here?"

"Who?" Annalisa moved to join her, and the girl pointed at a photo of Vicki Albright, dressed to kill, standing with a guy in a tux who frankly could use a shave. They had their arms around each other. The picture had no caption so she had not identified the man yet.

"You know, the climate activist guy," Naomi said. "He founded the C-squared green initiative . . . they had a big march last year. I gotta say, he cleans up fine." She and Cassidy giggled together.

"What else do you know about him?" Annalisa asked as she pulled down the picture for a closer inspection.

"Not much. There are rumors that he's, like, a real du Pont. Like filthy rich. If it's true, I think it's cool of him to spend his time fighting for the planet." Naomi paused to take a sip. "If I live, I'd kinda like the earth to still be here."

NINE

ANNALISA HAD HER PHONE PROPPED UP ON THE EGG CARTON, HER MOM ON VIDEO CHAT, AS THE BOILING POT OF WATER STEAMED HER FACE. "How much salt am I supposed to put in here?" she called to her mother.

"Enough to taste it," Ma replied, and Annalisa rolled her eyes. Her mother did not use any recipe books. All her food was made with a "pinch" of this and "enough" of that.

"Numbers, Ma. I need numbers." She waved a set of measuring spoons at her mother's face, causing the older woman to scowl.

Ma held up her hand to the camera. "Cup your hand like this. Put the salt in your palm. That's enough."

Annalisa did as she was instructed and added the potatoes she'd peeled and cubed earlier, as per Ma's instructions. "I don't know how you learned any of this stuff if no one ever wrote it down," she groused.

"I learned cooking from my mother," Ma said.

"Yeah, so how come I never learned it from you?"

"You never sat still long enough to listen. You and your brothers, all of you, came to the table at suppertime, inhaled your plates, and disappeared again like that whirling cartoon devil."

Annalisa had no argument for this. It was one reason she'd given up her job as a police detective: the Chicago PD no longer owned all her hours. She had married Nick again, and this time, they were supposed to start a family of their own. Someone needed to tend the home front. "You can go now, Ma, thanks," she said over her shoulder as she moved to the fridge. "All I have left is the salad, and I think I can handle that much."

"Do I smell something burning?" Her mother's voice floated across the room.

"Ma, you're twenty minutes away," Annalisa yelled from where she bent over the veggie drawer. "Not even your nose is that—" She broke off as the acrid smell hit her, and she whirled to see smoke coming out of the oven. With a string of curse words, she ran to pull the meat loaf out just as the smoke alarm started blaring overhead.

"I've got it." Cassidy, who'd been doing her homework at the kitchen table, got a dish towel and started fanning the alarm as Annalisa waved her arms by the stove, trying to dispel the smoke. The meat loaf looked like a charred football sitting in a lake of grease.

"Is it okay?" Ma called anxiously from her place by the eggs.

Annalisa gritted her teeth. "It's fine, Ma." They could always order pizza. Again.

"We'll try again tomorrow, eh?" Ma said, her shrug philosophical. "Maybe something simpler, like chicken piccata."

"Sure, Ma, thanks." She clicked off with her mother and Cassidy got the alarm to stop its shrill complaint. Annalisa surveyed the damage to the meat loaf as Cassidy joined her by the stove.

"Just the outsides are burned," Cassidy said. "I'm sure the inside is fine."

Cassidy may have grown up without Nick around, but the kid sure inherited his optimism. Annalisa poked at the meat loaf with a fork. "I don't know. I think the victim may be burned beyond recognition."

"I'll make the salad, at least."

Annalisa scraped the meat loaf while Cassidy chopped vegetables. "Shoot," Annalisa said as she noticed the potatoes again. "I forgot to ask Ma how long to cook those."

"Until you can put a fork through one," Cassidy replied as she demonstrated. "See? They're done."

Annalisa watched as the girl drained the potatoes and added milk and butter to the pan. "How did you learn how to do that?"

Cassidy's ears turned pink. "Uh, my mom," she muttered, head bent over her work. "She kinda put me through domestic boot camp when I was thirteen. I swear we did *Joy of Cooking* from cover to cover."

Annalisa immediately grasped the math. Three years ago, Summer Weaver was diagnosed with ALS and knew she had limited time with her daughter. "Ah," she said. "Well, I'm grateful for your help."

Cassidy hunched her shoulders as she mixed the salad. "I can help for real, you know," she said after a beat. "With your work. I wouldn't ask for the assistant's position if I didn't think I could handle it. You can let me do other stuff besides fetch the coffee."

Annalisa hesitated a moment. "Okay," she said, wiping her hands on the back of her jeans. "Here's something you can help me with." She picked up her cell phone and texted Cassidy the close-up picture of the wind chimes from Vicki Albright's apartment. "I'm trying to figure out where these were made and purchased," she said. "So far, I've had no luck."

Cassidy took out her own phone and blew up the photo for a closer inspection. "They look handmade to me," she announced. "Not mass-produced." Cassidy was into art, so it was possible she saw something Annalisa did not.

"Great," Annalisa said flatly. "So I'm looking for a crafty killer."

Cassidy's eyes flew open wide. "A killer made these?"

Annalisa didn't get a chance to reply because the front door opened and a second later, Nick came into the kitchen still wearing his leather jacket. "Something smells good," he said with a grin, pausing to kiss Annalisa on the cheek as he shrugged out of his coat.

"Liar," she returned, flicking him on the rear end with a dish towel.

"Hey, I didn't see the fire department out front. That's an improvement." He slipped an arm around Cassidy and squeezed. "Hi, kiddo. How was school?"

She barely looked up from her phone. "Boring."

"Yeah? Maybe you'll like this better." Nick took the phone from her and proceeded to juggle it along with a whisk and an onion he snatched from the counter.

"Hey!" Cassidy grabbed for the phone but Annalisa saw the girl was smiling. "Give that back."

Nick handed her the phone. "Time to wash up for dinner."

Annalisa put her hands on her hips and regarded the charred meat loaf. "If you can call it that."

Nick mashed the potatoes while Cassidy set the table, and they made the best of it. Annalisa found that half-burned meat loaf paired well with merlot; or at least by the second glass, she no longer cared. "No phones at the table," Nick admonished Cassidy, who was texting in her lap.

"It's for Anna," Cassidy said. "For work."

"For work?" Nick echoed, pinning Annalisa with a hard gaze. "I thought we agreed that wasn't happening."

Annalisa replayed the conversation in her head and affirmed she had not agreed to anything. "She's just looking something up on the internet for me," she told Nick. "Not running surveillance."

Nick did not argue further at the table, but the look he shot Annalisa suggested they would be discussing it again when they were alone. "I've got the dishes," he said, clearing them away. "Who wants ice cream?"

Cassidy didn't look up from her phone. Nick raised his eyebrows in silent surprise while Annalisa raised her hand. "Always," she said.

"I think I've found it," Cassidy said a minute later, holding out her phone. "The artist is Lily Rubin. This is her Etsy store, see?"

Annalisa grabbed the phone. "How did you find it so fast?"

"I belong to a few chat groups for local artists. I posted a picture of the wind chimes and someone recognized the woman who makes them. I don't see an exact match in the store, so maybe the set you have is custom ordered. See? If you blow up the pic, you can even see Lily's initials by the jaguar's leg in the photo you sent me."

"Someone ordered the wind chimes from her online?"

"I just messaged her store to ask her about them. She already wrote back. She said the jaguar was sold from a local boutique along with a bunch of her other pieces. She doesn't know who bought it."

"But she does know where?"

Cassidy took the phone for a moment to call up the information. "The boutique is on East Ohio Street." She showed its location on the map, and what Annalisa noticed was Craig Canning's hospital sitting there only a block away.

"Don't tell me you're still on about the wind chimes," Nick said from his place at the sink.

"What do you care? Your case is closed. You said so yourself."

"Yes, but—"

Nick's protest was cut off by Cassidy's phone ringing. "It's Melanie," she said, glancing at it. "I have to take it."

Melanie was Summer's best friend and primary caregiver. When Summer passed, Cassidy was to live with Melanie. Annalisa watched as the girl said a cautious hello. Her own heart squeezed in response. Her father had Parkinson's and so she knew what it was like to dread bad medical news on the end of every phone call. Cassidy's face turned pale. "But when? How? She was fine when I left this morning . . ." She turned anguished eyes to Nick, who took the phone from her.

"Mel, what's up?"

"My mom's in the hospital," Cassidy whispered to Annalisa. "I've got to go."

"Oh, honey, I'm sorry." Annalisa reached for the girl, but Cassidy shied away from her touch. Annalisa watched helplessly as Cassidy flew around the room, gathering her things while Nick got the details from Melanie.

"I have to get to the hospital," Cassidy said to Nick, her voice quavering.

Nick returned her phone to her. "I'll drive you. Come on." Annalisa stood to go too, but Nick halted her with his keys in hand. "You don't need to come."

The words felt like a slap. He must have heard it too because his expression softened. "I meant there's no need for all of us to go. You can stay and clean up if you want."

"I'm coming," Annalisa said swiftly, and Nick hesitated before giving a slight smile.

"Okay then, let's go."

....

Summer was unconscious when they reached the hospital. No one could say why. A distraught Melanie explained that she'd been making tea in the kitchen, and when she returned to the bedroom, she'd found Summer unresponsive. The doctors were trying to figure out what had triggered the coma. "But she's going to wake up, right?" Cassidy kept repeating the question when none of the adults would answer her. "She's going to be okay."

"I hope so, baby," Melanie said tearfully, enveloping Cassidy in a big hug. "We have to see what the doctors say."

Cassidy let out a sob against Melanie's chest. "I'm not leaving until she's awake. I'm not leaving."

Melanie cast a helpless look at Nick over the top of Cassidy's head. Nick turned away. "No one's going anywhere right now," Melanie said in a soothing voice as she rubbed Cassidy's back. "We're all right here for you and your mom, okay? We're going to wait to hear from the doctors see how it goes." She led Cassidy across the waiting room to sit down.

"I hate this," Nick said under his breath to Annalisa.

She put a hand on his arm in sympathy. "I know." Nick was a fixer, and there was no fixing this. Summer might regain consciousness this time, but her illness was terminal.

"You see why I don't want her getting mixed up with your work? She's got enough going on right now. She doesn't need to be worrying about some socialite who took a swan dive off her balcony and if a 'nice' psychopath is responsible. Which he's not, by the way." He glared at her and Annalisa took a steadying breath. He was stressed and lashing out.

"Cassidy approached me," she reminded him. "Not the other way around."

"Yeah, and why is that?" he snapped.

She blinked. "What do you mean?"

"I mean . . ." He faltered and looked over at Cassidy. "I'm her father. Why's she chasing after you?"

She blew her bangs off her forehead in frustration. "Probably because you didn't have a job opening down at the station. Also, you're right—I'm not her father. I'm not as emotionally loaded. Sixteen-year-old girls are supposed to give their parents hell. Trust me, I did the same thing at her age."

"You idolized your father." He eyed her.

"Yeah, and look how that turned out." When he didn't reply, she rubbed his arm again. "Give it time."

"I don't have time," he said, his voice turning tight again. "She'll be a senior next year, then she goes to college."

"So, she goes to college. It's not like she's leaving for Mars."

"I want her to live with us." He blurted the words and froze for her reaction. She didn't even breathe. "It would be for just a year. Until she goes to college. I know Melanie is supposed to take her, but I'm her father. She should be with me."

TEN

....

Aｎｎａｌｉｓａ ｗｅｎｔ ｔｏ ｇｅｔ ｃｏｆｆｅｅ. That's what she told everyone she was doing, and she did plan to return eventually with a bunch of coffees to go around, but what she really wanted right now was space. She took herself on a tour of the hospital, from the cafeteria in the base- ment to the fancy lounge on the top floor. It stood empty so she went to the large windows and admired the twinkling lights of the city below. When she and Nick had talked about having a family together, she'd imagined starting with an infant and working her way up to a teenager. Now he wanted to move one in without even discussing it first. *Trying to fix it,* she thought. *As usual.* Cassidy was losing one parent, so he thought he'd slide into the gap and Cassidy wouldn't miss a beat.

Annalisa drifted from the windows to admire the large framed pho- tos on the wall. They showed kindly, smiling doctors tending to grateful patients. A female physician consulted with a mom, showing her an X-ray while a little boy looked on with his arm in a purple cast. A male nurse adjusted the blankets over an elderly woman. Annalisa stopped short at the third photo. Craig Canning waved a dragon hand puppet for a little girl who had a bandage around her head. His cheeks puffed out like he was making the dragon blow fire and the girl clapped her hands at his antics.

"Her name is Fatima. She's in high school now."

The deep voice behind her made Annalisa startle. Craig Canning had materialized as if gazing upon his likeness somehow summoned him from the ether. "What are you doing here?" The words escaped her before she had formed a conscious thought. She had not heard a single noise before he spoke.

"This is the physicians' lounge. The real question is what are you doing here?" He looked amused and took a step closer to her. She could smell cigarette smoke on him now and surmised he must have been out on the terrace behind her.

"I, uh, I'm here visiting a sick friend. I went for a walk and ended up here. I'm sorry, I didn't realize this was a private space."

He waved her off and she saw a silver lighter in his hand. There was an etching on the side, some sort of a jungle cat. A jaguar? "No worries," he said with a broad smile. "Now you're here as my guest." He nodded at the photo of himself and the little girl. "Would you like to see a more recent picture?" He didn't wait for her answer. Withdrawing his phone, he summoned up an email from Asif Shamon with the subject line "District Champs!" It read: *Dear Dr. C., Fatima's lacrosse team took home the big trophy this year, and she scored the winning goal. You would never guess this girl couldn't walk until age three. Now, she flies. Mashallah.—Asif*

The photo showed the same dark-haired girl, sweaty and grinning, dressed in a burgundy lacrosse uniform and holding the stick high over her head.

"She had a cerebellar tumor," Canning explained. "Noncancerous but it was large enough to interfere with her motor function. I removed it."

"That's amazing," Annalisa said, meaning it. What it must feel like to restore someone's health to them. *Mashallah,* Annalisa knew, was a blessing that translated roughly as *God wills it*. God might have willed Fatima to walk again, but Craig Canning made it happen. No wonder he had an ego on him.

"Your sick friend," he said as he tucked his phone away. "Is there anything I can do to help?"

He looked legitimately concerned. "No," she said. "She has ALS."

He winced. "Ah, I'm sorry. That's a tough one."

"The worst," she agreed.

"At least let me buy you some sustenance," he said. "A sandwich? Coffee and a donut?"

"Coffee would be great, thank you."

"Excellent. Right this way." He extended his arm in a gallant fashion. "I just have to make one quick stop along the way." She followed him two floors down to a patient wing, which appeared dedicated to children. The walls showed murals of various sea creatures and the nurses wore scrubs with cartoons on them. One female nurse wearing bunny ears smiled and waved as Canning passed by.

"Evening, Dr. C."

He halted and put a dramatic hand over his heart. "Nancy, with those ears, I swear you could be moonlighting at the Playboy mansion."

Nancy giggled, clearly used to this humor. "Oh, you stop it."

"Is Malcolm still up?" he asked, turning serious.

She raised her eyebrows. "Is the Cubs game still on? Then yes."

Annalisa trailed Canning down the hall to a room with an octopus tentacle painted across the door. Canning knocked and poked his head in. "Who's winning?" he asked as he entered.

"Pirates, four to two," said a dejected voice on the other side.

Canning motioned for Annalisa to join him. She saw a small boy, maybe ten years old, wearing a Cubs cap and lying in bed watching the television. He had a glove with him and a raggedy stuffed dog. Under the cap, he appeared to be bald. Canning squinted at the screen. "All is not lost," he said in a hearty voice. "Cubs are up in the bottom of the ninth, the heart of the order."

"Yeah," the kid said. "They could still pull it out."

"You should be resting up for your surgery tomorrow," Canning told him.

"I am resting," the kid complained. "I never get out of this bed."

"Soon," Canning promised.

The kid rolled his eyes. "That's what they all say. Nothing ever changes."

"You can't give up," Canning replied. He beckoned Annalisa closer. "Look, I brought someone to meet you."

The kid glanced her over, his gaze skeptical. "Yeah, who?"

"This is Detective Annalisa Vega from the Chicago Police. She caught the Lovelorn Killer." An icy sweat broke out across her back. He knew who she was. Maybe he'd known all along. Maybe he'd looked her up after their chat. Either way, he was wise to the fact that she wasn't a lowly insurance investigator. He looked to Annalisa with a gleam in his eyes, enjoying the *gotcha*. "Annalisa, meet my good friend Malcolm. He's kicking cancer's ass."

Annalisa forced a smile. "Nice to meet you, Malcolm."

His small, pale face scrunched up. "Who's the Lovelorn Killer?"

"A very bad man who murdered a lot of people," Canning said, making his voice ominous. "No one could catch him for years, not even the FBI, but Annalisa stopped him. Now he can't hurt anyone else ever again. Isn't that amazing?"

"Wow, for real?" The kid gaped at her. "Did you shoot him and stuff?"

She threw an annoyed look at Canning. This was not an appropriate bedtime story for a young boy. "Uh, yes," she confirmed to Malcolm. "He's gone now."

"I bet Malcolm would like an autograph. Wouldn't you, Malcolm?"

"Sure," the kid agreed, his attention already back on the television.

Canning produced a pen and a small notepad, and he stood there smiling as Annalisa wrote out a short note with her best wishes. Malcolm accepted it without a glance, peering around her as the Cubs hitter worked a leadoff walk.

"See?" Canning told him with a nod at the screen. "There's always hope. Get some rest. I will see you tomorrow morning."

"'Night, Dr. C.," Malcolm mumbled as they left.

In the hall, Annalisa turned to face him. "You've been reading up on me," she said.

"On the contrary, I knew who you were the moment you walked through my door. You're the most famous detective this side of the Mississippi, Ms. Vega. Don't tell me you really thought you could do undercover work?" His dark eyes danced with mischief. "I confess I did miss your change of profession, which I gather is a recent development. No more badge and gun?"

"No more badge," she clarified.

He outright laughed, a charming rich baritone that almost had her smiling along with him. He was right, of course, that she could expect to be recognized. The Lovelorn case had made national headlines for weeks. "Touché," he said. "Shall we get that coffee now?"

"I really should be getting back."

"One cup," he pressed. "My treat."

She wasn't sure when she'd have this easy opportunity to talk to him again, so she agreed and let him lead her to a small café. When they had their beverages, they sat at a table for two and she regarded his hand where the bandage had been in the CCTV footage from the hospital parking garage. The skin had largely healed, she saw, so the wound could not have been that deep. "Did your scalpel slip?" she asked, indicating the red line on his palm.

"Hmm?" He looked down. "Oh, no. There was a broken bottle near my rear tire the other day and I cut myself removing the pieces. I had to run back in to change my clothes and was nearly late for surgery. Ghastly sin, littering." He turned his hand so she couldn't study it. "Tell me, what was it like bringing down a serial killer?"

She could tell he wanted gory details. Almost everyone did. "To be honest, the whole thing was pretty terrifying."

"Is that why you left the job? No fun chasing killers?"

She sipped her coffee. "Who says I've stopped chasing killers?"

He grinned again and raised his paper cup to her. "Still on the hunt, eh? Maybe you'll tell me the truth then about Vicki Albright. It's not the insurance company who hired you."

"Insurance companies hire private investigators all the time."

"But not you," he said shrewdly, leaning across the table.

Don't tell him who hired you, Mara had said, but Annalisa felt Canning would keep digging until he had an answer. "Okay, you've got me," she told him. "I was hired by Vicki's brother, Gavin. He's worried someone may have murdered her."

She wanted to see his reaction to this bit of news, but he gave nothing away with his mild frown. "Murdered," he repeated. "How terrible." His dark eyes were guileless as he regarded her. "Did you find any evidence to support this claim?"

"Not yet."

"Hmm." He fingered the edge of his cup and looked thoughtful. "Perhaps I could be of some use to you. I live in Vicki's building, as you know. I could ask around about her."

Everyone wanted to be Annalisa's assistant these days. "Oh, that won't be necessary, thank you. Unless . . ."

"Unless?"

"Well, you told me you didn't know her. If you did have some sort of relationship with her, then you might have access to information I can't get easily."

He didn't bite. "Too bad then," he said with regret. "I didn't know the girl. But you should consider my offer of help anyway. I'm a trained researcher. A Howard Hughes scholar. There's really nothing I can't find out."

Her skin prickled but she gave him a polite smile. "No, thank you."

She saw a brief flash of anger in his eyes. He wasn't used to being told no. He recovered and mirrored her placid expression, but his voice had an edge to it when he said, "Your loss."

ELEVEN

....

MARA WAS ALREADY AWAKE WHEN HER PHONE RANG AT TWO IN THE MORN-ING. She couldn't sleep with Paul's snoring practically sucking in the drapes from the bedroom. She'd fled to the den and was idly flipping through late-night TV when the phone screen illuminated with the number for campus security. "What is it?" she said by way of greeting.

"Dr. Mara Delaney?" said a male voice on the other end.

"Yes, this is she. What happened? What's wrong?" She closed her eyes and clutched her phone.

"I'm sorry to tell you there's been a fire, ma'am. It's been extinguished but your office sustained a fair bit of damage."

"A fire?" She sat up straight. "What kind of fire? My books are in that office. My computer . . ."

"The investigators will have to sort out the cause. We just wanted to alert you as soon as possible to the problem."

Mara hung up with the officer and dashed upstairs to throw on some clothes. Paul heard her stumbling around and sat up in bed. "Where's the fire?" he asked as she slid into her jeans.

"At my office," she told him.

"Seriously?" He reached for a tissue and blew his nose. "A real fire?"

"That's what they tell me. I'm on my way over there now."

"I'll come with you," he said, moving to get out of bed.

"No, honey. You stay here and rest. There's nothing you can do to help right now." Finally dressed, she went and kissed him on top of his balding head. "I know you've been feeling poorly."

"Tree season," he said and sneezed on cue. "It gets worse every year."

"My poor baby." She grabbed a fistful of tissues and dropped them, fairylike, over his lap. "I'll call you if I need you."

She drove to campus with her heart in her throat. They had put out the fire but how much damage would she find? The stone building had stood for centuries—she had no fear for the structure—but the inside was nothing more than wood, drywall, and piles of paper. When she reached the building, she felt a stab of relief to see it appeared relatively normal on the outside. Four walls. Windows intact. It wasn't even smoking, although she could smell fire in the air. Bits of ash blew in her face as she got out of the car.

Normally the academic heart of campus would be dead at this hour, but it looked like a rave right now with a collection of emergency vehicles circled around, each with their own flashing lights. Mara grabbed the first guy in uniform she could find. "Excuse me, I'm Mara Delaney," she said. "That's my office in there."

His eyes widened, a flash of white in the dark. "Delaney?" he repeated, like her name was familiar. "You should talk to Steve Laughton . . . that's him over there." He pointed out a short, squat guy with a yellow helmet on. The guy was saying something into a walkie-talkie, which he lowered as Mara approached.

"I was told to talk to you," she said. "I'm Mara Delaney."

"Dr. Delaney." He shook her hand. "You didn't need to come down here in the middle of the night like this."

"Of course I did. This is my office. My work . . ." She trailed off and turned anxious eyes to the building. "I had to see what happened."

"Passing patrol spotted the smoke and called it in," he replied. "Damage is limited to the east side."

"Where my office is," she said tightly, cinching her belt as the wind picked up.

He gave her a curious look. "Yeah, about that . . . come take a look." He went to the back of a truck and picked up two large flashlights, handing her one. "Power is shut off right now," he said as he led her to the darkened building.

She hesitated at the door. "Is it safe to enter?"

"Oh, yeah, my boys have been back and forth a bunch. These old buildings are like fortresses—marble floors, stone walls. Tough to burn. Most you're going to get is a little water on your shoes."

It was creepy going down the hall with no lights on. Water dripped from the ceiling and the smell of smoke made her cough. "Try not to breathe too much," he advised her, like she had a choice in the matter.

"What is it you want me to see?" She wheezed as the chemicals hit her lungs.

"Over this way." They reached her office and her stomach sank at the sight of the huge mess. Her bookcases had half melted. Her desk was charred. The computer and keyboard were drenched in water. Steve shone his beam in the corner, and she could see scorch marks on the walls and a pile of ash on the floor. "Check out that charcoal pattern . . . like an alligator's skin," he said. "That's where the fire started."

"Here? In my office?"

"Nothing's official yet, but it looks that way. You had something flammable stored in the corner there?"

"My book," she whispered. The first printed copies. She'd had two cartons of them stored in the office. "Someone burned my book? Who would do that?"

Steve shrugged, causing his beam to skitter around the office. "Guess someone who didn't want anyone to read it."

THERE WAS NOTHING MORE TO BE GAINED FROM STANDING IN THE RUINS OF HER OFFICE. Mara returned home and took a thirty-minute hot shower, shampooing twice to try to remove the scent of smoke from her hair. When she emerged and dressed, watercolor streaks of dawn crossed the sky and Paul had a cup of tea waiting for her, served on their fancy china. "You're too good for me," she told him as he kissed her cheek and set the delicate cup in front of her. It had a rose design, not her choice. The set had belonged to Paul's mother, and her mother before that.

"Tell me what the investigators said," Paul commanded her as he took the seat opposite her at the table. "They really say it's arson?"

"Nothing is official, but it looks that way. Someone set the boxes of my books on fire."

"Who would do such a thing?" Paul frowned, pursing his lips, and Mara turned her head so she wouldn't see his disapproval. He had never believed in the book. *Glamorizing deviant behavior,* he'd said when she told him the subject matter. *Are you sure you want to do that?* He had even questioned the idea of hitching her wagon to Craig Canning right from the start. *You say he's a good sociopath, that you have ways of measuring these things, but darling . . . what if you're wrong?*

"There's Miles Dupont, for one," she told Paul. "His book is being delayed to give mine a larger printing and he's furious about it. Plus, he loves stunts. Remember when he dumped a pile of dead fish into the Chicago River?"

"Must have missed that one." He sipped his tea and set the cup down on the saucer again. "What about your little friend? Maybe he's having second thoughts about his coming-out party."

"Are you talking about Craig? He can't get enough of the book. He'd put it on billboards all over the city if he could. The publisher wanted to use a stock image on the cover but Craig said no, he wanted his own face. Besides, Craig knows that burning a few cartons of books will stop nothing—they are being shipped to stores by the thousands. He can't burn them all."

"No, he burned yours," Paul said meaningfully. "Or someone did, maybe trying to rattle you. To make you rethink this book. If there is anyone who could call off the project at this point, it would be you, darling."

"I think you're projecting," she said tartly as she swooped up her cup and took it to the sink. "If I didn't know you were snoring here all night, I might think you burned those books. You're the one who's been against it from the start."

He came up behind her and put his hands on her arms with a gentle squeeze. "Against you? Never. I'm merely worried about you, about your safety. This is a direct attack on you, Mara."

She suppressed a shudder. She couldn't let him see the truth. Later, she would meet with Annalisa Vega and learn what she had found out about Craig and that poor woman's plunge off the balcony. If Annalisa had a favorable report, everything could proceed exactly as planned. But if she didn't? Mara swallowed hard and turned in Paul's arms. "I really don't deserve you."

"Nonsense," he said, and then sneezed into her hair.

"Paul, honey . . . you're sure you're not sick?" She withdrew as though he'd punctured her hazmat suit in a biohazard lab. The last thing she needed right now was a cold.

"Just extra sneezy," he replied, his tone apologetic as he dabbed at her head with a handkerchief. "Maybe I've developed a dust allergy."

She forced a smile. "As long as you don't become allergic to me," she said lightly, and then she went to take another shower.

At campus, she felt brittle and on display on the stage of the auditorium. Normally she loved standing in front of the students, holding their attention, widening their worlds. But today, the lights made her sweat and she kept scanning the shadows to see if Craig Canning had crashed her lecture. Twice she lost her train of thought and had to endure the snickers from her students as she fumbled around with her notes. Paul said the fire had been meant to rattle her and she refused to let anyone see it had worked. "As you can see in this fMRI, the limbic system is . . ." She trailed off again as a male figure appeared at the back of the room. He stood there in silhouette and they stared at each other long enough that a few students turned in their seats to see what had attracted her attention. "Can I help you?" she called out.

The figure moved into view and she felt relief when she did not recognize his face. Then she saw the uniform. He was campus security. "Ma'am, I've been asked to bring you to headquarters immediately," he said.

She blinked in surprise. He had a gun. Did they all carry guns? She had never noticed before. "I'm in the middle of class," she said, gesturing to indicate their audience.

"I realize that, and I'm sorry. I need you to come with me right now."

She let out a humorless laugh. "Surely I'm not under arrest . . ."

He looked uncomfortable. "No, ma'am. Just a conversation."

When she realized he would not budge, Mara dismissed her class, reminding them of their reading ahead of next week's quiz, and followed the officer to his car. He drove her to a modern building she'd never entered before. Inside, she found Lewis Ralston, her dean, and a ruddy-faced middle-aged man wearing an ill-fitting suit jacket who introduced himself as Howard Dombrauer, head of campus security. Her phone buzzed in her pocket, but she ignored it as she shook hands with the men. "You've pulled me out of my lecture to be here, Lewis," she said with a tight smile. "I hope it's important."

"It is," Lewis assured her. He did not smile back. "Please have a seat."

Both the men were standing in Dombrauer's cramped office, so Mara elected to stand as well. "Is this about the fire?"

Dombrauer exchanged a glance with Lewis and cleared his throat. "Yes, ma'am."

She didn't like the energy in the room. The way they stood stiffly and didn't quite make eye contact with her. "It's doctor," she told him. "Or professor." She wasn't even forty. Too young to be called ma'am, especially not by either of these two guys who were both old enough to be her father.

"Professor." Dombrauer corrected himself as he shot Lewis another look. "We've pulled the camera footage from last night's fire."

Her pulse picked up. "There's a camera?"

"Not in your building. At Smith Hall, next door. But we can see the entrance to Keaton in the background, and well . . . this is what it shows." He turned his computer monitor around so she could view it.

Mara held her breath and leaned down for a closer look. What would it show? She watched a bunch of dead footage for a few seconds. It showed the brightly lit entry to Smith Hall in the foreground and the dimmer entry to Keaton in the back. Keaton had no overhead lighting. Only a nearby pole with a lamp atop it provided any illumination. After a beat, she saw a figure appear on the screen. It was dressed all in black, including a hood, and she could not see a face. The person hurried past Smith and went up to the door of Keaton, where they paused to withdraw something from their pocket. They waved it at the scanner and the door opened.

Mara drew back. "Who is that?"

"Keep watching," Lewis instructed.

The figure was inside Keaton Hall fewer than five minutes. If they turned on any lights, she did not see it. She waited anxiously to see the person emerge because their face would be turned toward the camera. But, almost like they knew the camera was there, the figure kept their head lowered as they exited from Keaton. They jogged away off-screen, but not before Mara caught a flash of silver in the person's left hand. "Is that . . . is that a lighter?"

"This was just past one in the morning," Dombrauer said. "We think this person went in and set some kind of delayed fuse—a string maybe, or a lit cigarette—something that would allow them to be far away when the fire got going."

"Well," Mara said, taking a deep breath, "it shouldn't be hard to tell who it was." The men stared at her again in the way that made her uncomfortable. Surely they hadn't missed the obvious clue. "Whoever it was, they badged into the building." She gestured at the screen. "It should be easy enough to trace."

"Yes," Dombrauer confirmed. He looked distressed. "We looked it up." He hit a few keys and the picture on the monitor changed to show the electronic log sheet for Keaton Hall. "Right there at 1:12 on the dot."

Mara leaned down. Her vision blurred and she shook her head, denying what was there in black-and-white.

"It was your ID, Mara," Lewis said grimly. "Your badge opened the door."

TWELVE

....

ANNALISA WOULD NORMALLY CHOOSE TO WORK AT HER NEW OFFICE. Her cozy condo, now on the market, didn't feel like hers anymore. Nick had not even bothered to move in much of his stuff, just left it in storage until they found a new place together. Tina, their Realtor, had advised them to move out all clutter and depersonalize the décor, so Annalisa had temporarily rehomed most of the plants she'd inherited from her neighbor. The front windows looked bare without them but Tina said it gave prospective buyers easy access to admire the view. No more family photos on the bookshelves. No drawings on the fridge done by her little nieces. The condo now looked like anyone could live there; or rather, like no one did.

This morning, however, Annalisa took her coffee to one of the few remaining pieces of furniture, the couch in the front room, and worked her laptop for any traces of Elizabeth Johnston, Naomi's erstwhile mother. Annalisa had no birthdate to work from, but she guessed the woman's age between thirty-eight and fifty-five, which helped to narrow her search. She no longer had access to the Chicago PD search engines, but she paid for an aggregating database that compiled all public records. She did not know if Naomi's mother still resided in the Chicago area, but she would start there and widen her search if necessary. Once she added in all the potential nicknames she could dream up for Elizabeth—Betsey, Betsy, Betty, Liza, Beth, Lizzie/y—she had three dozen potential candidates. Several had current driver's licenses with accompanying addresses. Others had minor arrests, with the most current a drug possession from last year. One was simply listed as a witness in a traffic accident from eighteen months ago, no additional information given.

Annalisa was compiling a list to check out when Nick walked through the door, looking haggard. He wore yesterday's clothes and a twenty-four-hour stubble. He flopped into the lone chair and lolled his head back. "Summer's awake," he told her, and Annalisa released a long breath as she unclenched at last.

"That's great."

"She's on a ventilator. They aren't sure . . ." He paused to scrub his face with both hands. "They aren't sure if she'll ever talk again."

Summer already used an iPad for most communication. "Still, awake is good. Right?"

He answered with a single nod. "Cassidy went home with Melanie. I'm going to see her later after my shift."

"Nick, you can't go to work. You haven't slept."

He forced himself to his feet. "We took two weeks off for the honeymoon, remember? I don't have any time banked right now."

"So call off sick."

"I can't. We don't know what's going to happen with Summer. I may need those days."

"But—"

"I've worked through worse." He paused to look her up and down. "It's the job, Anna. You know how it is."

He probably didn't mean this as a barb, but she felt the sting anyway. They had been partners, watching each other's backs, until she'd quit and left him on his own. "At least let me make you something to eat. I've got coffee on already."

He gave her a wan smile. "Great. You got a needle? I'm going to need mine by IV today."

She fixed him eggs and toast while he showered and changed. He emerged looking clean but tired, with dark smudges under his eyes. She sat with him at the counter while he ate. "Did you talk to Cassidy? I mean, about her moving in with us . . ."

He shook his head. "Not yet."

"Good," she said, relieved, and he looked sideways at her.

"Good?"

"She has a lot to deal with right now, with her mom in the hospital."

"I know that. Don't you think I know that?" He pushed his plate away. "But maybe knowing she's got a home waiting for her might help with that."

"She does have a home waiting for her. She has Melanie."

"Melanie's not her father."

"No, but she's known Cassidy her whole life." *Not just the past six months of it,* she added silently.

"That's not my fault," Nick protested, gesturing broadly like the Italian he was. "I didn't even know Cassidy existed until recently."

"None of this is your fault," she said, laying a hand on his chest to calm him. "It also means it's not up to you to fix it."

He pulled away from her. "If you don't want her to move in here, just say it."

"I'm not saying that. I'm only trying to help you think things through."

"I have," he insisted.

"You haven't. What about her school, for one thing? We live forty minutes away, Nick, too far to commute every day. She'd have to change schools her senior year. What kid wants to do that?"

The surprise that flickered over his face told her he hadn't considered this. "We're moving anyway," he muttered, renewing his argument. "We can make it work."

Annalisa frowned but didn't argue the relative merits of buying property farther from each of their workplaces for one year of a kid's schooling. Nick was spiraling enough already. "We can talk about it more later," she said, rubbing his arm in a comforting fashion.

He didn't shrug away from her this time. He hung his head and spoke so softly she almost didn't hear him. "I need you with me on this." When she didn't reply, he turned to look right at her. "If Summer or Melanie thinks you're not on board, they'll never agree. Let alone Cassidy."

"We can talk about it," she said lightly.

His mouth tightened but he nodded. "Okay, later then." He got up to clear his plate while she sipped her cooling coffee. "How's it going with your friendly psychopath?"

"I met him in the hospital last night, actually." He halted to give her a questioning glance and she shrugged. "His patients love the guy. The nurses about eat him up. Hard to argue he isn't doing good in the world, regardless of his psychological makeup."

"But?"

"I see what Mara said about the veneer. His shtick almost feels performative. Nothing I've found suggests he tossed Vicki Albright off her balcony, though."

Nick closed the dishwasher drawer and turned around, wiping his hands on the back of his jeans. "About that. I did have one piece of information that might interest you. After our, uh, talk the other day, I had the lab run the wind chimes for prints."

She almost fumbled her coffee cup. If Craig Canning's prints were on the wind chimes, she'd have something solid to take to her meeting with Mara Delaney today. "And?"

"Nothing." Nick scratched the back of his head with one hand.

"No trace of Craig Canning, you mean."

"No, I mean no prints at all. Not even the victim's."

Annalisa sat back, momentarily stunned. "But how could Vicki's prints not be on the wind chimes if she'd been hanging them at the time of her death?"

"That's not a question I can answer." She knew he meant it both ways, that he had no idea and also that it wasn't his case anymore. He stopped on his way out to kiss her forehead. "Just remember a nice sociopath is still a sociopath."

She held him in place for a squeeze. "Thanks for believing me."

"I always believe in you."

She caught the slight difference. "Be safe," she told him, stretching her face for a real kiss. "Call me later."

"I'll be at the hospital."

"Then that's where I'll be too."

Annalisa still had a few hours before her meeting with Mara Delaney, so she tried contacting as many Elizabeth Johnstons as she could identify with a phone number. "Elizabeth Johnston?" she said when she connected with a female voice.

"Yes, who is this?"

"My name is Annalisa Vega, and I'm a private investigator. I'm working for an attorney who is trying to locate an Elizabeth Johnston for estate purposes."

"You mean like an inheritance?" The woman perked up and she dropped her cautious tone. "Someone died?"

"Yes, ma'am. We need to track down the heir, Elizabeth Johnston. Could you please tell me your full name and date of birth?"

Like a rube, the woman gave it to her. "How much money are we talking about here?"

"I'm not at liberty to discuss further until we've confirmed you are the Elizabeth Johnston in question. Tell me, do you know a Ken Na-kamura?"

"Who? Is that the guy who died?"

Annalisa took a pen and struck a line through this Elizabeth John-ston's details. The real one should recognize Naomi's father's name, since he was her ex-husband. "I'm sorry," she said, "I'm afraid you're not the person I'm looking for. Thank you for your time."

"Wait, maybe I do know this Yakamuri guy. I think we went to school toge—"

"Goodbye." Annalisa clicked off with her and tried the next number on her list, using the same ruse of an inheritance.

"I know a Ken Nardini," the next Elizabeth Johnston said when An-nalisa asked about Naomi's father. "Is that close enough?"

"No, I'm sorry. Thanks for your time."

She went through all her available numbers and got no hits. For the rest of the names, she would have to figure out a different mode of con-tact. *Except,* she thought, squinting at her list. *Maybe this one.*

The Elizabeth Johnston listed in the car accident report had been a passenger at the time of the crash. The driver's name was Henry Hig-gins, and there was a number listed for him. Annalisa decided to try it. After two rings, a brusque male voice answered. "Yes?"

"Henry Higgins?" she asked.

"Hank," he corrected. "Who's this?"

"My name is Annalisa Vega and I'm a private investigator. I'm trying to locate a woman named Elizabeth Johnston."

He hung up on her. Annalisa pulled the phone away from her ear to confirm the call was dead. Then she smiled as she circled this Elizabeth Johnston on her list. Ken Nakamura wanted nothing to do with his ex-wife Elizabeth, and apparently Hank didn't have fond memories of his Elizabeth either. It wasn't a complete confirmation that they were the same woman, but it was an intriguing lead. She searched her databases and discovered that Higgins's car, a Honda CRV, had survived the crash. She used its registration number to pull his address and, from there, his place of employment: Ibex Manufacturing.

....

A NNALISA DROVE ACROSS TOWN TO IBEX MANUFACTURING, WHICH TURNED OUT TO BE AN UNREMARKABLE SQUARE BRICK BUILDING NEAR I-94. She entered and found a woman about her age working at a computer. The woman looked at her in a puzzled way that suggested Ibex Manufacturing did not receive many unexpected visitors. "Can I help you?"

"Uh, yeah," Annalisa began as she looked past the woman to an open door. A man in a sweatshirt and ball cap stood there studying a clipboard. "Hank," Annalisa called, and the man looked up. She'd found him. "Hank Higgins?"

He walked through the doorframe and she saw he was at least six feet tall. He did not look pleased to see her. "Who's asking?"

"I'm Annalisa Vega," she said, drawing out one of her brand-new business cards. "We spoke on the phone? I'm trying to locate Elizabeth Johnston."

The woman at the desk hunched up like Annalisa had invoked the devil. Hank's face darkened. "I don't know where she is and I don't care to know. Goodbye."

"Wait," Annalisa pleaded as he turned around to leave. "It's urgent that I find her. It's about her daughter, Naomi."

Surprise flickered over his features. "Lizzie's got a kid?" He snorted as he digested this bit of information. "Good luck to her."

"I take it you and Elizabeth did not part on good terms."

"You might say that." He fixed her with a hard look. "That crazy witch tried to kill me."

THIRTEEN

·············

ANNALISA LOOKED HANK HIGGINS UP AND DOWN AND SAW NO VISIBLE SCARS, SO WHATEVER ELIZABETH JOHNSTON HAD DONE TO HIM, IT LEFT NO OBVIOUS TRACE. "I'm sorry," she told him. "But I still need to find her. Any information you can give me about where she is would be really helpful."

"I don't know where she went. I don't want her to know where I am. I don't even want to breathe her name. You feel me?"

"I hear what you're saying, but—"

He held up his hand. "No, you're not hearing me. You really don't know what kind of she-devil you're chasing here. This woman, she looks regular, same as you and me. But she's wired up wrong. Something's missing—a soul, a feeling, any basic humanity. She'll laugh when you get hurt. She'll cry but there's no tears. She'll tell you whatever you want to hear so you'll let her into your house and then she'll burn it down when she leaves."

Annalisa waited a beat after he'd finished his rant. "Is that what she did to you?"

Hank looked at the woman at the desk. "Patty, why don't you take your break now, okay?"

Patty grabbed her purse and scurried away like she couldn't wait to be out of the room. When she'd left, Hank took a deep breath and began his story.

"I met Lizzie at a bar—nothing fancy, just my neighborhood joint where I'd been going for years. My buddies and I, we'd watch the game and throw darts, that sort of thing. We didn't get many unattached women in the place, definitely none like Lizzie. She was already there when I showed up, holding court by the dartboard. Guys were buying her drinks and she was challenging them to a game. Twenty bucks if she could beat them. She had a tight red shirt and her hair in pigtails, like she was Dorothy from Oz. She even said she came from a farm, her father's place, where she'd only had pigs for company. A couple of the guys, they were snorting at her after that, and she laughed and laughed. But she kept taking their money. I sat at the bar, drinking my beer and watching her, and after a while, I figured out her game. See, initially I thought she was using the game to get them to keep buying her drinks, but that ain't it. She wasn't even drinking those rounds because if she did, she'd start missing with the darts. She was taking their twenties—the booze was just a cover."

"She was hustling them," Annalisa concluded.

"Yeah, and they probably even knew it, somewhere deep down. But they were enjoying the female attention so I guess they were willing to keep the charade going. When she finally got tired of it, she took her winnings and came to sit down next to me. Chatted me up a bit, asked if I wanted to play a round of darts with her. I told her I don't play that game, and I wasn't talking about the darts. She laughed and said she'd buy me a drink for getting wise to her act."

His chin lifted with pride. He still had this much, she saw. Whatever else Lizzie Johnston had done to him, he'd seen through her at one point. "So you started seeing her?" Annalisa asked.

His face fell. He reached out and adjusted the stapler sitting on the desk. "My mistake was thinking I was different," he said gruffly. "That I wasn't one of her marks. Yeah, we were hot and heavy there for a while.

She was fun. Lizzie would do crazy stuff like go to the ladies' restroom and come back with her panties off. She'd stick 'em in my pocket and lick her lips like I was the juiciest fruit she'd ever seen. We ordered fifty-dollar steaks because she convinced me you only live once. I never ate like that. But Lizzie, she'd say, what are you saving it for? No one gets out alive so live while you can."

"Happily spending your money."

"Mine and whoever else's she could get her hands on. She moved into my place. It was okay at first but she turned out to be a real slob. She didn't clean, didn't cook. Just lay around all day playing on her phone or watching TV. I'd come home and there'd be dishes all over the coffee table. Trash on the floor. I told her I didn't want to find her with my place messed up like that, and the next night I came home, she was gone. Found out later she'd been smoking weed with the college kids upstairs. When I discovered my petty cash fund missing, that was the last straw. I told her to get out."

"I bet she loved that."

He gnawed at his lower lip for a moment. "She started choking herself with both hands. In between squeezes, she'd yell, 'Hank, stop! You're hurting me!' I hollered that I wasn't laying a hand on her. She was doing it to herself. She called 911. Tells them her boyfriend is trying to kill her and gives my address."

"She didn't."

"The hell she did. Then she hangs up, cool as a cucumber, and waits for the cops to roll up. What could I do? If I picked her up and threw her out, it's assault. She'd file more charges on me. I couldn't touch her."

"Did the police come?"

His nostrils flared with the memory. "Oh, yeah. I guess I'm lucky they didn't come through the door shooting at me. Lizzie sobbed and gave them a story about how I was abusing her. The cops looked at the marks on her neck and hauled me out of my own place in handcuffs.

They perp walked me past all my neighbors while Lizzie practically waved from the window."

Annalisa had searched Hank's record and knew it was clean. "What happened?"

"Lizzie didn't show to file a report. When they sent a car to pick her up, she was gone. She took my stereo and laptop with her, I might add. Since there was no hospital record, nothing to show she was ever injured, they dropped the charges. But my lease was up the next month and the landlord didn't renew it because I'd caused a 'terrible disturbance' that made the rest of the building feel 'unsafe.' What a load of bullshit. That witch cost me my apartment and a bunch of expensive stuff, but at least I didn't get pumped full of lead because of her lying ass." He took a deep breath, his shoulders rising and falling as if a heavy weight had lifted from them. "So if it's true that Lizzie has a kid, trust me when I tell you that kid is better off without her."

"Still," Annalisa pressed, "if you had wanted to find her, where would you have looked?"

He shook his head at her in dismay, like it was her funeral. "Once," he said finally, "I came home to find her with another girl in the apartment— an Asian chick she introduced as Cherry. They were drinking the last of my whiskey and playing Mario Kart on my TV. Cherry had on a faded T-shirt advertising the Liar's Club." He peeked at her. "You know it?"

"Can't say I've ever been."

"Caters to the punk and goth scene. Place shakes like an earthquake every Friday and Saturday night but in between it's a ghost town filled with freaks." He paused to make his point. "That's where I'd look for Lizzie."

....

ANNALISA MADE NOTES FROM HER CONVERSATION WITH HANK HIGGINS, BUT SHE DID NOT FOLLOW UP ON THE NEW LEAD IMMEDIATELY. Before meeting Mara, she wanted to check the boutique where Cassidy had traced the wind chimes. If Annalisa could somehow prove Craig Canning had bought the set found in Vicki Albright's house, she had a shot at linking him to Vicki's death. She drove to the store and saw it was definitely convenient for Canning, only one block away from the hospital. A merry bell tinkled as she opened the door. The place smelled like lavender, citrus, and sandalwood. Scarves in riotous colors hung like snakes on a wood tree. Carvings in the shapes of zoo animals lined various shelves, along with candles, little porcelain dishes, and glass beads. The art on the walls had a Pacific Northwest vibe, with stylized whales, caribou, and fish. The only other customer appeared to be an elderly man in a plaid cap examining the rows of rings at the counter. Annalisa came to stand next to him, and the young woman sitting on the stool by the register leaped to her feet. "Can I help you?"

Annalisa withdrew the picture she had of Vicki Albright's wind chimes. "I'm hoping you can give me some information about these," she said as she showed the woman the photo.

"Oh, this is Lily Rubin's work. I love her stuff."

"It is beautiful." Annalisa cast another look around, trying to find anything similar. "Do you have any more?"

"Um, I don't see any right now, and they usually hang over there," the woman said, pointing at a blank space on the wall. "Let me check for you." She went to the computer and punched a few keys. "No, I'm sorry, we sold the last one yesterday."

"Gee, that's too bad. I was really hoping to replace this set. They belonged to my sister, and they got damaged in an accident."

"I can give you Lily's card, if you want. She might be able to make you another set."

This wouldn't really help her, but Annalisa took the card anyway. "Thanks. Hey, do you think you could help settle a bet for me? My sister got these from an anonymous sender. I think her boyfriend bought them for her, but my mom swears it was our cousin Bobby. Neither one will 'fess up."

"Uh, without the tag on it, I don't know."

"I think they were bought recently . . . within the past few weeks." Annalisa nudged the picture of the wind chimes across the counter again.

"They don't look familiar to me, so I don't think I sold them. Let me ask Fran. She's in the back."

The girl disappeared and Annalisa wandered the store while she waited. She picked up a handmade leather wallet Nick might like for his birthday. As she studied it, she had a prickly sensation like someone was watching her. When she glanced up, she saw Craig Canning at the storefront window. He took a drag from his cigarette and blew the smoke out in her direction. Then he grinned and gave a friendly wave.

She ignored him as the clerk appeared with Fran in tow. Fran was older, with a neat white bun, and she took out her glasses to get a better look at the photo. "Oh, yes, I remember selling these. A nice young fellow."

Annalisa figured that meant anyone under fifty. "A man bought them? Do you remember what he looked like?"

"We get so many people through here . . ." Fran studied the wind chimes. "I remember he said he was buying them for a lady friend."

"That means it was your sister's boyfriend, right?" The young clerk piped up. "Do you win the bet?"

Annalisa held up a forestalling hand. "Did he pay with a credit card?"

"Cash, I think. Oh, yes. I remember now. He said to keep the change even though it was more than ten dollars. That counts as a big tip around here." Her blue eyes glinted with humor. "Don't worry, though, because I know he can afford it."

Annalisa leaned closer, intrigued. "What do you mean?"

"Well, he was wearing scrubs. I presume he's a doctor, from the hospital down the block." She looked triumphant at her resilient memory.

Annalisa held back her rising excitement. "Really," she said, "that's such a coincidence. Do you think it could have been that gentleman over by the . . ." She turned around to gesture at the big front display window and her hand sagged in midair. Canning was gone.

FOURTEEN

··········

ANNALISA STOOD ON THE SIDEWALK NEXT TO HER CAR, SCANNING THE BUSY STREET FOR ANY SIGN OF CANNING. The shop clerk's last words still rung in her ears. *Was it him? Did you win the bet?* Annalisa could not be sure. She had shown Fran a picture of Canning on her phone, but Fran could only say it might have been him who bought the jaguar-themed wind chimes found at Vicki's place.

Annalisa's phone buzzed and she saw it was a message from Mara Delaney, asking to change their meeting place to her campus rather than Annalisa's office. *There's something here you need to see,* she wrote. Annalisa drove the short distance to campus and found Mara outside her office building, surrounded by reporters and cameras. Mara did not look like the polished woman who had shown up in Annalisa's office. She wore grubby jeans, a university sweatshirt, her glasses and sneakers with black stains on them. Her hair was in a messy twist and she had what looked like soot on her cheek, but she was holding a copy of her book. "Do you think the fire was an attack on you or on your book?" a male reporter asked her.

"I'm harmless," Mara replied. "An ordinary assistant professor. Why would someone attack me? No, the person who set fire to my office did so deliberately to destroy my book."

"Why do you think they did that?" a female reporter asked.

"Because of the message," Mara said as she held up the book for the cameras to see. "We're trained by Hollywood and popular opinion to see sociopaths as murderers and con men, but the truth is more complex. Society can't function if we're all bleeding hearts."

"Are you?" the female reporter followed up. "A bleeding heart?"

Mara glanced over her shoulder at the office building. Annalisa could see damage on the right side—the boarded windows and char along the roofline. Mara sniffed back emotion as she turned around again. "Someone tried to make me bleed. To—to try to frighten me into canceling the book. But I won't be cowed and sociopaths surely won't stop doing what they do. They are here among us, whether my book ever hits the shelves or not. They are born with a unique human makeup that can be used for society's good or society's ruin. I know which one I'd want them to choose. Don't you?"

Annalisa waited to the side until Mara had finished her little press conference. "I gather you had some excitement," she said when Mara finally approached her.

"Thank God you're here." Mara grabbed Annalisa in a fierce hug.

She smelled like smoke. Annalisa hesitated, taken aback by the display of affection, before returning the embrace. "What happened?" she asked.

Mara sniffled into her shoulder. "My office burned down last night. Well, not to the ground, as you can see. But the place is a total wreck. Worse, they think I did it."

"What?" Annalisa stepped back abruptly.

Mara nodded to affirm the bad news. "Can you imagine? Setting fire to my own office?" A hysterical laugh escaped her. "I feel like I'm in a nightmare."

"Stop," Annalisa said. "Tell me everything."

Mara walked her through the story, from getting the phone call to coming down in the middle of the night to find fire engines and the smoky ruins of her office. Annalisa followed Mara inside for a look. The firefighters had arrived quickly so most of the damage was limited to Mara's office and the two on either side of her. The whole place was waterlogged and stunk of chemicals, ash, and burned plastic. Annalisa agreed with the fire investigator's initial impression that the blaze had started in the corner of Mara's office where the boxes of books had been stored. Mara told her the video showed an unidentified figure in a hoodie entering the building shortly before the fire. "Whoever it was, they used my ID to get in. It's gone from my bag. I don't know who took it."

"Is anything missing from your office?" Annalisa asked as they surveyed the ruins.

"I—I don't know. Why?"

"Arson is often used to cover up some other crime."

"My computer monitor is destroyed," Mara said, gesturing at it. "The laptop, I had with me at home, thank goodness. There really wasn't much of value in here otherwise, just books and little knickknacks."

"Your ID," Annalisa said as they walked back outside into the fresh air. "How would someone get that?"

Mara gave a helpless shrug. "I don't know. Someone must have stolen it from me because I can't find it anywhere. I usually wear it on a lanyard or keep it loose in my bag. I didn't need it yesterday so I'm not sure when it went missing."

"I'd like to get a look at that CCTV footage," Annalisa said as she eyed the outside camera on the building across the way.

"I demanded they give me a copy. Let me send it to you." She took out her phone. "Do you think I should get a lawyer? It all seems so crazy."

"What do the cops say?"

"I only talked to a campus security officer so far. He seemed interested in whether I have any angry students."

"And do you?"

"No more than usual." She tapped away at her phone for a few moments. "There, I sent you the file. It's not long and it doesn't show much."

Annalisa viewed the clip on her own phone. At this size, it wasn't much help. She would take it back to the office and view it on a larger screen. What she was most interested in was the direction the intruder took when they left the building. The road forked and the hooded figure took the left-hand path. "Let's go," Annalisa said, setting off in the same direction.

Mara hurried to keep up. "Go where?"

"Wherever he went."

"He," Mara repeated. "You think it's a he?"

"Statistically, most arsonists are male. Also, the figure from the video is approximately five eight to five ten—you can tell that from where the head reaches relative to the doorframe as they enter the building. Tall for a woman, but not impossible."

Mara was quiet for a moment. "I'm five eight," she said.

"So am I," Annalisa reassured her. She bent to pick up a short stick, after which she approached the nearest public garbage receptacle and started poking around inside it.

"What are you looking for?"

"Not sure yet." Annalisa found only partially eaten food, plastic coffee cups, and other trash. She walked farther down the path, keeping her eyes on the ground for anything unusual, until she reached the next can. Mara stood there fidgeting while Annalisa surveyed the trash again. "Tell me how you got into studying sociopaths," Annalisa said to distract her companion.

"Oh, you know," Mara replied scuffing at the pavement. "I met one."

Annalisa straightened up from her garbage excavation. "Met a sociopath?"

"Yeah." Mara grimaced. "The bad kind."

"What happened?" Annalisa asked as they walked onward.

"It was back in college. I had this roommate, Donna Jo. She was sweet and oh-my-gosh so smart. Everyone called her Watson, after that supercomputer who was so popular at the time? Anyway, Donna had her heart set on getting some prize that came with a scholarship to the University of Oxford, to study there for a year. She'd never been abroad before and she really wanted to go. She worked her ass off on the application. You had to take a special exam and write a big paper. The finalists had to interview with the committee that decided the prize. I told Donna she had nothing to worry about, but she said there was this other guy, named Brent, who wanted the scholarship too."

"So who won?" Annalisa asked as she poked around in the next trash can.

"Well, that's the thing . . . Donna said her submission wowed the committee. She was a finalist but so was Brent. It came down to the interview. The day before the committee was to do the interviews, Brent approached Donna and asked her out. He said they should have a nice dinner, on him, to celebrate the end of the whole long process. May the best man win, and all that jazz. Donna didn't have a lot of money. Brent did. He offered to take her somewhere fancy so she agreed, and I guess the first part of the evening was amazing. He bought champagne and they toasted each other's hard work. But the next morning, she woke up naked in his bed. Had no memory of how she'd gotten there."

Annalisa halted and looked at Mara with alarm. "He spiked her drink?"

"We think so. She'd only had two glasses of champagne. Not enough to black out."

"That's assault," Annalisa pointed out. "She should have reported him to the authorities."

"She was embarrassed. She said every college student should have a one-night stand at some point anyway. But it wasn't the rape that bothered her. Whatever drug he gave her, it caused her to oversleep and miss her interview with the prize committee. Brent showed up. He got the award."

"Donna must have argued the decision."

"She tried. The committee said it was her fault for missing the interview. She confronted Brent but he said he'd thought she was just hungover. She couldn't prove he'd drugged her. There was nothing she could do. Then, over that summer, she found out she was pregnant. Her parents were total puritan conservatives. She couldn't tell them what happened. When she contacted Brent, he told her to have an abortion. He was in Oxford already. It wasn't his problem."

"That's awful," Annalisa replied.

Mara swallowed hard. "It gets worse. Donna felt trapped. I told her I'd go with her to the clinic if she wanted. She didn't answer me. I texted and emailed her a bunch of times over the summer, but she never wrote back. When she didn't return for senior year, I discovered the truth— Donna had taken her own life."

"I'm sorry," Annalisa said, pausing her search to regard Mara with sympathy. "Did anything ever happen to Brent?"

"Of course not," Mara said bitterly. "I saw him at graduation, strutting around campus, totally fine. I wanted to kill him, but more than that, I wanted to understand him. I thought maybe there was a way to prevent guys like Brent from existing in the first place."

"Is there?" Annalisa asked, curious.

"No." Mara sighed with regret. "Sociopaths are usually born that way. The best we can hope for is to nudge them into productive arenas where their talents benefit society. You can't fix Brent but maybe you can minimize the damage so he doesn't go through life like a wrecking ball, leaving a bunch of Donnas in his wake."

"You mean like Craig Canning."

"Exactly like him." Mara bit her lip. "I hope. Have you found anything linking him to Vicki Albright's death?"

"No," Annalisa answered truthfully.

"Whew. Well, that's a relief."

"But I haven't found anything that proves he didn't."

Annalisa spotted one more trash bin by a small parking lot that had a sign indicating faculty parking only. She took her stick over to it and poked at the trash. "Hello," she said as she spotted something black and made of fabric. She used the end of the stick to raise the garment from the garbage. It was a black hoodie, like the figure had worn in the CCTV footage.

"You don't think that's his," Mara said, her blue eyes round. "Would he be that careless to throw it away here?"

"It was a disguise for the cameras," Annalisa said, glancing around. "Once he was here, he didn't need it anymore." Whoever it was who burned the office, they knew they would blend into the campus surroundings.

"Looks pretty generic," Mara said, wrinkling her nose at the sweatshirt. "Cheap."

"I'm sure you can buy it anywhere," Annalisa agreed. She wished she was still on the job so she could have it analyzed for trace evidence, maybe even DNA. She turned it around to examine the back and saw a silvery blond hair stuck to the shoulder. Mara saw it too.

"It wasn't a man," she whispered as her eyes grew wide. "It was a woman?"

"Someone with your hair color," Annalisa observed grimly.

"No. Wait. You don't think . . ." Her face grew pale. "That's not my hair. Is it?"

"If someone got close enough to you to grab your ID . . ." Annalisa trailed off and Mara put a hand to her forehead.

"I feel sick. Who would do this?"

"I don't know. But I think you were wrong back there, what you said to those reporters. Whoever is doing this, it's not about your book or its message. It's about you."

FIFTEEN

....

M ARA'S ID HAD BEEN USED TO ENTER THE BUILDING TO SET THE FIRE. The
hoodie disposed of in the trash can nearest the faculty parking
lot. Now a blond hair on the sweatshirt certainly seemed like a visual
match to Mara's. "I assume you park nearby?" Annalisa asked as she
carefully folded the hoodie in on itself to preserve any other trace evidence.

"That's my car over there," Mara said, indicating a black Nissan
Rogue only twenty feet away. "In my assigned space."

"Someone definitely wants it to look like you set that fire," Annalisa told her as they started walking back to the burned office building. "Someone with a personal grudge against you. Any ideas who it
could be?"

Mara made a pained face. "Maybe Miles Dupont."

Annalisa halted in surprise. "The climate activist guy?"

"He teaches here. His office is in the building across from mine, the
one with the cameras. He had a book slated to come out the same time
as mine but his has been pushed back to make room to print more copies of my title. He's, uh, not taking it well."

"What does that mean?" Annalisa asked as they resumed walking.

"Oh, he came to my office the other day to yell at me about it. Stomped around a bunch and waved his fists. I figured he was letting off steam since there is nothing he can really do about the printing schedule. The publisher puts a clause in the contract that allows them some room to shift things around. It's not like his book is canceled, just delayed a bit."

"But whoever broke in targeted your book, and they want to make it seem like you set the fire. What would happen if the publisher decided you were responsible for the fire?"

Mara chewed her bottom lip, slowing her steps. "Publicity would probably dry up. They wouldn't be pleased. There is a morals clause in the contract that says they do not have to go forward with the book release if I'm convicted of a crime. You know, I can't believe I'm saying this, but Miles swore he'd stop my book no matter what he had to do and making me into a criminal might be the only way to do it at this late date."

"I'll have a talk with him. See what I can find out."

Mara turned anxious eyes to the sweatshirt in Annalisa's hand. "What are you going to do with that?"

"Hang on to it for now."

"You won't take it to the police?"

"Not unless they ask me for it." Annalisa paused at her car to remove a paper evidence bag from the trunk. She bagged the sweatshirt and sealed it, just like she would have on the job. She didn't know what other secrets it might yield. "Miles Dupont knew Vicki Albright," she said to Mara. "Well enough that she kept a picture of them together in her apartment. Were you aware of that?"

"Goodness, no." Mara put a hand to her throat. "Knew her how?"

"No idea. But you can be sure I'll ask him when we chat."

ANNALISA FOUND MILES DUPONT IN HIS OFFICE WITH A CADRE OF RAPT UNDERGRADUATES. He'd come out from behind his desk to sit with them in a cozy nook with a futon and rattan furniture. A half dozen overgrown plants threatened to make the place into a jungle. "The government databases are only a place to start," Miles was telling them. "You have to dig deeper to find what the government doesn't want you to see."

"Professor Dupont?" Annalisa asked.

He glanced up at Annalisa's intrusion. "Ah," he said, regarding her with a curious expression. "Here's the government now. The enforcer branch." The kids looked blank so he filled them in. "Detective Annalisa Vega of the Chicago PD."

A kid with a tight Afro and polo shirt sat up with interest. "The Lovelorn Killer," he said. "You caught him."

Annalisa never knew how to react when someone pointed out what was supposed to be her greatest success. She was glad to have the Lovelorn Killer off the street, but given the personal costs—the scar on Nick's abdomen, the wrecking ball the case took to her family—she viewed it more as a tragedy than an accomplishment. She spread her hands to illustrate she came in peace. "I'm no longer with the department," she told Miles. "I'm a private citizen, just like you."

"Ah." He gave a tight smile like he didn't quite believe it. "So what brings you to my office, Comrade Annalisa?"

"Mara Delaney. She's a friend of mine. I'm sure you heard about the fire in her office."

He held her gaze for a long moment without saying anything. Then he abruptly slammed the book closed and stood up. "That's going to be all for now," he told the students. "Email me if you still have questions about the final."

He moved with a fluid grace, and as he got closer to her, Annalisa saw he wasn't especially tall for a man, perhaps five feet nine or so. He could be the figure in the video. "So," he said when the students had filed out, "Mara sicced the dogs on me, eh?" He went behind his desk to make a show of straightening it.

"I don't know what you mean."

"She called up her gestapo friend to come interrogate me about the fire. She thinks I did it, right? Of course she does."

"Did you?"

He paused his paper shuffling to glare at her. "Don't be ridiculous."

"She said you're angry about her book taking precedence over hers."

"I am angry." He slammed down a folder. "Everyone should be angry. My book is about the most pressing issue of our time, the health of our planet. It concerns us all because we all live here together, whether we like it or not. Her book is embarrassing psychobabble drivel about how psychopaths are actually cuddly and friendly. But guess which story the media is eager to cover with breathless interviews?"

"The press was here today," Annalisa observed.

"Yeah, and who do you think called them?" When she didn't answer, he rolled his eyes. "Mara, of course. She can't get enough of the spotlight. She was nothing, just another junior professor struggling to get a research grant, before she hooked up with that pet psycho of hers and invented this book idea. She probably burned the office. Or he did."

"Why would he do that?"

He shot her a meaningful look. "He's a psycho. Why do they do anything?"

"Where were you last night between midnight and two a.m.?"

"Where I usually am at that hour. In my bed sleeping."

"Anyone with you?"

His lips curled in a sardonic smile. "Why Ms. Vega, are you making a pass at me?"

"I'm a married woman." She showed off the ring on her left hand. The circle of tiny diamonds was flashier than she would have picked for herself but she felt a gratitude whenever she glimpsed their sparkle. Diamonds were special because of the tremendous pressure they'd withstood, the same as her and Nick.

"The ring is symbol, not a chastity belt," Miles replied airily.

She noticed his hands were free of any jewelry. "Maybe for some," she said. "Not for me."

"Maybe for your friend Mara." He gave her a cheeky glance to see how she received this suggestion.

She kept her tone neutral. "I don't know," she said. "What have you heard?" She didn't know Mara that well. If Mara was having an affair, that person would be a good candidate for setting her office on fire.

Miles gave an exaggerated shrug. "She and the pet psycho. They're awfully close."

"Craig Canning?"

"Does she have another psycho she's cozy with? She probably does, given her affinity for them."

"Have you actually seen them together or is this rumor and supposition on your part?"

"I try not to see them together." He made a gagging face.

"Who do you see?" she asked, and he chuckled.

"There you go again with your interest in my personal life . . ."

"Vicki Albright," she tossed out. "You see her?"

His humor vanished like smoke in the wind. He started moving items around on his desk again, this time with less surety. "Vicki," he murmured. "Shame about what happened to her."

"So you did know her."

He gave a short nod. "We went out a few times. Nothing serious. She, uh, she won me in a charity auction last year." He gave a self-conscious smile, dropping his egotistical act, and Annalisa had a flash of what

Vicki might have seen in Miles. "I did it as a favor for my childhood pal Bridget, who was raising money to rehab children's playgrounds. It's not my usual arena, but Bridget said the playgrounds counted as green spaces and I'd be saving them from getting plowed over for parking lots. So, I agreed." He shrugged. "Incidentally, that's where I first encountered Mara's pet psycho."

"Craig Canning was there?" Annalisa's interest perked up. This meant she could prove he'd been at the same party as Vicki Albright.

"Oh, yeah, working the entire room, if you know what I mean."

"Did he talk to Vicki?"

"He must have. I don't remember any specifics."

"Did she bid on him?"

"I don't remem . . . actually, wait. She did. She said something about being glad she lost out on him because she got me instead."

Vicki could also work a room, Annalisa thought. Miles must have read her face because he thinned his lips.

"I know what you're thinking. She was just being nice, assuaging my preening ego. Well, it wasn't like that. My ego is microscopic compared to Canning's. Early in the evening, he started making this joke about how he was going to take home the crown for the bachelor with the most bids. He was, like, begging the ladies to help him on this epic quest. 'Make me the king, won't you, please?' Everyone laughed and thought it was sort of funny, although I counted it as more pathetic."

"Of course," Annalisa said, suppressing her eye roll.

"Anyway, his ploy for sympathy worked. He had the most bids out of all the men. One from nearly every woman in the room, if I recall correctly. He got up on the stage with Bridget and asked her for the crown. She tried to laugh it off, but turns out, the psycho wasn't kidding. He really wanted a crown. Bridget realized he wasn't leaving the stage without one so she said something to her assistant and the girl went scurrying off. She came back a minute later with a circle of branches with leaves and berries on them. Bridget put the thing on his head and the man got a standing ovation for it. Can you believe that? He bullied Bridget into making him king and then everyone applauded him for it. Only when I was leaving did I see where the crown came from—it was a decoration from the hotel's lobby. The branches were ringed around the bases of the fake candles, and they were every bit as fake themselves. But the psycho got his big moment, I suppose. It's his world and we're just living in it. Like background characters in his video game."

"Do you know who won his company at the auction?"

"No, but I can ask Bridget if you want."

"Please do, thanks."

He made a note to himself. "Whoever it was, you can bet he engineered it that way."

"You're saying he rigged the winner?"

"Of course," he replied like it was obvious. "He got himself a crown that hadn't even existed. You think he left his future date up to chance? That man calculates the angle on his breakfast order. That's why I feel a little bit sorry for Mara."

"What do you mean?"

"She thinks she picked him for this project. I guarantee it's him who picked her."

Annalisa absorbed this insight without comment. Whoever had set the fire left campus via the closest faculty parking lot, maybe to frame Mara, but maybe because he or she parked there themself. "You have a parking spot on campus, Professor?"

His expression turned self-satisfied. "Yes, but I don't have a car. I use either public transportation or an e-bike, which I keep on the rack outside. Unlike with Mara and her book, the earth isn't some PR project for me. We can all pretend like the planet isn't cooking us alive. But as much as we don't care about the earth, the earth doesn't care for us either. It was here before we humans showed up, and it will be here spinning when we're gone."

"Speaking of gone," she said, "who broke off your affair with Vicki Albright?"

"It was a mutual parting. She was generous with her charitable donations, don't get me wrong. I was able to draw her attention to a few local groups that greatly benefited from her funding. But Vicki liked parties—big, loud parties with lots of people and even more waste. Food thrown away uneaten. Plastic decorations. Washing for linens and silverware and plates, and all for what . . . so rich people can entertain themselves for a few hours?"

"Rumor has it you're one of those rich people."

"Don't put your faith in rumors, Detective. I'm a Dupont in name only. My father was a carpenter. My mother a social worker. I've had to work for every penny I've got."

"A struggling grant writer," she said. "Like Mara."

"I guess you can say she and I have that one thing in common."

"Maybe more than that," Annalisa observed lightly.

"Oh?" He raised an eyebrow at her.

"Craig Canning is her meal ticket. Vicki Albright could have been yours."

A stain of anger appeared on his cheeks. "I don't use people. I'm not like Canning or Mara. Vicki wasn't interested in my work, not at a serious level, and I don't have time for unserious people, no matter how much money they might have."

"I'm getting that," Annalisa said drily. She had no doubt now that Vicki had been the one to end things. "I also think maybe you aren't much fun at parties."

She left Miles Dupont's office and walked back toward her car, pausing to recycle a plastic water bottle someone had dumped on the path. When her phone rang, she saw Nick's name flash on the screen along with the time, which said it was almost six o'clock. She'd promised to be at the hospital by now. "Hey," she said, quickening her pace. "Sorry, I'm running late. Someone set fire to Mara Delaney's office and I—"

"Is Cassidy with you?" Nick cut her off.

She halted with her hand on the car door. "What? No."

"She's not here at the hospital like she said she'd be, and when I called her school, they said she never showed up today. She's not answering her cell."

"Given everything going on with her mom, it's not surprising she might want to blow off school. Have you tried her friends?"

"Melanie's been texting and calling around for a couple of hours now. No one has heard from her." The panic was rising in Nick's voice. Annalisa sympathized with him, but she'd been a teenage girl once and her parents had not known her whereabouts at all times, often on purpose.

"I'm sure we'll find her," she said soothingly as she got into her car. "What can I do to help?"

"Go by the condo. See if she's there?" Cassidy had a key to their place.

"Sure, I'll go right now."

They hung up and she'd started her engine when her phone buzzed again. She snatched it up, expecting it to be Nick calling back with the news that Cassidy had turned up. Instead she got Craig Canning's voice on the line.

"Detective Vega," he said. "I hope I'm not catching you at a bad time."

She had never given him her cell number. "Actually, I'm in kind of a rush at the moment."

"That's too bad. I really wanted to have a chat with you. I've been waiting at your office for some time now under the assurances that you would be turning up here soon. Frankly, we were starting to get worried."

A chill went through her. "We?"

"I've been in the hands of your capable young assistant. Cassidy."

SIXTEEN

....

Annalisa cursed and slapped the wheel of her Civic, wishing she had Miles Dupont's nimble e-bike as she inched through Chicago rush-hour traffic like sludge through a drain. *He's a good sociopath,* she tried to tell herself every time she pictured Craig Canning alone with her teenage stepdaughter. *The harmless kind.* Then she remembered the woman who'd dubbed him a "good" sociopath had also hired Annalisa to investigate him for murder and she hit the gas pedal a little harder—only to brake hard as she met the bumper of the car in front of her. Getting up North Milwaukee Avenue was slow, slow, and then fast as it opened up into Jefferson Park. Annalisa drove like she still had the light and siren. When she finally reached the squat brick building that housed her office, she slammed to a stop behind Canning's fancy Jaguar, her heart lurching forward as she did so. She pounded up the stairs into the office waiting room, where relief flooded through her as she heard Cassidy's voice, perfectly fine.

"She was an artist who also wanted to be a doctor," Cassidy was saying. "I'm the same way."

"You could do both," Canning replied. "Why not?"

Annalisa burst through the door and Cassidy froze like she'd been caught doing something worse than drinking tea. "No," Cassidy said to Canning as her fingers tightened around the mug. "I have to choose."

Canning turned at Annalisa's arrival. "Ah," he said with a smile. "At last."

Annalisa ignored him as she advanced on Cassidy. From the used tea bags sitting on the tiny table, the girl had been entertaining Canning for a while. "What are you doing here? You're supposed to be at the hospital. Your father is worried sick."

Cassidy's color heightened and she began clearing away the mess. "I'm going to the hospital later. But we agreed I work here in the afternoons, remember?"

"Not if you're skipping school." Annalisa snatched the trash from Cassidy's hands. "And why aren't you answering your phone?"

"I didn't want to talk to anyone. I was working on Naomi's case and I found something you should see."

"No." Annalisa cut her short. "We'll talk about this later. Get your stuff and wait for me in the other room. I'll take you to the hospital in a minute."

Canning checked his shiny watch. "I can give her a lift if you want. I have to be over there soon myself."

"You've done quite enough, thank you."

He lifted his eyebrows at her and held up his palms. "As you wish."

Cassidy hadn't budged. "I may have a way to find Naomi's mother. Aren't you even a little bit interested?"

"I think you should focus more on your own mother right now." The clipped words came out harsher than Annalisa intended, and Cassidy paled from head to toe. "Cass, I'm sorry . . ." Annalisa reached for her but Cassidy went rigid. She picked up her backpack and marched out to the waiting room, slamming the office door behind her.

As Annalisa stood frozen in the reverberations, Canning resumed tidying up her office. "You don't need to do that," she told him dully.

"It's no bother." He took the trash from her gently and deposited it all in the can. "I'm guessing her mother is the sick friend you mentioned." Annalisa hesitated before giving a short nod. Canning looked at her with such sympathy she couldn't believe what Mara had said about him, that he had no real feelings. "I'm sorry," he said.

She gathered herself, self-conscious at his pity. "You wanted to talk."

"Yes." He gestured vaguely. "I'm sorry if I intruded. Cassidy answered when I knocked earlier. She said she's your assistant."

"She's my stepdaughter." Annalisa had never said the words aloud before. "She's, ah, a bit eager. But she should know better than to let strange men into the office when she's here alone." She drifted off as she realized he'd been seated with a prime view of her murder wall. All the photos from Vicki's apartment were tacked up there for him to see. The wind chimes. The impossible timing that meant he could not have been present at the moment Vicki tumbled off the balcony.

"I wouldn't hurt her," Canning said, his intense blue gaze trained on Annalisa.

She jolted her attention back to him. "You said you wanted to talk to me."

"I thought it was time we had a real chat, you and me. Come clean, so to speak."

For a flash, she thought he might admit everything. "What do you mean?"

"The young man who works the booth at the hospital parking garage. He stopped me this morning and asked about the damage to my car. I had no idea what he was talking about. I said there was no damage and he must be confused. But he insisted an insurance agent had been to inspect my spot and view camera footage of me parking there the day Vicki Albright died. He didn't know the meaning of the date, of course, but I did." He tilted his head at her. "You suspect me of murdering her."

Annalisa figured it was pointless to argue with him at this stage. "I told you I was investigating her death."

"Yes, hired by the brother," he said, walking closer to her. "He has suspicions, you said. But why on earth would he suspect me?"

She shrugged. "It's just a theory."

"But what is the basis for the theory? I told you I didn't know the girl. Why would I toss her off a balcony?" He stepped into her personal space, studying her face intently. She said nothing. He narrowed his eyes a moment and then smiled. "It's Mara, isn't it?"

She held her breath. *Don't tell him I hired you,* Mara had said.

"Mara's book," he clarified. "The one that says I'm a sociopath."

Annalisa exhaled slowly. "She says you're a good one. I confess, in my line of work, I don't know that I've ever encountered such a thing. The sociopaths I've known all have a body count on them."

"So I must be the same, hmm?" He seemed amused. "I've lost a patient here and there, Detective, but I'm betting you've killed more people than I have." She blinked. He could be right. He watched her doing the math and his ghostly smile returned. "Are you a sociopath?" he asked her.

"No." A sociopath would pull the trigger and not care what happened afterward. Annalisa woke some nights sweating with the echo of her own gunfire in her head. She'd left the job, but she feared it would never leave her.

"But you have killed before," Canning continued. "The Lovelorn Killer is just one example. I know there are others."

"You've been researching me?"

"Why not?" He indicated her murder wall. "You've done the same to me."

She didn't want to engage him on the specifics. Not until she had more ammunition. "Help me understand," she said, gesturing for him to take a seat. "What does it mean to be a good sociopath?"

He waved her off. "That's Mara's label. Not mine."

"Tell me how you see it then." She took the chair Cassidy had vacated. She appealed to his ego, but the truth was she desperately wanted to hear what he had to say. The question had haunted her since Mara Delaney first posed the suggestion: could someone with no empathy, no emotion, somehow still be a good person?

Canning seemed intrigued, fingering the back of his chair as he considered her offer to speak. "What it's like to be me? That's what you want to know?"

"Everything you can tell me," she said, leaning forward like an eager student.

"Okay. Okay, if you really want, I'll be completely honest with you." He sat down, and mirrored her posture so their heads were close together. "What it's like to be me," he began in a philosophical tone. Then he whispered near her ear: "It's fucking awesome."

His breath on her cheek sent tingles across her skin. She sat back with a jolt and he cackled at her.

"Oh, come on. My life is objectively amazing. I'm a god at work, operating at the top of my game. Physicians around the world call me for consultations. I can have any woman I want, age eighteen to eighty. I'm in the best shape of my life and it's only getting better. Who wouldn't want to be me?"

She couldn't argue him on the merits, but his position seemed hollow. She probed him with her gaze. "But surely you have some . . . regrets. You must. Everyone does."

"I could have bought Amazon stock back in 2002, if that's what you mean."

"No, I mean like patients you lost. Mistakes you made."

"I don't make mistakes." A sharpness came into his tone. He must have heard it because he paused and relaxed back into a smile. "Of course, I hate to lose a patient. It's awful. But I sleep at night knowing I gave them everything I could, the absolute best chance to survive. If fate couldn't take it the rest of the way . . ." He ended with a slight shrug. "It's not on me. You, though, you have much bigger problems."

"Oh?"

He indicated the photos and notes tacked up on her wall. "First, you're chasing your tail on a murder that may not even be a murder at all. Just a brother, who, in his grief, can't let go. He's paying you to keep Vicki alive somehow. As long as you're thinking about her, as long as there is something more that can be done for her—call it justice or maybe revenge—then she lives on. Meanwhile, you can keep cashing his checks."

Annalisa understood now why Mara found him so fascinating. If he didn't experience normal human emotions, he certainly grasped their psychological underpinnings. He'd just ascribed a primal hunger to Vicki's brother, a searing connection that Mara insisted Canning himself could never feel. As if to underscore that point, he'd finished up his argument by saying Annalisa must be in it only for the money. His imagined humanity didn't extend to her. "Let's say for argument," she began slowly as she stood up. "Let's say it was a murder. Someone deliberately threw Vicki off her balcony. How was it done?" She might never have another chance to keep him talking, and this technique had served her well when interrogating ordinary suspects. *Okay, you say you didn't do it. But let's pretend you did. What would be your motive?*

Canning rose to join her at the wall. "It's not very elegant," he said with a slight frown. "Anyone with sufficient physical strength could have accomplished it."

"They would need to gain entry to the apartment."

He pointed at the picture of wind chimes. "A gift. A Trojan horse."

"It would have to be a gift from a friend. She wouldn't let a stranger come hang wind chimes on her balcony."

"I heard she liked to entertain men and that she wasn't too particular. If he was a handsome stranger, she might let him in."

"She would have let you in, is what you're saying?"

He looked at her with a gleam in his eyes. "I bet she would have, yes. But as we've seen, I can't have done it. Your own work here on the timeline precludes me as the murderer."

"You admit you went back into the building. You had a cut on your hand. One could argue that's suspicious."

"I admit? That phrasing makes it sound like I had something to hide. I told you I cut my hand on the broken bottle by my tires. But even if I grant you your suspicions, I still couldn't have been at Vicki's apartment at five to nine and pulling into the hospital at five past. Not unless I've mastered time travel or have some underground tunnel. It would have to be the perfect murder."

He had her on the timing. It was impossible. But the way "perfect murder" rolled off his tongue with such glee. He was enjoying her frustration if nothing else. "Maybe Ruth Bernstein is wrong about the timing," she suggested.

"No way," he answered flatly. "That woman is like an automaton. The whole building sets its clocks by her and her habits. If someone threw Vicki off that balcony at five to nine every day of the week, then Ruth Bernstein would be there to witness it Monday through Sunday."

Huh, thought Annalisa. *Almost like you could it plan it that way.* Then something else occurred to her. "You said 'first,'" she told him.

"Hmm?" He was still looking at the photos of Vicki. Was that sympathy in his eyes or pride in a job well done?

"You said I had bigger problems. Vicki's death is the first. That implies more than one."

"Oh," he said, shaking himself loose from his contemplations. "That girl out there." He gestured to where Cassidy waited for her in the next room.

Annalisa's heart froze. "What about her?"

"Her little friend, the one who's sick? You're meant to be tracking down the mother as I understand it. Trust me when I say it's pointless."

She thought he meant from a medical perspective. "The doctors say she needs a kidney transplant and then she'll be fine. It's entirely possible her mother is a match."

"Doesn't matter." He shook his head. "She'll never give it up. The kid's been sick for years now. You think the father hasn't asked the mother already? Of course he has. I see parents with deathly ill children all the time, and there is literally nothing they wouldn't do to save their kids. That father, if he has even an ounce of love for the girl, the first thing he did when he wasn't a match was hire someone like you to track down his ex. She's already said no, and he's just refusing to tell the girl. He can't bear to tell her that her mother doesn't love her. That she won't ever love her. She can't."

Annalisa was catching on. "You're saying Naomi's mother is the bad kind of sociopath. Is that it?"

"Your label," he said as he picked up his coat. "Not mine."

"So there's no changing or stopping her."

He scoffed at her naivety. "Come on, Vega. People don't change."

"What do you think should be done with them then . . . the bad sociopaths?"

He considered a beat and then stretched his lips into a humorless smile. "You already know the answer. You've lived it." He made his hand into a gun, pretended to fire it at her, and blew imaginary smoke from the barrel. The light returned to his eyes. "Goodbye, Detective, and . . . good luck."

SEVENTEEN

··········

CASSIDY SAT ON THE FAKE LEATHER COUCH, HER BACKPACK ON HER LAP, WATCHING THE SECOND HAND SWEEP TIME AWAY ON THE OLD-TIMEY CLOCK MOUNTED ON THE WALL. Annalisa hadn't picked the clock; maybe the previous guy hadn't picked it either. It could have been nailed there when the building was built in 1944. Everyone had a phone or a digital watch now. Cassidy saw these old-fashioned clocks only in school or town squares. Her mother had taught her how to read one even before she started school, had delighted in how quickly her daughter figured out what "quarter past" meant. They had laughed together at the child's riddle: what has two hands and a face, but no eyes? A clock! Now Cassidy resented the old clocks that made you puzzle out what they meant rather than just giving you the numbers. She didn't have time for this nonsense. That's what her mother always said when Cassidy was growing up, and not just when Cassidy dillydallied putting on her shoes. Her mom said it to inanimate objects like a key that wouldn't fit straight into the lock or a cup that crashed to the ground. *I don't have time for this nonsense.* Her mother had managed her life down to the second. She had to. She was a single mom with a job. She had worked at a

bar with Melanie—that's how they met—then she became the manager
and eventually she and Melanie bought the whole place. Come to think
of it, the bar had an old-timey clock too in the back office. Cassidy had
done her homework under it, sitting on the ratty green sofa, eating stale
popcorn and drinking the Shirley Temple that Mom made for her.

I don't have time for this nonsense. Cassidy hadn't noticed at first
when her mom began saying it more often. Mom just seemed extra
clumsy, stumbling on the sidewalk and dropping silverware in the
kitchen. Her mother didn't tell her about the first doctor's appointment,
or even the second. In fact, she'd only spilled the truth about the
follow-up visit to the neurologist because the man left a voicemail on
their shared landline at home. If Cassidy's mom hadn't been such a
hard-ass, making her daughter wait until she was thirteen to get a cell,
who knows when Cassidy might have found out her mom was sick?

Cassidy stared at the unceasing second hand as it counted off the
minutes. Minutes she would never get back. She felt like she couldn't
breathe. *I don't have time for this nonsense.* Just as Cassidy was about
to bolt, Dr. Canning emerged from Annalisa's office. Cassidy knew Annalisa would chew her head off about letting Dr. Canning into the office
when Annalisa wasn't here, but it's not like he was some dangerous axe-
murdering stranger. He was a doctor at the same place that was treating
Cassidy's mother. Plus, he was pretty hot for an older guy. "Sorry to
keep you waiting out here like this," he said. He smiled directly at her
and she felt her face go warm. At school, the guys acted like she was
invisible, and the truth was, she liked it that way.

"No problem," she mumbled as she tucked a lock of hair behind her
ear. She wished he'd ask her again if she wanted to ride with him to the
hospital. He'd be way better company than Annalisa. At least he'd been
interested in her theory about Naomi's mother and how to find her.

"You know . . ." He leaned down and lowered his voice so Annalisa
wouldn't hear. "You're a bright girl. Don't let your wicked stepmother

get you down about cutting classes, hmm? I don't think school has much left to teach you. In fact, I bet you're on the right track as far as Naomi's mother is concerned." He slipped her a business card. "Let me know what you find out."

"Really?"

Annalisa appeared and Cassidy shoved the card in her jacket pocket. "I thought you were gone," Annalisa said pointedly to Dr. Canning.

"All the way gone, to hear some tell it," he said with a sardonic smile. He tipped an imaginary cap to Cassidy. "Ladies."

He left then and Annalisa took out her keys to lock up the inner office, something she had not bothered to do before. "When I gave you the security code for this place, it was so you'd have somewhere to hang out and do homework if you wanted," Annalisa said as she armed the alarm for the outer door. "Not so you could conduct business on your own."

"He showed up here. It wasn't my idea. What was I supposed to do, ignore him?"

"Yes. You tell him to come back when I'm around."

"Whatever." Cassidy hunched under the weight of her backpack as they walked down the stairs. "It's not like he's dangerous or anything."

"You don't know that." Annalisa grabbed Cassidy's shoulder and spun her around. "Maybe your dad hasn't taught you this yet, but trust me when I tell you that bad people look the same as good ones. You have to be careful."

"Don't trust anyone, is that it?"

Annalisa looked startled by this pushback, but she folded her arms and stood her ground. "Not before you get a chance to know them."

"How am I supposed to ever get to know them if I don't trust them enough to have a conversation? That's all I was doing with Dr. Canning, you know. Talking." He spoke to her like she was a real person with her own opinions, not a kid with a dying mother. Someone to be pitied.

"I know that." They reached the car and it beeped as Annalisa unlocked it. "Just . . . stay away from Craig Canning, okay? He might seem nice, but he's got an agenda."

"Yeah, curing sick kids. What a monster." Cassidy rolled her eyes as she got into the passenger seat. "I don't know why you're so down on Dr. Canning. He likes you even if you don't like him."

"Oh, he said that, did he?" Annalisa said wryly. "How nice."

"He said you were the best, like he's the best. He respects that. He thinks it's too bad you quit the force and gave up your power." Cassidy knew this would needle Annalisa, and she watched with a little thrill, her sideways gaze catching the slight tightening of Annalisa's hands on the wheel.

"This is quite a wide-ranging conversation you two had."

"You were gone awhile."

Annalisa grunted and zoomed through a yellow light. "For the record, I didn't give up my power. I'm still solving cases. Now I get to pick which ones I take on rather than the city telling me what to do with my time."

"Yeah, but you can't arrest anyone. If you saw someone robbing a store or something, you couldn't do anything about it."

"I could call your dad."

"Right." Cassidy hugged her backpack to her chest, self-satisfied. "No power."

Annalisa glowered but didn't argue further. "I thought we could hit Starbucks on the way."

"Whatever you want." Cassidy looked out the window at the deepening sky.

"I figured you might be hungry. We know you didn't get a school lunch."

Cassidy turned her head to stare at her. "You don't need to act like my mother."

"I'm not trying to."

"I don't need a backup mother. Mom already got me one of those. So you'd be, like, at best in third place." She felt mean and dirty, talking like that, but she had all these awful feelings and nowhere to put them.

"Just offering you a coffee or a sandwich," Annalisa replied. "That's all."

Cassidy's stomach rumbled at the suggestions but she didn't give Annalisa the satisfaction of a reply. "Don't you even want to know what I found out about Naomi's mom?"

"No," Annalisa said firmly. "You're off that case."

"But—"

"No buts. I'm serious. You are to leave anything regarding Elizabeth Johnston to me. Are we clear?"

Cassidy hugged her backpack tighter. It contained her laptop and the secret she'd unearthed. Naomi had sent her every picture she had of her mom and none of them yielded any hits on the internet, which wasn't too surprising if her mom didn't want to be found. But Naomi had added in one sort of yellowed picture of herself at two years old, on a swing at the park. Her dark hair was in little sprouted pigtails and her smile lit up like the sun. *My mom's not in this one, but my dad says she took it. Look how happy I am. I wouldn't have been this happy if she hadn't loved me, right?*

Of course, Cassidy had written back. *Of course she loves you.*

"But you're still going to look for her," she said to Annalisa. "You'll find Naomi's mom?"

Annalisa didn't answer right away. "Honey, I think you need to prepare yourself for the idea that Naomi's mother might not agree to be tested, even if we found her. Giving up a kidney is a major deal, and she hasn't exactly shown a lot of interest in her kid for the past sixteen years."

"She doesn't even know Naomi is sick. She could save her life." Cassidy would do literally anything if it could change her mother's fate.

Drop out of school. Chop off her own arm. Of course Naomi's mom would want to save her.

"She could," Annalisa agreed. "But she might choose not to. I know that's hard to accept . . ."

Cassidy's voice rose in stubborn insistence. "Once her mom understands how sick Naomi is, I'm sure she'll agree. Just because she hasn't been there for every second of Naomi's life doesn't mean she doesn't care about her. Dad wasn't around for the first fifteen and a half years of my life, remember?"

"I know that," Annalisa said quietly. She pulled into an open spot near Starbucks. Cassidy didn't get out.

"Mom thought the same thing, you know. About Dad. That he wouldn't care. That's why she didn't fight harder to find him and tell him she was pregnant with me, because she thought he wouldn't care if he had a kid. But he did." She slammed her body back against the seat, defiant. She repeated the words to herself, softer now. "He did." Shit, was she crying? She swiped furiously at her face.

Annalisa wordlessly took two tissues from the console and handed them to Cassidy. She balled them into her fist. "Maybe you're right," Annalisa offered. She touched Cassidy's hair, stroking gently. Cassidy hated how much she liked it. Her own mother hadn't been able to do this for months now. "Maybe you're right that Naomi's mom will agree to do the test," Annalisa said. "Now, let's get something to eat, huh?"

Cassidy got out with her backpack and followed Annalisa into the café. She didn't tell Annalisa what she'd found. She didn't admit she already knew that Naomi's mom was not a hundred percent nice person. Cassidy had taken that picture of toddler Naomi and searched it on the internet, just on a whim. Cassidy had been shocked to get a hit. The picture was attached to a GoFundMe-type of page. *Help me care for my sick daughter.* The text said the mother, Liza Guffman, was caring for her daughter, Naomi, who had leukemia. There were details about the kinds of treatments and expenses the girl had, and how Liza couldn't work because she was too busy taking care of Naomi. The goal amount was ten thousand dollars, and the campaign had already earned more than seven grand.

Cassidy burned with rage on Naomi's behalf. Her mother was pretending that Naomi was sick with cancer, an illness she didn't have, lying to people, profiting from it, when in reality her daughter was deathly ill and she couldn't be bothered even to visit her. Cassidy's first instinct was to forward what she'd found to Naomi. Her friend deserved the truth. But then Cassidy thought Naomi deserved something more: she deserved a life. The crowdfunding site had a contact email for "Liza Guffman" but Cassidy wasn't stupid enough to believe the woman would answer her. What it also had was an associated PO box in the Chicago area and Cassidy planned to use it to track "Liza" down.

Maybe Naomi's mother would be moved to help when she found out about her daughter's true predicament. Cassidy still believed it could play out this way. Her own mother was laboring to breathe, to linger on this earth a little longer so they could be together a few more days. Surely Naomi's mother felt some echo of that. But if she didn't agree to the test or the eventual transplant, Cassidy now had a way to make her agree. The woman was a fraud and she was breaking the law, collecting money from people under false pretenses. Annalisa was right—sometimes you didn't need a badge to have power. You just needed to know how to call a cop, and Cassidy had one ready and waiting.

EIGHTEEN

....

R UTH COULDN'T SLEEP. This had happened to her often since Marty had passed. The doctor had prescribed her little pink pills to help with the problem, but Ruth didn't like the vivid dreams they gave her or the hungover, sluggish feeling she had when she awoke. She typically solved the issue by getting up and doing chores, but there were no chores left to do. She had exhausted them all in an effort to distract herself from Duchess's absence. Indeed, so spic-and-span was her apartment that one might question whether a white cat had ever lived there at all. No hair could be found on the hardwood floors. No trace of kibble on the mat in the kitchen. Only the little ceramic bowl with Duchess's name and her tufted cat bed in the living room signaled her strange vacancy.

"You can always get another cat," her daughter, Meredith, said on the phone when Ruth had again lamented the loss of her pet. "There are hundreds in shelters who would love to come home with you."

"I know." She couldn't bear the thought of another cat sitting on Duchess's bed. Not when Ruth didn't even know what had happened to her. "But your father gave me Duchess. He picked out her name."

"I know," Meredith had echoed, her voice full of sympathy. "And maybe she'll turn up. I read online the other day about a cat who was missing for seven years before he found his way home to his family."

"Seven years." Ruth didn't have that kind of time. But she'd said, "Send me the link."

Absent any chores, Ruth decided to get some exercise. She wouldn't leave the building at this hour, but she could walk the halls and do a couple of flights of stairs. Damon was on the night shift, so he would be working in the lobby. She hesitated near her closet, trying to determine what one wore on a midnight jaunt. Did she redress in the clothes she'd removed at 9 p.m. or put on tomorrow's outfit early? "What do you think, Duchess?" she asked the silent room and startled when she heard a meowing in reply.

She whirled, her gaze darting about the bedroom. It wasn't the first time she'd thought she heard the cat. Once she swore she even saw a puffy white tail swishing around the corner. "Duchess?" Ruth held her breath but heard nothing this time. *I'm going mad,* she thought. *Hearing and seeing things like a batty old woman.*

Ruth did not believe in ghosts. She didn't believe in an afterlife. Marty was right where she'd left him at the Zion Gardens Cemetery. *Ashes to ashes, dust to dust.* Fifty-seven years together would have to be enough—God, she was trying to make it be enough—but Duchess was only four and a half years old. Ruth had thought it was safe to love this cat. She'd expected to be the first one to go.

She decided to put on yesterday's clothes, tweed trousers and a camel-colored sweater. She added an overcoat before remembering she wasn't actually going outside. She went to put it back but then decided to keep it so it might look like she was going out if she ran into any of her neighbors. She didn't want them to think she was haunting the hallways. Her hall stood empty when she opened the door; it had already seemed quieter since Vicki died, but now it was silent as the grave. Ruth walked to the end and took the stairs down one flight. In the staircase, she found the tape had come loose on her LOST CAT flyer and it was flipped upside down. She righted the poster and stopped to admire Duchess's adorable little face. "I haven't given up," she whispered to the photo. "You don't give up either."

She walked three floors at a slow pace, telling herself she was conserving energy, but in reality, she was listening at each passing door for a familiar mewling. Duchess was often awake at this hour, even if Ruth wasn't. Ruth initially thought perhaps the animal had become trapped inside a different apartment by accident, but with the dozens of flyers she had plastered around the place, Duchess's new keeper would have to know the real owner at this point. Once, Ruth had even knocked on a door when she heard meowing, only to find a tall bald man and his tortoiseshell cat on the other side. He'd promised to keep a lookout for Duchess. Everyone had. Everyone was looking. No one was finding.

Ruth found Damon at the front desk cutting up an apple with a pocket knife. "Mrs. B," he said with surprise. "What are you doing up at this hour?"

"Checking the locks," she said with the barest smile.

Damon looked confused. "Beg your pardon?"

"Oh, that's what Marty would say to me whenever I caught him wandering around our apartment in the middle of the night. 'Just checking the locks, dear.'"

"That's sweet." Damon crunched a piece of apple. "You were together with him a long time, huh?"

"Since we were sixteen," Ruth replied as she leaned on the counter.

"Man, I'm twenty-five and I still can't get it right." He shook his head at his poor luck. "You want some apple?"

Ruth looked down at the plate of cut-up fruit. "I don't eat after eight p.m.," she said. "What happened to your special lady friend? The one who helped you with the criminalistics class?"

"Ghosted."

"My word." Ruth clutched her throat. "She died?"

"Oh, no. Sorry, Mrs. B. She's fine as far as I know. I meant she stopped returning my texts and stuff. No explanation. Just won't talk to me anymore."

"That's extremely rude," Ruth said, drawing herself up to her full height.

"Ain't it, though," Damon agreed. "That's what I mean. It's hard to find someone out there, someone real who cares about you. You and Mr. B had it lucky."

"Yes, we did," Ruth mused. She took a piece of apple and bit into it. "I'm still not used to rattling around in that place by myself."

"Is that why you're out walkin'?"

"Maybe." She hesitated. "I guess I'm also hoping to find Duchess. You've had no word on her?"

"Believe me, I'd run right up to tell you."

"I know." She sighed and took another bite of apple. "I keep thinking she must be in the building. You would have noticed someone walk out with a cat under their arm."

"Normally, I'd say you're right, but that day, it was chaos. All those EMTs and cops coming in and out, front and back of the place. It was like Brooklyn down here. Maybe she slipped out behind someone's boots and no one noticed it happen."

That would be fitting, Ruth thought. *My heart tiptoed out the door and no one even noticed.* Aloud, she said, "I suppose that's possible. Say, you have a master key, don't you? A way to enter the apartments for repairs and such."

"Not me," he said as he snagged another slice of apple. "The super takes care of that stuff."

"The super," she mused. "Yes. I should ask him if he's seen Duchess in any of the apartments."

"Mrs. B," Damon said gently, "I think you should face facts that

Duchess isn't in the building. If she was, someone would've seen her by now."

"Unless they kept her on purpose."

He gave her a reproachful look. "Now who's going to steal a cat from a sweet old lady?"

Who indeed? Ruth felt tired all of a sudden, her bones wilting. She really was an old lady. "Thank you, Damon. I'm going up to bed now, I think. Don't let your 'ghost' haunt you too much. You are better off without her."

"I won't. 'Night, Mrs. B."

Ruth dragged herself to the elevator, and blessedly, it was there waiting for her. She stepped in and hit the button to close the door. "Wait," called a male voice, and a large hand curved around the door to stop it from going shut.

"Dr. Canning," she said as he stepped into the elevator with her. His dark jacket had beads of water on it. "Is it raining out?"

"Pouring cats and dogs," he told her. He stepped to the side to ensure he didn't drip on her dry clothes. "You didn't notice?"

"I was having a nice chat with Damon. You must have worked late tonight."

"Car accident. Subdural hematoma."

"I don't know what that is, but it sounds bad."

"Not anymore," he said with a smile. The elevator glided to a stop at his floor. "Have a good night."

Ruth wished him well and continued on her journey back to her apartment. She needed sleep. She needed to find out what happened to Duchess, or at least some kind of peace so she wouldn't keep imagining her everywhere. Like just now, she could have sworn she saw little white hairs on the back of Dr. Canning's jacket.

NINETEEN

....

ANNALISA HAD TEXTED NICK THE MOMENT SHE'D LEARNED CASSIDY WAS AT HER OFFICE, SO HE WOULDN'T BE SURPRISED TO SEE THEM ARRIVING TO-GETHER AT THE HOSPITAL. In fact, he waited for them in the lounge, crushed coffee cup in his hands and worry lines creasing his face. "Finally," he said when he saw them. "What took so long?"

"Traffic," Annalisa replied before Cassidy could say anything. She didn't want Nick to worry about Craig Canning's visit. Cassidy looked at her sideways as she made the excuse, hearing the omission and judging Annalisa for it with a slight narrowing of her eyes. Whether it meant cool points for her or not, Annalisa couldn't say. "How are you?" she asked, giving Nick a quick hug. "How's Summer?"

Nick moved around her to frown at Cassidy. "I've been trying to reach you for hours."

"My cell is off."

"Well, keep it on from now on, okay? We need to be able to reach you. And why weren't you in school today?"

"Who says I wasn't?" Cassidy flopped down into one of the gray fabric chairs. She picked up the nearest magazine and began leafing through it.

"I called the school and they told me you never showed up."

Cassidy froze but the glint in her eyes said Nick had screwed up. Oh, this was a trap, Annalisa realized with a frisson of horror. She reached for Nick's arm but he didn't notice her as he stepped closer to Cassidy. She squinted up at him. "The school isn't supposed to talk to you," she said. "You're not on my contact list so they aren't supposed to give out any information about me. Only to Mom and Melanie. It's like, a law or something. Were you breaking the law?"

Nick flushed hard and Annalisa felt a pang of sympathy for how out of his depth he was here. "That's—that's not the point," he stammered. "The point is you skipped school."

"There's no name listed for my father on any of the forms," Cassidy continued as if he hadn't spoken. "There never has been, not in my whole life. So you must have told them you were a cop, right? That's how you got them to talk to you."

"I was worried about you," Nick mumbled.

"God," Cassidy said, tossing the magazine aside. "If Stacey Billings was in the office, it'll be all over school. A cop calling to ask about me. Thanks so much, really. That's just what I needed right now."

"Cass," Nick said, his tone turning conciliatory.

She leaped up and brushed past him. "I'm gonna go see Mom."

Nick, speechless, watched her go. Annalisa rubbed his arm. "Wow," he breathed after a moment. "What the hell was that?"

Annalisa gave him a wry smile. "Still keen to have her move in?" At his sharp look, she held up her palms. "Kidding." She took a deep breath and tugged him to sit down with her. "She's sixteen and her mom is dying. That's what it is."

"But I could help her. She just needs to talk to me."

"She will." Annalisa paused. "When she's ready."

"When will that be?"

"Can't say. Only Cassidy can decide. What's the latest on Summer?"

Nick slumped in his chair and scrubbed his face with both hands. "She's stable but her temperature is still elevated. They're trying another antibiotic, and of course, she's still hooked up to the ventilator so she can't talk. They think that's probably how it will be from now on—once the patient needs a ventilator, they don't go back. They got her a computer she can use with her eyes to communicate, but she hasn't said much. I wanted to ask Melanie today about the possibility of Cassidy coming to live with me but then Cass went radio silent and we've all been dealing with that problem instead."

Convenient, thought Annalisa as her phone buzzed with a text. She dug it out to read it. *The wind chimes are gone,* Mara wrote. *The ones from my office.*

Are you sure? Annalisa texted back. She thought they might have been destroyed in the fire.

Yes. Glass shouldn't burn that easy. Someone took them.

Canning? Annalisa wrote.

Mara was typing something but then the floating dots went away. A moment later, her reply appeared. *You tell me.*

"Anna?"

Annalisa jerked to attention when Nick nudged her arm. "Sorry."

"I was asking if you wanted to grab a late dinner." He leaned over to try to get a look at her phone, but she tucked it away.

"Dinner sounds good." She'd just had a sandwich with Cassidy, but she didn't want to mention that. "Do you want to eat here or . . . ?"

"No," he said quickly. "I . . . I need to get out of here for a bit. Let me tell Cassidy and Melanie we're taking off, okay?"

Annalisa answered with a distracted nod as she pulled out her phone to look at Mara's texts again. Canning should want the book to do well, so it didn't make much sense for him to set fire to the copies in Mara's office. Unless, like Miles Dupont had suggested, it was a ploy to get more publicity ahead of the launch.

Nick wanted to eat at home so they agreed to meet there and discuss a delivery option once they had time to decompress. Annalisa once again found herself slogging through city traffic, although it was lighter now. She liked the familiarity of glancing in her rearview mirror and seeing the glow of Nick's headlights. He got caught at a red light she eked through on the yellow, and when she next stopped, she looked eagerly in the mirror to see if he'd caught up. The car behind her now was silver, not race-car red like Nick's coupe. The headlights were rounder and brighter, almost hurting her eyes. Disappointed, she took her gaze off the mirror and headed for home. But the bright lights turned with her. She didn't think much of it until they made the next turn with her as well, and the one after that. She tried slowing her pace to give the other car a chance to pass her, but it kept trailing behind. Was it following her?

Only one way to find out, Annalisa thought, gripping the wheel. At the next light, she signaled for a right turn and slowed down as if to make it, only to surge across two lanes, cutting off a blue Honda and veering left at the last second. She gunned it up the random side street, watching behind her to see if the other car followed. When she spotted a small parking lot, she jerked the wheel, parked the car facing the street, and cut her own lights. A moment later, she saw a silver sedan with bright headlights inching down the street as if searching for something. She ducked down as it went by and then popped up to try to get a look at the plate. She only saw the first three numbers, 423, but the plate holder was a shade of yellow she recognized from her years on the job. The car was a rental.

She started her engine and edged back into the street to try to follow it, but it had disappeared. She watched her rearview mirror the rest of the way back to her place, but the bright lights did not show up again. Maybe she had been imagining things. At home, Nick had a bottle of merlot open already. "Pizza okay?" he asked her as she walked into the kitchen.

"Yes, fine."

He placed their usual order while she hung up her coat. She drifted to the front windows, still uneasy about the silver sedan. Their street was not enormously busy but it was still in the city. Cars passed by often. She watched them with the rapt attention of a cat under a bird feeder.

"I don't think delivery will be here that fast," Nick said.

She jumped when he touched her and then turned in his arms. "Sorry . . . just wondering about something. Did you happen to notice a silver sedan on the way home? It's rented with a partial plate number of 423. Could be a Lexus or maybe an Acura."

"No. Why?"

A black Kia whooshed by outside. She really was being silly. The silver car was a rental. Probably they were just lost, not out to get her. She forced a smile and pecked Nick on the cheek. "No reason."

···········

NICK TOOK A SHOWER WHILE THEY WAITED FOR THE PIZZA TO ARRIVE. Annalisa positioned herself on the couch where she could keep one eye out the front window. With the other, she read some of Mara's book, *The Good Sociopath*. It opened with a banger. *What's the line between mutilating a corpse and conducting an autopsy?* Annalisa thought of the various pathologists she had worked with in her career as a cop, men and women who had withstood the stink and the gore of an autopsy bay to provide Annalisa with hard-won evidence needed to arrest the perpetrator. To her, they were frontline heroes on the battlefield for justice. She would never want the job herself. It was bad enough to show up at a murder scene spattered with blood and brain matter; to spend hours with the unseeing victim, digging around in their intestines, required a fortitude Annalisa did not possess. *Intent,* she decided. That was the line. People who mutilated corpses for fun did not have the same noble intent as the professionals who were there to aid the victim. The former was causing harm while the latter was working to correct one.

As she read on, Annalisa found more fascinating information. For example, most sociopaths didn't know they were sociopaths. They assumed everyone else had the same shallow emotions and selfish motivations that they did. Winning mattered more than anything. Defeat was like death. Annalisa wondered if this explained why Canning refused to adopt the label of sociopath for himself, even as he was pictured on a book about the subject. He didn't accept Mara's characterization of him, but if he was going to be considered a sociopath, he would be the most famous, the best, the poster boy for all of them.

"You're seriously reading that junk?" Nick came out, toweling his wet hair. He wore only a T-shirt and boxers with hearts on them.

"I guess I'm answering the door for the pizza guy," Annalisa replied as she eyed his attire.

"Why, you think I'm too much man for him?" He flexed an arm and then joined her on the couch. "Tell me you're not buying that crap about good sociopaths."

"Hey, it's interesting stuff. Mara says there are two main categories of sociopathic traits. The primary cluster is narcissism, low anxiety, grandiosity, manipulativeness, and a lack of empathy. The secondary cluster is impulsivity, disregard for social norms, and a failure to plan."

"Failure to plan? Give me a break. That's every street punk in existence."

"You have to have the whole group of traits to be a sociopath. Although, that's an interesting question. What if you had some of the traits but not others? Maybe you can be a 'sorta' sociopath?"

"Yeah, it's called being an asshole."

Annalisa read a little further as Nick played with his phone. "Oh," she said. "I was right, kind of. Mara says that the so-called good sociopaths tend to be the ones with the primary traits—narcissism, manipulation, that kind of thing. The poor planners and the ones who say 'screw you' to society's rules are the ones we put in jail."

"And Canning's the good kind," Nick said, still skeptical.

"Hmm, maybe." She returned to the text. Her conversation with Canning still niggled at her, how he had pointed out she had killed people while he saved them. *You have more bodies on you than me.* She wanted to keep defending herself. *They gave me no choice,* she imagined herself saying to him. She could almost picture his smile and hear his answer. *There's always a choice.* She put the book aside and turned to Nick. "Have you ever killed someone?"

He looked annoyed and kept scrolling through his phone. "I told you to stop reading that."

"Have you?" She pulled his arm toward her so he had to stop scrolling.

"No."

She blinked. "Really?" She knew he hadn't had to shoot anyone in the years they had been partnered, but he'd been on the job much longer than she had and she didn't know much about his time working in Florida.

He took a deep breath and shifted to face her. "My first year on the job, I put a sixteen-year-old kid in the hospital. I busted him on a simple burglary charge, and he pulled a knife on me. I threw him into a wall. It was instinct, you know? Him or me. He had a cracked skull but he made a complete recovery. Since then . . ." He shrugged. "Nothing."

"But you would shoot," she said, "if you had to."

"If I had to, sure."

Annalisa curled into the couch cushions. He made it sound so easy. The men she'd killed were violent predators bent on ending her life. Like Nick had said, it was her or them. When the sound of her own gunfire woke her at night, heartbeat stinging in her chest, she did not feel remorse. She felt terror. And fury. They made her into a killer. They made her carry the awful memories. She had made the correct choice when she'd pulled the trigger, but it was not a victory and she did not win. She reached over to stroke the glossy cover of Mara's book. Nick caught her hand and kissed it.

"You're nothing like him," he said.

She smiled. He always could read her mind. She scooted closer and he wrapped his arms around her. She put her hand over his so she could admire their matching rings. "I hope it's true," she murmured at length. "That there are good sociopaths."

"Really?"

"Why not? The argument is that they're born this way and can't change. Wouldn't you rather they be neurosurgeons and CEOs than serial killers?"

"I'm not convinced those are the only options."

She burrowed closer, encouraging Nick to tighten his hold on her, and he obliged. Canning acted superhuman, like a god. Maybe he was. "It might be easier sometimes," she confessed in a whisper. "Not to care so much."

After the pizza, they went to bed early. Annalisa took a pill beforehand and was rewarded with a hard, dreamless sleep. She woke slack-jawed in the dark, her mind blank. Nick lay motionless beside her. She felt something had awoken her and reached for her phone to see if it had made a noise. Nothing. She put it back on the nightstand and punched the pillow, determined to get more rest. But no, she heard it again. A faint tinkling.

She got out of bed and went into the kitchen, squinting as she turned on the lights. The pizza box and dirty wineglasses sat on the counter. Nothing looked disturbed. She made a pass through the front room and all was quiet there too. Only when she checked the rear of the condo did the noise get louder, and as her hand closed on the back door, she finally placed the sound. Wind chimes. She yanked the door open and a blast of wind hit her in the face. When she stepped out into the shared courtyard, she saw the wind chimes hanging from the nearby skinny tree, dancing in the stiff breeze. Her feet froze on the cold concrete patio. She should get her phone to take pictures, but what would they prove?

She inched closer, strangely hypnotized by the colored glass glinting in the dim light. The melodic tinkling took on a frantic beat as the wind picked up. As the wind whipped past her face, she smelled it. Cigarette smoke. She whirled at the smell, expecting to see Canning, but a different man sat lounging on her patio furniture, dressed all in black. He had two empty beer bottles lying at his feet and the remnants of a six-pack on the table. He took a long draw on his cigarette and blew it out in her direction. "Annalisa Vega," he said. He shifted and she noticed a gun in his lap.

"Who the hell are you?"

His thin smile cut his face like a knife. "You ought to know. You're the one telling people I hired you to find my sister's murderer."

TWENTY

....

G AVIN ALBRIGHT," ANNALISA SAID.
He pointed a finger at her. "See? You do know me." He palmed the gun as he sat up. "I figured if you were messing around in my life without consulting me, you wouldn't mind if I did the same. Nice pad, by the way. I see it's for sale."

"You've been following me," she realized. "You're the one in the silver rented sedan."

"You drive like a she-devil," he said, sounding impressed. "I almost lost you like three times."

"You can't be here. This is private property."

He took a final drag on his cigarette and dropped it onto her patio, crushing it out with his boot. "I want to know why you've been telling people Vicki was murdered."

The back door opened, lights flicking on, and Nick emerged. "Anna?" he said, his tone cautious. Before she could reply, he caught sight of Gavin Albright and the gun. Nick had his own weapon, and he raised it in a flash, training it on Gavin's chest. "Drop your gun."

Gavin remained relaxed in his chair, his cool gaze taking in Nick's bare legs and boxer shorts. "Boyfriend?" he asked Annalisa.

"Husband," she told him. "He's a cop."

Nick hadn't lowered his gun. "You know this guy?"

"We go way back," Gavin replied.

"He's Vicki Albright's brother," Annalisa explained. "He just showed up here."

"I don't give a fuck who he is," Nick said, still looking at Gavin. "He's got two seconds to put the gun down or I will shoot him."

Annalisa shrugged at Gavin. "I think he means it."

Gavin glared at Nick but he put the gun at his feet and nudged it away with the toe of one boot. "Satisfied?"

Nick collected the gun without saying anything. He checked it briefly and looked to Annalisa with surprise. "It's not loaded."

Gavin lit another smoke. "Good thing you didn't shoot me. Can I have it back now please, Mr. Officer, sir?" He extended his hand for the gun but Nick ignored him.

"He's still trespassing," Nick told Annalisa. "We could call it in."

She was tired and irritable and didn't want to deal with the paperwork. "Let him go," she said. "This time."

Gavin flicked his cigarette in their direction. "Hey, I'm not going anywhere until you tell me why you're saying Vicki got murdered. That cop who called me said it was an accident, that she was standing on a chair hanging something off her balcony when she fell."

"You're that cop," Annalisa pointed out to Nick. "You want to tell him?"

Nick looked at the sky. "Screw it. I'm making coffee." He handed Gavin back his gun and went inside the condo. After a beat, Annalisa followed. She held the door behind her.

"You might as well come in," she said to Gavin. He started for the door but she dragged it closed. "No smoking."

He made a show of crushing out the cigarette and she let him inside.

True to his word, Nick had started a pot of coffee, but he only took out two mugs. "As long as we're chatting," he said to Gavin, "let's start with how you lied to me. You said you hadn't seen Vicki in months. You were out in L.A., you said. Hadn't visited since Christmas. But you were here six weeks ago."

Gavin looked from Nick to Annalisa and back again. He spread his arms. "I forgot. Came in for a buddy's bachelor party one weekend. In and out real quick. I didn't even talk to Vicki."

"The doorman at her apartment building remembers you showing him a picture of you at a recent Oscars party," Annalisa told him. "So cut the crap."

Gavin glowered at her. "You first, lady. You're the one lying to people, telling them I hired you to find Vicki's murderer. So you tell me . . . was she murdered or not?"

Nick and Annalisa exchanged a look. He gave her a tiny shake of his head. *Don't do it.* She took a breath and leaped in anyway. "We don't know," she admitted. "That's why I'm looking into it."

"Looking into it for who? Who really hired you?"

"I can't say."

He pounded his fist on their counter so hard the coffee cups jumped. "Bullshit. I want some answers."

"And I'm trying to get you some," Annalisa told him. "Calm down."

He unclenched his fist one finger at a time and then ran his palm down their counter. "Our parents are dead, you know? Vicki was all I had left." He swallowed hard. "You've got to tell me the truth about what happened. Why do you think it was murder? Who killed her?"

Annalisa knew he was in a better position to answer this question than she was at the moment. "Who do you think might have hurt Vicki?" she asked. "Did she have any enemies? Any ex-boyfriends she was worried about?"

"Vicki had a lot of exes," he admitted. He shot Annalisa a defiant look, daring her to judge. She kept her gaze steady. "I didn't meet most of 'em," he continued when she said nothing.

"Did she talk about them to you at all?" Annalisa still hadn't proved that Canning and Vicki ever interacted. She hoped maybe Gavin could connect the dots.

"They weren't worth talking about." He pulled out a stool and sat down as Nick poured the two cups of coffee. "She wasn't serious about any of them."

"What if they wanted more? Anyone mad when she moved on?"

He considered. "One guy, a little while back. Nerdy dude. I think he was a professor?"

"Miles Dupont?"

"Yeah, that's the guy. He's some earthy-type activist. Save the whales and hug the trees. I told her those guys don't even use deodorant. They're, like, foul." He made a face and shook his head. "She gave him money. Vicki gave everyone money."

"Including you," Nick interjected. "Isn't that right?"

"Fuck off," Gavin replied, immediately angry again. "It was my money too. Vicki just held the trust."

"Because you couldn't be counted on to handle it, right? That's why you were in town." Nick pressed him. "You wanted more money from her."

"You don't know what the hell you're talking about." Gavin shoved back from the counter and stood up again. "I told you why I was here. My friend was having a party."

"We're getting off track," Annalisa said, signaling for peace. "Tell me more about Miles and Vicki."

"There's nothing to tell. They were together for a bit, and then she cut him loose." Gavin took out his cigarettes, remembered he couldn't light one, and began fidgeting with the pack instead.

"How'd he take it?"

Gavin looked at her like she was an idiot. "How d'you think? He'd lost a hot girl and a money pot. He was pissed. But it's not like he could force her to go out with him." He halted his twitching. "You don't think he killed her?"

"I told you we don't have evidence supporting any particular theory right now. We're looking at all possibilities."

"If he hurt Vicki, I'll break his neck."

"You stay away from him," Nick warned. "Or I will arrest you."

"Yeah, yeah, whatever you say." Gavin shoved his cigarettes back in his pocket. "Sounds like you're stirring up shit for no reason," he said to Annalisa. "I ask you for evidence about Vicki's murder and you tell me you've got none. But that makes no damn sense. See, I looked you up, Vega. You're smart and you don't scare easy. You caught that squirrely Lovelorn asshole while the rest of your department stood around yanking their dicks." He glanced at Nick. "No offense."

"None taken," Nick replied as he gave Gavin the finger.

Annalisa knew what Nick had lost in his fight with the Lovelorn Killer. She ached to defend him but she didn't want to stop Gavin from talking.

"So I'm thinking you've got to have something," he continued, emphasizing the last word. "Some sort of proof. Something you're seeing that the other cops missed."

Annalisa hesitated. She didn't have proof. Gavin might be her best shot at getting some. "What do you know about Craig Canning?" she said eventually.

Gavin's eyes bugged out. "Holy shit. It's that guy?"

"You know him?" Annalisa asked.

"He's a brain surgeon. Thinks he's hot shit. Maybe he is." He started pacing. "I can't believe it. I had him. I fucking had him and I let him get away."

"What are you talking about?" Nick asked, irritated.

Gavin halted and looked them over as if debating what to say. "That guy, Canning . . . he saved this lady's life. Her and I were in a car accident and her head got cracked or something. Canning put her brains back together, so I guess he really is some miracle worker. I didn't know it was him who operated on her at the time. I only knew the lady survived."

"Saving you a potential vehicular manslaughter charge," Nick said as he sipped his coffee.

"It was icy that night."

"And you were doing eighty."

"Hey, I paid my fine, okay? I paid her medical bills too."

"You mean Vicki paid them," Nick shot back.

Gavin lunged for him, but Annalisa stepped in between the men. "Not worth it," she said, shaking her head at Gavin. "He can still shoot you, remember?" Nick had his gun on the counter to his right.

Gavin eased off. He rolled his shoulders to relax them. "Anyway Vicki went to some charity auction thing last year where the women compete to buy the guys—like for one night. Canning was there. I guess he and Vicki chatted, and she found out he was the doc who'd saved that lady's life. She wanted to buy him dinner to thank him."

Annalisa held her breath. Even Nick looked intrigued. Here was the connection she'd been seeking, proof that Vicki and Canning knew each other as more than neighbors. "And did she?"

Gavin pulled out the stool and sat again. "That's the thing. I don't know. I mean, I thought I knew, but then you're telling me maybe he murdered her . . ."

"I'm not saying that," Annalisa broke in impatiently. "I just want to know if Vicki had contact with him."

"Yeah? Well, there's debate about that." He eyed the coffeepot. "Do I get some of that or what?"

Annalisa signaled for Nick to get another cup. He rolled his eyes but complied. "Tell me more about Vicki and Craig Canning," Annalisa commanded as Nick slid the coffee cup to Gavin.

"They made arrangements to meet for dinner. That's what she told me. She goes to the restaurant and he's not there, so she has a drink at the bar. Maybe two drinks. That's where the story gets off track. She said Canning showed up. That's the last thing she remembers. He was there and ordered her another round. The next thing she remembered, she woke up naked in her own bed."

"He roofie'd her?" Nick asked.

"That's what she told me." Gavin cupped his hand tight around the mug. "I said I'd break his face, and that's what I came here to do."

"Your visit last month," Annalisa guessed.

He nodded. "Vicki told me not to, but no way I'm letting some asshole do that do her and get away with it. I went to Vicki's building and waited until he pulled his fancy-ass car into the garage. Then I took out my piece to say hello." He looked at Nick. "Unloaded, of course."

"Of course," Nick said, totally unconvinced. "Go on."

"I told him I was going to break his nose and then help Vicki sue him for everything he's got, from the car on up. He freakin' raped my sister! But this guy, he started telling me that Vicki's making the whole thing up, that he never met her for dinner, never bought her a drink, never touched her. I said why would my sister lie like that, and he said maybe she was confused. Maybe someone else spiked her drink and her brain got mixed up and thought it was him. I said she seemed pretty clear on who did it. But then . . ." He took a deep breath. "He said memory is funny and plays tricks on us. He knows because he's a brain doctor. He says he was at the restaurant that night and he did say hello to Vicki but that's it. He there was having dinner with some other woman, an author he's writing a book with."

"Mara Delaney," Annalisa said.

"That's her. He said I could call this lady and confirm his story." He shrugged. "So I did."

"What did Mara say?" Annalisa wanted to know.

"He gave me her number and I called her right there in the garage.

She said the same thing as Canning, that they were at the restaurant together. They'd had dinner and talked about the book. He didn't leave longer than to go take a piss, and they left together around the time the place closed down for the night. She said there was only one other couple left, an old man and his wife. No Vicki."

"Did you tell Vicki this?" Nick asked.

"Of course I did. She said Canning must've been right that someone else spiked her drink that night. Vicki just couldn't remember who it was."

"She didn't report it?" Nick said.

"To the cops?" Gavin scoffed. "What the hell would you do?"

"The restaurant might have had surveillance video to see who else was with Vicki that night," Annalisa said, frustration creeping into her voice. "But that's likely gone now." Regardless, Gavin had potentially revealed a big motive for Canning wanting to silence Vicki. True or not, her story about being drugged and assaulted could have made big trouble for him.

"I've told you everything," Gavin said, leaning forward on the counter. "Now you talk. What makes you think Vicki was murdered? Who hired you?"

Annalisa couldn't break Mara's confidence. "The wind chimes Vicki was supposed to be hanging at the time of her death," she said. "They have no fingerprints on them."

"Wind chimes?" He widened his eyes and then made a disgusted face. "You mean like those tacky noise pollutants you've got hanging out back? Vicki never would've had something like that."

Nick looked at Annalisa. "We have wind chimes outside?"

"I thought he brought them." She nodded at Gavin.

He held up his hands in a gesture of innocence. "Not me, man. I wouldn't even know where to get such an ugly thing. I swear to you—they were here before me."

TWENTY-ONE

....

D UE TO THE FIRE, MARA HAD TO WORK FROM HOME, WHICH SHE DIDN'T ENJOY
SINCE HER "OFFICE" WAS A NOOK SQUEEZED IN BETWEEN THE LIVING AND
DINING AREAS. Paul had the real office with a door and a window and a
full-sized oak desk. He didn't even work from home often, just made
infrequent calls or typed away on some research manuscript for *Podia-
trists Monthly,* but he made the larger salary, the one that paid for their
luxury town house, so that meant he got the office. Once, Mara had
approached him about taking over their spare bedroom for her work-
space, but he had nixed that idea because then where would his mother
stay when she came to visit at Christmas?

Mara checked her email, half dreading a message from the dean
saying she was being suspended over the fire investigation. She'd made
sure to get ahead of him with the TV appearance outside the building,
looking tearful and angry for the cameras. Annalisa seemed convinced
that someone had set the fire as a personal vendetta. Mara was ready to
show them how personal she could get. With grim determination, she
clicked open her inbox and felt a sparkle of delight when she saw the
first message was from someone at *People* magazine. The subject read:

"Let's talk profile." She also had messages from the *L.A. Times,* in which the reporter wanted to check a couple of facts for the feature piece they were writing about her and Craig, and the university press team wanted to set up another meeting. They were being overwhelmed with requests. Mara clasped her hands together and beamed at her glowing monitor. All her hard work, her years of investment . . . it was finally paying off.

Her puff of pride evaporated with the next ding from her inbox. The sender's name was MisterX and the subject line read: "I KNOW WHAT YOU DID." No message. A chill went through her, making her flesh ripple.

"Blue stripes or red dots?" Paul materialized behind her as if from nowhere, making her jump.

"God, you scared me. I thought you'd left for the hospital already."

"Early patient canceled," he said, holding up two ties for her inspection. "Which do you think?"

"Does it matter? You're going to put on a white coat over the whole outfit anyway."

"I'm meeting with the department chair this afternoon."

"And he cares about your tie?"

"She," he corrected her with a knowing smile. He wanted her to think she had some competition. Ha. Mara squinted at the ties in turn so it looked like she was considering.

"What color does the department chair wear?"

His expression went blank. He clearly had no idea what the woman wore because he'd never given her a second glance. Mara had no competition at all. "Uh, I think she favors blue," he said at length.

"Then go with the blue stripes." She gave him her most dazzling smile and he smiled in return. He crossed the room to kiss her cheek.

"You always know the right move." As he stood up, he noticed her necklace and gave her a quizzical glance. "Is that new?"

She touched the chain and crystal pendant self-consciously. "This?"

"Yes, I don't remember it," he said as he slipped a finger under the chain for closer inspection.

"It's a gift," she said, and he stiffened. She put her hand over his. "From me to me. To celebrate the book." When he said nothing, she added. "Don't worry, it wasn't expensive."

"Don't be silly," he said, his voice growing warm again. "You deserve it. You deserve everything."

"I have everything." Her eyes went to the clock. She had to get Paul out of the house soon. Craig would be arriving in a half hour so they could give a joint phone interview to the *Seattle Times,* and she didn't want him encountering Paul again. "You'd better hurry, darling. It's getting late."

"Hmm? I guess you're right." He went back up the stairs, pausing once to sneeze. Mara winced at the sound and turned around to her work again. The horrid email still sat there unopened. Several more mundane missives had arrived in her inbox since, making the threatening one seem smaller and less powerful. I KNOW WHAT YOU DID. It was laughable, really. What could they know? Nothing. It wasn't possible because there was nothing for anyone to know. Most likely Miles Dupont had sent the email. He'd outright accused her yesterday of torching her own office in some vainglorious attempt for publicity. She'd accused him right back. If anyone wanted to set her book on fire, it was him. If the dean dared ask her questions again, she'd sic him on Miles. She clicked open the email.

I know you have a micro penis, she wrote. She clicked send and then blocked the sender so he couldn't reply. Sad, stupid little man.

The doorbell gave a sonorous bong and her heart rate picked up again. Craig was here, and Paul was still in the house. She answered the door and found Craig decked out in sunglasses and a charcoal Armani suit. "It's a phone interview," she told him as she let him inside. "They didn't send a photographer."

"This is all for you, baby," he replied, gesturing at himself as he made kissy noises at her. He didn't seem like someone out to get her, but that was the illusion, she had to remember—the Craig he presented to the world and the Craig he really was were two different people. She trusted that her training would keep her safe, that she knew the difference, but she had to remain alert. She needed him on her side for a little while longer.

"Behave." She gave him a playful shove toward the living room. "My husband's home."

"Oh?" He looked up the stairs, obviously interested. "And here I came early hoping I could . . . come early." He reached for her and she dodged his hands.

"I told you that was a mistake. One I don't intend to repeat. Let's just get ready for the interview, shall we?" She cast anxious eyes at the stairs. Paul would be down any minute.

He took her hand and squeezed it. "We have plenty of time."

"No, we really don't." She jerked away. "Honestly, you can have any woman you want. Why are you bothering with this?" She knew even as she said the words the reason why. She'd said no. He didn't like no. Craig wanted to win, always. *At all costs,* she reminded herself as she steeled her shoulders.

"You owe me, Mara."

Her heart stopped at his words but she didn't have time to reply because Paul came down the stairs, ready to leave for the hospital. "What's this?" he said, not pleased when he noticed Craig standing in his living room.

"We have an interview," Mara said, going to him, smoothing his tie.

"Another one?" He peered around her at Craig, who had moved to the liquor cabinet.

Craig opened the cabinet and poured himself a bourbon. "What can I say, Paul? The world can't get enough of your wife."

Paul looked from Craig to Mara, askance. "It's not even ten in the morning," he said to her.

She hoped he was so horrified by Craig's day drinking that he wouldn't notice Craig hadn't had to ask where they kept the liquor. "I've been up all night," Craig said as he swirled his drink. "That makes this fair play."

"You operate in a suit?" Paul asked.

"Who said I was at work?" Craig countered. He raised his glass to Paul. "Cheers."

Mara intervened before Paul could carry on further. She had to get him out of there. "Darling, you don't want to be late." She stroked his smooth, pudgy cheek. "Will you be home for dinner? I'll cook the roast lamb you like."

He looked surprised. "You'll cook?"

"Why not? I'm working from home all day." She patted him and his eyes welled up. For a moment, she thought he was moved by her offer of domesticity. Then his nose wrinkled and she realized he was getting ready to sneeze. She backed off before the spray.

"Goodness," Craig opined, deadpan.

"Bless you," she corrected darkly as she handed Paul a tissue.

"I'm going to get a stronger prescription," he said, blowing his nose.

"Feel better," she said as she sent him off with a pat on the shoulder and a small wave. She barely had time to catch her breath before Craig sent her spinning again.

"I know it's you."

She froze for a fraction of a second before forcing herself to relax. "Of course it's me," she said briskly as she gathered her notes for the interview. "It's my house, remember?"

"You hired Annalisa Vega to try to pin Vicki Albright's death on me. Vega gave me some line about how Vicki's brother hired her because he thought she was murdered. That punk has already come after me once when he thought I drugged Vicki, so if he's gunning for a murderer, I knew I'd be first on his list. But funny story—I had my secretary call and pretend to ask him about some billing issue for Annalisa's services, and he had no clue what she was talking about. He didn't hire Vega." He took a sip, his dark eyes boring into hers. "You did."

Her heart started pounding erratically. They were alone in the house. She had to be very careful with her next words. "Why would I do that?"

"Beats the hell out of me." He set the glass down and started advancing toward her. She took a step back. "Why would you do that?"

"I—I wouldn't. You're wrong." He came close enough that she could smell him, a suffocating mix of cologne and bourbon. She screwed her eyes shut as he laughed in her face.

"I'm never wrong. I can ask her directly, you know. Vega? She might try to lie, but I'll know if she's lying. What I can't figure is what you hoped to get out of this little plan. The book launches in three weeks. It's your big break. If I go down then so do you."

"That's right," she said, squirming away from him. "So I had to be sure."

He grabbed her arm and yanked her close again. "And are you? Sure?"

"Let go of me."

"I can't. We're stuck like this, remember? You and me forever." His fingers bit into her flesh. "Tell me what she's found."

"I said let me go." She struggled in his grasp but he held her tight. Her arm started to ache as he cut off her circulation.

"Tell me."

"Nothing," she said with a gasp. He released her and she scrambled backward from him, rubbing her arm. "Vega's found nothing." It was the troubling truth. Annalisa had no answer for her either way, and time was running out.

Craig's face relaxed as he became himself again, the version he wore as tightly as that suit. "That's right," he told her, his voice dangerously soft. "She's found nothing. And she won't, not if she searches from here to eternity. Best you call her off then, hmm? We wouldn't want anyone to get wind of her snooping." He traced one gentle finger down the front of her blouse, catching on each button and lingering like a lover. "What would happen to your book if it came out that you suspected your good sociopath of murder? The whole project would be ruined."

Mara turned her head so he wouldn't see the truth in her eyes. "Yes," she whispered. "That would be bad."

"And think of Annalisa."

"What about her?"

His tone remained hypnotic. "Well, if Annalisa is right and someone did throw that poor girl off the balcony, she's looking in the wrong place for the murderer. She wouldn't see the real killer coming before it's too late. We wouldn't want her to get hurt."

Mara pictured Vicki as she fell to her death, blond hair in the wind and her scream echoing off the building. "No," she said to Craig, forcing herself to smile for him. "We wouldn't want that."

"So we're agreed," he said, sounding pleased. "I'm sure we have time before that interview, yes? You could show me the upstairs."

Mara shut her eyes briefly, resigning herself to her fate. She had a way out. She couldn't use it yet. "Yes," she said as she took his hand to lead him to the stairs. "We have time."

TWENTY-TWO

....

I N THEIR CRAMPED BATHROOM, ANNALISA ARGUED WITH NICK ABOUT TAKING THE WIND CHIMES FROM THEIR YARD TO THE FORENSICS LAB FOR EVALUATION. He refused to do it on the grounds that there was no official report to justify the analysis.

"So we file a complaint for trespassing," she said as she twisted her hair into a knot at the back of her head. "Then there's a report."

"Come on, Vega." Nick ducked out of the way of her elbow and then spat his toothpaste into the sink. "You know the lab is slammed with requests 24/7—homicides, shootings, assaults, and burglaries. You think they're going to make a trespassing case a priority?"

"They will if you tell them to." She knew even as she said the words it wasn't true; he'd be laughed out of the precinct.

"Even if you're right," he said, wiping his mouth with a towel, "even if they found Craig Canning's fingerprints on the wind chimes, it wouldn't prove anything."

"It would if they're the same chimes taken from Mara Delaney's office at the time of the fire."

Their eyes met in the mirror. He looked more concerned all of a sudden. "Are they?" he asked tentatively.

"I don't know. I damn sure plan to ask her." She had a whole bunch of questions for Mara Delaney, starting with the wind chimes and then moving on to why Mara hadn't said anything about Vicki Albright accusing Craig Canning of date rape. "What do you have going on today?"

"First, I am taking Cassidy to school and making sure she gets inside. After that, I'll worry about the real delinquents of the world."

He hugged her from behind and she put her hands over his. "Go easy on the kid, okay?"

"I just want her to be safe." He squeezed her one more time. "I want the same for you. Got it?"

"Home safe," she said, hugging his arms and repeating their usual pledge. "Got it."

Annalisa did not expect much trouble from Mara Delaney, but she wanted the advantage of surprise, so she did not contact the woman before showing up at her town house. Mara answered the door wearing a gray blouse and a tailored peacock-blue skirt, nicer clothes than Annalisa would have chosen if she was working from home. She seemed confused to find Annalisa on her doorstep. "I'm sorry, did I miss a meeting?"

"No, I had an important development crop up and thought we should talk right away."

Mara glanced once over her shoulder before stepping out onto the stoop and closing the door behind her. "We can't," she said, keeping her voice low. "Craig is here."

"He's here?" Annalisa turned to scan the street and kicked herself mentally when she spotted Canning's Jag parked half a block down. She had been thinking about Nick and Cassidy and failed to notice her surroundings. "What does he want?"

"We had a couple of interviews to do. He'll be leaving soon." Mara hugged herself and looked uneasy. "What is so important?"

Annalisa took out her phone to show her a photograph of the wind chimes that had appeared in her backyard. "Are these yours?"

Mara grabbed the phone with both hands. "Yes. Where did you find them?"

"Someone put them up outside my house."

"What?" Mara's eyes grew round. "Who?"

"I don't know. Presumably whoever took them from your office."

"I don't . . . I thought Miles did it." She put one hand to her head as she thrust the phone back at Annalisa. "He knows the wind chimes were a gift from Craig. I thought he did it to make a point."

"What kind of point?"

"Oh, that he hates Craig and everything he stands for . . . and me, of course, for publishing the book about him." She bit her lip. "But I don't know why Miles would come after you."

"Leave that aside for now," Annalisa said. "Why did you lie to me about Canning and Vicki Albright?"

Mara appeared genuinely perplexed. "I didn't lie."

"You lied by omission. You said nothing about Vicki accusing Canning of drugging and raping her."

"Oh," Mara said, dismayed. "That."

"Yes, that." Annalisa kept her voice down but her tone was clipped. "That's motive. It goes a long way to answering why a successful neurosurgeon might toss a socialite off her balcony when they otherwise didn't seem to know each other. How could you not think that's relevant?"

"Because he didn't do it."

Annalisa held her breath and counted to three. "Didn't do what?" she said slowly, enunciating each word.

"Didn't drug and rape her. Vicki must have been confused, maybe because of the drugs, I don't know. You see, Craig was there at the restaurant where she said it happened, but he was with me, not her. I never even saw him speak to her. He certainly didn't have time to . . . to do what she said he did."

Annalisa stared at her hard. Mara's blue eyes were open and honest, eager to please. Maybe a tiny bit contrite. She knew she'd screwed up. "Even still," Annalisa told her, not yet mollified, "you should have mentioned it. The accusation alone might have been enough to anger someone like Canning. He could have tossed her over the balcony in revenge."

"Oh," Mara said as though realization was just dawning. "Yes, I see what you mean. I'm sorry." Her gaze grew worried again and she glanced at the door. "I should tell you something else," she confessed. "He knows I hired you."

"What? How?" Annalisa had never said a thing.

"He figured it out somehow," Mara said with a helpless gesture. "I told you he's brilliant. He's pissed, of course, but oddly also calm about the whole thing. I hadn't considered it before, but his finding out about you might even help me in the coming weeks."

"What do you mean?"

Mara gave a tight smile and fingered the necklace at her throat. "Even good sociopaths hate to be wrong."

"Yeah, he's mentioned that to me," Annalisa remarked drily.

"Right. So here I am, a supposed expert in the field, suspecting him of doing a terrible deed. He'll want to show me up. Show everyone how I'm wrong and he's right. He'll probably try to make himself into Superman, running into a burning building to save a kitten or some such lunacy—all to prove how wrong I was to doubt him."

"I'm not so sure you were."

Mara's face fell. "Don't tell me," she said, bracing herself against the railing. "You found proof?"

"Nothing about Vicki Albright," Annalisa said. "But about the fire." When Gavin Albright had denied bringing the wind chimes to her house, Annalisa had immediately suspected Canning. Once Gavin left and Nick returned to bed, Annalisa spent the better part of an hour blowing up various frames from the CCTV footage around the fire. She never got a look at the hooded figure's face, but she had managed to enlarge a shot of their hand holding something silver—something with what looked like the face of an animal on it.

"Ladies." The door whipped open and Craig Canning stepped out between them. "I hope you don't mind if I smoke."

"Uh, n-no . . . of course not," Mara stammered. "I was just telling Ms. Vega that I won't be needing her services anymore."

He turned to Annalisa with a glint of mischief in his eyes. "Ah, so you've caught the murderer, have you?" She watched as he took out a cigarette and his silver lighter, the one with the head of a jaguar on it.

"No," she said. "Not yet."

TWENTY-THREE

....

Nick Carelli hadn't bitten his nails since high school, but he had his thumb in his mouth, chewing like a piranha as he watched the elevator doors on the fifth floor of the hospital. Each time they opened, he narrowed his eyes to study the faces of the people spilling out into the hall. None were Cassidy. He had been quite clear with her that she was to go nowhere else but the hospital after school, but classes had ended an hour ago and she was nowhere to be seen. He'd texted her, but his message sat unread. Ignored. He felt his agitation rising but there was nothing he could do about it. As the kid had pointed out, he had no authority over her.

Melanie came into the lounge, looking exhausted. Her hair was flat and greasy, her shirt wrinkled, her face devoid of makeup. She had not left Summer's side since her friend was admitted. Nick admired Melanie's commitment and stamina. He knew Summer only casually and it was hard for him to look at her in the bed, her limbs twisted, tubes coming out of her skinny body. Melanie had to watch her best friend vanish before her eyes. *This is love,* he thought. *Doing the hard thing because it's right. Because you care that much.* He was counting on Melanie to understand he was doing the same thing when it came to Cassidy.

Melanie shuffled over to refill her thermos from the water cooler and sank into the chair next to his, white-eyed and boneless.

"How's Summer doing?" he asked.

"She's sleeping. Other than that, no change."

He cleared his throat, trying to inject some energy into his voice. "I'm here for a while, you know, waiting for Cassidy. If you want a break—"

"No." She cut him off forcefully, then rubbed her head like it hurt. "No, I'm fine."

He nodded, not challenging her. They sat in silence for a long moment. Nick knew he had to tell her he wanted custody, and there was no easy way to say it. No way to make it feel nice. He grimaced and sat forward. He hated to upset people, hated being the bad guy, but he also felt the ticking clock. If Summer died, all her preset arrangements would go into effect, including Melanie's custody of Cassidy. Nick had run his situation by a lawyer friend and his buddy told him he needed to get Summer to change the papers while she was still alive.

But I'm the father, Nick had protested. He had a DNA test to prove it. *Wouldn't a judge be on my side?*

Maybe, his friend had told him. *But the kid's almost eighteen. By the time you get it sorted in the courts, she could be a legal adult and the whole thing would be moot. Plus, then you're the guy who dragged her into court after her mother died. You want to be that guy?*

Nick covered his face with his hands. He didn't want to be that guy. He just wanted to be a dad. *Do the hard thing,* he told himself. "I want Cassidy," he blurted into his palms.

"Hmm?" Melanie's answer was a tired hum. He glanced back and saw she'd lolled her head against the wall, eyes closed.

"I want her to stay with me."

Melanie's eyelids dragged open. "Like for the night? That's fine if you can take her to school again in the morning."

"No, I mean I want her to live with me after . . . when her mom . . . She should be with me."

Melanie folded her arms and stared at him a long moment. "Why?"

"Why?" He sat up straight like he was testifying. The evidence was on his side. "She's my kid. I'm her father. If she can't be with her mother, she should be with me."

"You're her father," Melanie agreed. "You're not her parent. You weren't there when she was born, or when she got scarlet fever, or when she won the third-grade spelling bee. You haven't cleaned up her vomit in the middle of the night or bandaged her skinned knees when she fell off her bike. You didn't spend six hours riding the subway, looking for her lost stuffed elephant. You haven't been to her art shows or her parent-teacher conferences or any of it. You had sex with her mother seventeen years ago. Yes, you're technically her father, but you damn well haven't earned the title."

"Whose fault is that?" Sleep-deprived, he sounded snappish. "Summer never told me. She went and had the baby without ever breathing a word that she was pregnant."

"She called you," Melanie snapped back.

"What?"

"You never called her back."

"No, I . . ." He searched his memory and came up empty. "Summer never called me," he said with vehemence. "We had one night together and I never talked to her again."

Melanie sighed, defeated. "She left a message at your house. She knew you were married so she said you left something at the bar and it was important you get in touch. You never did."

Left something at the bar, he thought. This had been one of his favorite excuses back when he was married to Annalisa the first time. *I've got to run out, honey. I left my wallet at the bar.* Or his keys, or his sunglasses. Nick was always leaving pieces of himself behind. "I never got that message," he said to Melanie as he absorbed the shock. Annalisa must have intercepted it.

"Look, Nick." Melanie laid a hand on his arm. "I don't think you're a bad guy. I'm glad Cassidy tracked you down all these years later, and you're right—she's going to need you. But her life is about to be upended in the worst way, and the last thing she needs is more uncertainty. Summer and I have had a plan in place for Cassidy ever since her diagnosis. Cassidy knows and approves of the plan. She's going to live with me."

Her words were sympathetic but final as she withdrew her hand. Nick tried not to flinch. Melanie dismissed him as a careless playboy looking to start over with a new insta-family. She didn't know anything about him, not really. She didn't know he'd sat outside an ICU before, at only eight years old. His father had shot his mother and she'd lingered long enough for her son to whisper his goodbyes. At least Summer was conscious. She could communicate with the aid of a computer. His mother's last words to Nick were a shout at him to hide while his father kicked in their back door. He'd run to the closet where he'd trembled among the coats, stifling his sobs with a wool sleeve. His father had frequent rages and the worst of them typically ended with screaming and bruises. He hadn't known his father had bought a gun, not until the shot echoed through the house, but he should have known there would be trouble. He should have run for help rather than sniveling in the closet. By the time he'd crawled out and found his mother bleeding on the kitchen floor, it was too late.

"I never agreed to this," he muttered now, looking down at his hands.

Melanie shook her head, pity in her eyes. "You don't get it. You lost your vote a long time ago."

"But—"

"No. We both know that Summer wasn't special. You tomcatted your way from Bucktown to Brighton Park, bedding whatever girl caught your attention for five minutes. You say you've changed and that Annalisa forgives you. That's fine. Your relationship is between the two of you. But you can't operate your sex life like a wrecking ball and not expect anyone to get hurt. Sorry if this one time that includes you."

Across the way, the elevator doors dinged and a fresh group of people shuffled out. Nick looked over automatically to check the faces, but Cassidy was not among them. He took out his phone and saw his texts to her remained unread. Maybe Melanie was right. He wasn't Cassidy's father; he never would be.

TWENTY-FOUR

....

CASSIDY IGNORED THE DIRTY LOOKS FROM THE GIRL IN THE APRON CLEANING TABLES AT THE COFFEE SHOP. So what if Cassidy had been sitting there for two hours with a single latte? It's not like the place was crowded. Cassidy had snagged a primo table by the window, big enough to seat four, but she was all alone. She had her laptop out, ostensibly to do schoolwork, but her attention remained focused on the post office branch across the street. This was the place that housed the PO box, the one attached to the crowdfunding effort Cassidy found with the old photo of Naomi on it. Yesterday, Cassidy had marched in and demanded to know who had the box and where to find them. The old man behind the counter had barely looked up from his sorting. "Can't give out that information," he'd told her. His bushy white eyebrows sagged down into his eyes, like even they were tired.

"But it's fraud," she had protested. "Whoever is using that box is committing a crime. Do you want to be associated with that?"

"Hon, I just sort the mail. It's not my business what's in it." He'd peered down from the high counter and raised those eyebrows at her. "Unless it's some kind of explosive."

She'd considered a moment. "If someone had mailed her an explosive, would you tell me who owns the box?"

"Nope." Dammit, his rejection sounded almost cheerful. "I'd call the cops." More hard-nosed peering at her. "Which is what I suggest you should do if you have evidence of a crime."

The last thing she needed was Nick or Annalisa getting involved, not before she had proof. She'd muttered her thanks and slunk away to the side to study the rows of metal boxes. There were a couple of hundred of them. She located the box that she believed belonged to "Liza" but there was nothing different or interesting about it. While she stewed about the problem, a man in a Cubs hat came in. He told the old guy at the counter he'd received a notice that he had a package at his PO box and handed the man a claim slip. The old guy shuffled away and returned with a square box. As Cubs hat man took his prize and left, Cassidy got an idea. She went to the nearest Walgreens, where she bought a box, a cheap pair of sneakers, and a roll of bright pink wrapping paper. Then she put the sneakers in the box and wrapped it in the hideous paper. On the outside, she addressed the box to Liza, and she returned to the post office branch to mail it.

Old guy had looked at her with some suspicion when she handed him the box. "What's this?"

"A package," she'd told him sweetly.

"What's in it?"

"I thought you didn't care."

He folded his arms and stuck out his chin. "I don't know what trouble you're playing at, but I don't want any part of it."

"I'm just sending a package to my friend. That's what you do here, right? Send packages?" When he didn't move, she rolled her eyes. "There's nothing explosive in it. I swear."

"Or otherwise illegal," he prompted.

"Cross my heart," she said, doing so to demonstrate her sincerity.

He snorted like he wasn't swayed, but he put the box on the scale. "That'll be eleven fifty."

Her jaw fell open. "But you only have to walk it over there," she said, pointing to the stacks of boxes from which he'd earlier retrieved Cubs hat guy's package. "It doesn't have to leave the building."

"Gotta process it all the same. You want to mail it or not?"

She'd handed him a twenty. Her last one.

Now she was on stakeout at the café across the street. Cassidy didn't know what Naomi's mother looked like, but she would recognize the package when the woman picked it up. Her surveillance meant skipping school so she could watch the post office branch, but Cassidy felt confident her mission was more significant than trigonometry or *The Catcher in the Rye*. She would never in a million years need to solve a cosine, and as for Holden Caulfield, she was pretty sure he'd approve of her plan. Holden hated phonies and Naomi's mother was the worst kind of phony that ever was.

The girl in the apron loomed over her. "Are you done with that?" she asked, pointing at Cassidy's empty cup.

Cassidy checked it for the dregs, which had almost completely dried up. "Not quite yet," she replied with a smile, and the girl sighed audibly as she returned to the counter. Cassidy had enough money left for a scone but not much more than that. She didn't have a job, unless you counted the work she was doing for Annalisa that so far did not pay, and she couldn't exactly ask her mother for more funds right now. She had to save every penny she could. Her laptop gave an alert from the messaging program and Cassidy diverted her attention to the screen. She'd turned off her cell so it could not be tracked, but she'd been trying unsuccessfully to reach Naomi for more than a day.

Her heart skipped when she saw Naomi's reply. *Hey, boo. Sorry for the radio silence. Guess where I am?*

Naomi sent a selfie showing just her face with a quizzical expression. Her hair was piled on top of her head in a messy bun and she wore no makeup, but her smile gave Cassidy a little thrill. The plain beige wall behind Naomi suggested some kind of institutional setting, but she should be out of school for the day. Maybe she'd stayed after for extra credit like the total nerd she was. *School?* Cassidy wrote back. *U know u can't get enough.*

Nah. Check out my fit. Sexy, right?

She sent another photo, this one taken behind her head showing her backside. The hospital gown parted to reveal a pair of pink striped panties. Cassidy also caught part of an IV pole at the edge of the photo. Her heart sank. *Hospital,* she wrote back. *What's wrong?*

Calcium levels are off. I win extra dialysis.

Sucky prize, Cassidy returned. *Should've picked door #2.*

What about u? Naomi wrote. *How's ur mom?*

Cassidy glanced out the window to see a heavyset guy carrying an awkwardly large box down the steps of the post office. A stab of shame went through her. Dodging Nick and Annalisa meant she wasn't communicating with Melanie or her mom either. She should be at the hospital. She knew she should. She just couldn't sit there in that hot little room listening for the heart monitor to stop. *Going to see her soon,* she wrote to Naomi.

Wish I could be there with u, Naomi said.

The words made tears well up in Cassidy's eyes and the screen blurred before her. She hadn't told her mother about Naomi, about how they were more than friends. It's not that her mother would care Naomi was a girl. She wouldn't like the fact that Naomi was sick, that she could possibly die. Mom was always shooing her out of the house or away from the hospital. *Go out and be in the world,* she would say. *Live your life.*

I wish too, she wrote to Naomi through her tears.

The computer flashed another alert as Naomi tried to video chat. Cassidy swiped at her face and quickly declined the connection. *Can't video now,* she wrote. *On subway.*

At least send a pic, Naomi wrote. *I want to see u.*

Cassidy hesitated a moment before leaning down close to the laptop camera. Her face filled the screen so Naomi wouldn't catch the background. She forced a smile, hit the button for a three-second delay, and put her hands together below her chin in the shape of a heart. Just as she got into position, her peripheral vision glimpsed movement across the street. She turned to see a man walking her bright pink package down the steps. Not Liza. Maybe a boyfriend?

Cassidy slammed her laptop shut right as it flashed to take the picture. She grabbed up her things and called out, "All set" to the sulky girl behind the counter. A brisk, spring wind hit Cassidy's face as she hurried outside, making her eyes tear up. The man had long legs and he was already half a block away. Cassidy shouldered her backpack into the wind and followed. As she scrambled after him, her mind whirled with doubts. Maybe she'd been wrong about who was behind the crowdfunding page. Maybe she was following some two-bit fraudster with no connection to Naomi's mom. But no, it couldn't be. Whoever had the PO box had access to the picture of Naomi as a child. This man, whoever he was, had to know her mom.

He took the stairs down into an L station and Cassidy fumbled in her backpack for her pass to follow him. The train was pulling in and she had to run for it, the doors almost closing on her. The man gave her a hard look from his seat. "You better watch it," he said.

Some detective, she chastised herself. She'd been on his tail for ten minutes and he'd already spotted her. She felt herself turn red as she slunk toward a seat at the back behind the man. She stared daggers at his bald head as they rode the train four stops. When he got up to exit, she did the same, taking care to remain at least twenty feet behind him as he exited the station. They reached the open world again, but she did not recognize the neighborhood. She did not have time to get her bearings or consult her phone because the man continued his brisk pace down the street. South Halstead, she realized as they passed an intersection. But where was he going?

He turned off the main road and the scenery got bleaker. Chain-linked fence and overgrown empty lots. One squat apartment building looked burned out, charred around the boarded-up windows. The sidewalks were uneven, and she tripped in her efforts to keep pace with the man. As she stumbled, she heard a rough laugh, and a man with straggly hair made kissing noises at her from a nearby stoop. He sat on the steps with a bottle in his hands. "Come here, little mama," he cajoled her. "I'll kiss it and make it all better."

Cassidy practically flew down the street. The man from the post office had disappeared. She ran to the corner and spotted him down the left block, entering a brick apartment building. She slowed her pace as she approached. The three-story building was old and might have been something in its day; the top had an ornate white crown and some of the façade remained near the front windows. But most had chipped away and the unit to the left of the front door was entirely boarded up. There was no yard, no trees, just a cracked sidewalk with weeds growing out of it. The man had used his key to get in the front door, which meant she couldn't get inside on her own. She walked the perimeter and estimated the whole building had maybe twenty units. The man could be in any one of them. Even if she could get inside, going door-to-door like a Girl Scout would be unwise. If "Liza" did live in one of the units but was not at home right now, Cassidy would give away her one important card, which was the element of surprise. The man had already seen her on the subway. He'd know she'd followed him home.

As she stared at the building from across the street, she saw a curtain move, like someone was looking out at her. She gasped and shrank back against the nearby iron fence. A black car sped by and some guys shouted at her through the open window. She couldn't keep standing here like an idiot. She stuck out like a preacher at a pride parade, as Melanie would say. Cassidy started walking back the way she'd come, her mind working on a new plan, when the black car circled around, slower this time. A man leaned way out from the passenger side, licking his lips. "Hey girlie, you wanna ride?"

Fear seized her. She picked up her pace and did not look at the men in the car. *You can't come back here,* her brain said. *You'll die.*

I just need proof, she argued back. *Proof that Liza is there.*

The horn honked, making her jump. The men in the car roared with laughter as Cassidy began to run.

TWENTY-FIVE

....

ANNALISA LEANED OVER THE SINK TO GET CLOSER TO THE BATHROOM MIRROR AS SHE ATTEMPTED TO APPLY THE BLACK EYELINER. Sassy, her best friend and sister-in-law, chortled from the laptop screen that Annalisa had sitting next to her on the vanity. "You're going to put your eye out if you do it like that," Sassy said. "You have to relax your wrist."

Annalisa made her wrist go limp, which made Sassy laugh harder. "I don't know how some women do this every day," Annalisa grumped as the eyeliner came out in a wide smear.

"Practice," Sassy replied, matter of fact. "You can't put on makeup once a decade and expect to be any good at it."

Annalisa surveyed her raccoon eyes. "I heard the zombie look is in this year."

"Well, then you nailed it."

Annalisa scowled and grabbed several tissues to wipe her face and start over. "This worked better when you could help me in person."

"Believe me, I wish I could. Gigi's been throwing up all day and Carla got gum in her hair that took me an hour to get out."

Annalisa paused to look at the screen. "Where did Carla get gum?"

"School," Sassy said wearily. "They use it like currency apparently, and Carla's a shark. I found thirty-seven pieces in her dresser."

"Now that doesn't surprise me," Annalisa said of her seven-year-old niece. "She's going to rule us all one day."

"Yeah, well today she got sent to bed at six-thirty. Mama's tired." Sassy yawned. "I barely remember my clubbing days. And you, you didn't go clubbing at all. How do you think you're going to pull this off exactly?"

"I'm just going to have a look around and see if I can get a bead on Elizabeth Johnston." Annalisa surveyed her handiwork in the mirror and decided it would have to do.

"Why?" Sassy said as she sipped a glass of red wine. "She sounds like a loser who wants nothing to do with her kid. Even if you find her, she's not likely to give up a kidney."

"No, I know," Annalisa said as she began teasing her hair. "I just . . ." She sagged with defeat. "I would die for Carla and Gigi. I know you would too."

"In a heartbeat," Sassy agreed without thinking.

"So maybe Elizabeth can be persuaded. It's her daughter's life on the line. Her own flesh and blood."

"Maybe if you offered her a ton of cash."

Annalisa looked at her sharply and Sassy's mouth fell open.

"Oh, my god, you're thinking of paying her?"

"No. I mean, I can't. Things are tight here as it is. But Naomi's dad might be willing if Elizabeth would agree to it. If I can talk to her, maybe I can feel her out on the subject. Or maybe she'll just agree to do the blood test."

Sassy shook her head like Annalisa was crazy. "See, this is why you had to quit being a cop. You still think people are good underneath it all."

Annalisa took a deep breath. "No," she said. "I had to stop because

I was starting to feel the opposite." She spun in a circle in front of the computer. "How do I look?" She had on a black T-shirt, jeans with a studded belt, and Doc Martens on her feet.

"Not bad," Sassy said with appreciation in her voice. "It'd be better with some ink."

"I'm not getting a tattoo. What else can you tell me about this place?"

"The Liar's Club? It's a dive but it's so fun. You'll find everyone from old punks to young hipsters—freaks and geeks and everything in between. Great music on the weekends. Oh, but it's supposed to be haunted."

"Haunted?"

"Yeah, some lady totally got murdered in the apartment over the club."

"Great," Annalisa muttered as she heard Nick come through the front door. "I've got to go. Wish me luck." She slipped on her leather jacket to complete the look.

"Have a tequila shooter for me," Sassy said, saluting her with the wineglass.

Annalisa found Nick standing in the kitchen and flicking through the day's mail. "Hi," she said, going around the counter to kiss his cheek. He didn't look up. "Did you come from the hospital?"

"Yeah. Cassidy finally showed, like four hours late." His voice was tight, his energy off.

"That's something. Have you eaten?"

"Yes, I took Cassidy for a sandwich in the cafeteria. When I asked her where she was all afternoon, she said she was at school helping to set up for the spring dance."

"That sounds nice," Annalisa offered.

"Yeah, but when I asked her if she was going to the dance, she excused herself to go to the bathroom and didn't come back for twenty minutes." He threw down the junk mail and looked at her for the first time. "What's with you?"

"You have to be patient with her," Annalisa said, ignoring him.

"I'm trying. It just feels . . . it feels like we don't have a lot of time to figure this out." He bopped the counter lightly with frustration. "She used to like me. I swear she did."

"She still likes you," Annalisa said as she gave his arm a reassuring massage. "You were just in your honeymoon period."

"Oh?" He softened a bit as he took her in his arms. "You mean like we're in our honeymoon period?"

Technically, they had ended the honeymoon three months earlier. "Must be," she said. "I definitely still like you."

He kissed her and she wound her arms around his neck. For a moment, she forgot she was supposed to be leaving. He fingered the edge of her jacket. "I like this outfit," he murmured against her neck. "What are the odds of getting you to take it off?"

She sighed and stepped back. "Not great right now. I'm about to head out to the Liar's Club. I'm hoping it may give me a line on Naomi's mom."

"Liar's Club? You mean that hole-in-the-wall joint over on Fullerton?"

"You know it?"

"Busted one of their regulars for armed robbery back in the day. Place reminded me of the alien bar from *Star Wars*."

"Well, now I can't wait to see it." She leaned in to kiss him. "Wait up for me?"

He caught her hand with his. "Better yet, why don't I tag along?"

"Mmm . . . okay, but . . ." She looked at his button-down collared shirt, gray suit pants, and scuffed-up shoes. "You need to look like you're there to party, not roust the place."

"Hey, I blend. I blend better than you."

Nick at least had some ink, although it rarely showed. An EKG readout that ended with a heart encircled his left bicep. If you didn't look too closely, it resembled barbed wire. Their first night together, Anna-lisa had asked about it and Nick had said it was to honor his deceased mom. The EKG made her think his mother had died of an illness, per-haps heart-related. Nick had not corrected her assumption. He'd fig-ured she wouldn't love the real him. She'd figured the same. With the pair of them pretending to be different people, it was no wonder their first marriage had failed.

"Well? Am I right?" Nick returned from his quick change and he really did look like a different person. He'd slicked back his dark hair, put on tight jeans, boots, and a Hellraiser T-shirt. His late-evening stubble completed the look.

"Is that . . . is that a safety pin in your ear?" She turned his chin with her fingers.

"Don't worry, I disinfected it first."

She grinned. Clubbing was different at forty, she supposed. You no longer expected to live forever. "Then let's rock."

They took Nick's sports car. "Well, did you prove Craig Canning is a bad sociopath yet?" he asked as he smoothly shifted gears.

"He did it. I can't prove it yet, but he did it. I think that's part of the fun for him, that I know. But Mara Delaney wants me to drop the case."

He glanced over at her. "She got spooked?"

"Canning knows I'm onto him. If anything comes out about him being a suspect, the whole book deal is in jeopardy. I don't blame her for being nervous."

"But if he's guilty, her book is a lie," he pointed out.

"It means he's not a good sociopath. It doesn't disprove the whole thesis."

"Don't tell me you believe this bullshit theory now too."

"I don't know." She looked out at the passing lights. "Maybe I want to believe."

The Liar's Club could not have been more unwelcoming from the outside, with its fifties-style yellow brick, narrow windows with iron bars on them, and battered metal door. They mounted the few concrete steps and were met by two bouncers on the inside. Nick paid the cover charge, and they were admitted to the interior. *If hell had a bar,* Annalisa thought, *this would be it.* The whole place glowed red. Red walls, red fez-hat lamps hanging from a black tin ceiling. Behind the bar, Elvis and KISS figurines presided over the action as two bartenders served up drinks to a crowded room. Vintage porn played on an old TV mounted in the corner. Nick stared like he'd never seen breasts before, and she squeezed his hand to get his attention. "Drinks," she yelled over the blasting sound coming from the dance floor in the next room.

They threaded their way through the bodies—black leather had been a good choice—to the bar. Nick ordered them each an IPA. Annalisa dropped a twenty in the tip jar in full view of the shaggy-haired woman serving them drinks. She looked about Annalisa's age, but with china-doll makeup and a spiderweb tattoo across the back of her right hand. "Thanks," she said flatly as she handed them their beers.

"I'm looking for a friend," Annalisa said, straining her voice to be heard over the din.

"Aren't we all," the woman replied.

"I think she hangs out here. Her name's Lizzie? Lizzie Johnston."

The bartender eyed Nick with speculation, like she wondered if Annalisa might be looking for a third. "I'm no matchmaker, hon. Good luck."

"No, no." Annalisa reached across the bar to grab her when the woman tried to return to her work.

"Hey, hands off."

"Sorry." Annalisa immediately released her. "I just, I really need to find Lizzie. Her uncle died and he left her some money, but the lawyer can't find Lizzie to give it to her. I'm trying to help her out."

"That's sweet of you, but it's got nothing to do with me."

"But . . ."

"Look. I serve drinks. I don't check name tags. You dig?"

Annalisa backed off, deflated. "Okay, thanks." She wished she could take her twenty back out of the jar. Beside her, Nick drank from his bottle and kept one eye on the nubile young women caressing each other on the TV. Annalisa elbowed him. "Are you that hard up?"

"Hmm? Sorry. It was your idea to come here." He looked around over the top of her head. "So what's the plan, Stan?"

She had no big ideas. Sassy had been right about the clientele at the club, which featured some college-aged kids and at least one guy dressed completely in leather who had obviously been around for the original punk age. He had thinning hair but what was left of it was dyed neon blue and gelled into a faux-hawk. Nick caught her staring and leaned over to speak into her ear. "If I've got any hair left at his age, I'm doing the same thing."

She laughed and gave him a light shove. "I'll dye mine pink to match."

A large inebriated man stumbled into her, causing her to bump into the person sitting at the bar behind her. She turned to apologize and found a thin man with a pockmarked face and golfer's cap over his bald head. "Sorry about that," she said, and he looked at her with eyes so pale they almost appeared white.

"You're asking about Lizzie," he replied.

Annalisa looked at Nick, who shifted closer. "Yes," she said. "Do you know her?"

He looked to the overflowing tip jar. "I might. Depends on who's asking, and how badly you want to know."

"I'm a private investigator," Annalisa said, handing him a card. "I was hired by a lawyer to find Lizzie. Her uncle left her some money but no one can find Lizzie to give it to her." She'd worked out a cover story that might persuade Lizzie Johnston to get in touch if it got back to her.

"How much money?" the guy asked as he studied her card.

"Don't know the exact amount, but it's got to be pretty big if they're paying my fee."

This seemed to satisfy him because he tucked the card into his shirt pocket. "My fee's a hundred bucks," he told her. "Flat rate."

She didn't have that much cash on her. "I can give you fifty."

Nick checked his wallet. "Make it ninety."

The guy considered. "Ninety and a drink," he said. "Johnnie Walker Blue."

He had a Pabst Blue Ribbon in front of him. Annalisa pursed her lips and took out her credit card to buy the man's drink. "Deal." When he reached for the cash in her other hand, she held it back. "Half now. Half after you tell me where to find Lizzie."

He laughed, a wheezy sound. "Fuck, I can't tell you that." The barmaid put his drink in front of him and he inclined his head like he was British royalty. "Thank you kindly, miss."

She answered with a good-natured roll of her eyes. "Shove it up your rear, Rory." When he grinned at her remark, Annalisa saw he had two missing teeth.

"Then what am I paying for?" she asked him.

Rory sipped his drink and smacked his lips. "Lizzie used to be a regular, yeah. But she hasn't been in for months now. Not since she hooked up with Big Tony."

"Who is Big Tony?" Annalisa asked.

"He's a big guy, name of Tony." He chuckled at his own humor.

"Where can I find Tony? What's his last name?"

"We were never properly introduced," Rory said with some bitterness. "And I don't know where he lives. Wherever it is, you can bet Lizzie's shacked up with him . . . and that he's paying the rent."

"They're dating?"

He snorted. "Yeah, dating. If that's what you want to call it."

"You've got to give me something more I can use here," Annalisa pressed him. She fisted the cash near his cheek. "I'm paying good money."

"Hey, I made no promises." His hungry gaze drank in the twenties and he licked his lips with a flicker, like a lizard. "Okay, here's one thing. Tony, he's decent-looking, all right? He wants to be an actor. Meantime, he shoves people around for money."

"What do you mean?"

"I mean if you've got a debt that needs collecting, Tony will collect it for you. Minus his fee, of course."

"Of course."

He took another sip and held up the glass to admire the amber liquid inside. "Mmm, that's the good stuff. Makes you glad to be alive, don't it?"

"I don't see how Tony's professional aspirations are helping me," Annalisa said.

"Then you're dumber than you look," he answered. He swiveled in his seat, narrowed his eyes at her and then Nick behind her. "I'm thinking you know some cops." Annalisa cursed inwardly, figuring she'd been made once more. She said nothing. "And I'm thinking maybe they can help you find Tony, given his backup profession."

"You're saying he's got a record," Nick said.

Rory gave an exaggerated shrug. "Tony breaks legs. That's something cops usually frown on, yeah? Lizzie . . . she's something worse."

"What's that?" Annalisa wanted to know.

Rory made a face into his drink. "Lizzie breaks hearts. Not the way you can put them back together. She puts them in a blender, turns them to pulp, and drinks it all down with a smile."

"You sound like you do know her," Annalisa said.

Rory stared at the red wall in front of him. "No," he said. "I never did."

NICK HAD A SECOND BEER WHILE ANNALISA TRIED TO TALK TO A FEW OTHER PEOPLE ABOUT LIZZIE JOHNSTON. No one else seemed to know her, unless Annalisa counted a young woman in a plaid skirt and combat boots who seemed friendly until Lizzie's name came up. Then she told Annalisa to fuck off and disappeared into the crowd. Nick eventually persuaded Annalisa to hit the dance floor, and it felt glorious to move her body to the pounding beat and leave her mind to float above it all. The air smelled like boozy sweat and leather. Nick grabbed her ass and held her tight against his body, his hard thigh between her legs. "That TV sure has you worked up," she said against his throat.

"It's not the TV." His fingers slipped into her back pockets, teasingly close to her bare skin.

She licked the salt from his neck. "Let's get out of here."

They drove home with his hand moving fluidly from the stick to her thigh, shifting her higher and higher. By the time they stumbled into the darkened condo, she was already pulling off her shirt. Her skin tingled everywhere his hands touched. She yanked the T-shirt over his head and he did the same, his mouth hot and eager on her breasts. Only when he moved to enter her did she slow down the action with a palm on his chest. "Wait, the condom."

He lowered his head to kiss her, pushing forward again. "We don't need it."

"Yes, we do," she said as she inched backward. "Come on." She reached for the nightstand and he tugged her arm away.

"Anna, we said we wanted kids. We said soon." He rained kisses on her face, making it hard to think.

"Soon," she said holding his head so she could look into his eyes. "Not right this second."

"It would be at least nine months."

"You know what I mean. We need a plan. We need to talk more about the timing. You're pushing for Cassidy to move in . . ."

He drew back. "What, so that means we don't have a baby?"

"No, of course not." She reached for him but he pulled farther away. "There's a lot of factors, a lot up in the air right now. I'm just starting my business. I currently don't even have a paying client now that Mara fired me."

"I can cover us short-term. You know I can."

"That's not the point."

"Then what is?"

"I . . . I have to be ready."

These were the wrong words because he rolled off her completely and sat on the edge of the bed. The slanting light from the window caught the tattoo on his arm, and his hunched shoulders made her ache inside. "It's not just about you," he said.

"I know that."

He twisted to look at her. "Do you?"

She drew the sheets over her naked body to protect herself from the anger in his gaze. "Nick, what . . . ?" She didn't understand where his emotions were coming from. He couldn't get enough of her on the dance floor. A moment ago, they'd been so in sync. All this over a condom?

"Summer called me."

She pushed up against the headboard, confused. Summer was off the ventilator? "Today?"

"Seventeen years ago. She called when she found out she was pregnant and left me a message to get in touch. I never got that message."

She clutched the sheet tighter. "I didn't either," she said forcefully. No way would she have forgotten a woman saying she was pregnant with Nick's kid.

"She didn't mention the pregnancy in the message. She said she'd found my wallet and I should call her. She knew . . ." He broke off and swallowed with effort. "She knew I was married."

Dread settled over Annalisa like a lead blanket. "Oh." She didn't remember the specific message, but Nick had lost a lot of wallets back then. She knew he was screwing around. He'd barely bothered to hide it. If Annalisa had encountered an unfamiliar woman's voice on the machine, asking him to call her back with such a flimsy pretext, she might well have deleted it. Deleted it and then tossed the whole damn machine.

"I could have known about Cassidy if you gave me the message." He punched the bed. "I could have been there from the start."

She tried to imagine what might have happened if he'd found out about Cassidy at the beginning. Their marriage would have been over, but it was already heading that way. He probably wouldn't have moved back to Florida. He would have stayed in Chicago with his kid. Would he have married Summer? Probably, she thought bleakly. He would have at least tried. Nick wanted to fix everything and so he would have tried to make a happy family. Maybe it would have even worked. Whatever the outcome, she doubted that he would have re-entered her life the way he did. They wouldn't be here now, married and naked in bed together. "I'm sorry," she said, stretching her fingers toward him.

"No." He sprang up from the bed, grabbing a pillow. "No, you're not."

He left her alone in the room, the air still vibrating with his accusation, and Annalisa scooted under the covers, drawing them up over her head so she could ponder the truth of his words in the dark.

TWENTY-SIX

....

ANNALISA AWOKE ALONE IN BED SOMEHOW MORE TIRED THAN SHE'D BEEN THE NIGHT BEFORE. When she shuffled into the living room, she found a pillow and folded blanket on the couch and an empty coffee cup in the sink. Nick had left early without a word, but he'd brewed enough coffee for both of them, so he didn't completely hate her yet. She poured herself a mug and sat on a stool at the peninsula, its cold black granite spare comfort. They kept it gleaming these days because the place could be shown at any time. Annalisa could make out the messy outline of her hair in the reflection but the shape felt unfamiliar, like she was seeing someone else. She had no active case to investigate, no job that needed her presence. PI work had appealed to her for its freedom. Freedom, apparently, to sit around in an old T-shirt by herself in the kitchen.

She couldn't ask Nick to look into the thug named Tony. Never mind that it wasn't technically his case; he obviously didn't care to talk to her right now. Mara Delaney had removed her from the investigation into Craig Canning. *You haven't found any proof he murdered Vicki Albright,* Mara said. *That's convincing enough for me.*

Absence of evidence is not evidence of absence. They'd taught her that at the police academy. Lack of proof did not equal innocence. Mara's fear of what Canning might do was evidence in itself, even if it weren't legally actionable.

Annalisa sipped her coffee and as the caffeine hit her veins, she perked up slightly. "Legally actionable." The phrase used to define her every move. On the job, her commander, Lynn Zimmer, would have certainly pulled her off the Canning case. No proof, no cause. The government could not pursue an investigation without demonstrating their right to intrude on a civilian's life. But Annalisa wasn't a government agent anymore. Mara had hired her and fired her, but she had no authority to block Annalisa from investigating Canning on her own time. Annalisa gulped down the rest of her coffee and dressed for the day with renewed purpose. If she hurried, she could make it to Vicki's apartment building before nine, the time Vicki had gone over the balcony.

The traffic gods smiled on Annalisa and she arrived at the Parkview apartment complex by a quarter to nine, about ten minutes before Vicki Albright had made her fatal fall. Annalisa went to the courtyard to study the spot where Vicki had landed, about fifteen feet clear of the building. The distance seemed large for a simple fall. She felt Vicki must have had some force pushing her outward as well as gravity pulling her down, like the woman had been pushed, or perhaps jumped.

Annalisa decided to work the scene as if Canning had murdered Vicki. She had two problems to overcome if she was to prove him guilty. The first was how he could have entered Vicki's apartment. Vicki had recently accused him of date rape, which gave Canning motive but it also meant Vicki wasn't likely to have opened her door for him, even if he had brought a gift of wind chimes. There was no sign of forced entry at Vicki's apartment. If Canning had been there, he had to have a way inside. Second, and more problematic, Canning was on camera arriving at the hospital ten minutes after Vicki's fall, and the hospital was at least twenty minutes away. Ruth Bernstein had witnessed Vicki's death. Her timing never varied.

As if to prove the point, Ruth Bernstein appeared at the edge of the courtyard dressed in a pale blue track suit. Annalisa checked her phone. Five minutes to nine, just like always. *We can set our clocks by her*, Canning had said. Ruth waved and made her way across the gardens to stand next to Annalisa. "I don't usually pass this way now," she confessed. "I stay on the other side of the courtyard. I don't even like being out on the balcony these days, especially since Duchess isn't there to keep me company."

"You haven't found her?"

"No, but I'm keeping my hopes up."

Annalisa smiled in sympathy but she figured the cat was long gone by now. "She had a collar, right? Maybe someone will find her."

"A breakaway collar," Ruth corrected. "I've searched the grounds but I haven't found it anywhere. She's got a microchip, though. Anyone who takes her to a shelter or a vet should be able to contact me." Ruth pursed her lips. "I still can't work out how she got free. I shut that door behind me. I know I did. It's almost like someone came into my apartment and took her."

Annalisa had only been half listening. She was squinting up at Vicki's balcony again, but she returned her attention to Ruth. "Could someone do that? Someone who had a key?"

"The building super keeps copies of all the keys in case work needs to be done. But I don't think he'd want to kidnap Duchess. He's allergic to cats."

"Who has access to those keys?" Annalisa asked. Canning lived here. He'd have provided a key to his own place, so he'd know Vicki had to have provided one too. Maybe he took it to get into her apartment on the day of her murder.

"Well, Mr. Irwin . . . he's the super. No one else as far as I know."

"Can you show me where the keys are kept?"

Ruth gave a decisive nod. "This way." Annalisa slowed her stride to keep up with the old woman, and Ruth glanced up at her. "You still think someone hurt that poor girl."

"I think it's possible, yes."

Ruth's face became pinched. "So awful. I keep hearing the scream and seeing her fall. Why did I have to be standing there?" Annalisa held the door to the lobby open for Ruth to pass through it. "Ah, Damon is working. He can help us. Hello, Damon!"

The young man at the front desk looked up from his textbook to answer Ruth's cheery wave. "Morning, Mrs. B. Right on time, I see."

"I'm taking a detour today," she informed him. "Do you know Ms. Vega? She's a private investigator looking into Vicki's death."

"PI, huh?" Damon looked at her with a slight frown as he realized she had not been honest with him in their earlier encounter. "What's the problem? I thought it was an accident."

"Maybe it was," Annalisa said. "That's what I'm trying to find out."

"She wants to see the keys," Ruth stated bluntly.

"I understand the superintendent keeps keys to all the units," Annalisa explained. "I was wondering if it might be possible for someone to lift one of the keys."

Damon's eyebrows rose. "You mean steal 'em? No way. Mr. Irwin locks his office when he's not in it. Always."

"Even if he's just popping out for a second?" Annalisa asked. "Like to use the restroom?"

Damon looked uncertain. "I don't think so. I mean, I've never seen the place unlocked unless he was in there."

"Is he in there now?" Annalisa asked.

"Nope. Won't be back until after lunch."

"Could I see the office?" Annalisa tried to look friendly and obliging. "Just to get a sense of where it's located?"

Damon hesitated and then shrugged. "Sure, it's back this way. But like I told you, it's locked."

Annalisa followed him across the marbled floor and down a short hall. Ruth trailed after them as well. Damon gestured at a windowless door that read SUPERINTENDENT on it. "Here it is."

Annalisa noted that the office had no view of the lobby, and thus persons in the lobby would have no view of it either. Total privacy. "Who else has a key to this office?"

"Me and Pete, the other doorman." Damon jingled the keys in his pants. "It's just for emergencies, though. I've never had to use it."

"What if someone needed to access an apartment and Mr. Irwin was away? Could you get to the keys then?"

"I'd text Mr. Irwin and he'd take care of it. He's never far away. And even if I open the office, I still couldn't get at the keys. He keeps 'em in a locked box on the wall."

"Hmm." Annalisa pretended to think. "I guess you're right. No one could access the keys. I'd like to make a report to my client about this, but I need supporting documentation. Do you think I could get into the office for just a second? To take a picture of the lockbox with the keys?"

"Oh, I don't think so," Damon said, backing up. "You better wait for Mr. Irwin."

"You said he's gone for hours yet. I won't touch anything. I just want a quick picture."

"A picture isn't going to hurt anything, Damon," Ruth urged. "You want to be an investigator yourself one day, right? Well, you're going to need this kind of help. Let Ms. Vega take her photo."

"I guess a photo would be okay," Damon allowed grudgingly. He dug out his keys and opened the door. "Just don't touch anything."

Annalisa noted the lock on the door was strong and fairly new; it wouldn't be easy to pick. It showed no signs of tampering. Inside, the super's office smelled like feet. Annalisa saw why when she noticed two pairs of old boots lined against the wall. The office was finely controlled chaos. Paper and folders piled everywhere—on the desk, on top of file cabinets. There was a chair with a pipe wrench on it and a window frame leaning on the wall. Mr. Irwin favored Dunkin for his coffee, according to his overflowing trash can. He had a framed map of 1930s Chicago on the wall and a half-eaten breakfast sandwich on the desk. Ruth muttered under her breath about the disgraceful mess as Annalisa moved deeper into the room.

"That's where the keys are," Damon said, indicating the large locked metal cabinet affixed to the back wall behind the desk. Annalisa went around the desk and tried to open the cabinet. As promised, it was locked. She took a quick photo. "Okay, great. Let's go." Damon sounded relieved their work was over.

"One sec," Annalisa said as she bent over the desk. Mr. Irwin was old-school. He had various sticky notes tacked on his computer monitor with reminders and passwords. Shortcuts. Or maybe he was just forgetful. She pulled open the narrow drawer underneath the blotter to find more chaos—pens, pencils, erasers, staples, old receipts and a small screwdriver. Also keys.

"Hey, you said you wouldn't touch anything." Damon strode over to the desk and Ruth filed in behind him, looking intrigued.

"What have you found?" she asked.

Annalisa plucked the small key at the top of the heap. A forgetful person would keep a backup, she reasoned. This one looked like it would fit the cabinet. Over Damon's protestations, she inserted the key into the cabinet and turned it. The door popped open. "Anyone who can get into the office can get to the keys," she said. "See?"

"Yeah, okay, I see. Can we go now?"

"One more picture." Annalisa held her breath as she nudged the door fully open with her finger. She expected to find Vicki's key was missing. But no, there it was, dangling on a tiny hook above the piece of tape labeled ALBRIGHT/148.

"Let me see." Ruth pushed in as Annalisa stared at the shiny key. She'd been sure this would be the answer as to how Canning had accessed Vicki's apartment. "Aha," Ruth cried, pointing at the cabinet. "I knew it! Someone took my key. I've been robbed."

"Robbed, Mrs. B?" Damon looked confused.

"Duchess," she said, her fury barely contained. "Someone stole her."

Annalisa's gaze slid from Ruth's empty hook to Vicki's key and back again. They were right next to each other, just as the apartments were. Of course. It all made sense now. How Canning got into Vicki's place. How he beat the clock. Even what happened to the damn cat. She could guess every last moment of what happened on the day Vicki Albright died.

Problem was, she could never prove it.

TWENTY-SEVEN

....

Annalisa drove to Mara's townhome. The woman had told her to back off, but she might change her mind when she heard what Annalisa had to say. More than that, Annalisa hoped Mara had some insight into how they could trip Canning up, for he seemed to have committed a near-perfect crime. Mara's face revealed trepidation when she opened the door, her gaze traveling beyond Annalisa to search for someone who could be lurking behind. Annalisa wondered again how much Mara had already guessed for herself. She suspected that Mara had seen a side of Canning that made her nervous, or she would not have employed Annalisa's services in the first place. Annalisa believed she had deduced what this was. It all went back to the wind chimes.

"Sorry to show up again without calling," Annalisa said. "It's important."

"Please, come in." Mara retreated from the entrance and made way for Annalisa to pass by. "Can I offer you something to drink? Tea or coffee?"

"I'm fine, thanks." She followed Mara to the living room where Mara's small desk sat with a laptop open on it. A copy of her book lay next to the computer. "Last-minute edits?" she asked as she picked up the book.

Mara gave a little laugh. "It's far too late for that."

Too late, Annalisa thought as she flipped open the first pages. She hoped not. "'For Donna,'" she read aloud from the dedication. "Who's Donna?"

"You remember. The friend I told you about."

"Oh, right. The one who was abused by the bad psychopath."

"Exactly."

Annalisa snapped the book shut and returned it to the desk. "If you were right," she said slowly. "If you were right about your suspicions and Craig Canning is a bad psychopath, what would that mean?"

Mara looked alarmed. She blinked in owlish fashion. "I'm not sure what you're asking."

"How did he get that way?" Annalisa asked with a trace of impatience. "What is he capable of beyond murder? Could you ever turn him from the dark side to the light?"

"Beyond murder . . . ?" Mara echoed, her mouth falling open. "Did you find proof, then?"

"No proof. Just suspicion, which is what drove you to my office in the first place. What I want to know is why."

"Why?"

"Why you saw the report of Vicki Albright falling to her death and thought Canning might be involved."

Mara's cheeks stained like wine. She sank into the nearest chair. "I knew she'd accused him of drugging and raping her. I also knew he couldn't have done it. But . . ."

"But?"

Mara gave a helpless shrug. "I had to know for sure."

"Because you were sleeping with him?"

Mara's head jerked up. "What?"

"He intimated as much to me, but I didn't take him seriously. I've seen him flirting with other women—even me, and he knows I'm married." She held up her left hand to illustrate. "Obviously a wedding band doesn't stop him. Then I remembered what you'd told me about the wind chimes being his go-to move when wooing a woman and I wondered why you had a set."

"We worked together on the book. We've been quite . . . close." Mara looked at her lap, and Annalisa waited her out with silence. When Mara raised her face again, she had tears in her eyes. "Please," she whispered, "you can't tell my husband."

"So you have slept with him. With Canning."

Mara turned her whole body away in shame. "Two years ago, we had a terrible rainstorm—with downed trees and high winds. I was on my way home from the university late at night when my car made this odd noise and stopped working. I maneuvered to the side of the road to call for help and my cell wouldn't work. I guess one of the towers must've gone down. I was standing there, soaked, trying to figure out if I could fix it myself or if I should walk for help when Craig Canning pulled over. He introduced himself and said he could give me a lift." She cast an imploring look at Annalisa. "He had scrubs on. He had a hospital ID. I didn't think he was dangerous."

"Of course not," Annalisa said. "What happened next?"

"I went to his place to use the phone and dry off. His apartment is impressive, elegant." She looked to Annalisa, who nodded. "Craig was smooth and charming. He made me tea and offered me clean scrubs while he put my clothes in the dryer. He . . . he gave me soup."

"Soup?"

"See, that's the thing, right? A guy who's putting the hard moves on you, he offers you booze, not soup. It was this delicious pea soup with mint. I'd never tasted anything like it. He showed me his record collection and we started talking about bands we'd seen. Paul was away at a medical conference in San Diego, so I didn't have to hurry home. We just kept . . . talking. I told him about my work. He was fascinated in a way that Paul never was. I felt . . . seen, really seen, for the first time in years."

"I see," said Annalisa. "Then what?"

"He kissed me." Mara turned red again. "I remember he definitely made the first move. But I didn't stop him. I think some part of me had been waiting for it to happen ever since he let me into his apartment. My heart was hammering, my palms were sweaty. I felt sixteen again."

"So you went to bed with him?"

"It was a mistake," Mara whispered, looking at her feet. "I knew that immediately. The next morning, early, Craig called for a tow and took me home. He wanted to see me again. I made excuses. I loved Paul. I loved our life together. I didn't want to ruin it all for one night with a brain surgeon."

"But you ended up writing a book about him."

Mara said nothing. She got up and went to the window, staring out at the brick wall of the house next door. Pink petals from a nearby dogwood floated down like rain.

"It was his idea," Mara murmured at length.

"About the book?"

"No, I'd told him about my idea for the book during the night we spent together. It was his idea to be featured as the main character. Craig pursued me, you see, after that night, asking me to go out with him again. He showed up at my office with those wind chimes. He even called me at home. I told him no, I couldn't see him anymore, but . . ." She paused to grimace. "You know he doesn't like to hear no. I told him he was behaving like the men in my book."

"And then he suggested the book could center on him," Annalisa said. It was blackmail of a sort, she realized. It gave him the "win" over Mara when she didn't want a romantic relationship with him.

"Yes, but it turned out to be an excellent idea," Mara replied in a rush. "I gave him all the tests and he passed them with flying colors. He's definitely a sociopath."

"Just not a nice one."

Mara winced. "None of them are nice," she admitted. "He's useful. He really is a brilliant doctor and he has saved hundreds of lives. He's just not caring of other people's feelings. He'll push to get what he wants and he doesn't mind if someone gets hurt along the way."

"Someone like you."

Mara licked her lips delicately. "He's threatened to tell Paul the truth if I don't split the advance money from the book. I guess he has a case. He's right that it wouldn't be getting the same kind of press without his participation. I—I can live with that, with sharing the money. I can't live with it if he really hurt that girl." She turned pleading eyes to Annalisa. "Please tell me he didn't hurt her."

Annalisa hedged. "I still can't prove anything . . . but I have an idea of how he could have done it. Someone stole the spare key to the apartment next door to Vicki's, which is owned by an elderly woman named Ruth Bernstein. Ruth takes a walk every day at exactly the same time. That time happens to be right around when Vicki fell."

"Ruth. I know that name. She was in the papers as a witness."

"Right. Ruth was just returning from her daily walk at the time Vicki went over the balcony. I think Canning planned it that way. Once Ruth left on her walk, he could enter her apartment and use the balcony to get from Ruth's place to Vicki's. But that was just part of the plan. He needed Ruth to see the death so she could put a timestamp on it. Everyone knows Ruth is in the courtyard at the same time every day. I think Canning arranged for her to be there a little earlier. He had the key to her apartment. He could have sneaked in shortly before the murder and adjusted the clock by the door. Not by much—maybe fifteen minutes ahead to give him the window he needed to complete the crime. Then when the clock bonged eight, it was really seven forty-five. Ruth set out on her walk and Canning enacted the second part of his plan. He went back to Ruth's apartment and used her balcony to access Vicki's unit. The edges of the two balconies are only a few feet apart. Anyone who is athletic enough could make the crossing easily. Vicki liked to keep her balcony doors open so she could wander in and out, so Craig was able to gain entry to her living area. He surprised Vicki, maybe knocked her out somehow. Then he dragged a chair over to the balcony, staged the scene with the wind chimes, and waited for Ruth to reappear in the garden at the end of her walk. He tossed Vicki so Ruth would see her fall. Only it wasn't 8:55 like she told the cops. It was more like 8:40, which would have given Canning enough time to return to Ruth's apartment to change the clock back, put on clean clothes, and hightail it to the hospital, where he could be seen on camera entering the garage slightly past nine."

Mara's eyes grew round. "That's diabolical."

"It's clever, I'll give him that."

"But . . . how can you prove it?"

"The time of the 911 call should help. Ruth said she was stunned by the accident and she didn't react right away. She's also eighty-five and not the quickest walker. Even still, the 911 call from the lobby should be closer to 8:40 than 8:55. That's evidence that Ruth got the time wrong but it doesn't prove much else."

"This is so much worse than I imagined," Mara muttered as she walked into the adjoining den and collapsed onto the sofa. Annalisa followed. She could try to convince Nick to search Ruth's place for Canning's fingerprints, but she'd bet he had worn gloves. After all, the wind chimes had no prints on them.

Annalisa looked at the nearby bookshelves, which featured various titles on psychology. One caught her eye. *The Born Psychopath.* "Is that true?" she asked Mara, gesturing at the book. "Are people like Canning born that way?"

Mara said nothing for a moment. "It's easier if I show you," she murmured at length. Mara removed a box of CDs from the television cabinet and inserted one into the CD player. Annalisa waited, peering around her as Mara fast-forwarded to one spot on the video. "Here," she said, resuming her seat next to Annalisa. "Watch this."

Annalisa saw a young girl, perhaps four or five years old, having a tea party with a doll and a teddy bear. The girl giggled as she served them pretend tea from a tin kettle. "Careful, it's hot!" she warned the doll. An adult woman entered the room and took a seat at one of the small chairs, appearing comically large amid the playthings.

"Hello, Emily," she said. "How are you today?"

"We're having a party," Emily replied in a cheery little voice. "Would you like a cookie?" She held out an empty toy platter.

"I'd love one," said the woman, who pretended to take and nibble a cookie. "Delicious. Did you bake them yourself?"

"With my mommy," Emily said. "I always put the sprinkles on."

"That's nice that you help your mommy. Do you like helping her at home?"

"Sure." She paused her play to bat her dark eyelashes at the woman. "I'm her best girl. She says so."

"I'm sure she does. What else do you do to help your mommy?"

"I clean up my room. I tidy the books. I give Devon his bottle."

"Devon, your brother?"

"Mmm-hmm. He's one. We had his birthday party and I got to open his presents because he's not old enough."

"What happened after the party?" the woman wanted to know.

"Devon had his nap. Mommy had a nap too. She was tired from the party. Daddy said I should be extra quiet and play in my room while

Mommy napped and he watched baseball on TV." She rolled her eyes. "Baseball is soooo boring."

"And did you play in your room?"

"Yes." Emily held up the doll for inspection. She smoothed the doll's dress and kissed her on the cheek.

"What else did you do?"

Emily returned the doll to its chair and poured it some more tea. "I went to check on Devon."

"Was he sleeping?"

"Yes."

"What did you do then?"

Emily hesitated for just a second. "I did an experiment."

"What kind of experiment?"

"I gave Devon a poke."

Annalisa looked to Mara, who sat forward on the couch, riveted as if seeing this for the first time. "What kind of poke?" Annalisa asked.

"Shh," Mara said. "You'll see."

"How did you poke him?" the woman asked Emily.

Emily took her finger and jabbed the air. "Like that."

"Did you use your finger?"

Emily shook her head. "No."

"What did you use to poke Devon?"

"A needle," she said sweetly.

Annalisa sucked in a breath. This kid was barely more than a baby herself.

The woman on the screen didn't react to this horrible disclosure. "What kind of needle?" she asked the girl.

Emily's chubby fingers played with the doll's blond ringlets. "The kind Mommy uses for knitting."

"I see. And what happened when you poked Devon?"

Emily made a face. "He got messy."

"Messy?"

"Yeah," she said, her voice upbeat again. "All his blood came out."

"You must have poked him pretty hard."

"Hard as I could." Emily looked at the woman, her small face earnest. "You don't see the blood unless you do it hard."

Mara froze the video. "Emily is four and a half here. This wasn't the first time she'd attacked her brother, but it was the first time her parents told anyone about it. They thought it was normal sibling stuff at first."

"My God," Annalisa whispered as she stared at the girl on the screen. "What happened to her?"

"This video is from several decades ago now. Her baby brother recovered from his injuries, but the parents wanted nothing to do with Emily once the doctors whispered 'psychopath' in the hallways. They released her to the state's custody, where she was eventually sent to a foster home without any indication of her psychological history beyond 'trouble bonding with other children.' I guess we should thank them for that small effort. She wasn't placed in a home with any other young kids."

"What happened to her?"

"She was fine for a few years. Then she set fire to the foster parents' home with them in it. After that, it was juvenile detention until age eighteen."

"You said this was several decades ago," Annalisa said. "She'd be an adult now."

"Yes. Emily is out there somewhere. She lost touch with the study's doctors a long time ago. The last anyone heard of her, she'd changed her name and moved to Portland, Oregon."

"But didn't they give her treatment? After the parents brought her in, after she hurt her baby brother. There must have been something they could do. Pills, shock therapy . . . something."

"If there is a treatment, no one has found it yet." Mara snapped off the TV. "If Craig Canning is like little Emily, then he's been this way since birth. He won't change. He can't."

"Then we have to stop him. How do we stop him?"

Mara considered this question. "Maybe . . . maybe I can get him to confess to it somehow. You saw how easily Emily revealed what she'd done to her brother. Sociopaths like to feel superior. They like to brag. It's no fun committing the perfect crime if no one knows you got away with it. Craig might tell me the whole thing, especially if he thinks I won't sink the book by revealing his secret."

Annalisa was tempted by this solution. "No," she said finally. "I can't ask you to do that. If he did do this murder, he's very dangerous. You can't confront him on your own."

"You can't either," Mara said, her eyes wide with alarm.

"Don't worry about me."

"He's already toying with you by bringing those charms to your house. If he thinks you're a threat, he'll happily have you eliminated." Mara got up to pace the length of the den. "There might be a way to get proof."

"What do you mean?"

"If Craig orchestrated a perfect murder, he'd want to remember it. He likely took a trophy." She fingered her own necklace. "Did Vicki have any jewelry that was missing? A hair tie? Anything from the body?"

"I don't know," Annalisa said. "Nothing that was in the report." A thought occurred to her. "Wait, there was one piece of the wind chimes missing. A crystal charm we never found anywhere. Could that be it?"

Mara looked intrigued. "Maybe. If it came from the wind chimes, it would be something he could look at to relive the experience."

"That's it then," Annalisa said. "Find the charm, and we've got him."

TWENTY-EIGHT

....

CASSIDY WAITED FOR THE MINUTES TO WIND DOWN ON HER AMERICAN HIS-TORY CLASS. The school had removed the clock from the wall some time ago—maybe it had broken, she didn't know—and now there was just an empty circle of slightly brighter beige paint to mark the spot above the door where the clock had been. The teacher at the front of the room droned on about Franklin Roosevelt. Next they would cover World War II. Cassidy knew from experience that this would be the end of the story. All her American history studies began with the Pilgrims and ended with the Allied victory in World War II. America won, case closed.

The teacher was a skinny old guy with gray stringy hair. He had to be at least seventy. *Maybe World War II felt recent to him,* she thought as she laid her head on the desk. *Part of his actual life.* He probably knew people who'd fought there. Cassidy understood that it was important to study Hitler and how awful he was so no one like that would ever rise to power again, but she got impatient with the ending. History didn't stop with white-hatted soldiers coming home to victory parades. Her generation still faced terrorism and poverty and the earth cooking itself under their feet. How had this happened? Who was responsible? It's like the books had a bunch of blank chapters at the back. She'd asked the teacher when they were going to cover 9/11 and he'd replied it was covered in the Current Affairs class, not History. Cassidy had blinked at him in confusion. Current Affairs? The towers had fallen years before she'd been born. She hadn't seen them and she never would. Nothing he talked about ever felt relevant to her *now*.

She held back a groan as she slumped across her desk. She was stuck here because she couldn't cut school for a fourth day in a row without triggering a sit-down with guidance and her guardian. *Battle of the Gs,* she thought. The school knew they couldn't drag in her dying mother, so they would call Melanie. *We'll have to contact your guardian.* Cassidy couldn't have that, so she endured a full day of school before moving ahead with her plan to confront Naomi's mom.

The bell finally rang—an electronic echo loud enough to signal World War III. Cassidy snatched up her phone to check on Naomi as she hurried for the exit. She planned to take the train back to the apartment building where she'd followed the man the day before. Cassidy halted on the cement steps of the school when she saw her last text to Naomi remained unread. She'd sent it more than seven hours ago. Naomi never went this long without checking her phone, not unless she couldn't for some reason. Cassidy's legs went weak as the other students rushed past her, jostling her with their arms and backpacks in their rush to flee the building. Her phone sagged in her hand as she staggered to the side of the stairs and sank down on their hard, dirty surface. *U don't wanna be with me,* Naomi had written the first time Cassidy had confessed her feelings to her over chat one night. *I've got an expiration date, remember?*

I don't care, Cassidy had written back. *I love u.*

The first part was a lie. Of course she cared. She felt like she was bleeding out right there on the steps. Naomi's illness was getting worse.

She needed a kidney. Cassidy had to find her mom, now, and convince her to do that test. She just had to figure out which apartment Naomi's mom was in without going door-to-door.

Cassidy's gaze traveled to the janitor hauling trash from lunch out of the building to the dumpsters in the back. The trash. The apartment building where the man lived had a line of trash cans at the back. She could search the bins to see if one of them had evidence of "Liza" in it. Junk mail, a bill . . . anything with her name on it. Then Cassidy would know the apartment number and could prove that Naomi's mom was shacked up in there. With fresh resolve, she heaved to her feet and started for the L station. She did not think about her last words to Naomi.

Miss u.

....

CASSIDY DID NOT GO UNPREPARED THIS TIME TO THE MAN'S SKETCHY NEIGH-BORHOOD. Melanie carried a can of pepper spray in her purse, and Cassidy had lifted it that morning before school. She transferred it from her backpack to her pocket as she left the subway station and began walking toward the apartment building. Maybe it was the confidence of her weapon or the purpose in her stride, but the people she passed did not give her any trouble. Even the guy sitting on his porch with the bottle just squinted and watched her walk by.

The rectangular brick building looked even more desolate today with the cloudy gray sky as a backdrop. Cassidy watched the front doors for a few minutes to see if anyone might appear, but no one did. She did her best to look casual as she walked to the side of the building and around to the trash cans. It must be close to pickup day, she figured when she saw some of them near to overflowing. The stench of rotting food hit her as she got closer and she almost gagged. *You can do this,* she coached herself as she lifted one grimy lid. *Gross.* She wished she had brought gloves. She held her breath and yanked at the knot on the top bag until it pulled free. Orange peels mixed with half a congealed pizza, used tissues, dental floss that got caught on her fingers and made her dry heave. She paused when she found a dirty diaper. Naomi's mother had left when Naomi was barely out of diapers herself. Would she really have another kid? Cassidy kept digging until she found a ripped envelope with a name on it. Yolanda Ramirez. Probably not the right place. She moved on to the next bin.

One by one, she excavated the refuse of people's lives. She found proof of humanity's inherent messiness, from used condoms to maxi pads, but also odd and sometimes beautiful pieces that made her wonder why they had ended up in the trash. Someone had thrown out a wedding photo, still in the frame. It wasn't cracked or otherwise damaged, but the frame was dusty and the picture showed a couple wearing dated clothes, maybe from the 1980s. They had big smiles, though, eyes shining as they held each other's hands. Cassidy carefully tucked the photo back in the trash. She searched the next bin and found a seemingly endless supply of empty bags of gummy candies. Also a ceramic foot with painted red toes. None of the papers she discovered had Liza or any other form of Elizabeth on them. She replaced the foot with a shudder and continued her search.

On the eighth bin, she coughed as the stench of stale cigarettes hit her in the face. Sure enough, she found butts galore along with a few empty bottles of vodka. Take-out containers, some of them still half-full, rotted at the bottom. Cassidy forced herself to root around until she found some mail. Resident, resident. *Hello.* A fashion catalogue addressed to Elizabeth Longmire. Cassidy held it out and dug into the second bag in the bin. Her fingers brushed what felt like hair and she momentarily recoiled. When she forced herself to reach back inside, she yanked out a blond wig. But it was a crumpled, handwritten note that convinced her she'd found the right trash bin. *I know you did it. You're going to pay.*

Cassidy felt the first tingling of fear since she'd started digging through the trash. She didn't want this to be the right bin all of a sudden. But her gaze caught something else in the bag, more crumpled paper, bright pink in color. It was the wrapping paper she'd used on the decoy box. She had definitely found the right trash can. The number on the bin said 308. She could go knock on the door and see who was inside. Make up a pretext like selling tickets for a school raffle. Or she could leave and try to convince her dad or Annalisa to investigate further. She hesitated with the note in her hand. This might not be enough proof for Annalisa or her dad.

Out of nowhere, she felt a sharp kick to her lower back. Right in the kidneys. She fell forward into the trash bin and hit her chin on the rough plastic edge, hard enough to leave a scrape. "What the hell are you doing, going through my trash?" The voice growled at her.

Cassidy struggled upright and turned, shaking, to find a woman, maybe forty but with some hard years on her, standing there with a death glare and a cigarette in her hand. "I was . . . I lost something," Cassidy said, her brain grasping the first lame excuse it could generate. "I was looking for it."

And I've found it, Cassidy realized as she took in the woman's rounded chin and high forehead. The elegant shape of her nose and the arch of her neck. Cassidy had spent hours contemplating Naomi's beautiful features, had traced the edges of Naomi's face with her fingertips and memorized the feel. Liza, Lizzie, Elizabeth . . . whatever name this woman called herself now, she was Naomi's mother.

"You're lying. I've never seen you before." The woman tossed her cigarette on the ground took a step closer. She smelled like alcohol. "What've you got there?"

Cassidy clutched the note. "N-nothing."

The woman grabbed her arm, fingers biting, and wrenched Cassidy's hand forward. "Fuck me," she said as she snatched the paper.

"You wrote this?" She fisted it and almost punched Cassidy's face. "You threatening me?"

"No, I found it."

"No, I found it," the woman mimicked. "Found it slipped under my door by some creeper, just like you're creeping around my trash. You're coming with me. We're going to talk to Tony."

"I can't. I have to go." Cassidy tried to get free but the woman's grip was shockingly strong. She started dragging Cassidy toward the back door.

"You'll like talking to Tony. And if you don't, it doesn't matter. Tony has a way of convincing people to talk."

"Let me go." Cassidy cast a desperate glance at her backpack, which sat next to the trash bins. It had her cell inside, but she'd turned it off so Nick and Melanie couldn't track her. *No one knows I'm here,* she thought as she struggled to get her arm free.

"You're trespassing on my property," the woman said as she worked to open the door and hold Cassidy at the same time. "That means I can do whatever I want to you."

"Let. Me. Go!" Cassidy screamed the words in case anyone might hear or care. She dragged her feet, trying to tip the woman's weight and throw her off balance. The move caused Cassidy's jacket to hit against her own leg and she felt the can of pepper spray in the pocket. She yanked it out and sprayed it at the woman's head. The woman screamed and released her.

Cassidy flew down the alley and grabbed her backpack while the woman hollered obscenities after her. She didn't look back but she could hear the woman's footsteps gaining on her. The street beckoned, getting closer. "Help!" she called. "Someone help me!" The nearest house was completely boarded up. Cassidy reached the mouth of the alley hoping to see a person, anyone, in any direction. Even that creepy guy with the bottle. But the streets were empty. In the fraction that she hesitated, her attacker caught up with her and grabbed her hair, yanking her back into the alley.

"You're going to regret that," the woman said, breathing hard.

Cassidy opened her mouth to scream again but she felt something cold and sharp against her neck. The woman had a knife.

"That's right," the woman said as Cassidy wheezed and closed her mouth. "I'm in charge here. Got it?" She hadn't let go of Cassidy's hair, pulling it so tight it hurt.

"Please," Cassidy whispered as tears stung her eyes. "I'm a friend of Naomi's."

She hoped the name of her daughter would move this woman to mercy, but she didn't even flinch. "Stupid girl," she spat out as she force-marched Cassidy back to the building. "You don't have friends around here."

TWENTY-NINE

....

THE FIRST THING ANNALISA DID WAS TO VISIT A MEDICAL SUPPLY STORE AND BUY A PAIR OF SCRUBS SIMILAR TO THOSE SHE HAD SEEN PEOPLE WEARING AT CRAIG CANNING'S HOSPITAL. She had learned by now that ginning up a cover story did not work; too many people recognized her. Adding the surgical face mask worn by hospital staff would offer extra protection, and she didn't expect her mission would take much time. She needed to blend in long enough to determine Canning's surgical schedule. Once she knew the exact hours he would be out of his apartment, she could find a way in to search for the missing crystal charm from the wind chimes.

Her plan in motion, she had the scrubs ready in her messenger bag when she entered the hospital, but she got distracted by a text from Nick. *I'm an ass,* he wrote. *I'm sorry.* She lingered in the lobby, her phone in her hand, trying to figure out what to say back to him. *You're right? Screw you?* These were the zingers they had thrown at each other near the end of their first marriage.

She checked the time and saw it was later than she'd thought. Cassidy would be out of school so there was a decent chance Nick was here at the hospital. She tucked her phone away and went up to the fifth floor, where she found him sitting alone, slouched in a chair in the waiting room. He stared at his phone without scrolling, probably because he waited for her reply. She crossed the room and plopped into the seat next to him. "Hi."

Naked relief flooded his face. "You got my text."

She patted her phone in her pocket. "Yep."

"I really am sorry," he said, turning in his seat to face her. "I—I shouldn't have pushed you like that. About having a kid."

"The big one or the little one?" she said gently, taking his hand.

"Both? Either?" He looked around the room searchingly. "I don't think it matters. Cassidy isn't here . . . again. She's not answering my texts, as usual. Melanie was right. I'm not Cassidy's father and I never will be. I'm just some guy who shares her DNA."

"Never is a long time." He snorted and pulled free to put his head in his hands. She rubbed his back in sympathy. "You are her father, Nick. You are. But you're not her mother, and that's where her emotions are vulnerable right now."

He gripped his own hair in frustration. "I know maybe better than anyone what's coming for her, you know? That's why I'm trying to stop it."

"It's not the same," she told him. "You lost your mom in a sudden ter- rible act of violence. Cassidy's known her mother's death was coming for a long time. She has Melanie and other supports, including you. It's terrible, yes, but she will be okay."

"I guess."

Neither said anything for a long moment. Annalisa steeled herself, preparing to own her role in the whole drama. "I wish I'd given you that message," she said finally. "When Summer called. I thought it was just another one of your flings. I'm sorry."

"Yeah, you didn't know. You couldn't." He muttered the words and stared blankly ahead, and she reassessed her phrasing. Here was the big apology he was supposed to have wanted from her, but it didn't seem to help. His jaw was set, his whole body tight like a coiled spring. He shook his head like he was disgusted with himself. "I wouldn't have wanted her," he confessed in a whisper. "Back then."

Annalisa sat still. She'd wanted raw honesty. Here it was.

"We were married," he continued in a strained voice. "Trying to patch things up, trying to keep going. If Summer had told me back then that she was pregnant, I would've tried to get her to end it."

"Oh." Yes, that's probably what she would have hoped for too. For the problem to go away.

"I mean, she may well have not listened to me. It would've been Summer's choice. But if she'd asked my opinion back then, I know what I would have said." He looked at her, stricken. "So maybe this is what I deserve. This rejection. But I want to make it right. I think of everything I've missed with her, everything I could still miss if she walks out of my life now."

"She's not going to do that," Annalisa interjected. "She tracked you down, remember? She wants you in her life. You just have to ease back, give her time. It doesn't matter what might have happened seventeen years ago. It matters what you do now." She hoped he understood she meant this advice for them as well as Cassidy. She took his hand again. "This isn't your last chance, Nick. It's your fresh start."

He hesitated before squeezing her hand in reply. "You would've handled it," he said. "If you found out about Summer's pregnancy back then."

She gave him a wry smile. "I would've thrown a plate at your head."

"Like I said. Handled it." He put an arm around her and she rested against his shoulder for a brief lovely moment before easing away.

"I've got to go."

"Still hunting Craig Canning?"

"On his home turf, no less. But you watch—I'll get him."

He grinned. "I have no doubt."

"Are you going to hang here?" she asked as she shouldered her bag.

"Yeah. Cassidy always slinks in eventually. Figure I'll stick around until she shows."

"I'm sure she'll turn up soon."

Nick turned worried eyes toward the elevator. "Yeah. Soon."

Annalisa skipped the elevator and took the stairs to the floor below the surgical unit, where she found an empty patient room and changed into the scrubs. She left her street clothes and her bag in the wardrobe cabinet, tightened her hair into a sleek knot, and affixed one of the hospital's surgical masks to her face. This was one bonus to the pandemic: there were boxes of masks everywhere, free for the taking. She poked her head out of the room, saw no one around, and darted for the stairs.

Upstairs, she held her breath as she passed the first white-coated doctor, but the woman didn't give her a second glance. Annalisa walked with authority, like she knew where she was going, even as she cast around for any sign of a schedule. At the nurses' station, a woman wearing similar purple scrubs as Annalisa was busy at a computer. Annalisa sidled up to the counter and lifted the nearest clipboard for a peek at the paper grid laid out on top. It was documenting check-ins with patients, not listing any operating schedule. She returned it and moved around the station to look at the whiteboard mounted on the wall. It had magnets with people's names on them and appeared to be a shift schedule. She did not see Canning's name listed anywhere.

"Excuse me," said a brusque male voice. She jumped out of the way as an orderly passed her with a cart. Heart hammering, she looked past him down the hall and deduced this must be patient rooms. She had to get closer to the operating room itself. She walked in the opposite direction, past the elevators to the east wing where she saw signs for the OR. The ratio of nurses to doctors changed, and now her scrubs stood out more. She avoided eye contact and continued to act like she knew what she was doing. *Aha,* she thought when a new whiteboard came into view. This one did have Canning's name on it. He'd been on since noon and was scheduled for OR time again at 7 p.m. His next shift was due to start at noon the next day and run until at least eight at night, so she had several opportunities to investigate his apartment.

Satisfied, she turned on her heels and bumped directly into Craig Canning. She tensed as he grabbed her shoulders to steady her. "Whoa, there," he said. "The hospital is full enough. We don't need to create more patients." He ducked his head, trying to look her in the face with his charm at full wattage.

"Sorry," she mumbled, keeping her chin down. She saw his features change to confusion and knew recognition would be next. She squeezed between him and the wall and began a brisk walk for the elevator.

"Wait," he called after her.

She sped up.

"Hold on there!"

She shifted into a sprint and threaded her way through the clump of people waiting by the elevator. She crashed through the door to the staircase, thundering down the steps. She heard the door open above her on the stairwell and presumed he was still in pursuit. She exited on the floor where she'd left her clothes and fled into the first available open room. An old woman sat up in the bed eating a bowl of pudding. She looked surprised and then pleased to see Annalisa. "Hello," she offered, waving her spoon.

Annalisa put her finger to her lips and ran for the bathroom. The old woman mirrored her *shh* gesture with a shaky hand. Annalisa shrank against the tile wall and listened for any sign of Canning. Moments later, she heard someone enter the room. The old lady said hello again. "Have you seen a female nurse come by just now?" Canning's voice interrogated her. "Dark hair, about this tall, wearing purple scrubs?"

Annalisa screwed her eyes shut. The old woman replied, "Oh, this pudding is delicious. Would you like some?"

"No," Canning said, sounding troubled. "No, thank you." Then he left.

Annalisa waited another few minutes before she crept out of the bathroom. "Thanks," she said to the old woman. "I owe you one."

"I lied," the woman said. "The pudding is terrible." She put her spoon down with distaste, and Annalisa peered in for a closer look at the congealed beige mess. She had to agree. "The one who came in looking for you," said the old woman in a quavering voice, "is he a bad doctor?"

"He's a good doctor," Annalisa admitted with a glance over her shoulder. "But he's a bad man."

"You'd better go then. Before he comes back."

"I will, thanks." Annalisa checked the hall for any sign of Canning, and finding none, went back to the room where she'd left her things. She swiftly removed the scrubs and changed back into her regular clothes. On her way out, she found a bin labeled DIRTY SCRUBS and added hers to the pile. She couldn't imagine wearing scrubs out of the hospital, although she had seen plenty of people who did, including Craig Canning. Wouldn't they have germs and other contaminants? Annalisa knew too much about the transfer of evidence to be comfortable with the idea.

As she hurried out of the building, she considered evidence transfer some more. Craig Canning said he'd changed his clothes on the morning of Vicki Albright's death. If she could figure out what he'd initially been wearing, maybe there would be evidence of his involvement there as well. Of course, if he were smart, he'd have ditched the clothes already, like the hoodie she'd found near the scene of the fire at Mara's office.

Annalisa halted in her car, her hand on the gearshift. The hoodie. Of course. She'd found Mara's hair there because that's what Canning wanted her to find. The pair spent so much time together, it would have been easy for him to pick up some of her stray hairs to plant on the hoodie. But if he'd worn it, his hair might also be there. Annalisa put the car into gear, the engine roaring beneath her as she peeled out of the hospital garage. She raced home as fast as she dared and fell upon the bag with the hoodie she'd saved from the day after the fire. She put on gloves before pulling out the sweatshirt. With a flashlight, she examined it carefully for short, dark hairs. She found none, but her eyes caught a silvery glint of something buried in the weave.

"Wait," she said as she put her face closer. "What's this?" She took her tweezers and extracted a white animal hair, thin and several inches long—as if from a purebred white cat.

THIRTY

....

MARA'S OFFICE BUILDING HAD BEEN CLEANED ENOUGH TO REOPEN ON ONE SIDE. Her hallway remained blocked off, awaiting repairs, and the dean had not offered her any temporary space in the interim. He still thought there was a chance she'd torched the place herself. Hazel Kennedy, the department secretary, had notified Mara of a box of items, things that the cleaners had rescued in their excavation of her charred office, so Mara dropped by campus to retrieve it. "Sorry about what happened," Hazel told her as she handed over the cardboard box containing a terra-cotta plant holder, now devoid of plant; scissors and a stapler; a round paperweight; and inexplicably, half a box of tissues. For this, Mara had braved afternoon rush-hour traffic? "Do they know who did it yet?" Hazel asked.

"It was Craig Canning," said a voice behind her. Miles Dupont. She repressed a sigh and turned to face him. His face was red and she saw he held a paper bag in his hands. "She knows it, she just won't admit it. She can't because then her whole book deal would go up in smoke just like her office."

"You don't know it was him. Neither do I." She didn't have the energy for a vigorous defense of Craig right now, not after what Annalisa had told her about Vicki's death. She wanted to go home and sleep for a hundred years.

"The hell I don't." He upended the paper bag and a creature fell out right onto Mara's feet. She yelped and jumped backward.

"What is that?"

"A dead frog. An American bullfrog, to be exact. I found it on my desk this morning, courtesy of your favorite psycho."

Miles really had lost the plot. "That's ridiculous."

"Is it? No one else calls me a frog-licker."

"Did someone say frog-licker?" Canning poked his head into the room, like he'd been lurking in the hall waiting for his cue. "Oh, there he is. Licked any good ones today?"

"You're a shithead," Miles said. "Killing an animal over a stupid grade-school prank. You're no genius. You're just a dumb bully."

"Whereas calling someone a shithead is an erudite response," Canning replied, amused. "Grade school indeed."

"See!" Miles pointed at him. "He admitted it. He admitted he murdered the frog to provoke me."

"I didn't hear that." Canning leaned over and helped himself to one of the wrapped mints on Hazel's desk. "Did you ladies hear any kind of confession?" He glanced down and recoiled at the sight of the dead frog. "Good lord, Miles. You're carrying them around with you now? Get help, my man."

Miles lunged for Canning but Mara stepped between them. "Don't," she told Miles. "It's not worth it."

Miles's eyes were wild. "You better to do something to stop him," he told Mara. "Or I will."

"Oh no," Canning said in falsetto. "Maybe he'll lick me to death."

Hazel tittered, her hand to her mouth. Mara urged Miles toward the door. "I will handle him. I promise."

Miles didn't look like he believed her. "Serial killers murder helpless animals," he muttered. "If he'd do it to the frog, he'd do it to you."

Mara managed to get Miles out of the building. When she returned, Canning sucked loudly on the mint and gave her the crazy eyes. "It's true," he told her. "I'm a wanted man. My bloodlust knows no bounds. Even now, my picture is up in frog post offices across the globe."

Hazel giggled some more, but Mara put her hands on her hips. "Shut up. Did you do it?"

"Do what?" All humor vanished from his voice. Mara's mouth went dry as his eyes bored into hers. She stammered and he stepped closer to her. "Do what?" he repeated, his tone dangerously soft. "Ask me what you really want to know."

She couldn't. "Get that thing out of here," she whispered, pointing down at the frog.

He picked up the creature by one leg and tossed it with a clean arc into the waste can. "Ew," said Hazel. "I don't want it here."

"Then dump it out," Canning said as he took Mara's elbow. "We need to talk."

"We can't," she said as he started marching her toward the door. "My office is burned, remember?"

He said nothing but pushed open the nearest door, the one that led to the stairs. His grip remained strong on her arm as he took her with him to the roof. The gray clouds that hung low over the city all day had turned dark. Wind blew her hair back and cut through her light spring jacket like a knife. She shivered but Canning didn't seem cold as he released his hold on her and went to the edge of the roof. "We have a problem," he said, his back to her. "Annalisa Vega."

"What about her?" She took a cautious step forward. Annalisa had told her not to confront Canning, but he was the one who'd forced this meeting. If she could get him to admit to something, this whole ordeal would be over. She slipped her hand into her loose pocket and activated her phone, glancing down long enough to ensure she had set it to record. "I took her off the case. You know that."

"She didn't get the message. I caught her snooping around the hospital today."

"What did she want?"

"I have no idea. You tell me. You're the one who put her on this crazy mission."

Mara concentrated on her breathing. *Look normal.* In, out. In, out. "She thinks you killed Vicki Albright," she said as neutrally as she could.

Canning whirled on her. "Whose fault is that? She thinks I did it because you told her I did."

"I never said that!"

"Come off it, Mara." He grabbed her again. "You hired her. You must have told her something."

"Ow, you're hurting me." She wriggled but he held her tight. "I hired her to make sure. I had to be sure. Vicki had accused you of rap—"

"I never touched that girl," he roared, shaking her. "Never. I don't know why she made up those lies."

"Stop it, Craig. Let me go . . ."

He looked down at his white fingers around her twisted arm and abruptly released his hold on her. She staggered backward, rubbing her bruised arm, while he stalked to the edge of the roof again. He scanned the darkening campus as though searching for something. "You have to make her stop. The hospital is already on edge about the book coverage. They're not sure a friendly psychopath is good PR."

"Too late for that."

He turned around to glare at her. "This is your career on the line too, I remind you. I go down and so do you."

She was well aware. She edged closer to him so the phone would be sure to catch what he said. "She's admiring of it, you know," she told him. "Annalisa. She thinks you pulled off the perfect crime."

"I'd have to. I was at the hospital when it happened. Maybe I've invented human cloning—look out, here comes another bestseller."

"She thinks . . ." She hesitated. She had to tread carefully here. Any admission would have to come from him. "She thinks she's worked out how you did it. How you killed Vicki Albright."

"Oh yes? Tell me then."

"Maybe you could tell me," she ventured, her hand skimming the cold stone edge at the top of the building. "I'm very curious."

He studied her a long moment before giving her an animal-like grin, one that showed his teeth. "I bet you are." He stretched out a hand and brushed her windswept hair from her cheek. "I see it now. What this is about."

She forced herself to remain still under his touch. "What's that?" she said, her voice catching.

"About your ego."

"My ego?" She felt genuinely shocked. "I didn't even know that girl."

"But you claimed to know me. You wrote a whole book on me. How could you have missed this?" He caressed her cheek as he spoke. "How could you have got me so wrong? You're supposed to be the expert. It must be so galling to think you'd misread me completely."

She swallowed with difficulty. Her gaze went to the door, some thirty feet away. It shouldn't be locked. Not unless they'd closed the whole building for the night. What time was it again? "You're saying Annalisa is right about you," she said, still trying to get him to admit something on record.

He withdrew his hand, looking disappointed. "All the time we've spent together," he said, "and you don't know the truth."

"What is the truth?" She almost begged him to reveal it.

He shook his head. "I think you know. I think you wouldn't be up here on this roof with me otherwise. What if I were to pitch you over the edge like Vicki Albright?"

Her heart sped up. Almost. Almost an admission. Had the phone caught it? She glanced at the door again, torn between running for it and moving closer to him to make sure the phone recorded all his words. She was so close. "You wouldn't do that," she said, trying to sound sure of herself.

He raised his eyebrows. "Wouldn't I? You should know, Doctor. You should know everything I'm capable of."

"There are witnesses." Even as she said it, she looked down to see the general area was desolate. Classes were done. This wasn't a residential part of campus. But they were also only about five stories high. "Also, I could live. Many people have survived falls greater than this one. Then where would you be?" She sounded braver than she felt.

He made a *maybe, maybe not* gesture with his hand. "I'd give you a fifty-fifty shot."

"Not great odds."

He looked amused once more. "For whom?" When she didn't reply, he leaned out over the roofline, peering down below. "Get Annalisa Vega to drop her crusade," he told her. "Or I'll tell your husband how we really met."

Fury rose up in her. "Fine, tell him," she said tartly, calling his bluff. They had a game of mutually assured destruction. "I'll get divorced but you're still totally screwed."

"I don't see how."

She laughed without humor. "Annalisa told me you'd looked her up. Did you fail to notice what she's famous for? The woman turned in her own father for murder. Her father. You think she'll ever stop coming after you?"

He looked taken aback for a moment, then storm clouds gathered in his eyes. "She'll stop when I stop her."

"Like you stopped Vicki Albright?"

He crossed over to her, close enough to kiss. For a moment, she thought he would. He traced her cheek with one finger, a lover's touch, but his mouth was twisted when he said, "Like I can stop you."

THIRTY-ONE

············

CASSIDY SAT ON THE COLD TILE FLOOR IN THE TINY BATHROOM WITH HER BACK TO THE DOOR. Her rear end had gone numb an hour ago. When Tony first shoved her into the room and barricaded the door, she'd ransacked the place looking for anything she could find to get her out of this situation, but the bathroom held only a chipped sink, a toilet with rust stains in the bowl, and a cruddy shower with a moldy curtain. There wasn't even a razor. Cassidy had tried banging on the window, but the small square wasn't even made of glass. The hard, clear plastic didn't budge no matter how hard she pounded on it, and Tony had heard her banging and hollered through the door. "You make another sound and I'll shove a sock down your throat."

A hot tear escaped her eye and she let it roll down her cheek as her head lolled back against the door. She had made so many mistakes. Coming here. Thinking she could fix things for Naomi. This was the worst part of the whole disaster: Naomi's mom was a psychopath, a criminal. She would never give up her kidney. Cassidy's efforts had been doomed from the start and now she'd maybe be killed herself as well as Naomi. *My dad is a cop.*

She clung to this hope. Tried not to think how silly it was. Naomi's mom, as awful as she was, had been with the family until Naomi was two and a half. Nick had known Cassidy six months. Sure, he seemed to like her okay, but he'd been just fine before she showed up and he'd be fine when she was gone. Still, Nick was a cop. She wrapped herself in this knowledge like it was a comforting blanket. He knew how to deal with people like Lizzie and Tony. His job was to find missing kids like her, and he was super good at it. "You shouldn't do this. My dad's a cop." She'd thrown the words at Lizzie when the woman dragged her into the building. Lizzie had told her to shut up but Cassidy had seen a look of fear in the woman's eyes. Nick would come for her, she knew it. She just had to hang on long enough for him to find her.

She pressed an ear to the door. She couldn't hear them talking anymore on the other side, and this was worse somehow than the furious shouting from before. They started screaming at each other the moment Lizzie burst through the door with Cassidy in tow. Tony sat at the kitchen table with a bunch of different-colored pills and plastic baggies. "What the hell?" he'd demanded, leaping to his feet.

"This little bitch was going through our trash. She knows. She knows something."

"She's a kid!"

"Help me," Cassidy had said, sending Tony a pleading look. She hoped she looked as helpless as she felt. "I don't know her. I don't know anything."

"Bullshit," Lizzie said as she'd grabbed her tighter. The knife had pressed closer against her ribs. "She knows my name. She knows who I am."

Tony wasn't pleased. "And now she knows me too. She's seen my face, the pills, the whole operation. Jesus, Lizzie, what the hell were you thinking, bringing her up here?"

"I'll go. I'll go right now. I won't say anything." Cassidy had even started inching for the door. Lizzie stopped her.

"She can't go. Her dad's a cop. She'll tell him everything."

Tony let out a string of expletives at this news. "A fucking cop? Way to go, Lizzie."

This was when Cassidy had ended up trapped in the bathroom. Her captors hollered at each other for a while, each blaming the other for the screwup. Cassidy's stomach churned at the silence. As long as they were screaming, they weren't doing anything to her. She got up and paced the narrow bathroom. She didn't know how long she'd been gone now, but the plastic window showed it was dark outside. People would be missing her. *You turned off your phone,* she reminded herself. *They can't track you.*

Nick can, she thought, tamping down her rising panic. Nick would find a way. Or Annalisa would. They had found the Lovelorn Killer. Surely they could find a couple of asshole losers like Naomi's mom and this Tony guy.

Yeah, Nick will find them after Tony dumps your body in the lake, the voice in her head taunted her. Cassidy clapped her hands over her ears and screamed internally.

She jerked her head up when she heard a door slam. The front door, meaning someone had left. Whoever remained paced around the kitchen, shoving chairs and slamming drawers shut. Maybe they were looking for a knife. A bigger one than Naomi's mom had pulled on her earlier. *I'm dead,* she thought. She went to the toilet because she feared she might throw up. Her mother's voice cut through the roar of blood inside her head.

Self-pity doesn't help. Take action and you'll feel better.

I tried. I tried. Cassidy whirled in a circle, searching again for anything she could use against her captors. She yanked on the shower rod with all her might and it pulled free, sending her sprawling backward. She grabbed for it with eager hands as the dingy curtain fell to the floor.

To her dismay, she found the rod was thin and hollow, not suitable as a weapon. She fingered the rounded O edge and wondered if she could sharpen it somehow. As she considered her lack of options, the door to the apartment opened and she heard voices again. She pressed her ear to the door to listen.

"I found her backpack by the trash bins," Lizzie said. "Her phone's off, so we have that on our side."

"But she could've told someone she was coming here. Like her dad, the cop?"

"I know that," Lizzie snapped. "That's why we've got to move quick. Look, she's got a laptop on her."

"Good, we can sell that."

"God, you're a moron. We have to destroy it when we get rid of her. It's traceable too."

"What do you mean, get rid of her?" Tony asked. Cassidy's blood went cold. *Get rid of me?*

"We'll have to leave. We can't stay here in this same apartment. Even if she didn't tell her father where she was going, she knows my kid. We can't take chances. We have to take everything and go."

"You have a kid?"

"Duh. You've seen the page I set up about her. The one people keep sending us all that cash for."

"But that's not real. You said she doesn't exist."

"Okay, so she does, all right? She exists. And apparently this kid knows her. Who the hell knows what they've found out about me? If this girl found me, Naomi can too. My ex . . . all kinds of shit could rain down on us."

Tony let loose more expletives. "This was not the plan, Lizzie. I never agreed to any of this."

"Hey, it wasn't my idea either. She just showed up here and now we've got to deal with her."

Cassidy shut her eyes and tried to think. Her time was running out and Nick wouldn't be coming through the door. This was how it would be now. She was on her own. *Think, think,* she ordered herself. There was nothing in the damn room. Nothing to fight with or draw attention to herself. The bathroom had just a toilet, sink, shower and . . . she noticed a drop of water fall from the faucet. Water.

She took the filthy shower curtain and placed it over the sink drain. Then she turned on the tap. Outside, Lizzie and Tony were arguing again, their voices rising.

"I'm not part of this. I can't do it," Tony insisted.

The small sink filled within a few minutes and water started spilling over the edge. The apartment was on the top floor of the building. Pretty soon, the water would find the cracks in the floor and drip down to the apartment underneath. *Please be home,* she prayed as the gushing continued. She backed up into the shower so she wouldn't get her feet wet. The water pooled on the floor and began forming a river to the back corner near the toilet.

"I can't kill a kid." Tony had stopped yelling but still she heard him clearly. She held her breath. He was close, on the other side of the door. He sounded so determined that Cassidy thought he might come rescue her.

But Lizzie's voice was close too. "Fine then," she said. "I will."

THIRTY-TWO

....

ALONG WITH HER OFFICE, ANNALISA HAD INHERITED A SMALL CABINET OF GOODS FROM SAM TRAN, THE PREVIOUS PI WHO HAD WORKED THERE. Some, like the fake beard, were not helpful to her, but she took the binoculars and a small can of sulfur spray when she went to Craig Canning's apartment building. She used the binoculars to scope out his place from the ground floor. She saw no illumination or signs that he was home, as expected. He was supposed to be in surgery at the hospital. Next, she knocked on Ruth Bernstein's door. She felt somewhat guilty about involving the sweet old lady in her plan, using her the way Canning had, but Ruth would sell the cover much better than Annalisa could.

"I don't understand," she said when Annalisa explained the plan. "Why do you want to get inside Dr. Canning's apartment?"

Annalisa hesitated, unsure of how much to reveal. "I think he may have been the one to let Duchess escape."

Ruth's white curls seemed to stand on end. "I knew it," she said.

Annalisa had not expected this. "You what?"

"The other day when we were in the elevator together, I saw white hairs on Dr. Canning's jacket. I thought I must be hallucinating because

I miss her so much. Dr. Canning doesn't like cats, so he wouldn't keep one for himself. But, I thought, maybe he knows something. And now here you are, saying he let her out? You think it was he who stole my key from the super's office?"

"I think so, yes."

"The devil," Ruth muttered, her hands clenched into fists. "Tell me again what you need me to do."

Annalisa went to Ruth's kitchen and sprayed the sulfur liberally in the air. Ruth made a face at the foul smell and Annalisa breathed through her mouth. "Call the front desk and report you have a gas leak. That should bring Damon up here to check it out."

"I'll do it right now."

"Wait two minutes for me to get back to the lobby first."

Ruth nodded as Annalisa turned to go. She stopped her with a hand on her arm. "You don't think . . . You don't think he could be keeping her?" she asked, a note of hope in her voice. "Maybe that's why he has the hairs on his clothes? Duchess is a terrible shedder."

"I will be sure to look."

Ruth seemed to hear what Annalisa did not say, that she did not expect to find the cat, because her face fell. Her thin lips set in determination. "Let's get him," she whispered as she gave Annalisa a slight push toward the door.

Annalisa raced down fourteen flights of stairs and arrived breathless at the lobby just in time to crack the door open and hear Damon receive Ruth's call. "Okay, Mrs. B. You're going to leave your apartment and wait for me in the hall, okay? Get out of there just to be safe. I'm coming up." Annalisa let the door fall back into place as Damon jogged over close to her to hit the elevator button. When he had gone, she hurried to his desk, where, as she had hoped, he'd left his keys sitting next to his travel mug and his open textbook. She took the keys and found the one that opened the super's office, where she then removed his key from his desk where she had found it earlier. She opened the cabinet with the keys in it and took Canning's from its hook. Holding the key tight in one hand, she used a bit of tape to keep the super's office door from locking and then replaced Damon's keys on the front desk. She took the elevator up to Canning's apartment, which opened with no problem when she inserted her stolen key.

She walked in without turning on the lights. She navigated to the main living area next to the big sliding doors that led out to the balcony. Directly across the courtyard, she could see Ruth's apartment lit from one end to the other. Ruth and Damon were just visible in the kitchen. Annalisa turned her attention from them and began her search of Canning's place. If he'd kept the missing charm from the wind chimes as a souvenir, it probably had a place of honor. Somewhere close where he could see it often. She turned on a flashlight and headed for the bedroom. Bracing herself, she searched his nightstand. Condoms, lube, a battery charger. A magazine cover that had his picture on it along with some other young professionals. "Chicago's Rising Stars." Annalisa felt along the edges of the drawer but only found loose change and what looked like an inexpensive wedding ring. She did not want to imagine what this might be a trophy for.

Moving on, she searched the dresser, pawing through his watches and cuff links. Nothing. She tried the adjoining bathroom next and also came up empty. She stopped briefly at his closet, pausing long enough to look his suit jackets over for any traces of white fur. She did not see any. With growing frustration, she shifted her search to the office. Canning had literal trophies here, everything from medical awards to a plaque for placing first in his age group in a half marathon three years earlier, but she did not see the missing charm. She searched the desk and in the top drawer found a gun with ammunition, which made her stop to take a closer look. She recognized the revolver because her father had owned one, a Smith & Wesson 57. The gun took a .41 cartridge and had been created with the police in mind, positioned between the lighter .357 and heavier .44, but they hadn't really caught on. Outside her father's, she'd only seen one other in all her years on the force. Her phone buzzed with a text, practically scaring her to death. Nick's name flashed on the screen. *Cassidy's missing. Need your help.*

The girl had gone missing practically every damn day this week. Annalisa ignored the text and continued searching Canning's apartment. The spare bedroom held more of his clothes and his golf clubs in the closet. The library displayed everything from serious medical texts and classic literature to detective thrillers and erotica. She picked up every little statue and knickknack, examining them for hidden compartments. She opened every drawer. Back in the living area, she even removed the couch cushions and felt under the edge of the coffee table. She was sweaty from her exertion, hair coming loose from its knot, and she stood up in the dark to take a moment to breathe. Across the way, she could see Ruth out on her balcony, watching the apartment. She could perhaps see the beam from Annalisa's flashlight as Anna gave a little wave.

At that moment, a slight breeze jingled Canning's wind chimes out on the balcony. He had two sets, one at each end, both done by the same artist who had made the ones found at the scene of Vicki Albright's death. His go-to move, Mara had said. Annalisa walked to the glass doors to watch the crystals twisting in the wind. What better place would there be to hide the missing charm than on a set he already owned? She slid open the door and walked onto the balcony, where she pulled the picture of Vicki's wind chimes from her back pocket. The crystals on her set had been tinted yellow to match the jaguar's eyes.

Annalisa shone her light at one of Canning's wind chimes and squinted for a better look. These crystals were darker, more green or blue. She moved to the other set. They featured a snow leopard at the top and the crystals appeared clear from her vantage point. Annalisa dragged a teak chair over so she could stand on it to get closer to the chimes. As she stood there close to the edge she had a moment's pause when she realized how similar her position was to the one Vicki Albright had been in when she purportedly fell. The chair teetered as Annalisa's balance wobbled, but she extended her arm downward to steady herself on the balcony's edge. The wind picked up, blowing the charms away from her. She righted herself and put one hand behind them to keep them still as she shone her flashlight on them with her other hand. She started the beam at the top and moved it gradually down each strand. The difference between clear and pale yellow would be difficult to spot. At the base of the third strand, she halted. This charm looked different. It was slightly larger and . . . she put her face close to it, tilting it back and forth. Yes. This one was yellow. She would have done a celebratory dance if she weren't perched on a chair fourteen stories in the air.

She couldn't take the charm with her as proof. She had no legal right to be here and Canning would argue she'd planted the thing to frame him. She snapped a few pictures of the charm with her phone, hoping it might be enough to convince Nick to reopen the investigation into Vicki's death so he could do a legal search of Canning's home. As if he'd heard her thoughts, Nick called, the phone ringing in Annalisa's hand. She did not answer. She had to get out of there.

She replaced the chair, turned off her flashlight, and prepared to go. Before she could open the sliding glass door, a light came on in the apartment. She froze. Canning appeared a moment later, looking relaxed as he dumped his mail on the coffee table and slung his jacket over the sofa. Annalisa shrank back against the side of the building. She had just been in the living room and knew that the glare from his lights meant he couldn't see out onto the balcony, but now she was trapped here unless he left again. Heart pounding, she looked at the four-foot gap between where she stood and the balcony next door. If Canning had made it across, so could she, but then she'd just be trapped on a different balcony. Still, that balcony didn't belong to a psychopathic murderer. She was willing to risk it.

She put one leg up on the balcony edge. *Don't look down.* In the second she took to gather her courage, the glass doors opened. Canning came out into the darkness. Annalisa stifled her gasp and remained stock still, pinned in her awkward position at the balcony's shadowed edge. He crossed to the front. She felt him only a few feet away, then smelled the lit cigarette. Her leg started to ache and she was sure he could hear her heart thumping through her chest.

"Are you going to jump or what?" he said, sounding faintly amused.

The breath she'd been holding came out in a painful rush. She released her position. "No."

"Pity," he replied.

She faced him. "You're not at the hospital. You're supposed to be in surgery."

"Patient coded." He paused to take a drag. "Sometimes they die before I can get to them, which I guess is bad luck for you. You've been following me. First today at the hospital, now here you are on my balcony. I should call the police."

"Do it." They probably wouldn't even write her up, but at worst, she'd get a trip downtown and away from here, where Canning stood between her and the door. She looked him over as best she could in the light pouring from the living room. He appeared mostly in shadow and she couldn't tell if he was armed. He had one gun she knew about and he could have more. Her own hand hovered near the weapon holstered at her hip.

He laughed gently at her enthusiasm. "Yes, I agree, Detective. The boys in blue are more likely to take your side than mine. So then . . . what? How do we resolve this little problem?"

Her phone rang again. Probably Nick. She ignored it and maintained eye contact with Canning. "You could move aside and let me leave."

"Ah, but you just got here. And you haven't told me anything about what you're doing here."

The phone stopped ringing. "I wanted to see if it was possible to climb from one balcony to another."

"If someone could have climbed onto Vicki's, you mean." He smoked as he considered and then moved closer to her to investigate the distance for himself. "It looks easy enough," he said before taking a drag. He blew smoke out in her face. "Is that how you think I did it?"

"I think it was part of the plan, yes."

He pondered this, tapping his ash off the side of the balcony. "Interesting theory. But you can't prove it."

She almost could. *Almost.* She wished she were recording this whole conversation. "It's a nearly perfect crime," she admitted. "The only real hint that something is up with the timeline is the 911 call that came in just before Ruth Bernstein said she witnessed Vicki's fall."

"Is that so? Still . . . a few minutes either way hardly proves anything. Clocks can be wrong." He smiled around his cigarette. "So can humans." Her phone rang again, and Canning removed his cigarette to gesture with it at her pocket. "Are you ever going to answer that?"

She flinched. He wanted her to answer it? It felt like a trap. Slowly, she used her left hand to comply, keeping the right one near her weapon. Of course it was Nick again. "Where are you?" he said as soon as she picked up. "I've been trying to reach you for more than an hour. Cassidy's missing."

She hadn't caught the time, but it couldn't be more than ten. The girl hadn't been gone that long. She was probably holed up in the hospital cafeteria, drinking bad coffee and waiting for someone to find her. Annalisa felt for the kid. She'd been that kid—the one bleeding inside because her family was coming apart and there was nothing she could do to stop it. You wanted to rage. You wanted to make people feel as scared and as hurt as you felt, so maybe they would understand. You wanted to run away and hide. Cassidy's little disappearing act accomplished all of that. Annalisa heard the fear in Nick's voice, the terror of a parent who couldn't find his kid. She hoped he realized what she knew, that he was definitely Cassidy's dad. "I'm at Craig Canning's," she said, keeping one eye on the doctor. He'd crushed out his smoke and was eavesdropping openly on her conversation.

"You're what?" The shock of her answer pulled Nick from his panic.

"We're having a chat."

"Well, wrap it up. I need your help. Melanie and I have called around and checked everywhere. No one has seen Cassidy since school today. She was in class but she didn't get on the bus."

"Where did she go?"

"No one knows." She heard traffic noises that told her Nick was in his car. "I'm driving around near the school, looking for her. Melanie's checking her favorite coffee places. We could really use another set of eyes."

"Okay, okay. What do you want me to do?"

"I don't know. Maybe check your office? That's where she went before."

"Will do. We'll find her, Nick. Don't worry."

"Yeah," he said, plainly not listening. "Call me if you find anything."

She hung up with Nick and looked to Canning. "I've got to go now."

He didn't move to unblock her path. "Trouble on the home front?"

"My stepdaughter didn't turn up after school today, so we're trying to track her down." She took a step forward and he shifted so she couldn't pass him. "Let me go."

"That's the young lady from your office, right? Cassidy."

Annalisa felt a prickle down her back. She'd forgotten they had met. "Yes," she said carefully. "That's her."

He nodded as if to himself. "I might know where she's gone." He paused and glanced down at her with a smug smile on his lips. "I might even be willing to tell you."

She bit back the urge to smack him. "Okay . . . so tell me."

"First you agree to leave me alone."

Bullshit. He was probably playing her anyway. The odds he knew something useful in this situation were slim. "Confess to killing Vicki Albright and I'll leave you alone. Otherwise . . ." She shrugged. "No can do."

"Good luck then, finding your stepdaughter." He moved aside. "She went looking for trouble. If she's not home yet, I'd bet she found it."

She should go. She'd have better luck driving the streets than getting help from a sociopathic liar. She moved to leave but stopped herself. "If you are what Mara says . . . if you're what she wrote in her book . . . then you should help me. A good sociopath, remember? That's your story. You're beneficial to humanity."

He narrowed his eyes at her. "You read the book?"

"I did. Tell me, Doctor. Is it fact or fiction?"

He stroked his chin as he thought about it. "It's about winning. It's about what's in it for me. Didn't Mara make that clear?"

"Convincing me you're a good guy is a win for you."

He grinned and shook his head like he'd been had. "You may be right about that." He waited another beat. "She's going after that woman, her friend's mother."

"Elizabeth Johnston."

He nodded. "She had a lead—a clever one. She said she was going to tell you about it."

Annalisa felt the words like a slap in her face. Cassidy had tried to tell her. She hadn't listened. Now she'd have to beg the sociopath. "You tell me," she said, her jaw tight. He made her wait. "Please."

He relaxed at her plea and smiled. "The woman set up a crowdfunding site for the girl. She was cashing in on her daughter's illness. Cassidy decided to track her at the post office box the woman was using as an address."

Annalisa bit back a curse. The post office would be closed for hours yet. "Okay," she said, heading for the door. She hesitated on the threshold and looked back over her shoulder in a moment of doubt. Maybe he was a good sociopath after all. "Thanks."

She didn't wait to pick up the phone. She called Naomi before she'd even left the building. The girl picked up before the first ring had completed. "Did you find her?" Naomi asked, sounding frantic. "Did you find Cassidy?"

"Not yet. Do you know where she went? The truth now."

"I don't," Naomi said with a groan. "I don't know anything. I texted her hours ago but she hasn't seen it. She isn't picking up her phone."

"Is your father there?"

Naomi went quiet. "My father?"

"I need to speak to him." Annalisa hit the cold night air. If anyone knew how to track down Elizabeth Johnston, she felt sure it would be him. His kid's life was on the line. Now Cassidy's was too.

"You said we could keep him out of it."

"That was before Cassidy went missing. She's out looking for your mom, Naomi. I need to know if your dad has any idea where to find her, and I need to know now."

"He doesn't."

"I want to hear that from him."

The girl hesitated another moment, and then Annalisa heard her moving. "Dad . . ."

"What are you doing up?" A male voice cut her off.

"Dad, listen. Cassidy's gone missing. Her stepmother is on the phone and she wants to talk to you."

"Me, why?"

Another stretch of silence. "She's a PI. I hired her to look for Mom."

Annalisa heard a muffled curse and then the male voice came on the line. "This is Ken Nakamura speaking."

"Mr. Nakamura, I'm Annalisa Vega. I'm married to Cassidy Weaver's father, Nick Carelli. I'm sorry to be calling so late."

"Yes, she's mentioned you once before, I think. How can I help you?"

"Cassidy disappeared this afternoon after school and we have reason to believe she's trying to track down Naomi's mother, Elizabeth Johnston."

Ken Nakamura's voice was tight and angry. "I told her very clearly she wasn't to do that."

"I understand, but Cassidy really cares about Naomi and she—"

"You think I don't?" He broke in with a raw cry. "You think I don't care about my daughter?"

"No, I'm sure you love her deeply. As . . . as we love Cassidy. That's why I'm calling to see if you have any idea at all about how to contact Elizabeth Johnston."

He said nothing for such a long time that Annalisa wondered if the line had gone dead. Finally, he said, "Go to your room. Go to bed."

"But Dad—"

"Do it now." He used the parent tone that brooked no argument. Annalisa heard retreating footsteps and then a door opening and closing. The noise of a passing car told her that Ken had gone outside. "I don't know how to find her," he said to Annalisa. "I don't want to find her."

"Not even if she could be a match to your daughter?"

He barked a laugh. "Lizzie is nothing like my daughter. You hear me? Nothing."

"I'm sorry. I know Lizzie is . . . challenging. I still need to find her."

"You really think Cassidy could be with her?"

"I think it's possible, yes."

He swore again. "I hope not."

"Anything," Annalisa said urgently, "anything you can tell me that would help me find her."

"I really don't know. I haven't seen or spoken to her in years. When we met, she told me she was from a little town in Idaho called Bonners Ferry. Her parents had a farm, she said, until they fell on hard times. Her father couldn't make the payments and they were going to lose the whole place. So he decided the government wasn't going to get him or his land. He shot the mother, shot Lizzie and her little brother, lit the place on fire, and then shot himself. Only Lizzie survived. She showed me the scar on her side, told me how she'd played dead on the floor of the barn and then crawled through the smoke and fire to get help."

"That's an amazing story."

"And a fictional one," he said curtly. "I found out when she ran out on me and Naomi. She didn't leave a note. Just emptied our savings account and ran. I thought maybe it was some post-traumatic thing connected to her childhood. She said she didn't have any family left, but I thought she might . . . I don't know . . . go home again. I went to Bonners Ferry to look for her. You should've seen the look on the sheriff's face when I mentioned her name. They remember her, all right. She shot her whole family at age fourteen and tried to pin it on her father. The farm wasn't going under. It was thriving. But Lizzie wanted to leave for the big city. Her father had said no, she wasn't going anywhere as long as he was in charge."

"So she shot him? Just like that?"

"And her mother and brother too. I guess she thought she'd inherit the farm and could sell it to start over somewhere else. She gave herself a flesh wound to try to sell the story but I guess the forensics didn't back her up. They arrested her within the week."

"What happened to her?" Annalisa asked.

"She did four years," he replied acidly. "She was released at eighteen and deemed rehabilitated. I guess she told them what they wanted to hear. Lizzie's good at that. Anyway, after what I found out about her, I wanted nothing more to do with her and I certainly didn't want Naomi mixed up with her. I—I can't believe she'd even be a match. There's no way. Naomi is nothing like her." He said this with such vehemence Annalisa felt her phone vibrate in her hands.

"I understand. But maybe you have some clue about where she might be? The last I heard, she had hooked up with a big thug of a boyfriend named Tony." It was a long shot, but long shots were all she had left.

"Tony? I don't know anything about him. Like I said, we're not in touch."

Lizzie had sent Naomi postcards. Maybe there was something there. "Could Naomi know? I gather this Tony was a wannabe actor. He'd appeared as an extra in some films."

"An actor? Like, a handsome guy?"

"I don't know what he looks like. Why?"

"Well, take this for what you will . . . I don't know Lizzie anymore. I'm not sure I ever did. But big, handsome guys were not her usual type. I found this out after she left and I started asking around about her. Lizzie went for the wallflowers, the shy or awkward-looking ones like me who didn't usually get noticed by a pretty girl. I guess she figured we're easier to manipulate."

Shy. Awkward-looking. I don't know Lizzie anymore. I'm not sure I ever did. Annalisa realized she had her lead already. She made an illegal U-turn on North Halstead and ignored the furious honk of the guy she'd cut off in traffic. Rory from the Liar's Club knew a lot more about Lizzie than he'd been telling. "Mr. Nakamura, thank you. You've been a big help."

"I have?" He blew out a breath. "I hope so. I hope you find Cassidy, and I hope she's not with Lizzie. If you find Lizzie . . ."

She held on and waited. "If I find her, what?"

"Watch your back."

THIRTY-THREE

....

CASSIDY STOOD IN THE SHOWER WITH HER BACK TO THE TILE, CLUTCHING THE BROKEN SHOWER ROD AS HER MEAGER WEAPON. The sink continued to overflow, water pooling across the entire back half of the bathroom, and she murmured a constant prayer that someone downstairs would notice. Nick had to be looking for her by now. She needed to hang on a little longer. Lizzie and Tony had ceased fighting and she heard footfalls approaching the bathroom. Someone was coming. Cassidy braced herself for the attack, and when the doorknob turned, she gasped and raised the rod over her head. No one appeared. She heard loud pounding.

Not at her door, she realized, dizzy with relief. Someone outside. She scrambled out of the shower, sloshing through the water on the floor. A woman with a Spanish accent was yelling in the apartment. "Water, everywhere! All over my place!"

"What do you want me to do about it?" Lizzie replied. "Call the super."

"It's coming from here! You've got a flood!"

This was her chance, Cassidy realized. "Help!" she shouted at the door, banging on it with all her strength. "Help, I'm kidnapped and they're going to kill me!"

"What's that?" The woman's voice turned suspicious.

"Nothing," Lizzie said. "The TV. Tony, go turn it down."

"Help me!" Cassidy screamed at the top of her lungs. "They're going to kill me."

Tony burst through the door, sending Cassidy backward into the wall. His eyes were wild, his face sweaty, like he'd taken the pills he'd had on the kitchen table earlier. "I told you to shut up," he growled as he grabbed her by the throat. Cassidy immediately began choking. Beyond the door, she could hear Lizzie making excuses to the woman.

"We'll check the taps and call the super, okay? Sorry for any trouble."

"Maybe I should check," the woman said. "See where it's coming from."

"Not necessary. I told you we're on it. Bye now."

Tony dragged Cassidy out of the bathroom by her neck. She clawed at his hands, trying to get free, but he was too strong. "Get the tape," he ordered Lizzie, and Lizzie opened a drawer to produce duct tape, which she fixed completely around Cassidy's head. Tony shoved her into a chair and Cassidy sucked in desperate breaths through her nose as her fiery lungs fought for air. Lizzie turned off the sink in the bathroom and reappeared with a towel in her hands.

"You see my point now? We've got to get rid of her."

Tony glared at Cassidy. "Yeah, but how? We can't kill her here."

"I know, I know. I'm thinking."

"Yeah? Well, think fast. Someone's going to come looking for her any second. Sooner if that bitch downstairs heard her screaming her head off."

Lizzie picked up Cassidy's backpack. "She won't call the cops. No one around here wants the pigs showing up. She'll call the super, though, and when he hears it's water, he'll actually get out of bed and come over here. We have to move her."

"Now?"

She shot him a look. "Right now. Get the keys and let's go."

Tony felt all over his body, checking pockets for the keys, which Lizzie retrieved from the counter and tossed at his head. He caught them one-handed. "This mess is all your fault," he complained, sulking like a fourth grader.

"That's why I'm cleaning it up," she said as she hauled Cassidy to her feet. "Come on now . . . and don't forget the knife."

THIRTY-FOUR

....

EN ROUTE TO THE LIAR'S CLUB, ANNALISA CALLED NICK FROM THE CAR. "Cassidy's trying to find Naomi's mom, Elizabeth Johnston. She may have located her through some post office box. I don't know the details. I'm on my way back to the Liar's Club to track down Rory and sweat him again for more information. I think he knows more than he's telling about Lizzie."

"Rory," Nick mused. "He said she'd hooked up with some guy named Tony, right? An actor who breaks people's legs on the side?"

"I think it's maybe the other way around," Annalisa replied drily.

"Okay, I can run the name Tony through the computers but I don't have a lot of hope unless we can get some more information to narrow the search."

"That's what I'm hoping to find out." Annalisa parked by the Liar's Club and went to the battered metal door. Immediately, she was met by the two big men serving as bouncers. They wanted the cover charge and she had no cash on her.

"No money, no party," the one in the leather vest said with a casual shrug.

"I'm not here to party." Annalisa wanted to scream. In her previous life, she could have just flashed her badge and gotten them to move aside, but she no longer had that option. "I'm a private investigator," she told them. "I'm trying to find a teenage girl who's been kidnapped."

"No underage girls here," leather vest guy said, frowning at the insinuation.

"Someone inside may have information on where the girl is. Please, let me in."

"Get your five bucks ready and we'll do that."

There wasn't an ATM in sight. "Look," she said, trying again, "the truth is that there's a guy in there, a regular by the name of Rory. When I was here a few days ago, he got rough with me. He—he assaulted me."

The bouncers exchanged a look and then the leather vest guy let his gaze linger over Annalisa. "You look fine to me."

She couldn't believe them. "Okay then," she said. "You're right. My dialing finger is just fine. I'm calling the cops and they can sort this out with Rory right here on the property."

Leather Vest put a beefy hand on her arm to stop her from dialing. "Wait."

"Why should I?"

Leather Vest nodded at his partner, who disappeared into the club. He returned in a minute holding Rory by the back of the skinny man's shirt. "What the hell did I do?" Rory protested, still holding his beer. "Get your hands off me."

"Both of youse . . . out." Leather Vest pushed Annalisa back out the door as his buddy tossed Rory in the same direction. Rory cursed as the beer splattered all over the cement steps.

"You again," he said to Annalisa. "What the fuck is this about?"

"Lizzie Johnston."

"Aw hell." He spun around and started walking away. "I told you what I know."

She grabbed his arm to stop him. "No, I don't think you did. I think you know Lizzie extremely well. I think you dated her. I think maybe you lost her to this Tony guy, but you know more about where she hangs out and what her angles are than you told me the first time. I want to hear all of it, and I want to hear it now."

"I don't feel like talking," he said petulantly. "And who are you to make me?" He yanked his arm free from her grasp and resumed walking. She hurried after him and blocked his path.

"Lizzie may have my teenage stepdaughter, Cassidy. I need to find her." She could only imagine how Lizzie might have reacted if Cassidy confronted her about Naomi and the kidney donation. The woman had shot and killed her own family. Cassidy would mean nothing to her.

Rory eyed her with suspicion. "Lizzie don't like kids."

"I know. That's what I'm afraid of." She tried for sympathy. "Please. Please help me."

"Ah, shit." He hesitated before turning back and lowering himself to the cement steps outside the club. He stretched over and retrieved his beer can, draining the remnants. Annalisa sat next to him. "Lizzie did me good," he said eventually. "She sold me a sad story about how her ex had beaten her and stolen her bank card. She had nowhere to go. I let her stay with me—on the couch. She crawled into my bed that first night and, what was I supposed to say to a sexy naked gal? No? She couldn't get enough of me at first. Then one night she brings home these pills. Says they'll make the sex insane, like from another planet. I took one and passed out for twenty-four hours. When I came to, she'd taken my TV and my mom's old jewelry. I didn't care about the TV but I wanted my mom's gold necklace back. I asked around until I found out Lizzie had hooked up with Tony. Part of me wanted to warn the guy, you know?"

"What's Tony's last name?" Annalisa broke in. "Where does he live?"

"I told you, I don't know his name or where he lives. But I saw him once dealing pills out of a car over in Pilsen. So I started watching the spot. I watched long enough to see some of the same kind of pills Lizzie gave me, and that's when I knew she already had Tony waiting in the wings when she ran off on me."

"Where in Pilsen? What kind of car? Did you get a license?" Annalisa would take any kind of lead.

He ran a shaky hand through his hair. "Allport Street, I think. Or maybe it was Cullerton. The car was a black two-door, that's all I remember. See, Lizzie showed up to get money off him. She brought him a sandwich, and—"

"From where?" Annalisa demanded.

"From where what?"

"Where did she buy the sandwich?"

"Uh, it was Potbelly's."

Annalisa repressed a frustrated sigh. None of this was helping so far. "Okay, then what?"

"Lizzie got the money from him and I followed her. I doubled back through an alley and surprised her from behind. God, was she shocked to see me!" He gave a little chuckle, pleased with himself. "She thought I wouldn't bother her, that I'd take what she did to me and not fight back. I told her I wanted my mom's necklace. She said too bad, she'd pawned it already. I told her she'd better get it back or I'd call the po-po on her old Tony boy."

"And did she get it back?"

"She called two days later and told me to meet her at this abandoned house in Hyde Park, that she had the necklace stored there for safekeeping along with some of her other junk. I told her to bring it to the club. She said if I wanted it, I had to meet her." He looked sideways at Annalisa. "I'm not an idiot. I knew it was a setup."

"What did you do?"

"I went there an hour earlier than she said. I broke in and found her stuff, which I searched until I found the necklace. I mighta took a couple other pieces off her too—you know, as payback." He waited for Annalisa to nod in agreement that Lizzie deserved it.

"Then what?" she prompted.

"Then she showed up with her knife. I was waiting with my gun. Man, if you could've seen her face. She didn't even know I had a gun. I never tell anyone about it unless I have to, you know? It's just good sense."

"Okay, sure."

"I told her we're even now. She leaves me alone, I leave her alone, and if I saw her again, I'd shoot her right between the eyes." He made a shooting motion with his hand and then stopped, satisfied. "Ain't seen her face since."

"Where is the house?" Annalisa asked. "The one you followed her to?"

"I told you. It's a little yellow place in Hyde Park, charred on one side like there was a fire. Boards on the windows. I don't know the exact address, but I can sketch it for you."

"I'd appreciate that, thanks." Annalisa removed her notebook and pen from her jacket pocket. "You're doing a good thing by helping me, Rory." She hoped he wouldn't want more money because she didn't have it.

"Oh, I know," he said as he sketched, his voice cheerful. "Because now, you and me? We're not even. You owe me." He handed her the notebook, a gleam in his eye. "And you seem like someone it's good to have a favor from."

Annalisa took his sketch back to her car, where she phoned Nick with an update. "I've got more than two hundred and fifty guys in the system between age twenty and forty who go by some version of 'Tony' and have a record for assault," he told her. "What a city."

"You can add dealing," she told him. "That might narrow it. Also Pilsen. If he's dealing there, he probably doesn't live too far away. I'm going to check the abandoned house in Hyde Park that Rory mentioned."

"I can meet you." She heard his radio crackle. "Hang on a sec," he told her and she listened as he took the call. "Carelli here. Yeah? When was this? Did they find her? Okay, give me the address." When he returned on the line with Annalisa, he sounded excited. "Forget the abandoned house," he told her. "Dispatch reported a call that came in a half hour ago from an apartment in Pilsen. A woman said the apartment above hers flooded, and when she went to investigate, she heard a girl screaming that she'd been kidnapped. The renter on the upstairs unit is Tony Rossi."

"Did they find Cassidy?"

"Responding officer said there was no sign of her. I'm still checking it out."

"Go, go," Annalisa said. "I bet you find her."

She hung up with Nick and continued driving south toward Hyde Park. She had Rory's sketch on her knee. Using Washington Park as a guide, she was able to find the street he'd indicated. Out of habit, she cut her lights and slowed to a crawl as she drove past the little yellow house. The scorch marks on the left side told her she had found the right place. It looked quiet, no signs of life anywhere around. The house next to it had been boarded up too. Annalisa might have driven away and gone to join Nick except she noticed a black car parked around the corner from the house—two doors, like Rory had said. She slid her Civic in behind it and went to feel the hood. It was warm.

Annalisa took out her weapon and went to the back of the house. She crouched low near a boarded window and listened. Now that she was close, she could hear the sounds of someone moving around inside and see a crack of dim light around the window. She tried the plywood covering the window and it did not move, so she crept across the back of the house to the next window. This one, the plywood was loose. She slid it aside and peeked in. Her heart stopped when she saw Cassidy slumped against the wall, her mouth wrapped in duct tape. A lantern sat on the floor next to her. The girl's eyes were closed and Annalisa couldn't tell if she was conscious. Just then, a woman's legs came into view. Lizzie. She was going through some boxes as if searching for something.

Annalisa held her breath as she widened the gap in the plywood enough for her to crawl through. Her adrenaline surged when she saw Lizzie searched the boxes with only one hand. In the other, she had a large kitchen knife. Annalisa got to her feet silently and crept up toward Lizzie. The warped wood floor creaked under her feet and Cassidy's eyes flew open. Lizzie whirled as Annalisa aimed the gun at her. "Stop right there."

"Who the fuck are you?"

"Drop the knife."

Lizzie tilted her head and her hand tightened on the knife. "This is my place. You're trespassing."

"This isn't your place. You live with Tony Rossi, and my partner is over there searching his apartment for evidence of a kidnapping. I think he's going to find some. What do you think?" She slid her gaze to Cassidy.

"You're a cop?" Lizzie actually relaxed, almost smiled. "Why the hell didn't you say so? You should arrest this little bitch right here." She gestured with the knife at Cassidy. "She broke into my place and maced me right in the face. That's assault."

"Drop the knife," Annalisa repeated, enunciating every word. "Right now."

"Okay, okay. Don't get your panties in a bunch." Lizzie put the knife on the floor.

"Kick it to me."

Lizzie did as instructed. "I'm telling you, I was terrified. I thought she meant to kill me."

"Cassie? Cass, honey, are you okay?" Annalisa called to the girl. Cassidy nodded her head. "Can you get up? If you can get up, do it now and come stand by me." The girl's hands were tied behind her back but she was able to use the wall for leverage and get to her feet. She moved to stand behind Annalisa. "Now lie face down on the floor," Annalisa ordered Lizzie. "Hands where I can see them."

"Me? You've got a beef with me? She's the one—"

"I said get down!" Annalisa shouted. Her arms shook. Like Rory had said, she wanted to put a bullet right between this woman's eyes. Lizzie had a knife. Annalisa knew very well what she'd intended to do with it. If she'd been a few minutes later, she'd probably have found Cassidy with her throat cut.

Lizzie lay on the floor and Annalisa pulled out zip ties to bind the woman's hands behind her back. Then she dug out her pocket knife and began cutting Cassidy free. The girl cried out as the tape ripped off her skin and Annalisa winced. "Sorry . . . sorry . . ." She didn't even try to get it out of Cassidy's hair. Someone would probably have to chop it off.

Cassidy launched herself at Annalisa, hugging her tight. She sobbed into her chest. "You were right. I shouldn't have tried to find her."

Annalisa held her in a fierce hug, holding the girl's warm head. She hoped Cassidy couldn't hear how fast her own heart was pounding. "It's okay. It's all okay now. Let's call your dad, all right? He's worried sick about you."

Cassidy buried her face in Annalisa's shirt. "He's going to kill me."

"No, honey. He loves you."

Cassidy peeked up at her. "He's really been out looking for me?"

"All night. He got a tip that there was some girl in a flooded bathroom, yelling her head off about how she'd been kidnapped."

Cassidy gave a tremulous smile. "That was me," she said, marveling. "I did that."

Annalisa looked down at Lizzie Johnston bound and lying on the filthy floor. "Yeah," she said to the girl. "You sure did."

THIRTY-FIVE

············

Tony Rossi and Elizabeth Johnston were both arrested. Nick reunited with Cassidy at the police station. She had dirt streaks on her face and duct tape in her hair but was otherwise unharmed. He gave her a long, wordless hug, and she held on tight. "I'm transferring the case to Rodriguez," his commander, Lynn Zimmer, told him as he held his daughter, "due to your personal involvement. He'll want to question the girl and get her statement as soon as possible, but we'll need to wait for a legal guardian to be present."

"It's okay," Cassidy said, her voice muffled against his shirt. She turned to look at Zimmer. "He's my dad."

Nick had sat through a thousand witness statements, heard hundreds of victims recount harrowing tales, but the worst was having to sit powerless next to Cassidy as she relayed her ordeal with Lizzie and Tony. Lizzie would have killed her; this was obvious to Nick. He kept looking at Greg Rodriguez's face as he asked the questions, willing him to understand. *Are you getting this? Do you understand this woman should fry for what she did?* Rodriguez used a cordial tone, his questions neutral. Just the facts. Cassidy kept her hands in her lap, her shoulders hunched, but her voice was clear as she detailed being locked in the bathroom while her captors debated her fate. After an hour of questioning, Cassidy asked to use the restroom.

"Of course, you can," Nick answered for Rodriguez. "I'll show you the way."

He ushered Cassidy down the hall and then returned to grill Rodriguez. "Well?" he asked as he stretched his arms across the doorway. "The case is solid, don't you think? They'll both go away for ten years, easy."

Rodriguez capped his pen and leaned back in his chair. "I don't know, man. I think kidnapping, second degree is probably a lock. Beyond that . . ." He shrugged. "It's dicey."

Nick glanced down the hall to check that Cassidy wasn't returning. Then he entered the interview room and shut the door behind him. "What are you talking about? Second-degree kidnapping is a second-class felony. Three years, out in half that time. These people are dangerous, Greg. You heard what Cassidy said. Lizzie dragged her into the apartment. She had a knife. We know she did because she had one with her when Annalisa found them. And the drugs . . . Cassidy saw Tony Rossi with all sorts of pills."

"We did not find any pills when we searched the apartment."

"So he got rid of them."

"Probably so. But it means we can't prove he had them in the first place. And Lizzie Johnston is saying that she never intended to harm Cassidy. That the girl trespassed into the apartment building and attacked Lizzie first by spraying her in the face with pepper spray, a fact that Cassidy doesn't deny. She admits she went there to confront Lizzie about the scam Lizzie set up about Cassidy's girlfriend."

"Cassidy only sprayed her when the woman attacked her," Nick argued. "She never went inside the apartment of her own volition. And what about the duct tape they used on her? That's assault."

"Lizzie said she taped her mouth to keep Cassidy from screaming about being kidnapped. She says she brought the knife to the abandoned house to open boxes, not to harm the girl. She intended to drop Cassidy off somewhere close to home after leaving the house. She says that's what she meant when she said she planned to 'get rid of her.'"

"Bullshit," Nick spat out. "That's bullshit and you know it."

"Calm down," Rodriguez said, holding up his hands. "I agree with you. I think Cassidy's version of events is the correct one. But you know how it is, Carelli—we can only charge what we can prove. Cassidy doesn't have a mark on her. Tony Rossi wasn't in possession of any illegal drugs. He and Lizzie detained a minor in their apartment when she wanted to leave—"

"They kidnapped her," Nick broke in, furious. "They were going to slit her throat and leave her in that house for some stray dog to find."

Rodriguez's face became troubled. "Funny you should mention strays. We talked to a neighbor of Lizzie's, a woman who says Lizzie poisoned her dog. She even wrote Lizzie a note saying she'd make her pay. Lizzie's saying she thought Cassidy wrote the threatening note and she's using that to justify her defense. The woman is smart, Nick. She's covered her tracks pretty well here. Believe me, I will make the argument to the DA that Lizzie needs to be locked up for good. I'm just trying to prepare you for the probable outcome."

Nick leaned over the table. "Well, let me prepare you the same way. If you don't find some way to get these people for what they did to Cassidy, then I will."

Rodriguez frowned and shook his head. "You're upset. You're not thinking straight. So I'm going to pretend I didn't hear that."

"Do what you want," Nick said coolly as Cassidy knocked tentatively and stuck her head back in the room.

"Everything okay?" she asked.

Nick stretched out an arm and brought her close to him. "Everything's going to be just fine, sweetheart."

············

Nick dropped Cassidy off at home, where Melanie awaited her. Cassidy hugged her too, grateful to be alive to do so. "Am I grounded forever?" she asked against Melanie's shoulder.

"No." Melanie pulled back and held Cassidy's face in her hands. "I think you've been punished enough. Let's get you something to eat, huh?"

"Nick got me a sub and soda at the police station," she replied.

"Okay, then. How about we fix this?" Melanie fingered the duct tape stuck in Cassidy's hair.

They went to the bathroom and Cassidy watched in the mirror as Melanie carefully snipped out the duct tape. "Remember when you had to do this after I got gum in my hair?" she said. "I think I was four."

"You begged me not to tell your mother."

"I wasn't supposed to have gum."

Melanie's smile crinkled her eyes. "Hon, she was going to be mad at me for giving it to you, not you for wearing it. Turn your head this way." She shifted Cassidy's head to the left.

"I guess she must've forgiven you. I mean, since she's giving me to you and everything."

Melanie's hands fell away. She met Cassidy's gaze in the mirror. "Sweetie, you're not a sweater or a box of chocolates. She's not giving you to anyone. She's making sure you have a safe place to be when she's gone."

"I know that."

"Do you?" Melanie squeezed her shoulders. Cassidy did not answer. Melanie sighed and put her hands against Cassidy's cheeks. "She loves you so much. So do I. So does . . . so does Nick. He's asked to take you when the time comes."

"What?" Cassidy turned around so she could look Melanie in the face. "He did? But I thought it was all settled. Like, Mom put it in her will or whatever."

"Yes." Melanie petted Cassidy's shorter hair. "But wills can be changed. I think what matters most is what you want to do. Where you want to live."

Cassidy's head swam. "I don't know. That's nice that Nick wants to have me, I guess, but I—I don't think Annalisa would want me there."

"What makes you say that?" Melanie asked with a new edge in her voice.

Cassidy bowed her head. "I can do the math, Mel. I know what happened. Nick cheated on Annalisa with Mom and that's how I was born. I don't blame her. I don't think I'd want me either if that's what happened."

"Annalisa doesn't hate you. I know it. I wouldn't let you be with her otherwise."

"No, but . . ." Cassidy bit her lip. "I think I'd be in the way."

Melanie brooded on this a moment. She took up the scissors again and began evening out Cassidy's haircut. "It's up to you. You have time to think about it."

Cassidy braced herself for the words she had not admitted out loud. "Not much time," she whispered. Her mom was dying.

"Maybe more than you think. They are making arrangements for your mom to go home. I've been waiting to tell you."

"Oh, that's great. So she's getting better?"

Melanie's lips tightened and she focused on her work. "A bit," she said at length. "Just a bit."

Cassidy reached back and grabbed Melanie's hand for a squeeze.

Melanie teared up and then used her free hand to fluff Cassidy's new chin-length 'do. "I think it's adorable. What do you think?"

Cassidy assessed her look with a cautious gaze. "It'll take getting used to. I've never had hair this short before."

"Well, I love it." Melanie leaned down so their heads pressed together. "I think Naomi will love it too."

Cassidy's face went hot. "Oh," she said, her voice tight. "You know?"

"You light up inside when you talk about her. That's usually a big sign."

Cassidy cleared her throat, embarrassed to be so transparent. "Does Mom know?"

"I don't know. Why don't you talk to her about it tomorrow?" Cassidy nodded, and Melanie circled her arms around her from behind, squeezing her in another hug. "Now it's time for sleep."

Cassidy went to bed but she couldn't sleep. She ran her fingertips over the raw places on her face where the duct tape had been. She had texted Naomi that she was safe. Naomi wanted to do a video chat, but Cassidy wasn't ready for that yet. What was she supposed to say? *Your psycho mom tried to kill me and there's no way she's ever giving you a kidney. I'm so sorry.* She knew Naomi would see the horror and despair on her face, and she didn't want to cry in front of her girlfriend. Naomi had enough problems to worry about.

Cassidy got out of bed and went to her closet for her denim jacket. She fished out the white business card from the pocket and tilted it so it caught the streetlight coming in from the window. DR. CRAIG CANNING, it read. It included both a business number and his cell. She took it to the bed with her and punched his number into her phone. He was a grown-up, a brilliant doctor, according to the news, so she used proper grammar in her text. *This is Cassidy Weaver,* she wrote. *I found my friend's mom. You were right. She wasn't what I was expecting.* She contemplated a moment before adding, *But you did. You knew already what she was.*

She hit send and waited, chewing her thumbnail as she stared at the glowing little screen. The dots danced. He was awake in the night, same as her. She held her breath until his reply came through. *I suspected. She was using her sick daughter for money. It takes a certain kind of person to do that.*

Cassidy felt a chill go through her. The news stories said he was the same. She'd seen the book Annalisa had about him. *The Good Sociopath.* Annalisa seemed skeptical about the concept, but she'd also said Dr. Canning told her that Cassidy was searching for Naomi's mom. He'd been the one to point her in the right direction. That was good, wasn't it? She tried to work up the courage to ask Dr. Canning what she really wanted to know. *I've read some stories about you online,* she wrote. *About your book.*

And you're wondering if it's true? he wrote back.

She gripped the phone in both hands. If he could be what that psychologist lady said he was and still save lives, maybe there would be some way to convince Naomi's mom to help Naomi. *I'm wondering if you think Naomi's mom is like you,* she wrote finally.

The dots flickered. Then: *I think you already know that.*

The phone slipped from her grip as a sob welled up inside her. She tamped it back down and forced herself to reply to Dr. Canning. *So there's no way? No hope of convincing her?*

I'm sorry, he replied. *Some people can't be saved.*

THIRTY-SIX

....

ANNALISA SAT ON A STONE BENCH IN THE COURTYARD OF THE PARKVIEW APARTMENTS. It had been two days since she'd broken into Craig Canning's place and photographed his wind chimes. She'd shown the pictures to Nick, hoping he could follow up legally and obtain the same evidence. Instead, he'd been furious with her. "You broke and entered? And he caught you? He could have shot you on sight and been perfectly within his rights to do so. We wouldn't even have arrested him."

"He doesn't want to shoot me. I think . . ." She broke off and tried to find the right words. "I think he wants me to figure it out. He wants me to admire him."

"You know what he doesn't want? He doesn't want to go to jail, Anna. If he threw Vicki Albright off her balcony because she accused him of rape, what do you think he'd do to you if he thought you could pin a murder charge on him? Jeez, come on. It was bad enough when you were taking chances like this with the whole CPD behind you. Now you're out there like some kind of Lone Ranger."

"So back me up. Go talk to Canning in his apartment. If you can state you saw the yellow charm from the wind chimes, that would be enough to bust him."

"To question him, maybe."

"It's proof," she'd insisted. "If it matches the set you took from Vicki's apartment at the time of her death. Vicki's brother, Gavin, will happily swear an official statement that Vicki had accused Craig Canning of drugging and raping her." What he'd actually said was: *When you finally strap this guy down and stick a needle in his arm, I want to watch.*

Armed with Gavin's statement, Nick had reluctantly agreed to go to Canning's apartment to question him. "Get close enough to see the wind chimes," Annalisa reminded him. "That's all you need." She sat below in the courtyard, waiting for the verdict. If Nick saw the chimes, there was a chance Canning could be arrested by the end of the day. She saw movement on the balcony and shaded her eyes to look up. Nick leaned over the edge and peered down at her. She spread her arms in question . . . did he get the goods? He disappeared from view without giving her any kind of signal—punishment, she supposed, for coloring outside the lines. Now she had to wait.

Ruth Bernstein appeared in the courtyard right on schedule. She spotted Annalisa immediately and walked over to join her. She seemed to be favoring her left leg. "Are you all right?" Annalisa said, rising to meet the old woman.

"Just a bit tired today," Ruth said as she leaned heavily on Annalisa's arm. "I haven't been sleeping well, I'm afraid."

"Sit down and catch your breath." Annalisa helped her to the bench and they both took a seat.

Ruth pursed her lips as she stared up at the balcony. "You didn't get him," she said.

"We will."

"He took Duchess. You can prove that much with the hair on his jacket. I've seen the crime shows on television. Animal DNA is traceable the same way a human's is. If I give you a sample—"

"Mrs. Bernstein," Annalisa began.

"Ruth," the woman broke in impatiently. "Mrs. Bernstein was my mother-in-law."

"Ruth," Annalisa corrected herself. "If he let Duchess out deliberately . . . even if he took her, it's not a major crime. It's a minor property violation."

"He broke into my apartment. That's a huge violation."

"And one we cannot prove yet."

Ruth folded her arms and stewed. "I won't let him get away with it. Mark my words."

"Leave Craig Canning to us," Annalisa said, rising as she saw Nick emerge from the building with his sunglasses on. He ambled across the courtyard, hands in his pockets. "Well?" she probed him as he finally reached her.

He tilted his head. "They're gone."

"What?" She looked up and saw Canning leaning out over his balcony. He gave her a cheery wave.

"No wind chimes in view."

Annalisa cursed and turned away. He had seen her examining them. Most likely he'd hidden them away or even destroyed the evidence. Nick was right; she'd been foolish to go in on her own. Now she'd blown the whole case.

"Is that it?" Ruth asked in a scratchy voice. "Is that your last chance to get him?"

"No, it's not." Annalisa looked at Nick, uncertain. "It can't be, right?"

Nick shook his head. "You've got nothing that will stick. No proof of anything. Hell, I'm even starting to wonder if maybe Mara Delaney's book is right, or at least half-right. Maybe he's not a sociopath at all. He seemed perfectly normal when I talked to him just now."

"The charm," Annalisa reminded him. She'd seen it on his balcony.

"Could have been a trick of light. Look, Canning's got an alibi for the time of Vicki's death. He's not covered in cat hair and he's been totally cooperative with any questions we've asked him. You should leave him alone now. For your own good."

Annalisa glanced up. Canning was gone.

Nick's cell rang and Annalisa held her breath. They were in limbo with Summer; she could still pass at any time. "What?" Nick practically shouted into his phone. "That's not possible. No. No, I don't care what the DA said. I'm coming over there right now."

Annalisa relaxed fractionally. The call was just a case, not a matter of life and death.

"You're not really giving up, are you?" Ruth asked her.

"Without more evidence, there isn't much I can do."

Nick returned to touch Annalisa's arm. His expression was serious. "I've got to go."

"What's going on?"

"No charges for Tony Rossi, and Lizzie Johnston made bail an hour ago. A hundred bucks."

"What?" Even Annalisa was shocked at this news. "But what about Lizzie's earlier crimes? That woman killed her whole family."

"Ancient history, apparently. Inadmissible. I have to go. I have to make sure Cassidy is safe. Without her to testify, there's no case at all."

"Go," she told him and watched as he sprinted across the courtyard, wishing she were rushing off with him. It was hard, no longer being partners. She brooded for a moment and then turned to Ruth. "Are you going to be okay?"

Ruth stared up at Canning's balcony. "Yes," she said. "I believe I will."

"Let me see you back to your apartment at least."

Ruth struggled to her feet, pausing a moment to catch her balance.

She forced a smile for Annalisa. "Don't you worry," she said. "I'll find my own way."

∙∙∙∙∙∙∙∙∙∙∙

THAT NIGHT, ANNALISA PREPARED A SIMPLE DINNER OF SALMON STEAKS, RICE PILAF, AND A SALAD. Nick had not answered her texts all afternoon, so she was eager to see what he had to say when he came home from his shift. Six o'clock came and went, but Nick didn't show. She tried calling. He picked up just before the voicemail would have kicked in, but he didn't say anything. Eerie silence stretched on his end. "Nick," she said. "Where are you?"

"In my car."

"In your car where? I expected you here a half hour ago. What's going on?"

She heard him shifting in his seat. "Melanie won't let me stay at the house. She says I'll scare Cassidy more than I already am."

Ah, so he was staking out the place from his car. "Nick," she said with sympathy. "Come home."

"They let Lizzie go. She's dangerous, Anna. Too dangerous to be walking around free."

"Look, Lizzie Johnston is more likely to skip town than she is to target Cassidy at this point. You said her charges were minor. She's out on bail. That's a win for her." Annalisa had read Mara's book entirely now, and it had information in it about criminal sociopaths too. They had the "good" traits but also impulsivity and a complete disregard for social norms. The impulsivity made them reactive but also lazy. They took the quick way out, the route with the least effort.

"She murdered her own family," Nick said. "You think she won't come for mine?"

Annalisa picked up Mara's book and flipped it open to the dedication. *For Donna*. A reminder at how much damage the bad sociopath could do. "What is the plan, then?" Annalisa asked Nick as she closed the cover with a sigh. "Sit outside the house in your car forever? You can't do that."

"I'm staying here until I think of something better."

"Come home," she begged him. "We'll figure it out together."

He clicked off, but when her phone rang two minutes later, she figured it was him again. Instead, it was Mara Delaney. "Did you see the news?" she asked Annalisa in a clipped voice.

"No, what happened?"

"Turn it on right now. WGN."

Annalisa went to the television and flipped it on. Ruth Bernstein was on the screen standing in the courtyard, gesturing at the balcony. "It was designed to look like an accident," she was saying. "He used my apartment to get into hers. That's why my key is missing from the superintendent's office. Craig Canning planned the whole thing—a perfect murder."

"Why would he kill Vicki Albright?" the reporter asked from off-screen.

"Because he had drugged and violated that poor girl. Go ahead, ask the police. Her brother made a statement. They have evidence, but not enough to prove it. Well, I say, if he did it once, he'd done it a hundred times. There have to be other girls."

"Oh no," Annalisa breathed.

"My phone is blowing up," Mara said, her voice fretful. "The dean. My publisher. Every place that Craig and I have done an interview. It's all going to hell and there's nothing I can do about it."

"I'm afraid there's nothing I can do either. Ruth can say what she wants."

"Does she have to say it on television?" Mara almost screeched the words.

The images on-screen shifted. The camera was pointed at the

hospital's front door, and then it cut to the parking garage. Craig Canning emerged dressed in street clothes. "Dr. Canning," the male reporter shouted at him as Canning barreled toward his car. "Dr. Canning, is it true you've been questioned by police in the death of Vicki Albright?"

"No comment," Canning snapped without slowing down.

"Is it true she'd accused you of assaulting her?" the reporter asked as the cameraman hurried to keep up.

Canning got into his car and started the engine even as he slammed the door. The taillights came on and he backed out in a swift motion, nearly hitting the reporter as he exited the garage. "Oh, this isn't good," Mara crooned. "He's angry now."

"He was already angry."

"Not like this. Everything we've done so far, he's had an answer for. He's been in control of the situation. Now the story's out there like a torpedo, and he can't dodge it fast enough. He's going to react. He's going to do something to show he's in control."

"Like what?"

"I don't know. That's the problem. Ah, hell. That's my other line again. I've got to go. Be careful, okay? Lock all your doors and windows."

"You do the same."

At Mara's words, Annalisa remembered her back door was unlocked. She had been out on the patio earlier, tending to the plants ahead of the storm rolling in. She raced through the kitchen to the back hall and nearly crashed into Craig Canning standing in her mudroom. He was soaking wet, and his face twisted into a mockery of a smile when he saw her. "This is how we do it, right? No knocking. Just come in."

She took out her gun but did not point it at him. He did not have any weapons in his hands, but he wore a long overcoat with big pockets. "What are you doing here?"

"I came to see if you were happy now."

"Why would I be happy?"

Rain dripped down his chin, almost like tears. "You must have seen the news. You fed that old woman a bunch of lies and she repeated them for the camera. She might have been a ventriloquist's dummy for all the original thought her story had. That was you talking, Ms. Vega. Not Ruth Bernstein."

"You underestimate her, I think."

He pondered this a moment and then shook his head. "No, I don't think so. But I have underestimated you." He spread his arms. "The hospital has suspended me pending an investigation. An investigation into what, I asked them? My supposed rape victim is dead. This isn't even a he-said, she-said situation."

"Convenient, isn't it?" Annalisa said evenly.

"Not from my perspective. I didn't do it."

"So you keep saying."

"You got your way. My career is ruined. Sometime soon, maybe even tonight, there will be a victim with a head trauma, or maybe a cancer patient with a tumor, someone whose life hangs in the balance, and I will not be there to cure them." He took a step closer, his gaze locked on hers. "Maybe it'll even be a child, like Cassidy's young friend. Someone who could have had their whole life ahead of them."

"Stay back," she said, aiming the gun at him now.

He kept coming. His voice rose. "You accuse me of playing God but it's you who is toying with human lives now, Detective. You think you are morally superior to me, do you? You have a conscience. You feel bad for your victims? How bad will you feel when they wheel in the next car-crash victim and I'm not there to put their brains back inside their head?"

"I said stop." She had him dead-center mass now. One pull of the trigger and he'd be gone.

He stopped. His tone grew soft. "You know it's true. One day soon there'll be a person bleeding out on a gurney, a person I could have saved, but thanks to you and Mara I'm not there. Who will be the one to die? What if it was you in the car crash? Or your husband? What if it was Cassidy? Would you feel bad then for what you've done?"

"I'm not responsible for your actions," she said coldly. "And believe it or not, there are other surgeons."

"Ah." He gave her a ghostly smile. "But none as good as me."

"That doesn't mean you get a free murder. The lives you've saved don't give you a pass to take another."

His forehead furrowed. "For the sake of argument, why not? If every human life is worth the same, my scale would still be vastly tilted in favor of society. I'd be at least a hundred to one. A thousand to one. Surely there's a number at which it would be illogical to question the math."

"No. Because you said it yourself. Every human life is worth the same."

He gave a bitter laugh. "You don't believe that."

"I do."

"Quit lying to me. Quit lying to yourself. Trust me, it's liberating to live your truth. You don't think all human lives are the same. You've taken more than one."

She swallowed and gathered herself, steadying her hands on the gun. "That's not the same thing."

"Isn't it?"

"Those men were killers."

"Ah, so you're saying it is possible to forfeit a precious human life, if one is evil enough."

"Something like that, yeah." She licked her lips. "I'd like you to leave now."

"Well . . ." His gaze dropped to her weapon. "If your logic is sound, you should shoot me right now. You have the grounds. I'm trespassing on your property. If you believe I'm a killer, you should want to stop me from committing any future bad acts."

"I plan to."

He leaned forward, his eyelids heavy and his voice soft. "Then do it."

Her hand grew slippery around the gun. Her finger slid along the trigger. "Get out of my house."

"I knew it." He grinned and righted himself. "You're not as certain as you sound. You're right about one thing—we're all the same, at least on the inside. I've cut enough people open to know it's true. We're all killers and we're all victims. It just depends on how the chips fall, and how you play the game. Our game, Ms. Vega, has not ended yet."

"Get out," she repeated. "Now."

"See you at the finish line," he murmured, and it sounded like a threat. Then left the way he came.

THIRTY-SEVEN

············

LIZZIE LIT HER CIGARETTE STANDING UNDER THE OVERHANG OUTSIDE THE PAWN-SHOP, NEXT TO THE HAND-LETTERED SIGN IN THE WINDOW THAT PROCLAIMED WE BUY GOLD. The night was cold and wet, rain still dripping down from buildings and trees, but she didn't want to go back to the apartment and deal with Tony. He'd been high and paranoid when she left. *That detective said you murdered your own parents when you were a kid.*

Lies, she'd told him. *You know how the cops operate. They make up all kinds of shit to get you to talk. They're trying to turn us on each other and we can't let them.*

You have a kid, he'd said. *You didn't ever tell me you have a kid.*

I don't. She's my ex's kid, not mine. Tony had believed her, or at least he'd wanted to believe. Lizzie had learned young how to hide behind her stories. She told people what they wanted to hear and that worked almost every time. It made it easier for her to cut them loose in the end. Chumps. Losers. Weak and stupid enough to believe her lies.

Tony was fading, though. That crazy girl had spooked him and Lizzie needed to get away before he had second thoughts and ratted her out to the girl's cop father. Good thing Lizzie had already been on the lookout for someone new even before the latest crap hit the fan. She watched the last of them shuffling out of the church across the street. Jeff, the chubby guy who drove a van for UPS, stopped to scan the area, and she knew he was looking for her. She turned away but it was too late. He'd spotted her.

He jogged across the wet street and joined her under the overhang. "You lit out of there like your ass was on fire," he said.

God give us the strength to accept the things we cannot change, Lizzie thought. Recovery meetings were great places to meet marks, even better than the bar. These people believed the worst about themselves, were desperate for someone to tell them otherwise. "Needed a hit," she told Jeff, waving the cigarette at him. "You know how it is." Most of the members smoked like chimneys.

"Yeah. You got another?" Jeff wasn't one of the nicotine fiends. He was looking for an excuse to keep standing there with her. She looked at his shoes. Cheap sneakers, half-worn. Jeans fraying at the cuff. No money to be had here.

"Sorry," she told him and forced a smile. "This was my last one."

"Ah." He waited for her to say something else. When she didn't, he heaved a breath. "Guess I'd better get going."

"Bye now."

He hesitated another beat, his neediness palpable, and she wanted to kick him like a puppy. Finally, he ambled off into the mist and she rolled her eyes before striding purposefully in the other direction. Her phone buzzed and she pulled it out to glance at the screen. Tony, wondering where she was. She put the phone back in her jacket pocket and exchanged it for her pack of cigarettes. She paused to light one and noticed something stuck to the wet sidewalk about ten feet ahead, near the mouth of an alley. As she got closer, she saw it was a twenty-dollar bill.

She hurried to grab it despite the fact that she was alone on the street. As she bent down, it seemed to come to life, blowing into the dark alley. Lizzie went after it. She had to halt for a moment to let her eyes adjust to the low light. Focused as she was on the ground, she didn't notice the man standing in the shadows until he spoke to her. "Hello, Elizabeth."

Her head jerked up. No one called her that. "Who are you?" she demanded, squinting to try to see his face.

He moved into the shaft of light and she saw he had a gun. She still wasn't afraid. What, this asshole thought he was going to mug her? She was the one chasing twenty bucks. "You're out of luck, buddy," she said, taking a drag from the cigarette. "I got nothing."

"You *are* nothing," he corrected, his voice so low she thought she must have misheard him. He took a step closer and aimed at her head.

She narrowed her eyes in confusion. What the hell? What was this guy's deal? "Look, pal, I don't know what your problem is. I don't even know you." She turned her back on him and went to leave.

The gunshot split the night, reverberating off the nearby buildings. Lizzie found herself on the ground unable to see even though her eyes were open. She felt no pain, only cold. When she tried to speak, blood foamed in her mouth. She felt the man taking something off her body. Years ago, when they had arrested her for what she did at the farm, the male cops wanted to make excuses for her. Maybe she's abused. Maybe her parents had been running a cult or something. They put her in a cell by herself as they tried to figure out what to do with her. The female guard had known what Lizzie was on sight, maybe the only person ever to see the truth. *They say everyone calls for their mama at the end*, she'd told Lizzie from beyond the bars. *Who're you going to call for?*

Lizzie had shot her mother from behind while the woman prepared a chicken for roasting. A kindness, she'd thought. Mama wouldn't have to know.

The man still stood over Lizzie as she lay bleeding on the pavement.

He wanted to watch her die. *Must've been someone I did wrong,* she thought hazily, unable to place him. *Fine then. You win.*

Pain arrived to seize her in its viselike grip. She heard the man's footsteps walking away. In the distance, a siren wailed.

A bright light filled her head, and she opened her mouth to try one last time to speak but her final word died in a whisper on her lips.

Mama.

THIRTY-EIGHT

···········

NICK CAME HOME AROUND MIDNIGHT. Annalisa wasn't asleep, but she laid still as he stumbled around in the dark, shedding his clothes until he could walk naked into the shower. While the water ran, she got up and found his discarded T-shirt, which she held to her face for a deep inhale. Back in the day, she'd do this and detect hints of makeup or perfume. This time, she smelled beer and . . . gunpowder? The water shut off and she dropped the shirt before crawling back beneath the covers. When Nick finally joined her in bed, she kept her eyes shut as he spooned up against her.

"What happened to the plan?" she asked him.

He snuffled her hair. "It's late. Go to sleep."

She didn't think she could. Her mind had been replaying her earlier conversation with Canning. The whole exchange was so bizarre that she might have thought she'd imagined it except for the puddle of rainwater he'd dripped in her back entryway. She could have shot him. She had the legal right. But not the moral one, not once she'd realized he was unarmed. Maybe this was how Canning would beat her. She still cared about right and wrong. *It's easier to fight the outer world than the inner one,* she thought wearily.

Somehow, she slept. She must have because the ringing of her cell phone dragged her awake again. She reached for it without opening her eyes. "H'lo?"

"Annalisa Vega?" said an unfamiliar and officious female voice. "I'm calling from Mercy Hospital. I'm sorry about the hour."

Annalisa came totally awake, bolting up in bed. She thought she must have somehow grabbed Nick's phone. "Is it Summer? Did something happen?"

"I don't know what you mean by summer. We have a patient here in critical condition and she was found with no wallet or usual identification. Your business card was in her coat pocket."

"I'm sorry, what?"

Nick sat up now too. He switched on a bedside light.

"We're hoping you could come here to the hospital and speak to us about this patient," the woman said. "We need to locate her family to make decisions about her care. Timing is rather urgent."

"You want me to come there to ID her?" Annalisa was already getting out of the bed, fumbling around for clothes. Who could have her business card? *Mara,* she thought. Oh, God, if Canning had gotten to Mara . . . "Does she have blond hair?" Annalisa asked the woman on the phone. "About five foot nine, one hundred and fifty pounds?"

"I'm afraid I can't discuss any details with you at this time. Are you able to come to the hospital?"

"Yes, yes, I'm coming now."

"Thank you. Please go directly to ICU on the fifth floor."

"I know where it is." Annalisa hung up and put the phone down so she could wriggle into her jeans.

Nick gave her a questioning look. "What's going on?"

"I'm not sure. A woman's in intensive care at the hospital and they don't know who it is. She had no identification on her, only my business card."

"Jesus," Nick said softly. "What happened to her?"

"I don't know. I'm going over there now."

"I'll go with you." He got tangled in the covers as he tried to get out of bed. Dressed now, she went around to his side and stopped him.

"You just got home." The bedside clock read 2:11 a.m. "Stay and get some rest. I'll fill you in as soon as I can."

As she drove, Annalisa mentally berated herself for not warning Mara that Canning had shown up at her place uninvited, that he was angry about being suspended from the hospital. If he blamed Annalisa, of course he'd also blame Mara. What could he have done to her to make identification an issue? A hundred gruesome scenarios played out in her mind, and by the time she reached the hospital, her stomach felt like it had turned to stone. She raced to the ICU desk and gave them her name. A Black woman appeared dressed in street clothes—a charcoal pantsuit similar to the kind Annalisa had worn in her previous job. "Ms. Vega, hello, and thanks for coming so quickly. I'm Kim Butler, one of the social workers here at the hospital. We spoke on the phone."

"Yes, thanks. Can I see the patient now?" Annalisa asked.

"Come this way." She looked over at Annalisa as they walked. "Normally we don't conduct patient privacy this way, but nothing about this situation is normal."

"What happened to her?"

"I can't share those details." She paused outside a hospital room. "She's sustained a serious injury and is on life support right now. This means her face is swollen and a machine is breathing for her, so she might not look as she typically does."

"I understand. Please just let me see her."

"Of course." Ms. Butler opened the door and Annalisa entered.

The woman lay motionless in the bed. Her head was bandaged, her eyes swollen shut. A tube snaked out of her mouth and over to the respirator, which performed regular compressions to force air into her body. Annalisa did not recognize her. Maybe it's a random coincidence, she thought, quivering as she got closer. Maybe this lady had picked up her card from somewhere and Annalisa had never met her at all. She forced herself to bend down and take a good look.

She drew back with shock as she placed the face.

"You know her?" Ms. Butler's excited voice floated from behind her.

"Her name is Elizabeth Johnston," Annalisa said.

"Oh, that's perfect. Thank you so much." The woman came forward and wrote something down on her clipboard. "Is she a relative? A friend?"

"No." Annalisa stared down at Lizzie Johnston. "She tried to kill my stepdaughter."

Ms. Butler stopped writing to gape at Annalisa. "I'm sorry?"

Annalisa's cell phone rang. The caller ID read Lynn Zimmer. Her old boss did not usually make phone calls in the middle of the night, and she certainly had no reason to be calling Annalisa now. *Oh, no,* Annalisa thought. *Oh, Nick, what did you do?* "Excuse me," she said to Ms. Butler as she left the room to take the call. "Commander?" she said into the phone.

"Tell me you're home in bed," Zimmer said by way of greeting. "Tell me you're in bed and Carelli's lying next to you."

"Uh, I'm at the hospital," Annalisa said. She could be there for a dozen reasons. "What's up?"

"Someone texted 911 three and a half hours ago saying they had been shot in the head. They proceeded to give the exact coordinates for the ambulance to respond. After that, the phone went dead. Responding units found it lying smashed in an alley next to a woman who'd been shot in the head. The tech boys were able to get the phone operational again and they ID'd the owner: Elizabeth Johnston. Greg Rodriguez is the detective assigned to her, so they called him. He took one look at the facts of the case before calling me. Now I'm calling you because we need to know: where is your husband?"

"Ah, not sure right now. Home. That's where I left him. In bed, like you said." She was intentionally vague about the time. Annalisa sank into a plastic chair in the waiting room. "You think Nick did this?" she asked Zimmer in a strained voice.

"Do you think Nick did this?" Zimmer countered.

Annalisa didn't answer for a long moment. "I hope not."

Zimmer sighed. "You say he's home now? Rodriguez is going to pick him up for a chat."

Annalisa didn't have time to process this before Kim Butler appeared in front of her with that clipboard again. "I'm sorry to bother you," she said, "but we really do need to find Elizabeth Johnston's next of kin. We need to get them here as soon as possible if they want to say goodbye."

"Goodbye?" Annalisa let the phone droop from her ear. "You mean there's no hope for her recovery?" Canning's words came back to her. *Who will be the one to die?*

Ms. Butler looked torn by what she couldn't say. "That's for the doctors to discuss with her family. So, I'm asking you: do you know her relatives or how we might be able to contact them?"

Annalisa looked beyond her to the room where Lizzie Johnston lay. "I know her daughter."

THIRTY-NINE

············

MARA LAY IN BED. The alarm had gone off at six as usual but she hadn't gotten up because there was nowhere she could go. Her office was burned. Her classes were canceled, per the university. She had a meeting with the dean at four this afternoon, and he was almost certain to fire her. A half dozen reporters waited, camped outside her home, desperate to document her shame. Foolish woman. Elitist professor blinded by her own arrogance. Craig Canning wasn't a good sociopath. He was a rapist and a murderer. How could she not have seen this?

Paul came and sat next to her. He wore a blue cashmere sweater over his shirt and tie. It brought out the blue in his watery eyes. "Can I get you anything, darling?"

She turned her head away. "A new career?"

"Oh, come on now. It won't be that bad."

"Paul, they're going to fire me today. The book can't come out. My reputation is in ruins."

He frowned before reaching past her to grab a tissue from the nightstand. "Craig Canning is the bad guy in all this. Not you."

"That's not how everyone will see it."

"It's how I see it." He leaned down to kiss her cheek. "It will blow over, sweetheart. You'll see. And in the meantime, maybe it's for the best."

"For the best?" She sat up, scrambling away from him and back against the headboard. "Just how do you figure that?"

"Canning is exposed for what he is. He's out of our lives. Face it, if that book came out, there would be pressure to continue to follow him. Updates. Sequels. We would never be free of him."

"How horrible," she said with biting sarcasm. "I might enjoy professional success."

"Is it success? If it's all a lie?" He patted her leg, affirming his answer. "I know you. You're like a cat, darling. You always land on your feet."

She resisted the urge to hiss at him. "Go out the back way, through the garage. The reporters will mob you otherwise."

The bed bounced as he rose. "They're not after me," he said reasonably. "Stay inside and ignore them. Tomorrow there will be some other scandal to grab their attention and we can return to our previously peaceful existence."

Mara got out of bed to watch him leave. True to his word, he marched out the front door without a care, barely slowing down as the reporters peppered him with questions. He got into his Lexus and drove off to his exciting world of podiatry. Peaceful existence, she thought as she let the curtain fall back into place. How dreadful.

She formulated a new plan as she dressed in casual clothes. Maybe she could win the battle for her job. Sure, the university was in the news, but wasn't that a good thing? The police hadn't actually charged Craig Canning with any crimes. Her thesis hadn't been disproven. The world did need people with steel nerves. People who didn't cry over every sad story. Well, she wasn't about to cry over hers. Resolute, she put on a soft gray hoodie and went down through the basement to the back exit. The place smelled like tuna fish and she made a mental note to tell Paul to take out the garbage.

She put on dark glasses and escaped out the rear, where she walked three blocks to a coffee house. She ordered a scone and a nonfat latte to go. No one in the place gave her a second glance. Paul was right. This would all be a distant memory soon. No matter what happened with the book, Mara would write her own story. She took her food to go, sipping through the hole in the lid, her mind forming arguments for her later meeting with the dean. She didn't see the figure lurking in the narrow opening between the two buildings before it was too late. She dropped her cup as he grabbed her, his hand clamping over her mouth.

"Shh," he said, releasing her.

She expected to see Craig Canning, but it was some other guy standing there. It took her a second to place him. Gavin Albright, Vicki's brother. "What the hell are you doing?" she demanded.

"You told me he'd be locked up. Canning. He'd be arrested for what he did to my sister. But he's still loose. No one's doing shit to avenge Vicki."

"I never promised you anything."

"You and Vega, you said if I swore out a statement against him, you'd back me up. You'd tell the cops that it was possible he slipped away from you long enough to drug her at the restaurant, that he could've doubled back and picked her up."

"No one has asked me to revise my statement."

He shoved her lightly. "No one should have to ask you."

"Keep your hands off me."

"You're the expert. They'll listen to you. Tell them you were wrong. Tell them he's a murdering psychopath."

"My opinion isn't evidence."

"That's bullshit!" He screamed at her and then turned away, punching the brick wall. "You don't care. None of you. Vicki's dead and nobody cares he killed her."

"That's not true," she said, moving toward him. "But the police have to follow the law. They can't convict him without proof. You have to be patient."

"Yeah?" He cast her a bitter look. "It's too bad Vicki isn't here, because she could tell you: that's not me."

"It has to be," Mara told him. "There's no other way."

"For you, maybe." He pushed past her. "Not for me."

FORTY

···········

Naomi got her mother's kidney. Someone else got her heart; others received her corneas, her liver, and her lungs. Annalisa didn't know whether Canning might have saved Lizzie Johnston from the gunshot wound to her head, but Lizzie's death saved a bunch of other people. Detective Rodriguez suspected someone had engineered it that way. He suspected it was Nick.

"Listen," he'd argued with her in the interrogation room for hours, the empty coffee cups piling up between them, "whoever shot Lizzie Johnston had crackerjack aim. They hit her right in the forehead and did enough damage to lay her out flat without killing her. The docs tell me if she'd been shot from behind, there's a good chance she would've stopped breathing before the EMTs ever got there."

"Fortunate timing then," Annalisa agreed.

"Fortunate my ass. It was planned that way." Rodriguez thinned his lips and used his thumb to bend back the waxy edge of his paper cup. "The shooter took Lizzie's phone and called 911. The voice on the phone sounds male. Whoever it was, they also texted 911 with her exact location. We know she didn't send the text herself. She was already unconscious. Why would someone do that unless they wanted her to be found?"

"Remorse, maybe," Annalisa offered. "When push came to shove, they couldn't watch her die."

"Or they wanted her to be in a hospital when she passed. That way her organs could be used in transplants. Her daughter could be saved."

"No one knew she was a match."

"They didn't know she wasn't," he countered. "Yes or no: Lizzie Johnston was Naomi's best hope for a kidney?"

Annalisa shrugged and toyed with her own cup. "You'd have to ask the doctors about that one."

"Yeah, well, let me ask you something else. Why was your card found on the victim?"

Annalisa hesitated. This she did not know. "I'd confronted her a few days before when she was trying to kill my stepdaughter. But then you already knew that." She narrowed her eyes at him but his smooth face gave nothing away. "Maybe I dropped a card at the scene. Maybe she picked it up. Who's to say how she got it?"

"No prints on the card," he told her, leaning across the table. His shirtsleeves were rolled up, revealing muscular arms. "Not even Lizzie's. Don't you think that's odd?"

"It's been chilly at night. Maybe she wore gloves."

"I think it's extremely odd," he continued as though she hadn't spoken. "Lizzie wouldn't be lining up for your services. So why would she keep your card? She wouldn't. It makes no sense. So then someone else must've put it there, and the lack of prints makes it seem like the shooter could've planted it. But why? Why you?" It was a rhetorical question. She already knew his theory.

"I had to ID her body."

"Ahh," he said, leaning back with a smile. "Exactly. You had to connect the dots so Naomi could get her kidney. Couldn't have Lizzie listed as a Jane Doe. Couldn't risk her kidneys going to someone else, not when her daughter desperately needed one. It's brilliant when you think about it. Two problems fixed with one bullet. Lizzie pays for what she did. Naomi gets to live. Now that's justice."

He watched her face to see her reaction, if she would agree with him. She said nothing.

He sighed. "I don't blame Nick for seeing this as a perfect solution. Hell, if he admits it, I bet the DA will even give him a favorable deal. No one wants to put him on trial. Sympathetic dad, trying to protect his kid, trying to save another kid's life? And the victim . . ." He tossed his cup aside and made a disgusted noise. "She's trash, right? Killed her own family. We're all better off without her. Nick's going to come out of this looking like a hero."

She stared at him, incredulous. "He'd be arrested. He'd lose his job."

"He'd maybe do some time, yeah. Not much. I'd lay odds he'd be home before your five-year anniversary."

"There's only one problem," she said. "He didn't do it."

Rodriguez scratched the back of his head. "I'd like to believe you. I really would. But facts is facts. Nick has no alibi. You said so yourself. He had the motive, means, and opportunity. That's three for three, Vega."

Annalisa fixed her gaze beyond him, at the gray-green wall. She could have said Nick was home with her at the time of the shooting. She could have lied. *Some lives are worth more than others,* Canning had argued. Nick surely trumped the horrid Lizzie Johnston. But Canning was right about her too. She had a conscience. "That doesn't make him the shooter," she said without looking at Rodriguez.

"No, but he knew Lizzie was out on bail. He knew you were looking at her as a possible donor for Naomi's kidney. He was angry and scared about what would happen to Cassidy. He had motive and opportunity galore. Not to mention, he failed the paraffin test. His weapon was recently fired. And of course, he had plenty of access to your business cards. Hell, I don't blame him, Vega. I get why he did it."

Annalisa turned her attention back to him, full-on. "It's a tidy story. You have one little problem."

Rodriguez rubbed his head, looking tired of the argument. "Oh, yeah? What's that?"

"No prints on the business card."

His forehead furrowed. "What?"

"You think Nick would shoot Lizzie with his bare hands so that he got gunpowder residue all over them, but then he'd put on gloves so he wouldn't leave prints on the business card? Come on, you're smarter than that . . . and Nick's definitely smarter than that."

He scowled at her backhanded compliment. "So he effed up. He never killed anyone before."

There was a sharp rap at the door and Rodriguez's partner, Andy Sullivan, stuck his head in the room. "Gotta talk to you," he said, waving a folder at Rodriguez. Rodriguez pointed at Annalisa as he got up to leave.

"We're not done yet."

"Oh, we're done," she told him, but she didn't move. She'd been on the job too many years not to recognize the edge in Sullivan's voice. He had new information, something important. She didn't intend to leave the station until she found out what it was.

Rodriguez reentered the room and closed the door behind him. He leaned against it, exhaling a long breath. "Ballistics came back," he told her. "The bullet removed from Lizzie Johnston is not a match for Nick's weapon. Not even close."

Annalisa exhaled too. "Told you," she said, grabbing her coat from the back of her chair.

Rodriguez blocked her exit, his eyes troubled. "You watch yourself, Vega."

"I'd like to go now."

"You didn't give Nick an alibi for the shooting, and that's fine. But it means he can't alibi you either."

"I'm not even going to dignify that with a response," she said, stepping around him.

She drove home to Nick and told him the good news. "I knew it," he said as he embraced her. "I knew it wouldn't match. I didn't shoot her."

"I know," she said against his neck. He'd been honest with her about his actions that night. Melanie had chased him away from stalking the house, and he'd bought a six-pack of beer. He'd drunk four of them and then taken the empties to a field and shot them off an old stone wall, one by one. If he hadn't turned off his phone to avoid talking to her, it would have been easy to show his whereabouts. In the end, the ballistics backed up his story. "I knew you didn't do it."

He rubbed her back and she drank in the closeness. "Rodriguez has a puzzle on his hands, then," he murmured as he hugged her. "There's probably a line of people from here to Peoria who would've liked to shoot Lizzie Johnston."

"It's his problem now," she said. "Not ours."

"I'm going to go to the hospital," he said. "Find Cassidy and tell her the good news."

"I'll join you after I shower and find something to eat."

He kissed her lips. "There's leftover pizza in the fridge."

She decided to eat first. She inhaled the cold mushroom and sausage pizza and then stood under the hot shower spray until her skin turned bright pink. Wrapped in a cozy robe, she meant to lie on the bed for just a few minutes. Sleep rolled over her like a stone. When she awoke, the sun was lower in the sky and her phone was ringing somewhere in the bedcovers. She felt around until she found it. "Hi," she said when she saw it was Nick. "Sorry, I took a nap."

"You earned it. I'm at work and the whole place is buzzing with how you put Rodriguez in his place."

She winced. "Great. My fan club is expanding."

"Yeah, he's madder than a wet hen. But I did get a look at the ballistics report. They've identified the weapon as a Smith & Wesson 57."

"What?" She gripped the covers with her free hand.

"Yeah, pretty unusual," he agreed. "Maybe it will be easier than we thought to find the shooter. A gun like that, you find the weapon, you got your killer. Rodriguez should be pleased."

"Uh, congratulate him for me," she said.

"Listen, I'm about done here. You want to meet at the hospital? We could grab a bite there."

"Yeah, sure," she said, her mind back in Canning's apartment. He owned a Smith & Wesson 57. What had he said to her? *It is possible to forfeit a life, if one is evil enough.* He knew about Lizzie. He knew Naomi needed a kidney. He certainly could have taken one of Annalisa's business cards when he was in her office.

Annalisa went through the motions of getting dressed without even seeing her clothes. This was perhaps her best chance to get Canning for something. She could tell Nick what she'd seen in Canning's apartment, fudging the details on when and how she'd run across the gun. With her statement, Rodriguez could serve a warrant and seize the weapon for testing.

When her phone rang, she answered it before checking the caller ID. "Hello?"

Canning's voice came on the other line. "Did you like my present?"

She halted in momentary surprise. "You," she said when she'd recovered her ability to speak. "You shot Lizzie Johnston."

He tut-tutted her. "I don't know what you're talking about. Someone shot her? I had no idea. I guess it's not surprising given her various criminal enterprises. Chickens come home to roost. She probably learned that on the farm growing up—the one where she murdered her mother, father, and younger brother."

"She wasn't a nice person," Annalisa said steadily. "You still didn't have the right to kill her."

"I just assured you that I didn't. Do we have a bad connection?"

"We have no connection," she told him, her voice sharp. "I didn't ask you to do this."

He chuckled. "You think I would do it for you? You told me you'd read Mara's book, Annalisa. I act only out of self-interest, don't you know?"

Her mind raced. He was right. But he had nothing to gain from Lizzie's death, unless it was some scheme to prove he should have been there to try to save her. "You said you'd left me a present," she reminded him.

"Flowers," he said smoothly. "Sent to your office. I hope you don't mind—I grabbed one of your cards to be sure of the address."

It was almost a confession. God, maybe this was the point of it all. To drive her mad. She tightened her grip on the phone. "Maybe this is your self-interest. To call me up and gloat. You pulled the trigger when I couldn't. You did what had to be done."

"Am I gloating? Hmm. The girl got her kidney, did she not?"

A thought occurred to her. "Oh my God, you knew. Somehow you knew Lizzie would be a match."

"Ms. Johnston had her appendix removed six years ago. A boring, routine surgery. Even a trained monkey could do it. But the bloodwork on file was quite thorough."

"So you shot her," Annalisa said. "You'd know where to do it, too. Keep her breathing long enough for the ambulance to come."

"I don't know what fantasy you're spinning. I was home all night watching the news destroy my hard-won reputation."

"It was your gun," she told him. "The Smith & Wesson 57? They've already done the ballistics analysis and they'll be able trace it back to you."

"My gun?" he said with exaggerated surprise. "That can't be."

"I saw it in your apartment. Don't try to deny it."

"Oh, I did have a Smith & Wesson 57 at one time," he agreed. "It belonged to my father. But funny thing . . . it disappeared from my apartment the other night. I think someone may have broken in here."

The hair on her neck stood up. "You lie."

"No, no. I'm quite sure of it, actually. Someone broke in. Did you know they have video cameras in the lobby? No one ever bothers to check it because this place is deathly boring most of the time. I suspect the super only uses it to make sure the doormen are minding their posts. But when I noticed my gun missing, I of course reported it as stolen. I also had that nice young man, Damon, pull the video from the night it disappeared. A woman, dressed in black, appears on the screen when Damon steps away from his desk. She goes back in the direction of the super's office and returns a moment later."

Annalisa sank down onto the bed. She hadn't noticed the cameras.

"Well, after that, Damon and I had to check the super's office. Funny thing . . . the only thing missing was my apartment key. Damon asked me if I wanted to report it and I said no, there was nothing damaged, no problems at this time. I would simply have my locks changed, which I did."

"I didn't touch your gun."

"So you say. But if the police come around asking questions about it, I'll be forced to show them the video. I'm sure they'll recognize the woman on it."

She squeezed her eyes shut. "So this was the plan? To frame me for Lizzie's murder?"

"Heavens, no. I'm not framing anyone for anything. But a good doctor always carries insurance. I'm sure the police will look for that gun, but I'm equally sure they'll never find it."

He'd probably tossed it in the river. Or maybe it was in a hiding spot somewhere, ready to be planted on her property if necessary. "What is it you want from me?" she said finally.

"An admission. You were wrong about me."

Her breath came out as a bitter gasp. "On the contrary. I think you've proved me right."

"Mark my words. When this is over, you and Mara will be the ones under the bright lights, dodging the uncomfortable questions. Your reputations will be in the toilet, and I will be fully vindicated."

"You're delusional."

"All human lives are not the same. Mine is worth more than most. You've tried to take it from me, to ruin my livelihood . . . well, I will ruin yours. You and Mara will be living in a box by the side of the road when I'm done suing you into oblivion for defamation of character. You think I'm a murderer? Go ahead then, prove it. The more you smear me, the higher the damages."

He hung up and Annalisa stared at the phone in her hand, his words ringing loudly in her ears. *Go ahead then, prove it.*

Problem was, she couldn't. If she fought him, he'd try to pin Lizzie's murder on her. He had her on tape practically breaking into his apartment. *Our game has not ended yet,* he'd told her, but she feared it really had.

She'd lost.

FORTY-ONE

···········

H ER DAD GOT A CAT. A kitten, really, a little striped fluffball he named
Jack. Cassidy loved it when he stretched across her lap and presented his belly for scritching. If she rubbed too long, though, he closed
his paws around her wrist like a claw machine at the arcade. She had a
dozen tiny scabs and every last one of them was worth it. Jack the Rip-
per, Annalisa called him. He'd shredded the end of Annalisa's leather
jacket and put teeth marks into one leg of the coffee table. With all her
harrumphing, Annalisa pretended not to like Jack, but Cassidy caught
her working on the couch with the kitten curled on her shoulder.

"That's how the Vegas operate," Nick had told Cassidy. "The more
they make fun of you, the more they like you."

Annalisa was polite to Cassidy. She did not make fun of her or give
her silly nicknames. She called Nick "Detective Smooth" sometimes,
like when he dropped a carton of milk on the floor of the kitchen. For
his part, her dad had taken to calling Annalisa "Magnum" now that she
was a PI. Cassidy knew her father was waiting for her to make up her
mind about where she wanted to live, so she was spending time at his
place, his and Annalisa's, trying to see if she could fit in there.

"Hey, kid." Annalisa looked up from her laptop as Cassidy entered the living room. "You ready to head to the hospital?"

"Yeah." Cassidy perched on the opposite end of the couch and Jack crawled down Annalisa's arm to come investigate the new arrival. She booped his little pink nose and he started to purr.

"He likes you," Annalisa observed as the cat went belly-up on the cushion.

Cassidy rubbed his whisper-soft tummy. "I think he does this for everyone."

"Not me. Today he tried to eat my hair." She shut down the computer.

"Melanie says Jack is a bribe," Cassidy said as she petted the kitten. "Because Dad wants me to come live here."

"Yeah? Tell her I think Nick's just baby crazy," Annalisa returned. She stretched out a hand and scratched Jack under his tiny chin.

"He wants to have a baby?"

"Like yesterday." Annalisa looked at her. "What do you think? Would you like a little brother or sister?"

Cassidy had begged her mother for a sibling for literal years. Mom worked so many hours in the bar, leaving Cassidy with sitters or setting her up in the back office all by herself. *Like I could handle two of you,* her mother always joked. Cassidy knew it was a joke because she never gave her mother any trouble. Once she got older, she'd understood the biology involved and realized it was never going to happen because her mother didn't date, at least not in any way Cassidy could discern. She didn't know if this was a reaction to what had happened with Nick or whether her mother had a secret guy stashed somewhere, but she'd long resigned herself to it being just the two of them. "Uh, sure. Maybe."

Annalisa gave her a wry smile. "You sound like me whenever he brings it up."

"You don't want kids?" Cassidy kept her focus on the cat. He nipped at her finger and chased it as she pulled it away.

"When I was your age, I wanted four."

Cassidy blanched, imagining four pregnancies. "Four's a lot."

"That's what I grew up with. It's what I knew. But life had other plans."

Cassidy drew her hands into her lap and went completely still. She knew she'd been one of the parts that went off-course, first when her mom got pregnant and then last year when she'd tracked down Nick and told him he was her father. "If you're going to have a baby, you definitely don't need me around here." The condo was cramped already.

"Cassidy . . ." Annalisa waited until Cassidy looked at her. "There will always be room for you. Always. We're selling this place, yeah? We'll find somewhere bigger. You can help us look if you want."

"Really?" Cassidy searched her face for the truth.

"Sure."

Cassidy leaned back against the couch cushions with a heavy sigh. "Nick wants me to live with you guys. Melanie wants me to stay with her. Mom set it all up, you know. Melanie would sublet her apartment and stay with me in the house until I go to college. I wouldn't have to move or change schools or anything."

"What do you want?" Annalisa asked her. Cassidy rolled her head around to meet Annalisa's gaze. What she wanted, she couldn't have. Annalisa nodded to show she understood. Jack wandered over to knead Annalisa's thigh and she scooped him up and positioned him so they were nose-to-nose. "I'll be the bad guy if you want," she said to Cassidy.

Cassidy's guard went up. "What do you mean?"

"I'll tell Nick it's too much to take you on full time, that we can do weekends and summer visits like usual." She glanced at Cassidy. "You could still have your own space, obviously. But you could stick with what your mom wants for you."

Cassidy turned this offer over in her mind. Annalisa would put it all on her. She wouldn't make Cassidy say no to her father and disappoint him when she'd only begun to know him. "You would do that for me? Why?"

Annalisa leaned over and squeezed Cassidy's knee. "I know what it's like to have a complicated relationship with your dad."

"Okay, thanks." Cassidy paused. "I'll think about it."

Annalisa got up from the couch. "We should get going. You might want to use the lint brush first." Cassidy looked down at her sweatshirt, which was covered in cat fur. "You look like a hair ball."

....

AT THE HOSPITAL, MELANIE LEFT TO GET FOOD WHILE CASSIDY VISITED WITH HER MOM. She knew her mother was being released soon, on hospice. She was coming home to die. Cassidy sat next to the bed with her laptop out but not open. Her mother had her own screen—one she could operate with her eyes. She typed out *Hi, doll*.

"Hi, Mommy." Cassidy leaned in for a careful hug.

Her mother's gray-green eyes moved back and forth as she selected more letters. Cassidy watched them with a pang in her heart. ALS had shrunk her mother's body, curled it in on itself, but her eyes remained the same. *You look furry,* her mother typed and then gestured with her eyes at Cassidy's sweatshirt.

"Jack is everywhere," Cassidy said with a laugh. "I have more pictures of him to show you. But first . . ." She opened the laptop and started the video call she'd planned with Naomi. Her heart was beating really fast, but it slowed when her girlfriend's face appeared on-screen. Naomi was out of the hospital after the transplant but she was still in isolation while her immune system rebooted itself. They had to make do with video visits for now. "Mom, I want you to meet Naomi," Cassidy said as she tilted the computer. "Naomi, this is my mom, Summer."

"Hi, Ms. Weaver." Naomi gave her sweetest smile as she waved on-screen. "It's nice to meet you."

Her mother lifted her hand a couple of inches and made a noise that might have been hello. They waited while she typed out a message. *Cassidy talks a lot about you. She says you have a new kidney.*

"Yes, I'll be good as new soon. It's like a miracle." Naomi's smile became fixed. Cassidy had not told her mother about the circumstances surrounding Naomi's kidney, about Lizzie getting shot. Annalisa had that book about sociopaths and Cassidy had read some of it. Naomi's mother surely fit the bill, but then someone else had murdered her. *Is it bad,* Cassidy wondered? *Is it bad that I don't care if she's dead?*

"Mom, Naomi asked me to go to prom with her."

Her mother's gaze moved from the laptop screen to settle on Cassidy. Cassidy felt her face warm under the scrutiny and she tried not to squirm.

"As her date," Cassidy added, and her mother's lips formed an *O*.

"It's not until June," Naomi said in a rush. "My dad said Cassidy could stay over at our place and he'd be there and you wouldn't have to worry about anything."

"So can I go?" Cassidy asked tentatively.

Her mother's eyes shifted to her communication device. *Of course. Take lots of pictures.*

Cassidy's eyes filled with tears and a choked sob escaped her. "We will. Thank you, Mom." She squeezed her mother's hand hard and her mother squeezed back. They all chatted about prom dresses as Naomi shared some photos of outfits she'd already been checking out online. Eventually, Cassidy noticed her mother getting tired and she signed off the call.

She's lovely, her mother typed. *Your girlfriend.*

Cassidy blushed again. "Sorry I didn't tell you sooner. With everything that's been going on, I just didn't know . . ."

Her mother shook her head. *Never be afraid to tell me. And never be afraid to love.*

Cassidy's throat thickened with emotion. She might never have another chance to ask her mother about her own love life. "Did you?" she blurted. "Did you ever love someone?"

Her mother was slow to answer. *Not Nick, if that's what you mean.*

Cassidy rolled her eyes. "I know that wasn't love. That was hormones."

Her mother nudged her with a fake reprimand and Cassidy giggled. "No, Nick loves Annalisa," she said after she'd sobered. "I think he must have loved her for a long time, if they got back together after everything that happened. I guess what I'm asking is . . . did you have someone like that? Someone who was the love of your life?"

Yes, her mother typed. *You.*

Cassidy buried her face in her mother's chest as she had as a child. Her mother could no longer hug her, but Cassidy felt a something like a kiss against the top of her head. She squeezed her eyes shut. She lay like that for the longest time, listening to the sound of her mother's heart as it beat out her name.

FORTY-TWO

....

ANNALISA SAT IN HER OFFICE WITH MARA DELANEY, STARING AT THE CHECK THAT MARA HAD JUST HANDED HER. "I'm not sure I've earned this," she admitted. Mara's book deal was over. The police had not arrested Craig Canning and it looked like they might never do so. They had no direct cause to investigate him for Vicki Albright's death and Annalisa couldn't imagine what evidence could emerge now that would prove his guilt. He had neatly boxed up and delivered Lizzie Johnston's death to her like a gift, as he had called it. Only inside the gift was a bomb. If she tried to report him for the crime, he'd show the detectives the video of her breaking into the super's office the night his gun was reported stolen. He would argue she or Nick had used the gun to shoot Lizzie and there was nothing she could do to prove otherwise.

"I'd say you've earned it two times over," Mara said. She was dressed in a gray pantsuit that suited the mood. "I'm sorry for dragging Craig Canning into your life. I sensed that I might be wrong about him, but I had no idea how wrong."

"You were right about his intelligence. He's engineered a kind of mutually assured destruction—if I go after him further, he'll come after me."

"Oh, it's the same with me."

Annalisa raised her eyebrows. Mara's book was canceled. She was suspended from the university. What more could Canning want? Mara reached into her bag and pulled out a large envelope, which she put on Annalisa's desk. "Never mind that Miles Dupont is still running around telling everyone I set fire to my own office. I guess I have Craig to thank for that too. But if I tried to fight back against everything he's done, he's sent another warning. I found that on the steps of my house this morning."

Annalisa opened the flap and pulled out a set of enlarged surveillance photos. They showed Mara and Canning looking cozy outside a restaurant. Davio's. Annalisa could see the name in script on the awning over their heads. Mara had her arm around him, and in the last photo, the pair shared an obvious lovers' kiss.

"Stupid, I know," Mara said, covering her face. "Acting like that with him in public. I'd had two glasses of wine with dinner and I guess I forgot myself for a minute. This was months ago now. I had no idea Craig had us followed and photographed, probably for just this occasion when he needed leverage. If I do anything more to anger him, he'll send the pictures to Paul. Game, set, match." She sat back in her seat, her expression morose.

Annalisa set the photos down. "There has to be a way to stop him."

"No, you can't risk it. At least he's on leave at the hospital. His reputation took a big hit and people are onto him now. He's so arrogant that he'll carry on with his usual bag of tricks, but maybe someone will catch him next time."

Years on the job had taught Annalisa that there was no such thing as a perfect murder. Craig Canning had to have screwed up somewhere. "We know he took a trophy from Vicki Albright's murder—the charm from the wind chimes. But what about Lizzie Johnston? Would he take something from her too?"

Mara perked up. "Probably. Was anything missing from her body?"

"Her wallet was gone." He'd needed Annalisa to be the point of contact, so he'd removed Lizzie's ID and left Annalisa's business card.

"Ten to one he has it then."

"Still, I'd need a warrant." She sighed and shook her head. "I meant Nick would need a warrant."

Mara gave her a tight smile. "Old dogs and new tricks, eh?"

"I guess. It was my job, you know, catching the bad guys."

"And it was my job to study them," Mara said, her voice wistful. "I guess we both lost this round."

"Maybe." Annalisa picked up the top photo, the one showing Mara and Canning kissing. "But I think maybe the game's not over yet."

....

IT TOOK HER THREE MORE DAYS TO FIGURE OUT THE MISTAKE. She visited the scene of Lizzie's shooting. She replayed the scene in her mind a hundred times. When she realized his error, it was so obvious she didn't know how she'd missed it before. "The phone," she exclaimed, sitting bolt upright in bed.

"Wha . . . ? Anna, what time is it?" Nick stirred beside her, squinting as she turned on the light. Jack, delighted to see someone awake in the nighttime, climbed her like she was a jungle gym.

"Lizzie's phone. You need to check it for prints." Canning would have used gloves for the shooting and to plant her business card, but he'd have needed to take them off to send the text to 911. Gloves thick enough to withstand gunpowder residue would not transmit a signal to a touch screen. "Canning had to use Lizzie's phone to text 911, which means he had to take the gloves off." She removed the kitten from her head and he rolled over in her lap, swatting at her with tiny paws.

"Okay, okay, I'll check with Rodriguez in the morning."

"Can't you do it now?"

"It's almost three. If I drag him out of bed to ask him about a print report, he's liable to arrest me for the murder."

"Don't even joke."

"If Canning's prints are on the phone, they aren't going anywhere. We can check it tomorrow."

·············

THE PRINTS WERE ON THE PHONE. Annalisa did a victory dance when Nick called to tell her. "It's a single print from Canning's index finger. He probably wiped it down quickly and happened to miss one. It'll be enough to get a search warrant."

"Look for Lizzie's wallet," Annalisa told him. "It's got to be there somewhere."

"We'd better hope so because it will be tough to nail him otherwise. You want to tag along when we serve the warrant?"

Annalisa could hardly believe the offer. "Really? You mean it?"

"Well, you can't come up while we serve the warrant, but the building's lobby is public enough. Anyone could happen by. No one could stop you from being there at about four-fifteen this afternoon when we plan to walk Dr. Craig Canning out in handcuffs."

Oh, she almost salivated at the thought of it. "Tell me you also alerted the media."

"Not me. I would never. But sometimes they get anonymous tips."

When Annalisa arrived at the appointed hour, she saw three news vans idling on the street. Rodriguez ran point on the operation, backed up by Nick and a half dozen men and women in blue. Annalisa felt a stab of envy, an ache at being sidelined as she watched them storm the lobby and head for the elevators. At the front desk, Damon watched the procession with nervous eyes. He looked wary when she approached him. "I owe you an apology," she said.

"You mean for breaking into the office? Taking Dr. Canning's key and going into his apartment like that?" He busied himself with tidying the desk, not looking at her. "It could've meant my job, you know."

"I know and I'm sorry."

He shook his head at her. "Maybe you ain't a cop no more, but you still think like one. Rules don't apply."

"If the super gives you any trouble, send him to me."

"And like, then what?" Now he did look at her. "What are you going to say to him? You don't have a badge. He don't have to listen to you."

"It must be okay so far," Annalisa ventured. "If you're still here."

"Yeah, but what's all this about?" He gestured after the officers who'd marched through the lobby. "No one's going to be happy about this."

"Can't be helped. Sorry."

He sucked in his lower lip for a moment. "Is it Dr. Canning? Is that why they're here? I saw the news about Vicki accusing him of . . . well, you know."

"Yes, they're here to speak to Craig Canning."

"So it's true?" His gaze turned worried. "The dude is bad news?"

Annalisa didn't get a chance to answer. Nick reappeared, looking spooked. He gestured to her and she excused herself to Damon. "What is it? Did you find the wallet?"

"Canning is dead," he told her in a low voice. "Gunshot wound to the temple. Gun at the scene."

"What?" She felt the blood leave her body. "Suicide?"

"Initially that's what it looks like. Obviously there will be an investigation. We didn't see any note or explanation. He's been dead for less than twelve hours."

A coroner's van rolled up outside as Annalisa tried to absorb the shock. Canning was dead and his threats had died with him. She was free. She should be happy. And yet . . . . "I don't believe it," she whispered. "Craig Canning wouldn't kill himself. He's the only person who mattered in his world. He was threatening to sue me and Mara into oblivion over the loss of his job, and he might've won his case."

"He had lost his job. The papers were calling him a possible rapist. Plus, we just found evidence that put him at a murder scene. If he thought the net was really closing in on him, maybe he took the only way out. We don't get to put him in jail. We don't get the satisfaction."

"He still wins," Annalisa murmured.

Nick touched her arm. "Look, I gotta get back up there. I'll see you at home?"

She nodded but did not move. She watched him cross the marble floor and disappear into the elevator. The press was being held at bay by a uniformed cop at the front door. She'd somehow slipped behind the blue line and she didn't want to give up her spot. She took a seat on the bench and tried to look inconspicuous. Eventually, Zimmer herself showed up on the scene. She eyed Annalisa and her lips thinned out, like she couldn't believe what she was seeing. Then she summoned Annalisa closer with a jerk of her head. "Vega," she said. "Why am I not surprised to find you here?"

"Because you're the smartest commander CPD has ever had?" Annalisa ventured.

Zimmer chuffed a noise of disbelief, but a smile tugged at her lips. She reined it in quick. "You were never a suck-up when you worked for me, Vega. Don't start now."

"Yes, ma'am."

"Carelli says you don't think this was suicide."

"He told you what I think?"

Zimmer appeared annoyed by her surprise. "You don't work with us anymore, but we're both acutely aware of your investigation skills. You've been tangling with this victim for some time. What can you tell me about him?"

Annalisa gave her the rundown on Canning's unproven murders, and Zimmer's only reaction was a slight frown. "Let's hope he left a long note confessing everything," she said.

"If there's a note, it probably tries to pin it on me."

"That's not funny," Zimmer told her.

"Who's laughing?"

The next day, Annalisa parlayed her keen investigatory skills into a special invitation to view Canning's apartment. His body had been removed and the whole place searched, top to bottom. Lizzie Johnston's wallet turned up inside a carved wooden box he kept in his closet. He had not left any note. The gun, a .22 revolver modeled after those in the Old West, was registered in his name. Annalisa had not found it during her earlier search of the apartment. "What does forensics say?" she asked Nick as she walked the apartment. "Was the gun in his hand when it was fired?"

"Definite powder residue on his right hand. Gunshot was delivered within inches of the right temple," Nick said, pantomiming the shot on his own head. "If Canning didn't pull the trigger, someone got close enough to him to make it look like he did."

"And the body was found here?" Annalisa indicated an armchair in the living room. Canning's last view was out the glass doors to the balcony, where the whole story began.

"He was sitting in the chair right there, yes," Nick affirmed. "No forced entry. Balcony doors locked from the inside. No evidence of anyone else at the scene."

Annalisa checked the bedroom. She wasn't even sure what she was looking for, what piece of evidence would make it all seem right. Canning's place had been tidy and well-ordered when she'd searched it. Now it looked like it had been ransacked by a band of rabid raccoons. She closed the drawers on his dresser one by one, then moved to the office where she did the same with the desk and cabinets. He had a dozen awards but no family photos, she realized. On his wall, he kept framed photos of his diplomas. He had a bachelor of science from the University of Wisconsin, where he graduated summa cum laude. Then he went to Yale for medical school. Craig Canning had a dizzying array of academic and medical achievements, but no human credential. No one to mourn him. She guessed maybe he'd preferred it that way.

"Well?" Nick asked from the doorway. "You find anything?"

Annalisa let her gaze linger on his wall of honors. "No," she said, dejected.

Nick waved something at her, and she saw it was Mara's book. "He's got like ten copies of this if you want to snag one. I bet they're going to go for big bucks on eBay."

For Donna, Annalisa recalled. Another one who never got satisfaction from her battle with a sociopath. She was such a sweet, trusting girl, Mara had said. The perfect roommate. "Roommate," Annalisa repeated to herself. Mara's voice floated back to her. They'd roomed together in Madison during college. Madison was in Wisconsin. "Let me see that." She took the book from Nick's hands and flipped to the back that showed Mara's picture and biography. Educated at the University of Wisconsin and then UCLA for her PhD. Had she been there at the same time as Craig Canning? They were about the same age.

"What is it?" Nick asked. "You got something?"

"Maybe," Annalisa said as she closed the book with an uneasy feeling. "Or maybe not. I need to talk to Mara Delaney."

FORTY-THREE

··········

ANNALISA TRIED A FEW TIMES OVER THE NEXT FEW DAYS TO REACH MARA. She left her a couple of voicemails. She texted. She even drove by Mara's town house but got no answer when she knocked. After four full days with no contact, Annalisa started to get worried. At the hospital with Nick and Cassidy, she remembered Mara's husband, Paul, worked there too, and she sought him out to ask about Mara. She had to wait almost an hour in a little reception area with only year-old *People* magazines for company, but eventually Paul appeared dressed in blue scrubs with a white coat over them. He paused to use the hand sanitizer at the front desk. "Ms. Vega," he said in a friendly tone. "Come on back. What can I help you with?"

"I'm having trouble reaching Mara," Annalisa said as she followed him to his office. Like Canning, he had a wall full of commendations and a medical degree from Rosalind State University.

"She went to visit her aunt Susan in the UP for a few days. Sue has a little cabin that she gets ready every spring and Mara went up there to help her. They don't get great cell service in the woods, but honestly I think it's good Mara's getting away for a while. The reporters have been relentless." He gave Annalisa a probing look. "I assume you know she's on leave from the university."

"Yes, I heard."

"Nasty business, all of it."

"Do you know when Mara will be back?"

"Gosh, I'm not sure. This weekend, maybe. Why do you need to reach her?"

"I had a question for her about Craig Canning." Idly, she examined his bookshelves. They were jammed with medical textbooks, journals, and various knickknacks. A snow globe with the Chicago skyline in it. A small bronze alligator. A stuffed badger wearing a red-and-white striped jersey with a W emblazoned on the front.

"Canning," Paul said with a distasteful downturn of his mouth. "He's dead. What more is there to know?"

"You didn't like him," Annalisa observed.

"Nor did you. Mara told me you were convinced he'd murdered that girl. What was her name? Vicki Albright."

"Nothing I could ever prove."

He shrugged. "He killed himself, yes? Guilt will out and all that."

"I'm not sure Craig Canning ever felt guilt. To hear Mara tell it, he was incapable."

"Yeah, well, Mara was wrong about him, now, wasn't she?" His eyes had started watering and he reached for a tissue immediately before sneezing into it. "Please excuse me. Allergies."

"You were saying about Craig and Mara."

"Craig and Mara," he repeated with biting sarcasm. "There was no 'Craig and Mara,' no matter how much he might have wished other-wise."

"You think he had a romantic interest in her?"

"I think he tried to nail every woman who crossed his path." He paused to eye her with a speculative gaze. "You would know better than me." When Annalisa did not respond to his insinuation he gave an annoyed sigh and sat forward across his desk. "Look, I'm not stupid. I know he was running his usual plays with Mara—little gifts, dropping by the house, expensive dinners at Davio's. She was so wrapped up in her book idea that she couldn't see the truth of what he really was."

"But you could?"

"I clocked his number the first moment I met him. A good sociopath my ass. Craig Canning was a brilliant doctor but a lousy human being."

Dinners at Davio's, Annalisa thought. "It was you," she told him. "You left those pictures for Mara. Craig wasn't tailing her with a camera— you were."

Momentary shock colored his features. He shrank back from her in his chair and cleared his throat. "What pictures? I don't know what you mean."

"The photos of Mara and Craig together. Mara was right—they were a warning to her, but not from Craig. You had her followed that night. Or maybe you even did the surveillance yourself."

"I don't know what you're talking about. I—I think you need to leave now. I have patients to see. I'll . . . I'll have Mara call you . . . when she gets home." He blustered as he rose from the chair, gesturing at the office door.

She took her time getting up. His scrubs were rumpled. Was that a bit of blood on them? On her way to the door, she paused to touch the stuffed badger. "University of Wisconsin?" she asked. "I didn't know you attended." It wasn't one of the degrees on his wall.

"Failed PhD," he said tightly as he held the door open for her. "I left and went to medical school instead. Mara graduated from UW. It's a gift from her."

"Is that where you met then?"

He looked confused by her question. "No, we met on a dating app ten years ago. Here in the city. Now, I really do need you to leave. I have a three-thirty appointment."

Annalisa left the office, musing on her meeting with Paul. He didn't seem at all concerned that his wife was off the grid. Annalisa had never seen him dressed in scrubs before, hadn't known he ever wore them. It gave her an idea. In the reception area, she went to the wall showing the doctors' headshots alongside their names. She snapped a picture of Paul. *Running out for a bit,* she texted Nick. Then she went outside the hospital and down the block to the boutique store where someone had purchased the wind chimes found at the scene of Vicki Albright's death. *A doctor,* the clerk had said. He was buying them for his wife or a girlfriend. Annalisa had been sure this was Canning who made the purchase, but perhaps she had been wrong.

"Hi," she said brightly when she reached the counter. "I was in a couple of weeks ago asking about the purchase of some wind chimes. I spoke to Fran. Is she here today?"

"Fran," called the young male clerk. "Someone's here to see you."

"Oh, hello," Fran said as she appeared from the back room. She recognized Annalisa, which Annalisa took as a good sign. "Are you still looking for those wind chimes?"

"More like I'm trying to find the man who bought them."

"I told you everything I know."

"Yes, I know. I just wanted to show you one more picture." She called up the snapshot she'd taken of Paul's face. "Could this have been the man?"

Fran put on her glasses and took Annalisa's phone. "Oh," she said. "Yes. He's much closer to the gentleman I remember. Friendly fellow."

"Thank you," Annalisa said as she accepted her phone back. *I clocked his number the first moment I met him,* Paul had said. Paul had recognized Craig as a sociopath. Maybe he had recognized this deviance because Paul was a sociopath himself. He'd known about Mara's affair. He'd hated Craig Canning. Now Canning was dead and Mara's absence felt more ominous.

Annalisa went back to Canning's apartment building. Damon did not appear happy to see her. "What kind of trouble are you making this time?" he asked as she leaned on the high counter in front of his desk.

"I need you to look at a picture for me." She gave him her phone with Paul's photo. "Have you ever seen this man hanging around the building?"

Damon frowned at the image. "Is he part of your association or something?"

"What are you talking about?"

"Like a PI club. He's one of you guys."

"You're saying this man told you he's a private investigator?"

"You're saying he's not?" Damon's eyes bugged out. "I knew you were bringing me more headaches. Man, this never stops."

"Tell me about this man."

"He came here maybe two months ago. Had a fancy camera on him. Said he was a PI hired by one of the building tenants after a break-in. He wanted to know about our security. I told him no tenants had reported any kind of break-in."

"Did you tell him about the security?"

"I showed him the cameras, told him about the keys. He seemed satisfied."

"Did he ask about Dr. Canning at all?"

Damon stroked his chin, thinking. "You know, I think he said something about him. We have that old newspaper story tacked up on the community board by the mailboxes. He saw it hanging there and said it must be nice having a celebrity in the building. Why?"

"No reason. Thanks, Damon. You've been a big help. I won't be bothering you anymore."

He pursed his lips. "Dr. Canning always seemed so nice. Guess you don't know anything for sure about anyone."

She gave him her card. "If you think of anything more about the PI, let me know."

He looked down at her name. "He wasn't a real PI, was he?" She regarded him with sympathy. He shook his head before she could answer. "Never mind. Don't tell me. I don't want to know."

"Call me anytime you need," she said. "I don't just make trouble. Sometimes I get people out of it."

"Yeah," he said, his tone grudging. He tucked her card away and nodded at her jacket. "You get a dog or a cat or something?"

She looked down at the white hairs dotting her jacket. "A kitten. He's shedding like crazy."

"Mrs. B can help you with that. She had that cat, Duchess, but I swear I never saw a hair on her. She knows the secret."

"Thanks, I'll ask her."

On her way out of the building, picking fur off her clothes, Annalisa stopped cold. Duchess. Paul's sneezing. Of course. She quickened her stride and called up Nick. "I need you to find a way to search Paul and Mara Delaney's place."

"What exactly am I looking for?"

"Evidence of a murder." She only hoped there wouldn't be signs that Mara was the latest victim. "Mara's missing. I haven't been able to reach her for days."

"She's an adult. She's allowed to be missing."

"I know that," Annalisa said impatiently. "But I'm worried about her. She hasn't answered a text or an email for almost a week now, and that's not like her."

"What does Paul say?"

"That Mara's in the UP visiting her aunt Susan."

"Okay, well, there you go."

"Nick . . ."

"Anna, I don't know what you want me to do here. You know the law as well as I do. Unless you have some specific reason to justify a search of the Delaneys' home, something more than a vague worry about Mara's safety, then there is nothing we can do right now."

Annalisa hung up in frustration and drove back to her office. She would track down this Aunt Susan and find out if Mara was really with her. If, as she suspected, Mara was not there, this would catch Paul in a lie and be enough to justify a warrant to search the house. She turned on the coffee maker and powered up her computer. By the time she'd drunk three cups and searched four databases, she had her answer. She called Nick back. "Get your warrant ready," she told him.

"What now?" he asked.

"I found an interview with Mara Delaney from the campus newspaper dating back to when she joined the university six years ago. She talks about growing up in foster care. Her parents were both dead by the time she was eight years old. She has no living family. Nick, Mara doesn't have an aunt Susan."

....

THE FICTITIOUS AUNT SUSAN WASN'T ENOUGH FOR A SEARCH WARRANT FOR THE DELANEY HOUSE, NICK ARGUED, BUT IT WAS ENOUGH FOR HIM TO REQUEST HER CELL PHONE RECORDS. When Mara's phone showed it had never left her home neighborhood, despite Paul saying she'd gone to the UP, Nick got his warrant.

"This is crazy," Paul said when Nick showed up with Annalisa and two uniformed officers. "Mara's not here. I told you, she's on vacation."

"Right," Annalisa said. "With the aunt she doesn't have."

"What are you talking about?" Paul said. "She's been up to visit several times."

"We can check closets, under beds . . . anywhere a person could be hiding," Nick reminded the officers.

"Hiding?" Paul waved the search warrant around. "You've lost your damn minds."

Annalisa looked in the coat closet, the kitchen pantry—even the narrow broom cabinet. Nick and his boys took the upstairs. Everything seemed to be in order, so Annalisa went down to the basement. The stinging scent of cat pee told her she'd hit her mark. "Duchess?" she called softly. "Duchess, are you here, girl?" No reply.

She took out a small bag of cat treats they had at home for Jack and rattled them in the shadowy room. "Here, kitty. I've got yummy snacks." She started shifting boxes aside. The longer she got no answer, the faster her heart started racing. "Here, kitty kitty." Duchess was the key to everything. If Paul had moved her, if she was dead . . .

Meow.

"Oh, thank God," Annalisa breathed when she heard the faint mewling sound. She yanked more boxes aside until she found a pathetic white cat curled in on itself in the corner. Duchess was thin but otherwise seemed okay. "Hey, girl," Annalisa said, crouching down and extending her hand. "I'm going to get you out of here, okay? Your mom is going to be so happy to see you."

Duchess gave Annalisa's fingers a delicate sniff and decided it was okay to unfurl her tail. She rubbed against Annalisa's leg and started purring. Annalisa scooped her up and took the stairs two at a time until she reached the men standing around on the first floor. "No sign of Mara," Nick said. "What's that?"

Annalisa looked to Paul. "Mara was right," she said as she cuddled the terrified cat. "They always take a trophy."

FORTY-FOUR

....

PAUL DELANEY DENIED EVERYTHING. He lawyered up quick and the lawyer put out a strong statement that Paul was innocent of any wrongdoing, which would become obvious when all facts were at hand. But the facts were few and Mara was still nowhere to be found. Nick dug into the couple's financial records and discovered that someone had transferred Mara's million-dollar book advance into an offshore account. The police suspected Paul had done this and then killed Mara. Paul argued Mara had done it and disappeared. Without a body, there was little the authorities could do to advance their case. They had a forensics team go through the Delaney home and found no blood or other evidence of harm.

"I know it's upsetting," Nick said to Annalisa over take-out Indian food one night. "But until we can prove Mara's deceased, we can't charge Paul with anything."

"He had Ruth Bernstein's cat!"

"He claims the animal must have gotten in through the broken window." Nick stirred his lamb saag with a fork.

"A heck of a coincidence, Duchess getting across town and happening to pick the town house of a murder suspect—a murder her owner witnessed."

"I agree, it stinks. Literally." The animal had been living in the basement for weeks.

"Other stuff makes so much more sense now," Annalisa said as she tore into some garlic naan. "Like why he wouldn't alibi Mara for the fire at her office. He said he'd sent her out to a late-night pharmacy to get allergy medicine. Yeah, so he could use her ID to break in and set fire to her office."

"What about the lighter?" Nick asked. "You said it looked like Canning's."

"Yeah, I can answer that." She got up and went to her bag, where she took out the photos Mara had left her, the ones of her and Canning canoodling outside the restaurant. "Look here at Canning lighting up his cigarette. You can totally see the jaguar lighter in his hand. It wouldn't have been hard for Paul to track down a similar model."

"I'll look into it," Nick said as he put aside the photo.

"Mara said sociopaths like to brag. They think they're smarter than everyone else so they sometimes slip up. I wonder if Paul could have been telling the truth about the cabin in the UP. Maybe it's real even if there's no aunt Susan. It could be where he took Mara."

"No other property is registered in his name," Nick said.

"A relative then."

"I'll check."

"I can do it."

Nick put down his fork. "Anna . . . you have to leave this alone now. If you go after Paul Delaney, he'll have you up on harassment charges and they would probably stick. I don't want to have to arrest my wife."

"Mara came to me for help," Annalisa said, her eyes downcast. "She hired me to help her and she ended up murdered. I never saw it coming."

"Neither did she," Nick said gently. "And she was married to the guy." He reached over and took her hand. "None of this is your fault."

Annalisa let him hold her hand but she did not relax. "I don't know how she could have missed that she had married a sociopath. She was supposed to be the expert."

"Love is blind."

Only, if the sociopath's profile was to be believed, Paul had never loved Mara. But he sure had hated her. Paul had plotted for months to destroy his wife's and Craig Canning's careers and then he'd taken their lives too. Nuked them from orbit, as Annalisa's niece would say. The sociopath's ultimate win.

....

ANNALISA WAS STILL STEWING THE NEXT DAY, SIFTING THROUGH THE FACTS OF THE CASE AT HER OFFICE, WHEN HER PHONE RANG. Her ex-cop father had always reminded her not to get too attached to any one theory, even when the answer seemed obvious. You never know what new bit of information will bring the whole thing crashing down, he told her. For Anna, that bit was Damon Young.

"You said I could call you," he reminded her. "About anything."

"Sure, what's up?"

"I've been following the news—you know, about Dr. Canning. That lady who wrote the book on him, now she's missing?"

"Yes," Annalisa said, her tone cautious. "Why do you ask?"

"Well, I been wondering: could they have been in on it together? Like, maybe she pushed Vicki off the balcony while he went to the hospital. It'd explain how he seemed like he was in two places at once."

Annalisa froze. "What makes you say that?"

"It's just a theory I had."

"Something must have made you think it."

He hummed a non-reply and Annalisa waited him out. Eventually, he muttered something that sounded like *fuck it*. "About six months ago," he said, "I was studying in this little coffee shop where I like to hang. They make a bangin' macchiato, way better than that nasty Starbucks crap, and it's quiet during the afternoon so I can get work done. Anyway, I had my forensic psych book out and this woman comes over to ask me about it. She was older than me, but smokin' hot. Classy-like. She said she'd taken the course, and if I had any questions about the final, she'd help me with them."

"Uh-huh," Annalisa said, wondering where this was going.

"We got to talking. She was funny and cool. Said she was in grad school studying to be an actual psychologist. Later, she came back to my place for a drink, and uh, we hooked up." He coughed and then sucked in a breath. "For a while, we were pretty regular. Then she up and ghosted me. No phone call, no text. After like a week, the phone went to an automated voice saying the number doesn't even exist. I mean, what the hell?"

"Sounds rough."

"Yeah, well, I didn't think too much more about it until I saw her face on the news. When, uh, when they said she was missing."

Annalisa almost dropped the phone. "I'm sorry, are you saying you had an affair with Mara Delaney?"

"Uh, that's the thing," Damon said, his voice hollow. "She didn't tell me her name was Mara. She said her name was Donna."

··········

*F*OR DONNA. Annalisa had a good couple of hours to contemplate the dedication of Mara's book while she drove out to the University of Wisconsin. It always struck her as odd that Mara would link her friend's tragic story to a book singing the praises of the good sociopaths. Donna had been victimized by a male sociopath while at the University of Wisconsin and now Annalisa suspected that sociopath was Craig Canning. The book wasn't a tribute to Canning. It was part of Mara's revenge tour. It explained so much, including how she'd known he was a sociopath before she'd ever tested him. She'd met him before, when he'd destroyed her friend Donna's life, and Mara set out to bring him down. First, she built him up, gave him a national profile. All those interviews. All that publicity. She'd used Damon Young to keep an eye on Canning, maybe even to gain access to his apartment. Damon had the keys. Annalisa figured the plan was to convince the world Canning was a good sociopath and then reveal the truth about what he really was. Annalisa wondered when Mara had begun to suspect she was in too deep. Was it when Vicki Albright made the accusation that Craig had drugged and raped her? That's what had happened to Donna. Mara would have known Craig had a history of this behavior. Then when Vicki had plunged off the balcony . . . no wonder Mara had been scared enough to start digging around on her own, why she'd hired a private investigator.

I'm not giving up, Annalisa told her mentally. *I'm going to find out what happened to you.*

She was sure it all went back to UW. Maybe Paul was mixed up in it too somehow. She'd called the university to ask about an incident that had taken place some years ago with a student named Donna Hawkins. That was the name Mara gave to Damon, so Annalisa figured it had to be the same Donna that Mara named in her book. Eventually, she was put in touch with a senior professor named Warren Bowman, and he agreed to speak to her about Donna Hawkins. She had been his student.

When Annalisa arrived at the large brick building, she noted Warren Bowman's name appeared on the floor of the psychology department. In his office, she found a man who looked more like Santa Claus than a college professor. "Welcome, welcome," he said, clearing aside books and folders from a chair so she could sit down. "I apologize for the mess. I'm retiring this summer and I don't know where I'm supposed to put my career."

Annalisa saw he had the usual framed degrees on his wall, but also a Degas print and some images that looked like brain scans. "I appreciate you taking the time to see me."

He made an expansive gesture. "All I've got right now is time. How can I help you?"

"As I mentioned, I'm trying to learn everything I can about a former student of yours, Donna Hawkins."

He frowned into his beard. "Donna, yes. Such an upsetting story."

"She lost out on a scholarship of some kind?" Annalisa asked. "I heard she took it hard."

"A year at Oxford," the professor agreed. "An amazing opportunity."

"I heard that the scholarship went instead to Craig Canning. Is that right?"

He narrowed his eyes at her and his tone grew more guarded. "Yes, I believe that's the year Canning won the prize. It's always a tough call, determining the awardee. We get at least a hundred applicants every year, and Donna was a strong candidate. But after what happened, there was no choice but to disqualify her."

"Because she missed the final interview?" A male rival had drugged Donna so she didn't make the interview, Mara had said. She never mentioned it was Canning.

"Missed an interview . . . ?" Professor Bowman gave her a quizzical look and then shook his head. "All of this is ancient history. Why are you asking about Donna now?"

"Did you know Craig Canning?" she countered.

He peaked his fingers together. "Not well, no. Canning had a concentration in biology, as I remember. I chair the psychology department. I would have interviewed him as part of the scholarship committee, but that's true of all the finalists. I heard he'd become a big-time surgeon in your neck of the woods."

"That's right."

His expression darkened. "I also heard he took his own life recently."

"That's the official finding, yes."

"Official finding," he said shrewdly. "But you think otherwise? That's why you're here asking these questions?"

"What about Mara Delaney or Paul Delaney? Did you know them?"

"The name Mara Delaney sounds familiar."

"She's been in the news."

He shrugged. "I don't follow the news. Dreadful stuff."

"She was also a student here at the same time as Donna. They were friends and roommates. Maybe you had a class with her?"

"I can check." He grabbed his keyboard and punched in some keys. While he worked, Annalisa let her gaze travel over the books he had stacked around the room. They felt awfully familiar. *Without Conscience,* by Robert Hare. *The Complexity of Psychopathology*—a compendium. *When Brains Go Bad.* And an older one entitled *Neurological Correlates of Psychopathology*, by Warren Bowman.

"Is this your book?" Annalisa tugged it from the pile.

"One of six, yes." He peered over the rims of his glasses at her. "But that's my favorite."

She read the description on the inside. "It's about brains of sociopaths?"

"Broadly speaking, yes. That's been my passion and pursuit for all my life. Why, are you interested in the topic?"

"I've been studying up recently," Annalisa replied. She read a few sentences. "Is it true you can tell whether someone is a sociopath by doing a brain scan on them?"

"It's not quite that simple. But there are certain patterns that are strongly associated with sociopathic traits. See that image up there?" He pointed. "The PET scan on the left is a control subject—no evidence of socio- or psychopathology. The one on the right scored high on the Hare scale of sociopathy. You can see the lower activity levels in the front part of the brain in the image on the right. That's the area that controls planning and moral reasoning. They also show reduced activity in the amygdala, a brain area that responds to fear."

"So if you saw someone with this brain scan, you'd know they were a sociopath?"

"I'd be wary of them, yes." He leaned forward and peered at his screen. "I'm sorry, we don't have any record of Mara Delaney here."

"She never took your classes?"

"Mine or anyone's." He turned the monitor so she could see. "No one by that name was ever a student here."

"But that's not possible. She has a degree . . . oh, wait. Delaney was her married name." She dug out her phone, wondering if she could access Mara's maiden name. It might even have turned up in her earlier searches someplace. She went to the cloud to pull down the files. She could search them if she knew what name to search for, but then if she knew the name, she wouldn't have to search. Her head started to ache and she put aside the phone. "Is there anyone else who might have known Donna at that time? Someone who could have known her roommate too?"

"I'm sure I don't know. I only knew Donna from my classes and my research."

"Research?" Her eyes went to the images on the wall. "She was a subject?"

"She helped run one of my early studies." He frowned. "I thought that was why you were here asking about the incident."

"Someone drugged Donna the day before her interview for the scholarship. Maybe that someone was Craig Canning. He was competing with her for the prize so he ensured she'd blow it."

"What? No." He looked horrified. "I never heard anything about an assault."

"Mara said the university covered it up. That they didn't believe Donna. That's why she killed herself."

"This is the first I've heard of any of this."

"You must remember," she pressed him. "Denying Donna the scholarship to Oxford."

"Yes, after what she did, we had no choice."

"After what she did?"

"Donna was one of the students working with me on the brain scan study. She couldn't do the actual PET analysis, of course. She administered the psychological tests and scored them. They were done in batches, though, with the subject's name detached. Each one was assigned a coded number to ensure the study was blinded."

"Blinded?"

"Donna didn't know the names of the students as she scored their psychological tests. Neither did the medical technicians doing the PET scans and evaluating them for signs of psychopathology. Only I knew who was who. At the end, once everything was tallied, we would line up those who scored high on the psychological analysis with those who showed brain patterns suggesting sociopathy to see if they matched."

"And did they?"

"We had to cancel the study. Throw it out." Years on, he still looked pained. "All that wasted time and money."

"What happened?" Annalisa asked.

"Craig Canning was one of our test subjects. Donna knew this and she used my credentials to access the computer files and look at his test results."

"After what he'd done to her, she probably wanted to see if he was a sociopath."

"She never said a word about him assaulting her. She never explained herself at all. But yes, she brought the results to the committee. She said we could not award Craig Canning the prize because his test results were strongly indicative of sociopathy. When I looked at the analysis, I had to agree, but there was nothing we could do about it. He'd broken no laws, no code of ethics that we were aware of. The science linking brain scan results to pathological behavior was still in its infancy. Even now, it's not precisely proven. Craig Canning was an exemplary student, just as Donna had been before this outburst. I removed her from the lab and the committee voted to award the prize to Canning. Donna was furious, but there was no one to blame but herself."

"If he had drugged and assaulted her . . ."

"I told you, she never said one word about that. Even if she had . . ." He broke off and turned his eyes toward the window. "I'm not sure I would have believed her."

Annalisa felt hot around the collar. Years of this, and it never changed. Women were never believed.

"After the prize was settled and the study was terminated, I went through the analysis anyway," Professor Bowman continued. "Just for my own edification. I matched everyone's scores on the test with their PET scan analysis. We had trouble recruiting for the study. The department wouldn't let us offer much in the way of financial compensation and the PET scan isn't exactly a fun procedure. So, everyone in the lab also underwent testing." He looked at her, his gaze troubled. "Donna's results also indicated sociopathy. One of the highest scores I've ever seen in person. She had the brain scan to match."

Annalisa sat back, gobsmacked. "What happened to her?"

"She got her degree and moved away. I didn't hear anything from her after that, like she'd disappeared entirely."

Disappeared entirely. Annalisa had a creeping dread curling in her gut like a boa constrictor. She had a feeling she knew what had happened to Donna. "Professor . . . do you happen to have a picture of Donna Hawkins?"

"Hmm, let me think. We did take photos at the annual holiday party. Let me check the files." He poked around for a few minutes and when he turned his monitor around again, Annalisa needed only one look to see the truth.

It was Mara.

FORTY-FIVE

....

MARA WAS IN THE WIND. She had her million dollars and could go wherever she wished. Annalisa imagined her on a Caribbean beach somewhere, a fruity drink in her hand, laughing about how she had fooled them all. Now that she had all the pieces, Annalisa could see how she'd been played. She'd fallen for Mara's manipulation from the start, when the woman came to her office and tearfully confessed her fears about Craig Canning. Annalisa would believe her worries because Annalisa had been there before, Mara said. Annalisa knew the damage a dangerous sociopath could do. It was all true. Mara was right. And still Annalisa had missed the sociopath sitting right in front of her.

Professor Bowman was sympathetic when she explained her plight. "They can be excellent mimics of typical human emotion," he said. "They know all the right moves, and they learn early that a lie is best hidden between two truths. You believe the truths and miss the lie. Mara would have known that you have a history with violent psychopaths. She would have known you have an unerring commitment to justice. She picked you precisely for those reasons."

"You're saying she saw me for a patsy," Annalisa said, her ego still bruised. "And she was right."

"You're hardly alone in that."

"I've read her book," she told him. "Hers and others. I know more about sociopathy now than I ever cared to learn, and yet I still don't understand. Mara Delaney killed Vicki Albright and set up Craig Canning for the murder . . . why? Because back in college he won a scholarship she didn't? It makes no sense."

"In her mind, he'd defeated her. He'd won something she wanted. She tried exposing him one way by taking his test results to the committee but we didn't believe her. Canning didn't pay for his sin of besting her, so she bested him."

"In every way possible." Annalisa sat among the stacks of papers and books in Bowman's office. She felt less at sea here, less alone. This man had written textbooks on people like Mara and yet he hadn't seen her coming either. "Do you think she killed Canning too?"

"I think it's more likely than him committing suicide."

Annalisa brooded. She believed this too. "She could get into his apartment easily enough. He'd open the door for her. He might even have trusted her enough to turn his back on her."

"You're forgetting one thing," Bowman reminded her. "Canning's test results indicated high degrees of sociopathy too. He didn't trust. He simply didn't think she would be capable of getting the better of him."

"He clearly didn't recognize her."

"Well, we can see she took some care to disguise herself from her university days," Bowman said as he picked up a photo they had printed out of Mara from the lab. "She dyed her hair blond. Somewhere along the line, she bought herself a nose job. But it's entirely possible that she could have altered herself not one whit and Craig Canning still would not have recognized her. She didn't matter to him, so he didn't remember her."

"But if he's a sociopath and she's a sociopath, wouldn't he be best positioned to see through her act?"

Bowman rocked back in his chair. "Ah, but that's the flaw in the sociopath's thinking—they believe they are the only ones with special powers. They are the smartest, the trickiest, the most enlightened people on the planet. Everyone else is a chump. If you sincerely believe you are a singular god, you never imagine there could be anyone else like you. In this way, ironically, Craig Canning would be the least likely to see Mara's deception. He simply refused to believe he could be duped. Mara only knew Canning's true nature because she had access to the brain scans. She understood him better than he understood himself."

So it fell on Annalisa to explain the inexplicable. She had no hard proof. Mara had seen to that. She'd set up both Canning and her husband, Paul, as fallback villains so thoroughly that any prosecutor would find it difficult to untangle the lies enough to make sense of them for a jury. No one wanted to believe a person like Mara could exist. Easier to accept a jealous husband or a rapist doctor covering his tracks.

Paul, it turned out, had inadvertently captured as much truth as they were likely to find. "I don't understand," he said when Annalisa visited him after the charges against him were dropped. "Mara asked me to purchase the wind chimes . . . as part of a frame for Canning?"

"Yes, I think so," Annalisa replied. "She didn't want to be seen buying them herself."

"But she was sleeping with him." Paul was still hung up on the infidelity. He didn't seem to grasp Mara had never been faithful, not in her heart. She didn't have one.

"She said Canning initiated a sexual affair," Annalisa admitted. "But at this stage, I have to think she planned it that way. She had to get him on board with the book. She was using sex to distract him from her real plan."

Paul gave a slow blink of disbelief. "Which was to frame him for murder?"

"Yes. In a clever trap, designed to look almost impossible—the kind of murder Craig might have done for himself." And, she suspected, the kind he had engineered when he killed Lizzie Johnston.

"But he did rape that girl," Paul argued. "The one who got killed."

Annalisa hesitated. Paul had lived with Mara as man and wife for almost ten years. Maybe she'd never loved him, but he had loved her. What she had to say to him would shatter every last illusion he had about Mara. "Your pictures," she said gently as she removed them from her bag. "From the night Mara and Canning were at Davio's. This is the night Vicki said her assault took place. Your photos show that Canning is telling the truth. He left when Mara did. See? Here he is getting in his car and driving away. Mara goes back into the restaurant."

Paul studied the pictures with a pained expression. "I thought she was having another drink."

"I think she was. I think she drugged Vicki Albright that night. She took her home, undressed her, and assaulted her. It was part of the frame. She needed Canning to have a motive to murder Vicki."

"My God." His voice grew thick with anguish and horror and he pushed the photos away. "She'd have to be a monster. Not human. A literal monster."

Annalisa did not debate him, but on this point, she thought Mara had told the truth. Maybe the only truth in the whole damn mess. Sociopaths were undeniably human. They preyed on the weak and used the warmest parts of humanity—the trust, care, and forgiveness—against itself. To believe otherwise meant you would never understand them. Never see them coming.

Only Gavin Albright, Vicki's brother, seemed calm in the face of the revelations about Mara Delaney. Annalisa met him for coffee by Buckingham Fountain on a warm, windy spring day. "I knew she was off," he said to her as they moved to stay upwind of the spray. "Her story always stunk. I thought she was protecting her pet psychopath because of the book project, but really, she was protecting herself."

"I wish I could tell you she'll pay for it," Annalisa said. The police had searched for her, but it was as if Mara Delaney had vanished off the face of the earth. She'd been planning her scheme for years; it was reasonable to assume she had an escape hatch.

"She'll pay," Gavin said as he crushed his empty cup with one hand. "My sister's murder made me a very rich man. I'll spend every last dime of it hunting that bitch down. She can't hide forever."

Annalisa was not rich. She had to keep working, which meant accepting jobs that actually paid her money. She signed on to take a government case. The state of Illinois wanted to put up a municipal building but they couldn't determine who held the deed to the land since the original owners were long deceased. Annalisa needed only a day of googling to track down the descendants, who had no idea they were even the current title owners. Then a single mom scraped together four hundred dollars to hire Annalisa to find her runaway daughter who had taken off with her loser older boyfriend. Annalisa found the guy in a run-down apartment and determined he'd traded the girl to someone else in a drug deal. When Annalisa caught up with her, the traumatized teen was only too happy to come home.

In her spare time, however, she obsessed over Mara Delaney. Her office wall looked like some crazy conspiracy board, with pictures, timelines, and sticky notes with arrows on them. Sociopaths liked to brag, but they were still human. They were as vulnerable to tics and mistakes as the rest of the population. Annalisa knew if she could think like Mara, she could figure out where the woman had gone.

All this, she thought one afternoon as she studied her wall, *because you didn't get a scholarship to Oxford.* Annalisa could think of a hundred better places to be. But, she realized, Mara had wanted Oxford.

Could it really be that simple? The more she considered it, the more Annalisa became convinced. Mara had wreaked her revenge on Canning and now she'd take her victory lap. She'd claim the prize she believed belonged to her all along.

"I don't know," Nick said when Annalisa pitched him the idea of going to England. "Even if you found her in Oxford, what could you do? We can't actually prove she did anything. You'd practically have to get her to confess."

"I think she wants to. Hell, she practically told me so herself."

Nick threw his hands in the air in surrender. "One week," he said. "That's all we can do." The condo had sold and they were moving soon. Expenses were high and time was short. She kissed his cheek, grateful for the gift he was giving her. "You're the best."

He kissed her back. "Just nail her ass, okay?"

Annalisa flew to England and took up residence at a hostel in Oxford. She only needed a bed for sleeping because the rest of her hours were spent scouring spots she might expect to find Mara Delaney. She had no idea what name the woman would be using or how she might have altered her appearance. She started with the most obvious: the University of Oxford, the place where Canning got to study instead of her. Annalisa bummed around campus for a few days but got no leads. She then tried Mara's other move, the one that had netted her Damon Young, which was hanging around in coffee shops. She went to a dozen shops and showed Mara's picture to the staff. On the fourth day, she got a hit. Yes, someone resembling that lady had come in for coffee more than once, only she had dark hair.

Annalisa took a table with a view of the door and sat down to wait. As surveillance work went, this was a pretty good gig. The place smelled like sugar and dark-roast beans. Colorful cartoon paintings of dogs and cats hung on the walls, and she wondered idly how Jack was doing. She sipped her coffee and touched the soft yellow rose petals in the tiny vase on the table. The roses were like Mara, she thought: beautiful to look at, ready to prick you underneath. Her rear end went numb as the afternoon hours stretched into early evening. She was considering a bathroom break when the door opened and in walked Mara Delaney. Mara went to the counter and placed her order without noticing Annalisa. She fiddled with her phone while the barista got her coffee ready, looking like any other harried customer. Only when she received her order and turned to the display of cutlery and napkins did she see Annalisa staring at her.

Annalisa was pleased at the look of absolute shock on Mara's face. She tensed, preparing for Mara to bolt, but the woman rearranged her face into a broad smile and actually approached Annalisa's table. "Well," she said, "I see I wasn't wrong about you. I told Craig you would never give up. You're like one of those ankle-biter dogs. But who on earth is financing this little trip?"

"Maybe Paul," Annalisa suggested, and Mara laughed.

"If you're an ankle biter, he's a manatee. Sad, slow moving, and too stupid to get out of the way of a motorboat." Mara looked like the million bucks she had stashed away offshore. Posh haircut framing her face. Pale blue silk blouse and stiletto leather heels. A familiar necklace glittered at her throat and she fingered it as she contemplated Annalisa. "You're wasting your time and money. There's nothing you can do to me."

"I know. I know everything now. Doesn't that make you kind of excited?"

A smile twitched on Mara's lips. "You've been reading my book."

"No, this was more of a real-life lesson." Annalisa gestured at the chair opposite her. "Sit. Have your coffee. You've more than earned it."

"No way. I'm sure you're wearing a wire."

Annalisa spread her arms. "No wire."

Mara narrowed her eyes and set down her coffee. "Prove it."

Annalisa went to the restroom with Mara and let the other woman examine her for any hidden microphone. When Mara was satisfied, they went back to the table and Annalisa set her phone in sight so Mara could see it wasn't recording. Still, Mara appeared wary. She sipped her coffee and did not say anything. Annalisa chose an opening gambit she hoped would provoke her.

"I've been thinking your book was right all along."

Mara's delicate eyebrows disappeared under her wispy black bangs. "Oh?"

"Craig Canning was a useful sociopath. A good one, if you want to call it that."

"He wasn't good. To hear the media tell it, he was a rapist and a murderer."

"Ah, but we both know the truth about that, don't we?"

Mara answered with a small smile that she hid behind her coffee cup. "He killed that woman," she pointed out. "Just to harvest her organs."

"I can't condone Lizzie Johnston's death," Annalisa agreed. "But she murdered her whole family at fourteen years old. I looked it up. She was six weeks shy of her fifteenth birthday, the age at which the state of Idaho might have charged her as an adult and she would have faced the death penalty. Six short weeks and the government would have done what Craig Canning finally did and punished Lizzie Johnston for her crimes. If you believe it's possible for a person to forfeit their right to life, then Lizzie was already living on borrowed time. Done Craig Canning's way, at least some good came out of it."

"Yeah, yeah, he's a real saint."

"Vicki Albright, though . . . she was an innocent victim. You tossed her off that balcony like a piece of trash."

"She was trash. All that money and what was she doing with it? Buying her way into charity balls where she could dress up in fancy clothes and find men to take to bed. I'm not saying I killed her, but it's not like the world will miss her very much."

The way she said this, calm and emotionless, chilled Annalisa to the bone. It still wasn't proof. "You must be so annoyed," she said. "Miles Dupont told everyone you torched your own office. No one believed him, but he was right the whole time. You didn't fool him."

"Miles Dupont is a self-aggrandizing little toad. It turns out when you spend your days screaming at the sky about the weather, people start to tune you out—even when you might have a point. Do you think he's learned his lesson? I don't."

"You think everyone is like you," Annalisa said. "Empty inside. Scheming endlessly to get what they want."

"Everyone tries to get what they want. Everyone." Mara's voice took on a hard edge. "Look at you, halfway across the world to try to get me. Don't try to tell me you have no ego. That you don't want to win."

"Not enough to kill for it."

"I know." A look of disgust crossed Mara's face. She thought Annalisa was weak. "I figured you'd take down Craig when you had the chance, but you couldn't do it."

"You had to take care of him yourself," Annalisa said, leaning over the table. "Did you tell him? Did you let him know how bad you got him before you pulled the trigger? He must not have recognized you from your college days. I saw a picture. Your hair was longer back then. You wore glasses—and of course, your name was Donna Hawkins. He was a subject in the study you were conducting with Professor Bowman, so you had probably met him. Craig was good-looking, athletic. On his way to the top. He probably would have won the Oxford scholarship even if you hadn't interfered."

"It was mine," she said with sudden vehemence. "He took it from me."

"Was he surprised when you told him? When you admitted who you really were?"

"He laughed. Can you believe that? He called me pathetic for caring about an old school competition."

Oh, Annalisa saw it now. *More disrespect.* "He turned his back on you. He still didn't realize what you were. You knew he was a sociopath, but he hadn't figured out there were two of you in that room. He sat down in his chair and probably said something dismissive. Maybe he told you to go. That's when you shot him."

"So you say." Mara turned coy.

"Come on now," Annalisa cajoled. "You must want to gloat. There's no one else here but you and me, and you know I'm not wired. Tell me how smart you are. Craig Canning thought he was the world's most brilliant doctor, but you framed him for a murder and then shot him dead in his own living room. You made him look really stupid."

"And you too, for believing it." Mara smiled. "I had you spinning in circles. Craig thought he rescued me from my broken-down car that night in the rain, but he never bothered to check if the engine was running. I knew his route home from the hospital. I knew he liked women. It was so easy to put on some tight clothes, get soaking wet, and let his libido do the rest."

"He was dead the moment he pulled over," Annalisa said. "He just didn't know it yet."

"I had to get my million dollars. I needed him for that."

The good sociopath, Annalisa thought. "That's how you knew what he was. From the old experiments."

"They never told him," she said, sounding surprised. "They never told him the results of the study, not even when I took them to the committee. I'm not sure he ever believed me when I tried to show him the truth." She set her coffee cup down and gave a small shrug. "None of it matters now. Craig's dead and I'm bored with talking about him. I think I'll be going now."

"Wait," Annalisa said when Mara started to rise. "I didn't tell you one thing."

"What's that?"

"You were right about the trophies. We found Lizzie Johnston's wallet in Canning's apartment." Annalisa paused, and Mara gave a smug smile.

"Told you."

"But we never found the wind chimes. The ones I saw that had the missing charm from the set on Vicki Albright's balcony. The ones you had your husband buy to set up Canning for the murder."

Mara's expression turned guarded. "He got rid of them, like you said."

"No, see . . . he wouldn't have. Because he didn't kill Vicki. He didn't understand their significance. Only you knew what they meant, and you came back to claim them. A trophy." Annalisa reached over and snatched the necklace off Mara's neck. She held it to the light and the charm turned yellow. "Who's stupid now?" she said, looking over at Mara's aghast expression.

"You—you can't prove anything with that."

"I can when I combine it with this." Annalisa lifted the rose free from its petite vase. Underneath it was the bug that had been recording the whole conversation. She could send it all to Nick and he would file the official paperwork. Mara looked horrified. Furious. Powerless. Annalisa smiled. "I guess you're right," she told Mara. "I do like to win after all."

FORTY-SIX

···········

SUMMER WEAVER DIED IN MID-JUNE, JUST AS HER SEASON BEGAN. The family celebrated her life with an Irish wake at the bar she had owned with Melanie. They closed the place to the public and put up pictures of her everywhere. In one, Summer stood in an apron with Melanie behind the bar, both of them doing Rosie the Riveter poses. In another, she sat with baby Cassidy in a field of wildflowers. Annalisa did a slow circle, taking in every image. This had to be the place, she knew, where Nick and Summer had met. Summer had been waitressing at the time. Annalisa searched out Nick around the room and found him talking with Cassidy and Naomi, trying to show the girls how to balance a spoon on their noses.

"You need to get him a baby soon," Cassidy had said last week when she visited their new bungalow and saw the catwalk Nick had erected for Jack around the ceiling of the living room. "He's turning into a crazy cat person."

"His love dial is always turned to eleven," Annalisa replied. "Whether it's plant, person, animal."

The new house had three bedrooms. One for them, one for Cassidy when she stayed over, and one sitting empty, its white walls a blank canvas. Annalisa liked the sunny front windows and the private yard where she could put her large planters, like the peony tree now in bloom. She had visited Ruth Bernstein a few weeks ago and found the old woman had a new planting herself: she'd put in a pink rosebush in the garden, near where Vicki fell.

"How is Duchess?" Annalisa had asked her.

"Fat and sassy. But she no longer sleeps alone. Wherever I am, so is she."

"I like the roses," Annalisa said.

"They were Vicki's favorite. Her brother told me. Now when I come through here on my walks, I see the flowers and not . . ." She glanced briefly at the pavement where Vicki had landed. ". . . you know. It also helps that woman is in jail for what she did."

Annalisa had not corrected her. Mara Delaney was out on bail, but under house arrest with an ankle monitor and awaiting trial. It might be a year yet before she got convicted and sentenced. In the meantime, Annalisa resolved not to think about her anymore.

She got a soda water from the bar and picked up a handful of pretzels before joining Nick and the girls. "The photos are all lovely," she said to Cassidy, "but I think the painting you did is my favorite."

Cassidy had painted her mother sitting at a table with a cup of coffee, her chin in hand, a dreamy smile on her face as she looked out the window. "We had a little playground outside the apartment building when I was a kid," Cassidy said. "She used to sit and watch me play in the morning before she had to go to work."

"She wanted you to go to art school," Annalisa remembered. "But you weren't sure."

Cassidy's cheeks turned pink. "I am now. I'm applying to the Art Institute."

"So you'll be local," Nick said with obvious relief. "That's great."

"Dad, I still have to get in."

"You'll get in," Naomi told her, giving Cassidy's arm a squeeze. Nick's phone rang, and he excused himself from the group to go answer it. He returned a couple of minutes later, looking serious. "I've got to go."

"Now?" Annalisa asked him with a frown. "It's a wake for your kid's mom." Selfishly, she wanted Nick to stay, for her and for Cassidy. She wanted to talk to him alone and give him the small present she'd arranged to mark the day.

"Sorry. I'll be back as soon as I can." He kissed both her and Cassidy before making his exit. Annalisa watched him go, chafing at her new role of the cop's wife. She used to be running out the door with him. *You chose this,* she reminded herself. *You wanted a new life.* She returned her attention to the party, making conversation with the girls, helping Melanie refresh the food table and then staying late to assist with the cleanup.

"Dad isn't back yet?" Cassidy asked with anxious eyes as Melanie gave the bar a last wipe-down.

"The job means irregular hours," Annalisa said with sympathy. "He'll be in touch soon."

"I know, but . . . it's Father's Day. Our first one."

Annalisa put down the silverware she was sorting and went to slip an arm around the girl. Father's Day was a complicated holiday for both of them, but she had hope it would improve now. "I know, honey. He wouldn't have left if he had another choice."

Cassidy shuffled her feet and looked at the door, as if Nick might come through it. "I didn't want to make a big deal about it today because of everything with Mom, but I have something I wanted to give him." She fetched a gift bag and pulled out a small framed painting she'd done of Jack the kitten. "Do you think he'll like it?"

"Oh, he will love it," Annalisa said with certainty.

"Can you give it to him? I'm going home with Melanie."

"I think you should hang on to it. Give it to him yourself."

Cassidy hesitated. "Okay." She gave Annalisa a quick one-armed hug. "Thanks for coming."

Annalisa held her when the girl tried to pull back. She looked directly into Cassidy's brown eyes, so like her dad's. But despite the holiday, today wasn't about Nick. It was about Summer. "Your mom would have been proud of you today." As she'd watched Cassidy navigate tough emotions all day, Annalisa had to admit Summer had done her job well. This was the point of parenthood, she supposed. To prepare your child for your absence. "And I know your dad is proud too," she added.

Cassidy gave her a tighter, tearful hug. "Love you," she whispered, and then she was gone.

Back at home in the new house, Annalisa knew she should tackle another moving box, but she was exhausted from the day. She picked at some cold Chinese food from the fridge and watched TV in bed with Jack dozing on her lap. Nick finally turned up at around eight. He had his late-day stubble and a thousand-yard stare. "Tough day?" she asked.

"You might say that."

"Can you tell me about it?" she asked as he flopped down next to her.

"Mara Delaney."

This was the last name she'd expected to hear and she scrambled to sit up against the headboard. "What about her?"

"She was found dead in her apartment. Hanged in the closet."

"What?" Annalisa lurched forward in shock, dislodging Jack from her lap. He mewled his protest and crawled over to Nick. "No. I don't believe it. Sociopaths don't commit suicide."

"Maybe when facing life in prison they do. We've got no sign of a break-in, no other bruising on the body."

"What about a note?"

"No note, but then half of suicide victims don't leave them. You know that."

"Mara would have." She would have wanted the last word, Annalisa was sure. She recalled Gavin Albright's promise to make Mara pay. He'd been present at her arraignment, radiating silent fury in the back. "Vicki Albright's brother . . . he wanted Mara dead."

"Him and a lot of other people. If the coroner rules Mara's death a homicide, then I'll start worrying about everyone's alibi."

"You don't sound too concerned," she replied, narrowing her eyes.

His shrug was philosophical. "What did your 'good psychopath' once tell you? Some people can't be saved." He leaned over to grab the carton of noodles she'd put on the nightstand, but halted when he saw a small wrapped gift sitting there. "What's that?"

"Oh." She'd momentarily forgotten the present. She braced herself for the future, for the leap of faith she was about to take. "It's, uh, it's for you."

He looked confused as he took up the package. "It's not my birthday . . . it's not our anniversary either." He lifted the lid on the box and his eyes got huge as he saw the positive pregnancy test she'd tucked among the tissue paper.

"No," Annalisa said as she snuggled up against him. "It's Father's Day."

ACKNOWLEDGMENTS

Books have one name on the cover but a whole team of people who make it happen. Annalisa and friends are fortunate to have a fabulous group of people cheering them on. First among them is my terrific editor, Sallie Lotz, whose eagle eyes and smart questions make every book stronger. If you've heard of this book and found it somewhere, that's probably due to the hard work of Kayla Janas and Mac Jones, whose creativity and imagination inspire me daily.

Thanks also to my intrepid agent, Jill Marsal, who cheerfully answers all my pesky questions.

I am especially grateful to readers, many of whom I've heard from and whose comments, questions, and concerns are always a joy. I love that a shared passion for the written word connects us all.

As ever, this writer gig is way more fun if you are a member of #TeamBump. Thank you for your feedback and encouragement. I am blessed to have a crackerjack squad of betas that includes Katie Bradley, Rayshell Reddick Daniels, Jason Grenier, Shannon Howl, Michelle Kiefer, Julie Kodama, Rebecca LeBlanc, Suzanne Magnuson, Jill Svihovec, Dawn Volkart, Amanda Wilde, and Paula Woolman.

Thanks as always to my wonderful family, especially Brian and Stephanie Schaffhausen and Larry and Cherry Rooney, for love and support.

Finally, if inspiration starts at home, I am the luckiest writer on the planet because I live with two varsity-level humans: my marvelous husband, Garrett, and our phenomenal daughter, Eleanor. They are the source of all my joy.

Joanna Schaffhausen

JOANNA SCHAFFHAUSEN wields a mean scalpel, skills developed in her years studying neuroscience. She has a doctorate in psychology, which reflects her long-standing interest in the brain—how it develops and the many ways it can go wrong. Previously, she worked for ABC News, writing for programs such as *World News Tonight, Good Morning America,* and *20/20.* She lives in the Boston area with her husband and daughter. She is also the author of *The Vanishing Season, No Mercy, All the Best Lies, Every Waking Hour, Last Seen Alive, Gone for Good, Long Gone,* and *Dead and Gone.*